M. J. Hollows was born in London in 1986 and moved to Liverpool in 2010 to lecture in Audio Engineering. With a keen interest in history, music, and science, he has told stories since he was little. He wrote his first novel, *Goodbye for Now*, as part of his MA in Writing from Liverpool John Moores University. He is currently researching towards a PhD in Creative Writing. *The German Nurse* is his second novel.

🐦 @MikeHollows
www.michaelhollows.com

Also by M. J. Hollows

Goodbye For Now

The German Nurse

M. J. HOLLOWS

ONE PLACE. MANY STORIES

HQ
An imprint of HarperCollins*Publishers* Ltd
1 London Bridge Street
London SE1 9GF

www.harpercollins.co.uk

HarperCollins*Publishers*
1st Floor, Watermarque Building, Ringsend Road
Dublin 4, Ireland

This paperback edition 2021

21 22 23 24 25 LSC 10 9 8 7 6 5 4 3 2 1

First published in Great Britain by
HQ, an imprint of HarperCollins*Publishers* Ltd 2021

PB ISBN: 9780008444969
TPB ISBN: 9780008456962

Printed and bound in the United States of America by
LSC Communications

For Marian, my number-one fan, & for Geoff,
the only level-ten G.

Prologue

12 February 1943

It had been a terrible mistake and Jack wouldn't make it in time. His boots pounded on the dry earth as he sprinted up the path, thumping with each footfall. He hadn't had time to collect his uniform, and his civilian clothes hung loosely on him, the ankles of his trousers flapping in the cool breeze.

The birds sung sweetly, completely at odds with Jack's current state of despair. He couldn't stop running. Even if his lungs gave up his feet would carry on.

There was a crack of a nearby door banging shut against its frame. The town felt almost abandoned in the evening twilight. Lamps lit the hedgerows and facades of houses, casting menacing shadows across the road. The people returning to their homes after a day's work eyed him warily as he passed. Being caught out after curfew was dangerous.

He was too out of breath to say anything. They weren't used to seeing someone running and they feared the worst. Even the local police weren't immune to the curfew the Germans had implemented, not without a pass. He hoped that they were too busy tonight to notice.

He could feel the old Fletcher woman's eyes on his back,

staring out of her front room window. For once he didn't care what she thought. She could report him if she wanted to – it wouldn't make any difference now. He was sick of being watched at every turn, by the Germans, by his own colleagues, even by his neighbours.

As he turned a corner, he saw Beth coming the other way. The smile dropped from her lips as he carried on running. He could trust her even less than the others. Not now that she was in love with a German officer. She stopped and turned to watch him go, her blue eyes following him along the road.

The road lowered down, breaking the horizon and giving him a view of St Peter Port and the sea beyond. From this distance he could only make out faint blurs of boats in the harbour, some masts rising above the surrounding buildings like cigars resting on the deep blue sea.

He jumped across a wooden fence and into farmland. He felt a momentary pang of guilt at disturbing the crops, but they were thin and bare anyway, stripped by the occupying forces and sent to the continent. The furrowed ground was dry and hard, rougher on his feet than the road had been, and he almost slipped several times.

They thought they could resist the Germans. They were wrong. He should have listened to the others. Now the occupiers had whittled them down and taken everything from them. Almost.

The soft wilderness turned to town as he kept running. He was almost out of breath, but as he passed the houses on the outskirts of St Peter Port it gave him hope. A 'V' scrawled on a nearby wall gave him strength. They were still resisting.

The harbour was down and to his right, through the main streets of St Peter Port. Time was running out, but he wouldn't give up now. Not while he still had breath in his body. Curtains shifted in houses as he ran past. The sky was darkening, and he was sure he would soon run into a German patrol. So far he had been lucky, but that luck would not last forever. He should never have left Johanna, not when she needed him most. They should have escaped long ago.

What more did he need when he had the beauty of home, the love of Johanna and his family? Death had come to the island, stalking them in field grey uniform and jackboots. All the place held for him now was horror. How had it finally come to this?

He crossed the road and made his way down a gravel path between houses, stones skittering away as his boots dislodged them. There was a shortcut between the buildings. He no longer had any pretensions of reaching the police station in time. Instead he hoped to head them off at the harbour. He had to stop them, somehow. That was all he kept thinking as he ran. No matter what it took, he couldn't let the Germans do what they were about to do, take the only thing he had left. Not like this.

The harbour opened up in front of him. The scene he remembered so well from that terrible day the Germans had invaded. It had changed much since then – fortified and bleak, fewer boats bobbed softly in their moorings. He hadn't stopped running, the breath almost gone from his body, but he pushed himself on, legs burning with the effort. He skidded and changed direction, towards the harbour proper. His attention had been drawn by a pair of lanterns moving along one of the piers that jutted out into the sea. The hum of a motor rose up into the air.

He jumped over a fence and almost slipped on the landing. '*Halt!*' a German voice shouted from behind him. One of the patrols had spotted him, but he didn't look back. As he approached the end of the pier he could hear voices, a soft pleading intermingled with clipped and harsh German. He couldn't make out the words as they boarded a waiting boat. He wanted to shout after them, tell them to stop, but his lungs burned and no sound would come. He realised for the first time how much his heart was thumping in his chest. Feet slipped on the wet pier, and he pitched forward with a clatter. His stomach hit the ground and he only just managed to shield his face with an outstretched arm.

The breath was knocked from his lungs. He tried to raise himself up, but something felt wrong. He'd broken something. With a groan he leant on his elbow and looked up.

He was too late. He always knew he would be, but he couldn't give up hope. Not until now, when he could hear the faint whirring of the boat's engine as it pushed away from the harbour. Even if he jumped in the icy water to follow her, he would not make it in time. Plunging to his death would not bring her back.

The sound of boots rang out along the pier, growing closer by the second, as he stared into the darkness. All he could see was the faint light of a lantern illuminating the boat as it rose and fell in the water, moving away from the harbour. There were a few silhouettes on board, some wearing the distinctive steel helmet of the Wehrmacht. He could just about make out a shape in between them, scrabbling towards the back of the boat. Was it a woman? A hand reached out to the shore, then disappeared into the darkness.

1940

Chapter 1

19 June 1940

Guernsey was beautiful in the summer: the rolling green fields, the vivid blue sea. It was what drew most people here, taking the boat from Weymouth, or a short flight across the Channel. It was a perfect spot for a holiday, but fewer people were visiting by the day, since the British Government had declared war on Germany. Far closer still was the coast of France, visible on the horizon to the south of the island.

The beauty was the only thing Jack could think about as he left the house he shared with his mother and grandparents. His mother's voice still resonated in his ears, speaking those hard and damning words.

'Don't make the same mistakes I made. Not with that woman! Jack? Jack?!'

He caught the door before it slammed shut, then let it click softly against the wooden frame. He didn't want to exacerbate things and draw the neighbours' attention. Taking a deep breath, he tried to forget his mother's words and stepped away from the house. The further away he was from there, the less it would play on his thoughts. It was a fine June day, bright blue sky and barely a cloud in sight, and his mother's mood couldn't change that. It would take something far worse, and even though war was brewing on the horizon, it hadn't reached them yet. Who knew if it even would?

Their house was typical of the buildings on George Street at the edge of St Peter Port, built from a stone that gave it a mottled, irregular look, and roofed in grey slate tiles. Some of the houses in the terrace were plastered and painted white, but Jack's grandparents had left theirs as natural as possible, less difficult to maintain and still impressive. They had once owned a farmhouse, as they never grew tired of telling him, but as his grandfather's health had deteriorated they had moved closer to the town.

He had been a great man with a booming laugh, always telling stories and like a father to Jack, but now he was a gaunt man almost always confined to his bed. The row of houses lined the way down to the harbour, and Jack knew every occupant by name. He stood for a moment looking at the navy-blue-painted door and wondering if his mother would follow him after their argument.

He and his mother had argued a lot more recently, but he knew deep down that she was only concerned. She meant well, but sometimes she didn't think before speaking. Like everyone, she was worried about what might happen to them. The ever-looming shadow of war seemed to grow closer every day. She couldn't forget the last war, how it had affected them all, and it had affected her more than most.

He turned and picked up his bicycle from the wall; he was going to be late if he didn't hurry. He wished he had time to go and see Johanna. Seeing her would cheer him up.

The sun beat down and he began to sweat. His clothes were close and hot, and it would be even worse when he put on his uniform at the police station. But it gave him a sense of pride to wear it, a sign that even in his short life he had already accomplished something many others could only dream of.

People were going about their business as usual in the morning, heading to work at the shops and eateries, fishermen coming back from overnight hauls, and he greeted them with a smile and a nod as he cycled past. They liked seeing their local policeman on the streets, looking after them, especially in these dark times when everyone was nervous and never far from fear. He was here for them. He was a public servant, no more, no less. He had dedicated his life to helping other people, and no matter what happened he would never forget that.

*

Jack entered the police station and the hot summer sun was immediately blocked out. There was always a musty, damp smell to the interior, as if it had been built on top of some sort of stream. It was muggy and even the collar of his linen shirt chafed at his neck.

'Morning,' William – the sergeant on the desk – called, looking up from some paperwork. 'You've heard then? They're in the briefing room.'

'Heard what?' Jack leant on the other side of the desk, waiting for the sergeant to explain. Normally the pair of them only exchanged pleasantries, but there was a look in William's eyes that Jack couldn't quite describe, like he was staring right through him.

'The chief's called everyone in,' he said a moment later. 'Something big's happening. I thought you'd got the telephone call. You'd better hurry.'

Jack nodded and headed through the main doors and into their changing room. He tried to spend as little time in the station as possible, preferring the wide-open grasslands of the island. He asked for patrol shifts that took him on the long walks that many of his colleagues would rather avoid.

Jack had heard nothing of the meeting that William had mentioned and it pulled at his imagination, as he folded his clothes into a cupboard. It could be anything, but his mind immediately thought the worst. Some hoped the war would stall far away in France like the last one, but many still worried. They wondered what to do, some leaving the island already and others stockpiling food and supplies. Even the soldiers had no idea. He thought of them as he pulled his uniform on. Their fear must be worse than the Islanders, not knowing when they would be called to fight.

The newspapers had reported on the happenings in mainland Europe, and every time Jack thought of it he could feel a tightening in his chest. No matter how often he told himself to be calm, that everything would be all right in the end, he couldn't ignore that indefinable feeling of dread.

Fully uniformed, Jack pushed open the door of the briefing room. He was immediately hit with the smell of cigarette smoke and body odour. The room was dark, with no natural light, only the faint glow of the kerosene lamps. The building only had electric lighting upstairs.

The room was full, seeming to contain the entirety of Guernsey's police force, all thirty-three men.

'Glad you could join us, Constable Godwin,' a deep voice said. The chief officer didn't even bother to look at Jack as he leant against the wall at the back. The chief's voice was thick and he cleared it, passing the phlegm into a white cotton handkerchief that he kept in his breast pocket. 'Well,' he continued. 'Now that everyone is here we can begin.' He picked up a few pieces of paper from his desk and shuffled them, apparently looking for something in particular. He fumbled with his glasses. 'The next few days are going to be incredibly difficult for us,' he said, fixing each of them with a look before moving on. 'The news we've all been anticipating has finally arrived. The envoy returned from the mainland this morning.'

There was a slight shift in the room as the local policemen objected to the description of England as the mainland. Jack often made the same mistake, treating Guernsey as an extension of England when most of the locals thought of themselves as their own country. The chief didn't seem to notice as he continued.

'The Prime Minister, Mr Churchill, has ordered the withdrawal of all military forces on the island,' he said, looking them all in the eye one after the other again, letting the implication of his words settle in. 'The British Government have decided that the islands are not worth the resources needed to defend them.'

There was a gasp from the assembled policemen. They glanced at each other, looking for reassurance. 'Does it really say that, sir?' someone asked amongst the mutterings.

'Not explicitly, but that's not the point. We've often been on our own. I don't see this as any different. We all have our jobs to do. We've also been asked to assist in whatever way necessary, to expedite their withdrawal from the island. There is expected to be a panic when the Islanders find out the army is leaving, and many will want to travel to the mainland. The states want this to be organised as efficiently as possible, and the press is already preparing to circulate the details in today's papers.'

He raised a copy of the *Star*. 'EVACUATION,' it read. 'ALL CHILDREN TO BE SENT TO MAINLAND TOMORROW. WHOLE BAILIWICK TO BE DEMILITARISED.' By comparison the *Guernsey Evening Press* had a more measured account of how the evacuation was going to be conducted. There was a sigh from someone to Jack's right. 'They're abandoning us and we've gotta help them do it? Fantastic.'

'Less of that, Sergeant.' The chief officer fixed Sergeant Honfleur with a pointed stare over the top of his glasses. 'We've all had to follow orders we didn't agree with before; this is no different.'

Jack only knew some of the soldiers by name, Henry and the others, and they were part of the local militia that had now been disbanded. Some of them had gone with the army to enlist in England and he couldn't shake the horrible feeling that they were leaving them behind. The Islanders had known the war would come for them sometime, but the forces that were stationed here were supposed to be for their protection.

'What now, sir?' the sergeant asked, crossing his arms and

leaning back against a desk. The atmosphere was tense and the policemen shifted in their seats. William played with his watch, and David squashed a cigarette in an ashtray as he lit another.

'Now, with luck, the lack of armed forces here will mean that even if the Germans get this far, they'll leave us alone.'

'Let's hope you're right, sir.'

'Well, we all have our normal work to do and you all have a decision to make. The islands are not defensible. We don't know whether the Germans will come, but it's a possibility.'

'How do we know, sir? What will they want with us? If the islands are indefensible, it'd be the same for them.'

'Maybe they're after your potato patch, sir.' That was PC David Roussel, a grin stretched across his face. They all laughed, lowering the tension in the room, but it was cut short by a glare from the chief.

'The states have appealed to the government to mount an evacuation.'

There was another murmur around the room, and Jack looked across at David who shrugged in response. The chief cleared his throat again. 'They've agreed,' he said. 'But those wanting to leave have to be ready immediately. I've just received a telegram. The boats for the children are coming tomorrow. Any child who needs evacuating to England has to be ready to leave by tomorrow morning. The first boats will arrive at two-thirty in the morning. Children of school age and under can register to be taken to a reception centre on the mainland.'

'What about their parents, sir?'

There were parents in the room, and they sat up straighter than before. He shuffled through the notices again, then finding the one he wanted he pushed the glasses up on his nose and took a closer look. 'Anyone wishing to be evacuated will have to register with the authorities and wait to see if there is enough room on the boats. There is no guarantee that everyone will be evacuated, except for the children.

12

'Those men wishing to join the armed forces on arrival in England may also register.'

He dropped the papers to his desk and looked at them over the rim of his glasses.

'Now, as honourable a decision it may be to go and join up in England, let us not forget the people whom we serve here. If you all go, what am I to do then? Even if the Germans don't come there will be anarchy on the island. Please consider that before making your decision. I expect every man to do his duty and continue in service of the island. If you leave, there will be no job to return to.'

There was a general hubbub as the policemen talked amongst themselves. The islands had been conquered a long time ago when the English had taken them from the French. It didn't mean that it would happen again. Jack couldn't imagine it. The islands were peaceful. If they didn't fight the Germans then maybe they could just get on with their lives in peace. Jack wouldn't leave anyway. He needed to be here. His mother had no one else, except his grandparents, and he had to look after them as well. They all relied on him. Then there was Johanna.

The chief cleared his throat. 'Dismissed,' he said. 'Get to work.'

The chief came over to Jack as the others were leaving and pushed his glasses back up onto the bridge of his nose. Through them his eyes were large and beady. They reminded Jack of an insect, and he fought a smile that threatened to turn the corner of his lips. Smirking at his superior officer wasn't a good way to start the day, no more than arguing with his mother.

'I remember your thoughts on war, but surely you aren't against helping these chaps get on their boats, are you?'

Jack didn't say anything. A few misplaced comments from Jack in the past and the man had assumed so much. He had learnt since then that it was easier to let him talk. The chief liked the sound of his own voice. 'We all have to do things we don't like in the line of duty. I have a special request of you, Jack.'

'Yes, sir?' he asked, already dreading what it might be.

'I want you ready first thing in the morning. On your way in, check on the evacuation of the children; make sure they have everything they need and that no one is causing trouble.'

'Yes, sir.' It wasn't the duty he had been expecting, but it could have been a lot worse.

'Good. Then I want you to be the first one down at the harbour. You and your colleagues will erect barricades to ensure that only those who are registered can board. We have to be careful – I have a bad feeling about this.'

It was true, things were only going to get worse as the tension on the island rose and people panicked. The chief nodded over his glasses and left Jack to his thoughts. He would need a good night's sleep, but he still had a whole day of work ahead. He sighed and went to find the sergeant to enquire about his duties.

*

After the briefing it had been a quiet day, which seemed to drag on into eternity as Jack patrolled the island, keeping an eye out for any trouble and helping with menial tasks when he had nothing else to occupy him. Many had been busy making preparations for the evacuation as word had spread quickly. Finally, later that evening, he returned home, ready for a good night's sleep. His legs ached and his feet were sore from standing all day, something that he thought he would never get used to. He didn't know why the boats had to come so early, but then he never really understood the methods of government. Leaving the island defenceless didn't seem right, but he had to believe they knew what they were doing, otherwise he might as well just throw his uniform away. He had worked so hard to get that uniform in the first place; he wasn't going to give it up now.

His way home took him past the town hall, which had been turned into a registration office for the evacuation. Jack had been past earlier in the day while they were preparing and now there was a long queue around the building. It moved slowly, but the tension was clear as people stood closer to each other than they would do otherwise, rushing forward every time a gap opened. Some groups chatted quietly; others stood in silence.

There was a scuffle between two men, and one of them was knocked to the ground. 'I was here first,' the standing man shouted, moving closer to his victim and pulling back a foot to strike. There was a gasp from the surrounding crowd, a quick intake of air as they recognised Jack, even out of uniform. The attacker hesitated, then reached out a hand to help his victim up. The other man refused and went to stand further back in the queue as his attacker eyed Jack warily. The knuckles of his right hand were grazed and pinpricks of blood stood out. Jack made a mental note to check on the man later, in case he caused any more trouble.

He nodded at the man, then worked his way around to the front of the queue, to see a man come back out of the door to the registration office, pulling his wife behind him. He didn't see Jack as he bumped into him and pushed his way past without so much as a 'sorry'. Given the stress that people were feeling, he decided to let it go. People in the queue looked after him, their eyes wide.

He flashed them a smile. 'Good evening,' he said, touching the brim of his hat. No one paid him any notice, but his smile didn't falter.

A woman appeared around the corner, walking at pace. She wore a light beige summer dress, which fluttered in the breeze, and a matching hat. It was a second or two before he fully recognised her, as he was lost in his own thoughts. 'Johanna,' he breathed, before stepping aside to make sure he was in her path.

She almost walked around him, shaking her head, before looking up and stopping in her tracks. 'Jack?' she asked, in the familiar way she said his name. *Jacques*. He loved the way she said it, with the soft 'J' much closer to the French. 'What are you doing here?'

She reached out a hand and rested it on the crook of his arm, and smiled.

'I was on my way home.' He smiled back at her, stroking her hand. 'I could ask you the same?'

'Me? Bah!' She snorted, remembering herself. 'I joined this queue to see if they would take us to England. But they said no and called me an "enemy alien". An enemy indeed! First they lock me up, now when they release me, this. What harm could I possibly do to their precious country? We have the same enemies! But they treat me like an enemy, just because I'm German. They wouldn't even let me work as a nurse, despite my training.'

Her cheeks were red and she shook her head, letting go of his arm. When the war had started the states had not been sure what to do with foreigners living on the island, and when the Nazis were getting closer to the islands they had locked up all the Germans in case they were spies. Johanna had only just got out. Jack looked around them and caught the eye of several in the queue watching their conversation. Without thinking he took a hold of Johanna's arm and pulled her gently along the street, down an alley between a pair of buildings, out of view and earshot.

'We're best talking here,' he said. 'Who knows who's listening?'

'Why does it matter?' she asked, looking up at him.

'These people are worried.' He gestured back the way they had come. 'They don't know what to do and they don't know what will happen. If we're not careful their worry may become anger.'

'I don't understand,' she said, a frown crossing her brow. It was that look that had first attracted him to her, the look of a furious intelligence. The curls of her auburn hair bounced as she shook her head. 'Why can't we go as well?'

He sighed. It wasn't that the question was a bad one, he just didn't know what to say. In a perfect world they could just live out their lives on the island in peace. He took hold of her hand.

He wanted to tell her he would run away with her, that he would always protect her, but where would they go? Europe was at war, and she wasn't allowed into Britain.

'There are conditions that need to be met before someone can register,' he said at long last. 'There's not enough room in the boats for everyone. It's only for parents who wish to accompany their children, and even then, I'm not sure they can guarantee space. And foreign nationals aren't being allowed into the country right now.'

'So they expect me to stay here?' She struggled her hand out of his grip and paced across to the other side of the alley. She leant against a wall, her back on the painted stone, and closed her eyes. 'What happens when the Germans come? I've already run from them once. What next? What if they find out I'm a Jew?'

Again, he didn't have the answer, but based on her body language he didn't think that she expected one. He moved closer to her, careful not to startle her. 'We don't know if they will come,' he said. 'The states are hoping that they will just avoid us, especially when the army leaves. Besides, I want to stay here. I don't want us to go anywhere.'

'You haven't seen the things I've seen, Jack.' It almost felt like an accusation, like somehow because he hadn't been there he couldn't possibly understand what she was thinking or feeling. She was probably right, but if she didn't confide in him, then how could he ever understand? She had mentioned her past, but had refused to say more when he asked. She didn't want to talk about it, but how was he supposed to understand her if she didn't? He often wondered what had happened to her in Germany, and he had heard plenty of rumours, but she would not speak of it.

'They won't stop at the French coast,' she said, seeing his hesitance. There were tears at the corners of her eyes.

'What if they don't?' he asked. 'We can't worry about that now. We have to take each day as it comes. They are just as likely to leave us alone. What need do they have of the islands?'

'You never worry. How can you be so calm, Jack? Teach me.' She reached out a hand to him as if beckoning, and he took a step closer. He intertwined his fingers with hers and thought about pulling her into an embrace, but stopped.

'When I was old enough to understand that my father had died, I was angry,' he said, his voice a soft whisper. 'It took me a long time to realise there was nothing I could have done.'

The town hall bell suddenly struck, ringing out across St Peter Port. It was getting late. He screwed his eyes shut, feeling suddenly weary.

'I have to go,' he said with a sigh. 'To get some sleep before the morning. The boats are coming at two-thirty in the morning, but the attorney general has managed to persuade them to delay boarding until six.'

Johanna let go of his hand and let out a deep breath. He tried to take hold of her again, but she pushed herself away from the wall and walked towards the end of the alley.

'Where are you going?' Jack called after her.

'To the hotel,' she shouted back over her shoulder. 'They need volunteers. At least I can be useful!' Johanna walked away, leaving him alone in the side street.

Chapter 2

20 June 1940

Jack awoke with a start, the faint light of morning framing his curtains but failing to give a sense of time. The dream he had been having disappeared as quickly as it had appeared, and a trickle of sweat ran between his shoulder blades. The anger he had felt upon waking subsided, almost forgotten. He knew it was aimed inward, but he couldn't remember why he had been angry with himself. He pulled the alarm clock off the side of his bed, noting that it was roughly five minutes before he had set it to go off. As usual it felt worse waking up earlier than intended, even though the extra five minutes wouldn't have made any difference.

He dragged himself out of the bed, barely sitting up as he did so. His sheets had been kicked to the floor during the few hours of unbearably hot sleep he had managed to grab. He pulled on some clothes, not caring that he had worn them the day before. It didn't matter anyway, as he would head to the police station to collect his uniform before going on duty. First he wanted to see Johanna, and she wouldn't care what he was wearing. He wasn't happy with the way they had left things the previous evening. He needed to speak to her, to assure her that he wanted her here, that he would do everything in his power to care for her.

Jack climbed down the stairs, careful with each step. He knew the creaks and groans, but sometimes an unexpected noise would betray him. By the time he reached the bottom of the stairs he could just make out the faint murmur of his grandparents either talking, or snoring in their room, and he was careful not to disturb them. His mother would likely already be stirring; she didn't sleep well and it was even worse in the summer heat. She was prone to night terrors, all her fears playing through her mind while she tried to sleep. He didn't have time to check on her, especially if he wanted to find Johanna before work. The front door clicked softly open as he turned the handle. He picked up his boots with one hand, thumb and finger clasping them together, so that he could put them on outdoors.

As soon as he was outside a gust of wind caught the door and its hinges squealed as it slammed shut behind him. He winced – so much for not disturbing his family. He had been meaning to fix those hinges for some time, and now they would be angry he had disturbed them. He didn't have time to worry about it now. The sun was just coming over the horizon, its warm glow slowly spreading across the island, and he had a lot to do before it had fully risen.

*

The Royal Hotel he was looking for was one of the main hotels in St Peter Port, near the harbour with easy access to the ferry and the shops. Prior to the war it had been one of the locations in which people had come to stay when they travelled from the mainland or Europe to experience the beauty of Guernsey. The businesses would surely be struggling to make ends meet, and he wouldn't be surprised if some of the proprietors joined the evacuation to try to find a new life on the mainland.

Now, the hotel was a scene of furious activity, as staff piled wooden crates that were normally used for groceries by the entrance. At this time of morning it would have been strange to see so many people at work, were it not for the current circumstances. Whether the staff had volunteered to help, or had been forced to by their employers, Jack didn't know, but he hoped it was the former.

'I'm looking for Johanna?' he asked one of the porters as the man dropped another crate on the pile. He waved Jack in the direction of the kitchen behind him and carried on his work without saying a word. As with a number of hotels on the island, the kitchen was in a lower ground floor, accessed by the side of the building allowing easy access for unloading supplies, and there was an almost steady stream of volunteers going back and forth. He dodged one of them as he stepped down the stairs to the main kitchen. There were more people inside working at counters, some in silence, others busy talking amongst themselves. The kitchen smelt strongly of breads, cheeses, and pickles.

He recognised her straight away, even from behind. It was the way she stood taller than everyone else and worked with a practised efficiency. It struck him that it was similar to the very first time he had laid eyes on her. He smiled to himself as he walked up behind her. She was working on her own at one side of the kitchen, away from the comings and goings of the regular staff.

'Johanna?' She turned and her smile made him weak at the knees. He had expected her to be angry, but as usual her anger had diminished as quickly as it had come. Her temperament was fiery, and he would not have her any other way. It had taken him a while at first to stop himself thinking that she hated him. In time she had shown him more love and passion than anyone else ever had.

'Jack,' she said, still smiling up at him and revealing perfect, white teeth. 'What are you doing here?'

He stepped closer to her, wanting to take her hands in his, but she was busy working, making sandwiches for the evacuees to take with them on their journey to the mainland.

'I wanted to say … to say.' He hesitated despite running the words through his head over and over again on the way to the hotel. The lack of sleep was playing with his mind and he wondered if he was doing the right thing.

'Yes?' she asked, looking up again and nodding at him to continue. Her curly hair had been tied up and there were bags under her eyes that spoke of a lack of sleep. The whites of her eyes were red, which made it look as if she had been crying. He second-guessed himself again. Would she really appreciate what he was trying to say? He convinced himself that her smile was genuine; there was a warmth there despite her tiredness.

'I wanted to say that I don't want you to leave the island,' he said, finally blurting out the words in a torrent. 'I don't want you to leave, not without me. I want you to stay here with me, and I will give everything to look after you.'

He couldn't gauge her reaction. Was it shock? His heart thumped heavily in his chest, and he felt sick. He thought about walking away and forgetting everything he had said, to save himself from the embarrassment. But he could never walk away from her; he didn't have it in him.

'Oh, Jack,' she said, tears forming at the corners of her eyes. 'You should have been a poet, not a policeman.' He wasn't sure if she was gently mocking him or not. She wiped away the tears with an index finger, then cleaned her hands on a nearby tea towel. 'The only thing that makes staying on this island bearable is the thought that I will be with you. Even if most people treat me like an enemy. I've been through worse.'

She tried to smile again, but another wave of tears took over. As always he wondered what it truly was that had happened to her in Germany, but he knew not to push her on the subject.

With a sudden rush of confidence, he took hold of her, wrapping his arms around her. Her head rested against his chest. It felt natural, as if she was perfectly built to fit into that space, like a piece of a jigsaw. As if God had made them for each other. The smell of her hair was overwhelming. He closed his eyes, breathing her in. 'I'm going nowhere,' he said. 'Not while you're on the island. When the war is over we'll be allowed to go to England or wherever we want and live out our lives in peace.'

They stood together like that for a few minutes, savouring the moment. Opening his eyes, he spotted the clock on the wall and gasped. 'Look at the time!' he said, loosening his embrace. 'I have to go.'

Johanna laughed, and let go of him. 'Bah, you're always running away from me, Jack Godwin.'

'I'm sorry,' he said, looking between her and the clock. 'If I didn't have to get to work, I would stay. You know I would. I can barely stand to be apart from you.' He bent down to kiss her, but she pulled away at the last second.

'Not here. I will see you later. Take this.' She picked up a brown, rectangular paper bag from the worktop and handed it to him. 'Tell no one.'

'What's this?' he asked.

'It's a sandwich. I know you won't have had anything to eat yet.' They hugged again, briefly, and he left the kitchen, almost running. Late again, he would be in trouble.

*

In the early hours of the morning, the school was dark and forbidding. An uneasy atmosphere rested over it like a black cloud. It was a place for learning, but on this occasion the parents would rather they were kept in the dark. When he had studied there it had been a different time. Parents were already bringing their children to the school, as Jack joined them. They arrived in small groups, sticking together, their short arms reaching up to clutch their parents' outstretched hands, tighter than they ever had before. Some were going with their children, but for the others, who knew how long they would be separated? None of them

23

could predict how long this war would last, how long it would be before the Germans expended their energy on their enemies' guns, how long it would take for someone to force them back.

None of them had been given enough time to prepare, or to soften the blow for the children. The shock was still clear in the eyes of most of the people Jack passed as he headed towards the school. He was careful not to be too present as a policeman; he didn't want to scare the children. More than one parent had a hastily bundled together collection of belongings to send with their children. Some of their cases had clothes poking out of the seams, ragged and fluttering in the wind. It was a sorry, desperate sight.

At the school gates, a group of teachers and other officials were checking documents and admitting those children who had the correct papers. As Jack walked up, a mother was hugging her son, who could have only been four or five years old. The officials, seeing Jack's uniform, stepped aside to let him pass, but he waited for a moment to see what would happen. He could tell that she was trying her best, but tears threatened to escape the corners of her reddened eyes. Her voice broke. Her son simply stared idly around himself, blissfully ignorant of what was going on. 'Now, you're going on a great adventure,' she said. 'Once you get there your aunt May will be looking after you for a while.'

She stopped, catching herself again. Jack couldn't bear to watch anymore. He couldn't possibly imagine what these parents were going through. How that mother could stand it, he had no idea, but she had put her son's life ahead of her own, and given the circumstances it was the right thing to do. Had Johanna's parents gone through the same emotions when she had left her home?

He smiled at one of the teachers, but it was forced. He felt only sadness. Inside the school was a similar scene, one he suspected was duplicated across the island. Hundreds of children were standing around, looking lost. Some stood with one or two parents, but others were on their own and teachers were rounding them up, with smiles plastered on their faces.

'We're trying to make sure that there is no panic, Constable,' a voice said from behind him. He turned to see a middle-aged man, dressed in a cheap brown suit. The man smiled at Jack, but like his own it lacked certainty. 'As you can imagine,' he continued, 'it's an uphill struggle. It's why we're making sure the parents say their goodbyes at the gate.'

He reached out a hand and Jack returned the gesture, receiving a vigorous shake. Jack was taken aback somewhat by the friendliness of the man. He remembered teachers as being sterner and more distant, and the usual reaction to the uniform was wariness.

'An unenviable task, Headmaster,' Jack said, nodding. 'Times are difficult, and we can only do our best.'

'Wise words, for a young man. If you don't mind me saying?'

Jack shook his head. It was always nice to receive a compliment, and his teachers had never been that complimentary when he was in school. He didn't feel that wise. 'Thank you, but I'm just here to do my job.'

'Of course. These children need escorting down to the harbour.' He looked at his wristwatch. 'The boats will be arriving soon and they won't have long to get everyone on board. The longer we wait the less chance we have of getting them over to England.'

'The boats will have to wait until they're full. We won't let them leave before they're ready.'

'Good luck with that. I'm sure the captains won't want to wait around too long. Who knows when the Germans will come?'

Jack noted that he had said, 'when', not 'if'.

A teacher looked over at the sound of their raised voices. She was kneeling down to talk to a child, and a frown crossed her face. The headmaster gestured for Jack to step back out into the reception. The early summer morning heat was coming in the front doors. 'There are buses outside to take the children. We will organise them all, but I would appreciate it if you could escort them.'

'Of course,' Jack replied.

25

Outside the school a number of buses waited, silhouettes in the early morning gloom. The drivers stood by one cab, smoking cigarettes and chatting. A few minutes later the children appeared at the front of the school, in a line two abreast. The headmaster led them from the front, and it reminded Jack of the story of the Pied Piper of Hamelin his grandfather had once told him when he was little. The concept of some mysterious figure leading an entire village of children off into the unknown had terrified him ever since.

The children were well behaved as they boarded the buses, either shocked into obedience by events, or encouraged by the teachers and attendant parents. Thankfully, the majority of the children had yet to work out exactly what was happening. That would not last forever. It took some time, but it was going more smoothly than Jack had expected.

*

The harbour was awash with activity. Men shouted orders at each other and soldiers rushed from one area to another making sure that everything was in place. The air stank of brine and salt, fish mingled with the sweat of those at work. Not everyone in the harbour was wearing army-issue khaki, as various merchant ships were either returning from fishing trips or preparing to leave for Britain. The sun had risen above the horizon and lit the scene in its warm glow, making the work that little bit harder for everyone.

As the children climbed off the buses, volunteers attached brown labels to their lapels and led them towards the boats. They were getting more nervous as the strange situation dragged on, young murmurings of concern growing louder. Some mothers had gone against the states' orders and come to the harbour to see their children off, unable to stay away. Mothers' tears added to the already salty sea air, and those children who were more aware than others cried, hoping against hope that they wouldn't be put on those horrible little boats that rocked against the tide.

There were queues forming at the ends of the piers, and people shuffled with impatience, waiting for the order to board. Some were being turned away as Jack went to join his colleagues. Whole families sat together on the ground, belongings piled up around them in the sweltering heat. Some had discarded their cars, unable to take them with them. None of them were sure that they would be allowed to leave, and it was clear on their faces.

Not everyone in the harbour was looking for a way to escape. Some were saying goodbye to loved ones who were going with the army, and Jack caught a glimpse of Beth as she said goodbye to her brother, who had been in the militia. Even though he was Jack's age, Jack knew his sister much better. They had fallen into the same friendship group, and she had always enjoyed bossing him around. On any other day he may have waved and beckoned her over, but not today.

A man propped his bicycle against a nearby wall and walked back up the road, a roll of paper tied up with string in his hand. He disappeared around the corner of a building, heading in the direction of the town hall. Nearby a couple were saying goodbye, pulling close together as the husband looked to board a nearby boat. The man played his hand through the ringlets of her curly brown hair, as he kissed her goodbye, his other hand resting on the hem of her pleated skirt, lingering longer than was strictly appropriate.

Jack longed to pull Johanna into a similar embrace, but he didn't know when they would get the chance to be alone. They should have been boarding a boat of their own, if only Johanna had been able to leave too. Deep brown eyes bore into his, wide with surprise, and he realised he was staring.

Jack yawned and thought about how much more tired he would be by the time all of this was done. He would sleep the sleep of the dead later. For now, he forced himself forward, one foot after the other.

A couple of his colleagues were manoeuvring a wooden barricade into place along the end of the pier. One of them, an older man, PC Frank Baker, was struggling to lift the crossbeam into the groove cut in a leg, and Jack rushed to help him. 'Thanks,' Frank said as they wrestled the beam into place, and he stopped to wipe the sweat from his brow. 'This probably won't help much if this lot get rowdy.' He threw a thumb over his shoulder in the direction of the growing queue. 'But at least it will make them think twice.'

A man walked past them, carrying three overfilled rucksacks and visibly sweating in the heat. 'There's no way he's getting that lot on a boat,' Jack said, looking over at his other colleague, Sergeant Honfleur, who nodded and grumbled.

'Glad you could join us, Godwin. You can man this barricade while we take a break.'

There was a loud crack as a wooden crate was dropped to the ground by two khaki-clad soldiers. Neither of them flinched. The navy's boats bobbed gently in their moorings as the materiel was taken on board. That both the army and the children were being evacuated at the same time was causing havoc with the harbour, and the men in khaki moved freely past the cordons the police had set up. Jack could see some of the civilians edging closer, looking to take advantage of the lapse.

A soldier with three chevrons stitched on to his sleeve stopped, put down a crate and used the break to stretch his back. He looked over at Jack and nodded. 'Good thing the weather is calm,' he said, his accent not from the islands. 'Or the trip to the mainland with this lot would be hell.'

'That's true, but they'll want to hurry up. They're getting in the way of the evacuation.'

The sergeant nodded. 'Aye, but it's not easy mobilising an army, my friend. Especially across the sea. We've got a lot to get on board that there navy ship out in the bay.'

'They must have known this was coming. You could at least leave us something.'

'Hah, don't assume anything. We were caught napping during the last war too. Chamberlain didn't fancy a fight, but now ol' Churchill's in charge. And no can do, friend.' He patted the crate he had been carrying. 'Can't leave anything behind that we may need. It's for your own good. If the Hun do come, you'll be best off if they think you're completely unarmed. I know it's not easy to hear, but that's how it is.'

'You're still abandoning us.'

The other man was silent for a moment, looking out over the sea. He nodded shallowly, before speaking. 'I can see why you would think that,' he said. 'Truth is, I reckon it's a question of winning or losing the war altogether. If the Germans come here, what can we do to stop them really?' He waved a hand around the harbour. 'We could defend bits of the island, but with no navy support we'd soon be overrun. Me and my lads can be put to better use somewhere else.

'And if we're not here, at least they won't come with force. No one will die for a few extra days' resistance.'

Jack scowled. This man had no choice but to go off and fight somewhere else, but Jack didn't have to like it. While there was still some hope, they could stop the Germans taking the island.

The other man's frown broke into a smile. 'Say what. Come with us. Young lad like you'd do well in khaki.'

Jack shook his head. What else could he say? That he hated war? He surely wouldn't appreciate it. Besides, that was an overly simplistic explanation. It wasn't war that he hated; it was death. Jack had lost everything as a child, and he had always blamed war for it.

'I can't. My family … I'm needed here,' he said. He would never forgive himself if he left his family to fend for themselves, and he knew that no matter what he said they would never leave the island. This was their home. This was his home.

'I understand,' the other man said, lighting a cigarette and offering the packet to Jack who refused. 'More than you can imagine. It's why I do what I do. Some of us don't have families to look after. Some of us fight to protect other people's families, those who have what we don't.' He took a long drag. 'I don't blame you for staying. I'd probably do the same if it was my home and I had anyone to stay for. I wish you luck.' With a grunt he lifted the crate up and trudged off down the pier, cigarette hanging out of the corner of his mouth.

'Thanks.'

A boat was pushing off from the harbour, wobbling as a soldier kicked at the mooring. When the boat moved suddenly, he almost fell but was caught by a companion. They laughed it off, but the boat was so overcrowded Jack didn't fancy their chances of staying dry during the journey. There weren't enough boats to take them all out to the SS *Biarritz* in the bay. Jack wondered if he did want to go with them after all, where would he even fit?

A few hours later, Jack watched the last of the boats leave the harbour. The *Biarritz* was already disappearing around the corner of the bay, the smoke from its chimneys the only blotch on the clear blue sky. There were still some fishing boats moored up in the harbour, but it was a shadow of its former self. The island felt quieter already, except for the soft sobbing coming from behind him as families went home to await their unknown future.

'*À bétaot*,' he said to no one in particular. *Goodbye*.

Chapter 3

26 June 1940

The windows of the house rattled to an irregular rhythm in their frames. At first they had thought a truck from one of the farms had driven too close to the house, but the sound had continued. There would be a long moment of calm, followed by the glass shaking a few times in quick succession. Some were quieter than others, then a large bang drifted across the sea as something bigger went up.

The crockery on his tray clinked with each movement as Jack carried bowls of potato soup to his grandparents, trying not to spill any on the floor. He had expected them to look concerned when he entered their room, but they sat up against the metal headboard of their bed, quietly muttering to themselves.

'I hear the Hun are at it again,' his grandfather grumbled as he spotted Jack, who was too busy concentrating on the bowls to reply.

'Thank you, dear,' his grandmother said as he put the tray down on the only table in their room, a dark-lacquered, old wooden side table. He passed a bowl to her. She lifted the spoon and moved it towards her husband, who scoffed when he saw what she was doing. 'I'm not an invalid,' he said, before a cough racked his body. She smiled wearily at him, but Jack knew that she would do anything for her husband. As he would do for Johanna.

He picked up the second bowl and there was another rumble from outside. Jack flinched as it rocked in his hands.

'Don't worry, Jacky,' his grandmother said, and Jack was unsure whether she was talking about the soup or the sound of warfare drifting in through the open window. 'You'll get used to it, just like we did in the last war.'

Jack wondered if this would be the same, that at some point the backdrop of war would become second nature to them.

'The Hun wouldn't dare,' his grandfather agreed, before another coughing fit. Jack wanted to do something to help him, the man who had been like a father to him in the absence of his own father, but nothing they had done had helped. Jack longed for the grandfather who had told him stories of better times and convinced him to join the police force, knowing that he could never do anything else but try to help people, that since his father had died Jack had wanted to prevent anyone else suffering the same heartbreak. His grandfather was the man who had helped Jack feel like a local, forget that he was born in England and fit in on the island. It was funny to think that all those things had led him to become a policeman.

'When are we going to see that nice young girl again, dear?' his grandmother asked, breaking his reverie. 'Jocelyn, Josie, whatsit?'

'Johanna,' Jack replied with a smile. 'Soon, I hope, but well … you know what Mum's like.'

She sighed, then took a mouthful of her soup. His mother's moods were an unspoken issue in the house. None of them truly knew what caused them, but all they could do was wait for them to pass.

'She will come around,' his grandfather said, joining in the conversation. 'You'll see – I'll have a word with her.' He managed to stifle a cough and his broad smile reminded Jack of past days.

'Thanks,' Jack said, smiling too, knowing that his grandfather would always come through for him.

The windows rocked again, causing a little dust to fall from the ceiling. Jack left his grandparents to their meal and went into the hallway. He opened the front door, the creak of its hinges lost in the din, as explosions lit up the coast of France. His neighbours stood on their doorsteps too and looked about, frowns etched deep on their faces. It wasn't supposed to be like this. The army had left only a few days ago, and the Islanders had hoped to be left alone now that they were no longer a threat. The newspapers had talked about the German advance, but no one had expected to hear it from here. Something terrible was happening over on the north coast. It seemed they wanted the whole of France for themselves.

Jack left his house and walked up onto the headland to get a better look. Some of his neighbours followed at first, but then drifted off after a while, unwilling to witness the reality of what was happening. From up there a person could see for miles, to the south across the bright blue sea, to the faint white hue of clouds on the horizon. Jack stood there for a time. He often enjoyed it up on the hills and grabbed a glance over the sea whenever he could. Sometimes he would sit; others he would just stand and think. It gave him a chance to compose his thoughts and a bit of distance from home. At times he was tempted to sketch the view, but he had no talent for it. His mother could draw, creating something that looked like a reasonable landscape.

The Cherbourg Peninsula was a muddy brown line along the edge of the sea, a land that seemed so far away. The wind was a south-westerly, blowing across him, threatening to take off his hat. The sounds had died out and been replaced by an eerie calm in which Jack could only hear his heartbeat and the occasional gust of wind. Over the few miles of sea blew thick black smoke, which left an acrid taste in his mouth. It was the taste of oil, strong and suffocating.

Often scents and smells would blow across from the mainland, the faint whiff of burning, of bonfires or wood stoves, but this time it was much stronger. It was a sign of things to come. Someone was burning fuel. He presumed it was so the Germans couldn't get their hands on it. The invaders wouldn't be far from the capital city now, and once there the rest of France wouldn't be far behind.

Jack stayed for a while longer, watching the French coastline. He feared for the people. While he hadn't been alive during the last war, he was aware of the damage it had caused. It had taken his father from him. People still refused to talk about it, but he knew how it had affected them. Another war was terrifying, but it wasn't their war. The Germans had wanted a fight, and now they were all on a course to be dragged into it. He only hoped that it wouldn't take anyone else from him, that he could protect Johanna from what she was running from.

After a while, when the smoke had blended with the clouds, he turned to walk back into town, taking one last glance over his shoulder at the coming darkness.

*

28 June 1940

'Mum?' Jack asked as he entered the living room. He hadn't spoken to her since Wednesday, and today was Friday. With everything that had been happening they had barely seen each other, and he was concerned that one of her moods might have taken her. Now that he had a day off, he wanted to make sure that she was all right. He had a few minutes before he had to leave and wanted to clear the air. She was sitting in her armchair, near the empty fireplace, knitting needles flicking back and forth as she knitted. She didn't respond straight away, just stared down at her hands.

'What are you making?' he asked as he sat down on the chair

closest to hers. She stopped what she was doing to push the *Guernsey Post* in his direction, but still didn't look up.

'It's happening again,' she said, her voice little more than a whisper. Jack almost hadn't heard what she said. He scanned the headlines, the fractured reports from the continent. He sighed, knowing that the mood he feared had arrived and that now there was nothing he could do or say to make a difference. It could last for days. It was at times like this that he worried for her the most, not knowing what he could do, but wishing. Wishing for something to change.

'We don't know that for sure,' he said, looking her in the eyes to get her attention. 'We can be safe here, even without the army.'

She frowned at him, then a smile bent the corners of her mouth. She reached out a hand and tucked his hair behind his left ear, the way she had always done when he was a child.

'How do you always manage to be so optimistic?' she asked, her features softening. 'You didn't get that from me, so it must be your father.'

'I just wanted to see that you were all right,' he said, trying to deflect the conversation. Talk of his father would only make things worse. She never admitted how much she missed him, but Jack knew it was like a hole in her heart. 'There's no point in worrying. We don't know what will happen. Besides I will be here.'

She patted his arm. 'Thank you,' she said. 'I will be fine as long as you are safe. You're all I have left.'

Jack reflected on her words for a moment, before leaning in to kiss her on the cheek. This was the reason he could never join the army, to follow in his father's footsteps. 'I will always be here for you,' he said, standing and walking to the door. It wasn't a good idea to dwell any longer than was necessary, and best to leave on a high.

'Where are you going?' Her voice was stronger than it had been before, an edge of concern creeping in. Jack didn't answer at first. He had finally managed to lift her mood and he didn't want to ruin it.

'You're going to see that woman, aren't you?'

He stopped dead at the door. 'I wish you wouldn't call her that,' he replied, trying to remain calm and not cause another shouting match. 'You would like her if you gave her a chance. She's a good person.'

'She's trouble. She'll be the death of you, just you wait and see.' She was shouting now. 'I wish you would choose things more carefully. You're just like your father, always running into danger.' He could feel her look of despair piercing the back of his head, as he kept walking, not knowing when he would come back.

*

A swift circled the harbour, wings forming a crossed silhouette against the clear blue sky. It wheeled again, searching, hunting, before disappearing from view behind a bluff. Jack cleared his mind and leant back against the harbour wall in the sunshine. These rare moments of being off duty were a blessing and he was determined not to take them for granted. Johanna would be coming to meet him soon, and he was looking forward to their time together.

A young boy played nearby, rushing around the narrow paving of the harbour, screeching with joy. He clutched a wooden toy in his hand. Jack knew the child, but only in passing. His father was a fisherman who had been out to sea when the evacuation had been arranged. His wife, who Jack knew even less thanks to her reclusive nature, hadn't known what to do and had decided to stay on the island. The boy was all she had. Others were heading down the hill from the High Street to the harbour after hearing the attorney general's daily briefing at the press offices, eager to see the last mail boat off. Perhaps there was some sort of morbid curiosity about it, but Jack was happy to sit and watch the birds.

36

The bird flew up above the harbour again, looking for more prey. A few seconds later it was joined by another, possibly a mate. They hunted together, whisking through the air with speed, before disappearing again in a hurry.

The air was pierced by the metallic whine of an engine, rapidly rising in pitch as it came nearer. Jack could tell from the timbre that it was some kind of aircraft, but at first he couldn't see it. The grey of its fuselage blended with the sky, but as it grew closer its yellow nose cone stood out. The first aircraft rushed past Jack, low, the black cross on its side a blur in motion.

Jack pushed himself to his feet, scanning the harbour as he did so. Others around him, including a group of men unloading tomato trucks by the harbour, stared up at the German aircraft. They had seen aircraft from a distance, but never this close. It could be a reconnaissance mission, simply getting a look at the island, before returning to France. Jack tried to convince himself of that, but something in the back of his mind told him he was wrong.

'The Germans! The Germans are coming!' a man shouted behind Jack. They had all feared it would happen soon, but why now? Jack was blinded by the glare as he looked up to see another plane. He hadn't expected them to come in force. They must have known by now that the islands were undefended, that the army had abandoned them. That bitter fact still troubled him. Why had they left, when they could have prevented this?

The other plane came around, the yellow cone of its propeller facing towards Jack. He resisted the urge to jump out of the way, as it zoomed overhead, the roar of its engine deafening in his ears. There were five other planes in its wake. Too many for reconnaissance, and too close to St Peter Port. Not even the Royal Air Force had dared fly this low.

A rising sense of dread left his stomach feeling empty and numb. There was a chattering sound as one of the plane's guns started up, peppering the road. Chips of stone flew everywhere, almost as deadly as the bullets. Those caught in the road ran or lay where they fell. One of Johanna's friends, a woman called Susanne, was running across the road. The plane banked, pulling up over the town and wheeled around for another pass. Susanne stumbled, her shoe caught in a gutter.

Jack didn't think; he ran towards her, grabbing her around the waist. He pulled her aside as she protested, and they fell together into the dirt at the side of the road, rolling down the shallow hill. The fighter roared overhead and away again, as bits of debris covered the pair. They kept their heads down. His face was close to Susanne's, and he could see the fear in her eyes. They were wide, pupils dilated. There was a moment of intimacy, the feeling of a shared life, safe for a second, before she shifted uncomfortably underneath him.

'Get off me, Jack, you *schwein*.' She pushed at him and it took him a second before he realised that he had been pinning her. He jumped up and helped her from the ground. Jack didn't know her that well. Like Johanna she had come over from Germany, but it wouldn't do to be seen this way.

'You should get out of here,' he said, guiding her in the direction of the town. 'There may be more on the way. Everyone needs to get to safety.'

'Where is safe?' she asked, walking quickly away from him up the road. He didn't have an answer. They would have to do something, and fast. He hurried to keep up. 'If they want to kill us,' she said, 'they will. Nothing here is going to stop them.'

'Just go, Susanne,' he shouted, over the din of the aeroplanes.

'What about you?' she asked.

Jack glanced back towards the harbour. There were still people in danger, and it was his job to keep them safe. 'Look after yourself,' he called back over his shoulder as he started to run. He didn't check to see if she had obeyed his command.

The young boy was the other side of the road from Jack, near one of the now-abandoned tomato trucks. He had been running about, playing in the dirt, but now was scampering in fear. Jack didn't know where the boy's parents were. The boy disappeared behind the truck. A horse whinnied as it bolted and took its cart with it, clattering along the cobbles towards town. A shadow crossed the sky and Jack felt a sudden wave of pressure. The truck exploded with a flash of flame. The shockwave struck Jack, pushing him back. A rush of heat washed over him as he hit the ground, and rolled, trying to put some distance between himself and the flames. The sound rang in his ears, drowning out everything else. He thought he could hear crying, but it could have just been the screech of breaking metal. He had never experienced anything like this before. It was like stepping too close to a bonfire. He felt his skin burning, like an intense sunburn that threatened to overwhelm him.

After a few seconds the heat subsided and he managed to roll onto his side. His body was bruised and scratched, and he felt weak. On the ground next to his hand was a small wooden toy, cut into the shape of a car, its varnish now covered in reddish-brown blood. The boy was nowhere to be seen amongst the debris and the flames. A timber yard's warehouse had been hit and thick black smoke spread across the harbour.

The planes disappeared into the clouds, the roar of their engines a faint hum, but he knew that wouldn't be the end of it. They were attacking an undefended island – nothing could stop them. As they circled back around, using the coast as a reference point, the machine noise of their engines grew louder again.

Jack pushed himself to his feet with a groan. He had to do something. He felt alone on the harbour now, as if everyone else had either fled or been engulfed by flames. The aircraft would be back in a few seconds.

Jack hobbled across the harbour to a boat and climbed over the hand rail. It was a wonder it was still floating, and so far the flames had not spread to its hull. He searched around the netting and supplies for something that would be useful, as he heard the plane's guns roar into life. He didn't have much time.

After a few moments scrabbling on his hands and knees, he found what he was looking for: a piece of white cloth, either a discarded piece of clothing or a sheet. He grabbed it and jumped back onto the pier, looking for the planes in the sky. The bright sun burned his eyes and he had to look away, blinking. The purple bruise remained behind his eyelids, a warning.

Using his ears to guide him, he ran up the pier in the direction of the aircraft. Others would say that running into danger was crazy, but that was who he was. He ripped the cloth in two, discarding one half. He raised it above his head and waved it back and forth a few times, hoping to catch the pilot's attention. The wind blew the cloth around his head, further obscuring his view and he ripped it again, pulling off a smaller piece this time. He tried again, not knowing whether it would do any good. Surely by now the pilots must have realised that there was no resistance, no one shooting back. The plane dropped its nose, pointing in his direction once again. Jack could see the barrels of its guns. He stood stock-still, holding the white cloth up in front of him. Sweat was pouring down his brow, but he didn't dare move. Fear and shock had glued him in place. Time stretched to eternity. Then in a rush of engine noise the plane zoomed straight over his head.

Jack turned on the spot, following its flight. Rather than banking and wheeling around to head back to the harbour, it maintained a straight course, flying over St Peter Port and gradually increasing in altitude. The other aircraft joined up in formation on its wings. Jack stood still as he watched them disappear over the island. He was left with the smell of burning fuel and the taste of iron on his tongue. The planes were gone for now, but he knew with a certainty he hadn't felt before, that the Germans were on their way.

Lifeboats

Despite the warm summer sun, the sea swelled as if a storm was coming. It rose then fell, throwing the lifeboat from side to side in anger. The wind blew across the ship, whipping the seven men on deck with white spray. Richard had sailed this way many times before, but never under these circumstances. The boat rocked and he set his face in grim determination against the salty wet spray as he thought of what he had been asked to do. After the British army had left the islands, the powers that be had thought about what else the island had in its possession and fell on the idea of their lifeboats. He'd received a telegram telling him that under no circumstances could the lifeboats fall into German hands. The only option left had been to collect them and deliver them into the care of the navy at the mainland.

As such, Richard had assembled a crew of seven men, who were now on their way to Jersey across the Roussels, the stretch of water between the islands, to collect their lifeboat, tie it to their own and begin the arduous journey over to England. They hoped they could be done before the Germans arrived, but they had no idea what was really happening on the continent.

One of his sons pushed a mug of hot tea into his cold hands

and muttered something that was lost in the noise of the engine. He moved away from the pilot's position, leaving Richard with his mug of tea, and spoke to his brother, patting him on the back in his usual manner. It wouldn't be long until they approached Jersey. He'd had someone phone ahead to tell them he was coming, so he hoped they wouldn't kick up a fuss about him taking their boat. They wouldn't be happy about it, either way. For communities that relied on the sea, a lifeboat was vital. Richard had rescued many a struggling fisherman from a tricky sea when things had grown out of their control. He didn't dare think what would happen without them.

He had considered simply hiding the lifeboat away somewhere, but had decided against it in the long run. He wasn't a good liar, and they would no doubt find the boats before long. He had been unable to think of an alternative and, as he stood at the prow of the boat he had spent so long working on, he wondered whether he should have simply refused and taken the consequences.

Suddenly there was the sound of an engine, rising in pitch, breaking through his reverie. At first Richard thought it was the lifeboat, but the rhythm was different, at a counterpoint to their own ship. He looked around for the sign of another boat, but they were alone in the seas not far now from Jersey. The sound came again, this time much closer. Richard crossed the front of the boat and finally saw it. There was a faint grey shape silhouetted against the sky. Then he saw another, its companion. They were getting closer, turning into the unmistakable outlines of aircraft. The German cross was clearly visible, black against the grey of the underwings.

Richard hoped they would be ignored, due to the giant red cross that was painted on the top of the lifeboat, but his illusion was soon shattered by a spitting sound. Spray jumped out of the sea in front of the boat like sprites in two parallel lines, getting closer.

'Get down!' Richard shouted as he heard the splintering of wood. Bullets hit the fuselage as he ducked down to find some cover. The crew cried out in surprise as they hid. There was a sound like a saw against wood. Shards of timber came loose as rounds cut through the hull, then the German aircraft rushed over them in a roar of engines. Richard didn't dare get back up, knowing there was another coming. A second later more bullets crashed around him, narrowly missing him, whistling past his ears. Then suddenly the other aircraft was gone, the pitch of its engines lowering in a Doppler shift.

It took a minute or so before Richard felt safe enough to lift his head. He looked up and the aircraft could no longer be seen. The faint hum of their engines was still audible in the distance, and he had no idea how long they had before the planes came around for another attack. The boat was heavily damaged, but still seaworthy as most of the damage had been done to the hull above the waterline. He pulled himself out of the netting, his legs aching from being squeezed into a small space.

The crew had clustered towards the back of the ship. They all stood now and, as he got nearer, he noticed a shape slumped across the stern bench. Impossibly his heartbeat rose and there was a pressure in his chest, a dull pain that was growing sharper by the moment. The shape was horribly familiar, and the crew pulled aside as Richard dragged himself nearer.

'My son?' The words escaped his lips, but he barely heard them over the beating of his heart. His son was lying there as if sleeping, but Richard knew he would never sleep on the job. His eyes were closed, but his chest didn't rise. There was a red mark on his temple and blood dripped down his sleeve. Richard fell to his knees. There was a wailing sound, but he didn't know where it came from until the motion of the boat caused him to close his mouth. He cradled his son's head in his arms, but it was too late.

Chapter 4

28 June 1940

Jack stayed at the harbour for as long as the flames from the ruined trucks would allow him. It was his duty to make sure that everyone else got away safely, at least, those who could. The clean-up operation would take some time, but that was the least of their worries. The German planes were dropping bombs on the rest of St Peter Port and the island, and he even saw one land near the hospital. Before long the planes would have to return to the continent to refuel, but they would be back, of that he was sure. He had grown almost accustomed to the sounds of explosions, but he had yet to see the full consequences.

There was still no sign of the boy who had been playing on the road. The tomato trucks that lined the way out of the harbour were ruined wrecks, some of which were still on fire. Their metal frames were a stark reminder of the terrible damage aircraft could cause. The few ambulances on the island had struggled to get through the wreckage and it had been some time since Jack had last seen one. If he found anyone else alive, he would have to either treat them himself, or somehow get them the help they needed.

He crawled under the wreckage of one of the trucks. It was still warm, like a fire late at night, and there was a smell of burnt tomatoes. As he crawled, his hand came up covered in a watery red paste. A pool of crimson liquid was spreading out, staining everything it touched. The cloth knees of his trousers were sodden, and he thought he would never get those marks out. It wasn't the only thing; the horror of the last hour would haunt him forever. Most of the colour was from the tomatoes, but he didn't doubt there was some blood mixed in there. He knew it wouldn't be the last of the islanders' blood to be spilt. He just hoped that wherever Johanna was, she had kept away from the bombs.

His search under the truck was futile. If any of the people who had hidden under the vehicles were still there, then they would need a lot more than a policeman to find them. The boy was dead and he couldn't do anything about that. There was no sign of his parents either, and Jack wondered if they had perished together.

He crawled back out from under the ruined cab in shock and wiped his hands on the thighs of his trousers. He looked up as he heard a scraping noise, instantly on guard. A man, only a few years older than Jack, was shuffling along the road, awkwardly dragging one leg as if he had been hit. He had a white cloth or piece of clothing tied round his head, in an attempt to staunch a head wound that was still bleeding. The blood stained his neck and shirt, and his skin was covered in a patina of black ash from the fires. He didn't seem to notice Jack as he passed, absorbed in his own personal hell. The man was far from the first walking wounded Jack had seen and he was sure the hospital would be inundated. The island didn't have much in the way of medical facilities, and the population was only small. They never expected it to come to this.

Jack moved closer and reached a hand to put an aiding arm around him. 'I'll be all right,' the man said, his voice barely a whisper, and shrugged Jack off with a wince of pain.

Jack let go, but the man stumbled. He managed to right himself, with a groan, but then the strength seemed to ebb from him completely and he dropped to one knee. The man sagged further before Jack could catch him. He was a deadweight in Jack's hands as he eased him to the ground and then knelt down to check his pulse. His heartbeat was still strong and he was breathing, if faintly. He would need medical help and there was no way that Jack could leave him there.

Jack looked around but he was alone, apart from a few firemen who were trying to put out the remaining fires. Jack cradled the man's head with one arm while he reached around his waist with the other and prepared to lift him up. He didn't want to risk his head dropping onto the hard road, but he needed to get a good enough grip. There was no way the man would be able to carry himself to the hospital. Bending his knees, Jack hauled him onto his shoulder. The man groaned like someone coming around from sleep. It was a lift they had been taught in their police training, but it didn't do much to displace the man's weight. It did, however, make him easier to carry and less likely to slip off Jack's shoulder.

He lurched forward, hoping that the man's weight would add to his momentum, but cautious not to let him pull both of them over. With each step Jack could feel his own wounds more, not just scratches and grazes, but bleeding cuts where shrapnel had hit him. They both needed help, and he would do his best to get them to the hospital.

*

As Jack arrived at the Country Hospital, there were still German planes circling in the sky. The smell of cordite and smoke was strong, but it didn't appear to be coming from here. The walk had been tough, more of a stumble, and he hadn't known whether he would make it.

He could already hear the hubbub of frantic noise coming from inside the hospital, and what sounded like someone shouting in pain. A pair of legs stuck out from under the engine of an ambulance and Jack could hear a hammering as the mechanic tried to get it going again. On a normal day Jack would have gone over to see if he could help, but he could be more use inside, even if he lacked much in the way of medical know-how. Johanna was far better qualified to help, but she wasn't here. He clung on to the hope that she hadn't been hurt in all this; she couldn't have been.

He crossed under the porch, walking as quickly as he could, his limbs exhausted. Unusually, there was no one other than the mechanic outside the building. It was as if the whole island had been abandoned, thrown into a silence of reflective mourning. Jack could hear the faint birdsong in the trees, enjoying the summer evening. It was strangely peaceful against the backdrop of such chaos. What care did the birds have that humanity was destroying itself?

Jack pushed his way through the hospital's double doors and was immediately hit with a wall of noise. He could hear people shouting down the corridors. A loud cry of pain was masked by the scream of an order or instruction. The hospital was almost as chaotic as the harbour had been.

Jack headed for the nearest room, looking for a bed for the man on his back. The room was occupied by a man with a white bandage wrapped around his head, sitting up calmly in the bed as if reading a book. Jack moved on, struggling to keep the man on his back, as if being in the hospital had given his body enough reason to give up. Nurses moved through the corridors, going from one room to the next. None of them seemed to notice him. He thought he saw Johanna's red-brown curls float past the end of the corridor, Johanna wearing a nurse's uniform. She was a trained nurse, but it couldn't be, because she didn't have a job. His mind was playing tricks on him.

There was a narrow bench in the corridor, which was typically used while waiting for an appointment. Jack leant over and laid the man down as gently as possible. The other man groaned as Jack moved him and his head rested on the cold metal. Jack wrenched off his Guernsey jumper, rolling it up, then placed it under the man's head. It was covered in dirt and blood, but at least it would be more comfortable.

He gently caught the arm of a passing nurse, but she fixed him with a scowl. He let go and apologised. 'This man,' he said. 'He needs help.'

Her scowl softened and then turned to a frown of concern. She reached out and checked the man's pulse, then carefully checked his wounds, before placing the rudimentary dressings back in place. She turned to Jack, concern still in her bright blue eyes. His heart thumped in his chest.

'He'll be fine,' she said. 'For now. We'll get to him as soon as we can. As you can imagine we are completely overwhelmed in here, and we currently have far more pressing problems with other patients. I will send a doctor to him as soon as I'm able.'

She turned to leave. 'I'm a policeman,' Jack said, stopping her in her tracks. 'What can I do to help?'

'Help?' she replied. 'You can see if any of the doctors need anything holding. A lot of our jobs are fetching, holding, but if you're willing to help …'

'Right.' Jack nodded.

'This way,' she said, turning and marching along the corridor.

He followed, glancing into the other rooms as he passed. The medical staff were treating more patients than he had ever seen in once place. Most of the doors were shut. The hospital was packed now, but what would happen once the Germans actually came? Would they continue attacking until there was no one left? He tried to focus on more immediate concerns. The shock of the initial attack was wearing off and his mind was racing. He wanted to do something, anything, to help, to take his mind off what was happening. The nurse stopped and pointed in the direction of a room.

'If the doctor needs any help,' she said, 'you'll be best placed in there.'

With that she was gone. Inside the room a middle-aged doctor in a white coat, its arms pushed up to his elbows, worked on a man who was lying on a metal gurney and bleeding heavily from a chest wound. The doctor was forcing gauze against the wound as a nurse handed him fresh materials, but the blood covered everything around it and it smelt strongly of iron. He said something to the nurse who rushed from the room. The doctor's hands were covered in blood, and a bead of sweat worked its way down his brow. Jack took a tentative step inside, not wanting to disturb the doctor in the middle of his important work.

'Who are you?' the doctor asked without looking up. He tied two ends of the fabric together in a quick knot with practised ease, then reached out to check the patient's pulse.

'Police Constable Godwin,' Jack replied, still in the doorway. 'I've come to see if I can help.'

'Well, don't just bloody stand there.' The doctor didn't raise his voice. He was used to being obeyed. 'Get over here.'

Jack rushed to the gurney. He'd had basic health training in the police, but it hadn't prepared him for something like this.

'Apply pressure here,' the doctor said as Jack stood over the patient. 'And here.'

The wound had been bleeding heavily and the bedsheets were brown with stains. The man groaned as he fought to stay conscious. Jack didn't know how hard to push, unsure if he would do more harm than good, but he kept a steady pressure while the man moved under his hands.

'Keep still, keep still,' the doctor murmured as he checked the other wounds. 'He may yet survive if we can stop the bleeding. But it'll be a long night for him. We'll have to be patient.'

He reached out to shake Jack's hand. 'Doctor Abbott,' he said, nodding as they shook hands. The man's close-cut brown hair was turning silver around the temples, which made him look older than Jack had originally thought. Jack knew most of the people on the island, at least in passing, but he had never seen this doctor before. He spoke with a mainland accent, but many of those in the top professions did these days. He had heard mention of a doctor returning to the island after working on the mainland for a number of years. Abbott must have been that man.

'Thank you, Constable,' the doctor said, wiping his bloodied hands on a cloth then putting it in a bin. 'I suspect our day isn't over yet.'

A crumble of dust fell from the ceiling as another explosion rocked the hospital, punctuating the doctor's words. He gave Jack a knowing look. 'Especially if they keep that up.'

Chapter 5

29 June 1940

Jack opened the front door gently, wary of the creaking hinges. It felt like days since he had been home but it was only yesterday. He half expected the furniture to be gone, the house forgotten and abandoned, with a patina of dust everywhere. However, the front room was exactly as he had left it, the only difference being that his mother wasn't sitting in her chair. A plate of forgotten breakfast food – a slice of bread and some jam – sat on the table, a pile of discarded papers next to it. He was still wearing his stained clothes, but before changing he wanted to check on his mother.

Jack could hear noise in the kitchen, broken by the occasional chatter and cough of his grandparents coming from their room. So he picked up the plate and went to look. His stomach rumbled, reminding him how long it had been since he had eaten. He was tempted to eat what was left on the plate, but he thought he'd check with his mother first. She had her back to him as he opened the door, but she didn't turn as he entered. She stood stock-still, as if waiting for something. He couldn't tell if it was his exhaustion, or whether she shook slightly as she stood.

'Mum?' he asked softly, so as not to surprise her. She was like a statue, cold and immobile, if not for the faint shiver that racked her body. He moved around the kitchen table, coming alongside her so that he could get a better look, to try to see into her eyes, to see what she was thinking. Still she didn't move. It was as if she was dead to the world. Her lips opened, silently whispering to herself. The repetition was like a mantra, as if she was reassuring herself of something. He couldn't work out what she was saying. He placed the plate on the side and reached out a hand towards her, trying to make some form of connection between them. She drifted further away from him every day. As his hand neared her shoulder, she shook it away, this time more violently, as if it offended her.

'I thought you weren't coming back,' she whispered.

It was faint, but clear enough once he could register the words. 'I heard the planes, the bombs.' There was more power in her voice this time, but it was still as if she was recalling a painful memory. She hadn't moved or stopped staring in the same direction. He had seen shock like this before in his work as a policeman, when people had been told – or seen – uncomfortable things. They would switch off, distance themselves from the world to stop themselves from believing it was real. Like shell shock, the results were often crippling. After the events of last night, he was sure that there would be many more people across the island feeling the same effects. The main difference was that he had returned, when so many others hadn't.

'I thought you were gone, that you weren't coming back,' she said again, more confident this time. Jack wanted to reach out and pull her into a hug, but he knew somehow that she would stand there like a statue, immobile and unable to feel his love through the embrace.

'I'm here,' he replied, tilting his head to the side and trying to get her to look at him. 'I'm here.'

'Are you?' she asked. 'Are you really?'

'Yes.'

He touched her shoulder, finally, hoping the sensation would back up his claim.

'Your father came to me too, through the darkness. I thought he was real at first, but then he went again. Like he always does. Like you always do.'

Jack wasn't sure what to say. His mother seldom talked about his father, least of all like this. Maybe it was because she didn't feel he was real that she was doing so now. He had tried before to get her to talk about the father he had never known, but even on her good days she had refused, saying it was too difficult for her. Everything he knew about the man he had got from his grandfather.

'Mum, look at me,' he said. 'I'm here, it's really me. I'm safe, I'm alive.'

She turned finally, and her eyes were glassy and distant.

'Are any of us really safe, Jack?'

So much had happened in the last few days that he no longer knew the answer to that question. 'I don't know,' he said. Even in his mother's fragile mental state, it wouldn't do to lie to her. She would see right through him. He also hoped it would make him more real to her. Would a spectre tell the truth, or would it tell her what she wanted to hear? 'I don't know if we're safe, and I don't know what's going to happen,' he continued, fixing his gaze on hers and keeping his voice clear. 'But as long as we stick together, we can come through this.'

'I thought the Germans had taken you, that you'd gone. Gone like your father. You're all I have, my son.' She placed the palm of her hand against his face as she looked up at him, her skin cold to the touch.

He gripped her shoulder, trying to be reassuring, but careful not to squeeze too tight. 'I'm here, and I will always be. I'm not going anywhere.'

The island was home, the people on it his family. His entire world was here, and he had never known anything else. Johanna had thought about leaving, but she knew that he couldn't, not while there was still something to stay for.

'You should go,' she said after a moment, her voice faint. 'Find safety. Go to England, at least the Germans haven't got there yet and they may never get there. Please, go!'

Tears were streaming down her cheeks and she was attempting to wipe them away with the back of her hand. Jack wasn't used to such an open display of emotion, but still he went to her and put an arm around her shoulders. 'I'm not going anywhere. Anyway, it's too late for that. I'm going to stay and look after you, Grandpa and Nan. Better here in our home than refugees in England.'

He held her for a while longer while the sobs subsided and his arm grew stiff.

*

The faint breeze fluttered the flag as Jack walked nearer, looking up into the bright summer sky. The Union flag was resplendent against the backdrop of the sun, its cord snapping against the pole with a sharp pinging noise. The rhythm was irregular, beaten by the whim of the wind. On other days the tinny noise would be irritating, but today it provided a sense of melancholy, the only sound against a sea of silence on an island that felt utterly abandoned. It had flown above the White Rock as long as Jack could remember, sometimes at half mast, but never removed.

Jack had volunteered for the task, but he didn't relish it. For some reason he wanted to save anyone else from the ignominious duty. He took a hold of the cord but hesitated. He wanted one last look at the Union flag flying over the island, to cement in his mind the time before, the time when things had seemed less fraught. It was entirely symbolic, the flag and everything else that went with it, but something in him knew that symbols were more important than he or most people ever imagined.

Finally, he pulled the cord and the flag lurched its way down the flagpole, jerking with each motion of his hand. He took his time and watched the wind against the cloth. It struck him then as odd. Here he was, a British policeman in uniform, striking the flag of the Union from the town's flagpole, removing it entirely. If the flag no longer applied to them, then what did the uniform mean? He was proud of his uniform and he had worked hard to earn it, but did it really make sense to go on wearing it? When the Germans got to the island would they strip them of their uniforms and responsibility, or would they make them wear something to represent the Reich?

They hadn't been told anything yet, but that only made Jack more anxious. All they knew was that they had to prepare for occupation, to visibly show their surrender and to remove all British flags from view. It left them in a weird state of limbo. Jack's job as a policeman defined him, and he had been obsessed with holding up the law since he was a child, but now he had no idea who he was in this new world.

Jack untied the Union flag from its cord and folded it. There were people on the island to whom the flag meant very little. They considered themselves Guernesiais rather than British, but it meant something to Jack. He didn't run up a new flag. It wasn't his responsibility. He wanted to be the last who remembered the Union flag and what being part of the empire had meant for them. He was supposed to return the flag to the bailiff, but he didn't think he would. They wouldn't miss it, and besides he couldn't trust them to keep it safe. He would take it home. There was a drawer beside his bed in which he kept many of his prized possessions. The flag would find a welcome home there, until it was needed again.

For now, the hour had come for them to face their fate.

*

30 June 1940

Jack had just sat down in the main office of the police station when the door flew open and the chief officer marched in. Jack's legs were weary from patrolling all day, but still he pulled himself from the chair and stood to attention as etiquette demanded. The others in the room did the same at various intervals and they all threw smart salutes. The chief saluted back, then turned towards the door as a man in the grey uniform of the German Wehrmacht stepped in, followed by an adjutant or aide similarly dressed. A surprised silence filled the room. The Germans had finally arrived.

'I would like to introduce the German Kommandant,' the chief said, stepping aside in deference to the man in the grey uniform, his peaked cap now tucked under his arm. 'He will be in charge of operations on the island, and I expect you to show him exactly the same level of respect that you show me.'

In normal circumstances someone would have cracked a joke at that point. Instead, the assembled policemen stood there, awkwardly awaiting orders. After a second or two those at the front of the room threw a stiff salute and the others joined in, Jack amongst them.

'Thank you,' the kommandant said with a thick German accent as he stepped forward to appraise them. The man was even older than the chief, twenty or thirty years Jack's senior. He had a thin nose and deep brown eyes, and his hair was cut close, more silver than black. His uniform was just as cleanly pressed as every other German Jack had seen, but made from a better quality grey wool. An Iron Cross was tied at the neck of his tunic and gold braiding decorated his collar and epaulettes. His aristocratic bearing was obvious from the way he looked down his pointy nose at everyone.

'I am happy to be here.' His English was stilted as if he had practised the words. It was as though he didn't really understand what he was saying, but had decided to say it nonetheless. Jack suspected that his command of the language was nothing to do with the reason he had been chosen for the position of commander of the occupation forces. Another German soldier stood at his shoulder, quietly looking over the assembled policeman. As on previous occasions when a French diplomat or some other authority had come to the island, they had been provided with an interpreter.

'But my English is not so good,' the kommandant continued. It was an unexpected admission for the kommandant, who had the air of a practised public speaker, a man who was never wrong, or allowed himself to be inferior. If it was a deliberate attempt to be disarming then Jack suspected that it had worked in a way. There was a relaxation of the tension around the room as the men realised that nothing they said would be understood by the German, and that his interpreter would probably not waste the time in translation.

He smiled at them in a way that didn't reach his eyes, then gestured for his interpreter to step forward. The kommandant spoke, then the interpreter translated into perfectly structured and accented English. Jack couldn't help feel that the interpreter was only paraphrasing what his superior officer was saying. He talked about how they had come in advance of the main force, their plans for the island, how none of them had anything to worry about as they were very fond of the islands and the Aryan people who inhabited them, and that they wanted it to be the very 'model' occupation they had all dreamed about.

When he had finished speaking, he smiled again, but Jack noticed that it was slightly more forced than the first time. Perhaps he had been expecting more of a response from the policemen, as they simply stood and stared.

After that he said something quietly to the chief that the interpreter relayed and then he walked around the various desks in the office, looking at them over the top of his glasses. A minute or so later, he stopped in front of Jack who felt his stance stiffen under the German's attention. If he had been uncomfortable before, he was even more so now. There was a look on the German's face that Jack thought was surprise. The kommandant rearranged the small glasses on his nose.

'Are you not young for the police?' he asked, speaking through the interpreter, then continued as if he didn't expect an answer. 'I would have thought a young man of your age to be with your army.'

'We're not subject to the same laws as the mainland, Kommandant,' the chief jumped in. 'That is to say, England has different rules to us.'

'Fascinating.' The kommandant turned, apparently now bored of the conversation. 'Then I suspect that very little will change at all.'

'Although,' he continued. 'It does surprise me that a young man such as yourself did not sign up with the British army to fight for your fatherland. Did you not want to defend your land? Perhaps you are a coward?'

Jack could feel his cheeks going red, but he stayed silent. The kommandant and his interpreter's voice droned on as Jack tried to concentrate against his growing anger.

'Or could it be that you are one of us and you welcomed us here? That you truly understood what the German Reich can bring? You are a true Aryan. The Führer would be proud to find such people in his new lands. Perhaps I should write to him of the great people of Guernsey and how they are looking forward to being part of the thousand-year Reich!'

The interpreter smiled at Jack when he finished speaking. It was a smile that spoke in volumes, a smile that on one hand told him that the interpreter thought that the kommandant believed his words, and on the other hand that Jack should ignore him completely. Without waiting for a response, the kommandant sat at the chief's desk and glanced through some papers. It was a clear show that he was keen on being involved in the day-to-day workings of the island, but it left the interpreter standing awkwardly by Jack. He smiled again and there was a warmth there that Jack wasn't expecting.

Jack shuffled his feet, praying for this situation to end as quickly as possible. The silence dragged on and he felt more and more visible as the seconds clicked away.

'Your English is very good,' he said to the interpreter, trying to fill the gap.

'Thank you. I studied in England, and it's a great opportunity to have a chance to practise it. It's a fascinating language, a mixture of German, French, and Latin. Fascinating.'

Jack nodded in reply, almost regretting the compliment. He didn't want to be drawn into a conversation with the man, but the silence was even worse. He shuffled again, suddenly feeling the weight of his legs. He realised the interpreter was waiting expectantly for a response. He racked his brain for something appropriate to say, but all he wanted to do was to scream *'get out!' The closer they were to him, the closer they were to Johanna.*

'Where did you study?' he asked instead, hoping that the conversation would end up with the kommandant drawing his interpreter away.

'Oh, er,' the interpreter mumbled, apparently surprised by the question. Jack wondered if anyone had taken an interest in him like this before, or had merely passed him off as an extension of the kommandant. 'At the School of Tropical Medicine in Liverpool. A fascinating place. Naturally since the war began I have had other duties to perform. I must attend to the kommandant. Excuse me.'

The kommandant had stood again, turned to leave, then stepped to the side, as if he had forgotten something. He snapped his heels together, while raising his right arm into the air with his palm outstretched. 'Heil Hitler!' he shouted.

The German liaison officer barely hesitated before he too clipped together his heels. 'Heil Hitler!' he returned with equal conviction.

There was an awkward moment as the kommandant appeared to

look around the room. The others appeared unsure, shuffled their feet and looked at each other for direction. David's eyes bored right into Jack's from across the room, and Jack shook his head with as little motion as possible. There was no way that he would salute. Sure, they were in charge now, but what did it mean to him? Who was Hitler to Jack? He may serve him in some way, but he wasn't about to debase himself like that. David seemed to be buoyed by Jack's response, and he took a deep breath before returning to work.

The kommandant let his arm drop, and nodded to the interpreter, before finally leaving the room, his highly polished boots clicking lightly as he walked along the tiled corridor floor. The interpreter followed a few steps behind and the sound disappeared into the distance. It was another moment before everyone returned to work and sound rushed back into the room like a coming tide.

Jack stood, strong in his decision. There was something about the kommandant that Jack couldn't quite identify, but something told him he would have to watch himself. He could never let them know about Johanna and who she truly was. He didn't think any of them could be trusted. His eyes went to the orders the kommandant had left behind, which had already been circulated to the press for the morning papers. Some of them would be almost impossible to follow.

ORDERS OF THE COMMANDANT OF THE GERMAN FORCES IN OCCUPATION OF THE Island OF GUERNSEY

1st July 1940

(1) All inhabitants must be indoors by 11.00 p.m. and must not leave their homes before 6.00 a.m.
(2) We will respect the population in Guernsey; but, should anyone attempt to cause the least trouble, serious measures will be taken and the town will be bombed.
(3) All orders given by the military authority are to be strictly obeyed.

(4) All spirits must be locked up immediately and no spirits may be supplied, obtained or consumed henceforth. This prohibition does not apply to stocks in private houses.

(5) No person shall enter the aerodrome at La Villiaze.

(6) All rifles, airguns, pistols, revolvers, sporting guns, and all other weapons whatsoever, except souvenirs, must, together with all ammunition, be delivered at the Royal Hotel by 12 noon today, 1st July.

(7) All British sailors, airmen, and soldiers on leave in this island must report at the police station at 9.00 a.m. today and must then report at the Royal Hotel.

(8) No boat or vessel of any description, including any fishing boat, shall leave the harbour or any other place where the same is moored, without an order from the military authority, to be obtained at the Royal Hotel. All boats arriving from Jersey, from Sark or from Herm, or elsewhere, must remain in harbour until permitted by the military to leave. The crews will remain on board. The master will report to the harbourmaster, St Peter Port, and will obey his instructions.

(9) The sale of motor spirit is prohibited, except for use on essential services, such as doctors' vehicles, the delivery of foodstuffs and sanitary services where such vehicles are in possession of a permit from the military authority to obtain supplies. These vehicles must be brought to the Royal Hotel by 12 noon today to receive the necessary permission. The use of cars for private purposes is forbidden.

(10) The black-out regulations already in force must be observed as before.

(11) Banks and shops will be open as usual.

(Signed) THE GERMAN COMMANDANT OF THE Island OF GUERNSEY

Chapter 6

1 July 1940

When he was walking home he couldn't help thinking that he hadn't seen Johanna since before the invasion. She had sent word to the police station that she was all right, but he longed to see her with his own eyes. When they had first met, almost two years ago now, they would spend their evenings together as often as possible, talking about everything and nothing all at once. That was before the war had come and changed everything. Since the attack he felt her absence more keenly. She had come to the island to escape her past, she had said, but now she was desperately trying to find work as a foreigner.

He was reminded of their early days together when he passed Creasey's department store at No. 9 High Street and spotted the window display. There were a pair of sapphire shoes in the window that Johanna had pined over when they had last been there. He looked at the price and sighed. There was no way he would be able to afford them on a policeman's wage, not unless he saved up for some time. With the war going on and now the occupation, he didn't know whether spending all his money was a good idea. He wondered what would happen to their money and the banks now that the Germans had taken over. Part of him thought that it didn't really matter anymore, their lives as they knew it were over, all they could do now was take care of themselves, while the other part of his brain told him the only way through it all was to stick together.

He entered the department store through the double doors and was immediately amongst the goods they sold, everything he could think of from musty-smelling leather clothing, to hat boxes and luggage. The shop had prided itself on selling everything the Islanders needed all in one place, and the inside of the store always filled him with wonder. Unfortunately he didn't get many chances to come here, except for the few times when Johanna and he were together, so now he walked amongst the racks and rows, taking it all in.

As he passed one counter a staff member looked up and spotted him. A smile broke out across her face and Jack mentally prepared himself for a sales pitch, but it didn't come.

'Jack Godwin,' she said, still smiling. 'What brings you in here?'

She stopped what she had been doing and placed it to one side. It took Jack a long moment to fully recognise her. It had only been a couple of months since he had last seen her, and it was amazing how much someone could change in that time. 'Madeleine?' he asked, uncertain. Her face had filled out since he had last seen her, and the shop assistant's dress made her look older. Her blonde hair was cut shorter than when they were children.

'For a second there I thought you didn't recognise me.'

Madeleine and Jack had first met as toddlers at the same school and, while he would never call them firm friends, they had always been close. He felt a wave of something pass over him, like butterflies in his stomach. He had had feelings for her then, but they had only been children. 'I could never forget you, I just didn't expect to see you here. I didn't know you worked here.'

'You charmer you,' she said, waving a hand idly in his direction. 'It's nice to see that one of us hasn't changed.'

She placed a hand on her stomach and for the first time Jack noticed the swell there. It had been hidden behind the counter, but as she stood up it was easier to see. He noticed the wedding ring he hadn't spotted before.

'Congratulations,' he said, forcing a smile onto his face. He was genuinely happy for her, but the shock had caught him off guard. He had never really considered that they were old enough to have children, nor thought about marrying Johanna himself, not really. He didn't know Madeleine had been seeing anyone, nor had he yet mentioned Johanna to her, even though they had been together for a couple of years now. Something held him back. He wished she was here now – she would know what to say – but Maddy seemed to guess the questions running through his head.

'Thank you,' she said, all smiles. 'It's all a bit sudden. But then isn't everything right now? My husband's in the army. He wanted me to go with him, but I had no one to go to in England and I couldn't leave my family. You know how it is?'

Jack nodded. None of them wanted to be refugees in England, with nowhere to go and no jobs, and they couldn't leave their families behind. He smiled, unsure what else to say.

'Well, good luck with everything.' The words stumbled out. 'Let me know if you need anything.'

'Thank you.'

'Disgraceful!' The woman's voice came from nearby at another counter, shrill and raised above the level appropriate for inside conversation. It was a voice Jack recognised well, and he closed his eyes for a second, sighing, before he turned around. At first Jack thought she had been referring to Maddy, but Mrs Fletcher was talking to another young woman at the other counter. The woman was clearly trying to finish something whilst doing her best to show interest in the customer. Jack nodded at Madeleine and went over to see if he could defuse the situation. He knew that Mrs Fletcher wasn't fond of him, but then she wasn't particularly fond of anyone.

Mrs Fletcher was one of his neighbours, and he would often

spot her staring out of a window, observing everything that went on in St Peter Port. She had a face that he could only describe as being full of hate. He could never imagine the sag of her jowls creasing into something even approaching a smile and her beady eyes behind her glasses always stared as if in silent judgement. Only her judgement was seldom silent. The dress she wore looked as if it would have been the height of fashion during the last war, but was now considered impractical and uncomfortable. Even though she made a point of presentation and appropriate etiquette, her mousy blonde hair always seemed as if she had mislaid her hairbrush, no matter how hard she tied it back. It was no wonder she was unhappy as the ravages of age took their toll, but was there really any need for her to be so mean to others?

'What's that you're working on?' he asked the shop assistant when he got to the counter. She had a needle and thread in one hand, while the other hand held a piece of material down on the desk. She was dressed in a similar manner to Madeleine, but with brunette hair that fell around her shoulders. Jack didn't recognise her. Even though the island was small, Jack didn't know everyone by name.

On the other hand, Mrs Fletcher recognised him immediately, her cold eyes fixing on him. She interrupted just as the assistant was about to speak, 'Oh, it's you,' she said. It wasn't a question, but more of an accusation. 'Have you seen what this girl is doing?' she asked, but continued before he could say anything. 'It's disgraceful, that's what it is.'

Jack raised his voice a little to make sure that he was heard, but not loud enough that she could accuse him of shouting at her. She had done that before. 'What is she doing, Mrs Fletcher? I'm sure she's just doing her job – isn't that right, miss?'

The woman nodded at him, apparently unable to find the words.

'Have a look for yourself, go on.' She thrust a thin finger towards the material. 'Disgraceful,' she muttered.

Jack moved so that he could subtly manoeuvre himself between Mrs Fletcher and the assistant. This time he spoke in a more calming tone. He was used to adjusting his manner as a policeman, and some people needed a gentler touch. He smiled, trying to give her the sense that this was between them and to ignore the Fletcher woman, but it was hard to express all that in a smile.

'What's the problem?' he asked, being deliberately vague so that she could give her version of events. The assistant hesitated, looking over his shoulder and then tried to form the words, but they only came out in a stutter. 'Take your time.'

She nodded, closed her eyes and took a deep breath. She smiled and then found her words. 'I'm one of the seamstresses here at Creasey's.' She almost struggled on the esses but managed to compose herself. Jack nodded. She started unfolding the material so that she could show him what she was working on. 'I've been asked to make a flag, see? A German chap came in here and asked for it specifically. They said he was the commander or something.'

She held up the red material for him to see and he finally realised. She had been stitching a white circlet in the middle of the flag, and the black cross of the German Reich lay next to it to be attached when she was ready.

'Well?' Mrs Fletcher butted in, and Jack had almost forgotten she was there. He couldn't help but agree with her, but there was no way he was going to say that out loud. 'Shouldn't your lot be doing something about this kind of thing? Make her stop.'

Jack resisted the urge to sigh. What exactly was he 'supposed' to do about the German invasion of Guernsey? They could hardly stand up to an army, and it was apparent that elements of the German invasion force were already making themselves known on the island.

'I can no more make her stop, than you can, Mrs Fletcher.' She looked as if she was on the verge of trying, but Jack made his presence felt between the two of them. 'The Germans have occupied the islands, and we will have to accept that. As for this flag here, there's nothing illegal about it. They have been paid for a service and they are providing one. The assistant here is just doing the job asked of her by her employer. If the German Kommandant wants a new flag made, then there is nothing I or any other policeman for that matter can do about it. It is his right as new commander of the island, as it is any customer's right to receive the service they have paid for.'

'Then what are we paying you for? Exactly whose side are you on?'

It was a question he had heard a thousand times before from many a disgruntled person, either being arrested, or wondering why the police refused to arrest them. Did the Fletcher woman really want him to put that poor girl in jail for doing her job? If that happened, then who would be next?

'I'm a policeman,' he said. 'I'm on the side of the people.'

Mrs Fletcher made a 'hmphh' sound, somewhere between a hum and a tut. When he turned, she had marched to the main door and was reaching for the handle. Nodding at the shop assistant and throwing a smile back in Madeleine's direction, he headed to the door as well. He wanted to make sure that the Fletcher woman wasn't going to cause any more trouble. When he stepped onto the pavement outside the department store, she was nowhere to be seen. The few people going about the town eyed him warily as they passed. Jack wondered whether everyone had stayed at home and bolted their front doors to keep away the Germans. If they had, they couldn't stay like that forever.

He realised then, that he had forgotten the shoes he had gone in for. He looked at the door of the department store, but he couldn't face seeing Madeleine again, let alone admitting that he had forgotten what he had gone in for. He would just have to pop in again another day, but then maybe Madeleine would think he had gone back to see her. He no longer had feelings for the woman, they had grown apart since they were younger, but it was still awkward, and he felt a certain sense of betrayal towards

Johanna for even being in the same room as an old flame. He would have to find a time when she wasn't working.

The shoes wouldn't be going anywhere, and he could always surprise Johanna another time. He thought of the joyous look she would give him when he gave her the gift, and he smiled as he walked away from the store.

*

Further along High Street on the corner that intersected with The Pollet, Jack was stopped by a scene that made his heart stop. A group of men walked along the street in his direction, tall men wearing pristine grey uniforms with rifles slung on their shoulders. They were calling to each other in German and cheering when they saw a local. Jack took a step backwards without realising. Part of him, some ancient instinct he barely had control over, wanted to run away, to be as far away from them as possible. Their very presence was intimidating, like the boys who had run the schoolyard. He forced himself to stand firm. He would not run.

If this was the invasion, then it was tame compared to what Jack and the others had expected. The bombing of the island and the harbour had been a horrible tragedy, bringing about completely needless deaths, but it had felt distant, even to Jack. Yet he had expected a proper invasion to be closer, more frantic, full of the sounds of gunfire and explosions ripping past him as he tried futilely to defend his home.

Instead, they walked past, some of them flashing smiles at the few locals who were around. They smelt like the British soldiers, but much, much stronger. Gun oil, boot polish, and a weird perfume that he couldn't quite place. They talked German softly between themselves as some broke off from the group to enter the shops and others stopped in pairs to smoke. The clean white cigarettes gave off a different colour of smoke than the local variants and only added to the feeling that these men were different, somehow alien.

They were shopping as if it was normal, as if they were locals going about their business, rather than invaders. Jack wondered whether it was all part of their plan, to act normally and build confidence in the local population. He couldn't feel anything but contempt for these men, even though he didn't know them. He needed to go to the police station, warn them that the rest of the German soldiers had arrived and were treating the town as their own. He looked around himself to see if any of them were watching, and then like a criminal he slunk away down the back streets to advise his superiors.

*

2 July 1940

The crowds were starting to gather outside and around the Royal Hotel, forming a line along the promenade facing out to sea. It seemed as if everyone wanted to get a look at the occupation force as it gave its first parade. Whether it was out of a sense of morbid curiosity, Jack wasn't sure, but they had come in numbers. The police had expected as much, and he had been posted along with David and the rest of his colleagues to stand guard along the route. It was more like a guard of honour than any real effort to prevent trouble. Despite the interest, there would be many who were unhappy with the occupiers, and some may take things into their own hands. Jack wasn't sure what he could do in that situation, but he would not refuse his duty.

He found it difficult to concentrate as the minutes dragged by, and his mind drifted to Johanna. What would she be thinking now that the Germans were here? He was lost in his own thoughts when he heard the shouting. He scanned the crowd, but there were too many people. He felt David tense and take a step forward beside him.

'My husband! My husband! Has anyone seen my husband?' The woman was close to running as she pushed through the crowd. She was looking around her, moving on with each glance. The more she looked, the more frantic she became, turning this way and that, going back on herself before seeming to change her mind. Her dress was frayed and torn and there was mud splattered up one side. Her brown hair was also in a tangle. It was unusual that someone would be seen out in public in this state.

'I'll look into it,' Jack said to David, who nodded in reply. Jack stepped out of the line to take charge, moving between the crowd of onlookers who stood gawping at the distressed woman. He didn't know her, but her face was faintly familiar. He reached out an arm to stop her running off in the other direction again and tried to soothe her with his tone of voice. It was something he had practised before. She stopped but still looked around, her manner slowing down with each passing second.

'What's wrong?' he asked, keeping his voice low.

'My husband …' was all she would say at first, until Jack pressed her.

'What about him?' he asked. 'Tell me what happened and I will try to help.'

'My husband. He's gone,' she said, her voice becoming a whisper, uncertain of what she was saying. Jack had to resist the urge to embrace and comfort her. He stood as close as was comfortable to hide her from the prying eyes of the crowd. 'I went home and he wasn't there. He was supposed to be there.'

He wondered how he would have felt if he were in this woman's shoes, desperately searching for Johanna. Relatively speaking, she was the very model of calm. Jack thought about taking her home, to delve further into the problem, but he was needed here. The crowds were already pressing in and if he left his post then there would be chaos.

'I want to help,' he said. 'But I need you to calm down and tell me exactly what happened.'

He led her aside to the mouth of an alley between two shops so that they wouldn't be overheard. She took a few deep breaths then looked up at him. Her deep brown eyes cleared as if seeing him for the first time. At first her words were difficult to fully discern, but as she spoke she grew in confidence. 'When the evacuation was announced,' she said, 'my husband and I, we decided that I should leave for England. We weren't sure if it would be safe here, and we didn't want to take the risk. So I signed up to go, but he … He had work here, work he had to stay for. So we decided that we would separate for the time being while the war was on. He stayed here and I caught a ship to England.

'Only, I couldn't stand it there, without him. Almost as soon as I got there I found a boat heading back. I couldn't bear to be away from him, no matter how dangerous it was. Now I'm back, I can't find him anywhere. Please help me.'

Sudden recollection dawned on Jack. He knew he had seen the woman before. It had been down in the harbour on the day the army were leaving and they were organising the boats to take people to the mainland. He had only caught a brief glimpse of the woman and her husband, but the image had stayed with him and he had seen the husband a few times since. 'Oh dear,' he said out loud, without realising he had spoken. Her mouth worked, trying to form a question. Jack saved her the trouble. 'Your husband is fine,' he said. 'At least as far as I know. But the terrible thing is … Well, I saw him boarding one of the last boats to leave for the mainland.'

'He … What?!' The colour drained from her face, and her mouth hung open in shock.

'I'm sorry,' Jack replied. 'He must have gone after you. He'll be safely in England by now.'

'I …' She stopped again, her eyes darting as her thoughts raced. 'I have to find a boat. I have to find a way off this island!'

She looked as if she was about to start running again, like an animal in flight. There was a wildness in her eyes that almost made Jack recoil. He wanted to do something to help, but he couldn't think what. With the parade due to start he wouldn't be able to leave his post without getting in trouble. There was only one thing he could think of.

'Try Petit Port,' he said, probably stating the obvious. 'There may still be one or two boat crews that want to get out before the Germans take over the whole island.'

She nodded, but it wasn't clear whether she had heard him, then she touched his arm. 'Thank you,' she said, words faint again. She picked up her skirts and ran off down the road, looking every bit like an actress from a film.

'Good luck,' Jack called after her before she was completely out of earshot.

*

Twenty or so minutes later, when everything had calmed down again and the crowds had pushed in, the Germans came marching along the road in groups, and into the centre of St Peter Port. Sergeant Honfleur walked at the head of the parade as they passed the Lloyds Bank on the corner, leading them along the route around the town. He looked about as happy to be there as Jack felt. The Germans' field grey uniforms blended in with the grey stone of the shops and houses, but the red banners they carried, centred with a white circle and the German hooked cross, stood out sharply. They marched in step, four abreast, throwing their legs up in front of them in a flamboyant way that Jack had never seen before. Their bands came between each section of troops, driving them on with a rasp of brass instruments.

The Islanders came out of their homes to line the roads. The Germans were stern, but proud, as if they expected the residents to welcome them. The bands were deafening in their marching pomp, resounding glory, but the Islanders simply stared back, unsure of how to react. The Germans behaved like heroic liberators, but were nothing more than conquerors, adding the islands to their empire.

Jack stood with his compatriots, watching. A thousand thoughts rushed through his head at once. He thought of what this would mean for the island, and for him as a policeman. Like his colleagues, he'd been ordered to stand along the marching route, to make sure that the civilians kept their distance from the German soldiers. He'd been stationed almost at the centre of the town by The Pollet, but he wasn't sure who to protect from whom, and he felt like he was standing between his countryfolk and their invaders. He had never felt more alone than at that moment, the only man visible in uniform, but not in the uniform of the German Wehrmacht.

He stood still and sighed deeply as another square of Germans goose-stepped past. He hoped Johanna was keeping herself away from trouble. It would be just like her to stand up to the Germans and cause some issue. They were seriously outnumbered, and there were very few places to hide.

'You ought to be ashamed of yourself!' A woman Jack didn't know pushed herself in front of him, coming within a hair's breadth of him. Under normal circumstances he would have been quick to show his authority, but tempers were rising. Jack simply stood his ground, as passive as possible, but the woman stepped closer to him. He could feel the tension radiating off her body like an approaching thunderstorm. She was close to spitting in his face. Even as a policeman he had never experienced such an open expression of anger. It wasn't the first time he had heard those sentiments in the last few days, but it hurt more for some reason. The crowd had pressed in between Jack and David and he was on his own. He stood up tall, the woman shaking with anger in front of him.

'Please step back,' he said, close to losing his patience. He didn't want to be there any more than she wanted him there, but he didn't have much of a choice.

'Whose side are you on anyway?' she replied, raising her voice so that everyone around could hear. The crowd stared at him, no doubt wondering what he was going to do.

'I'm on no one's side, madam,' he said, speaking low so that those prying couldn't hear. It was a standard police response, but on this occasion it didn't seem right. He was on a side, but he wasn't sure which it was.

'Don't madam me,' she continued, just as loud as before. 'I suppose you're just going to let them march all over the island and take what they want. Aren't you supposed to be upholding the law? Or do you just do what they want now?'

Jack took a deep breath and put his arms out, trying to guide the woman away from the crowd. She scowled at him and took a step backwards.

'They're not breaking any laws,' he said, feeling pathetic. 'There's really nothing I can do, no matter how much I want to.'

The woman stopped and looked up at him again. She sighed, as if she was taking his words for an admission. They probably were, but he hadn't meant them to be. 'One of these days, you'll have to pick a side,' she said, before tutting loudly and pushing her way back into the crowd, leaving Jack standing on his own in the middle of the road between the Germans and his fellow Islanders.

Chapter 7

7 July 1940

'Oh, William. Have you got that money you owe me?' David asked as he and Jack were leaving the police station to go on duty. He spoke quietly so that his words could not be made out by the policemen in the room next door, separated only by a thin wall. Jack frowned a warning.

'I thought I'd paid you back?' William grumbled from behind the desk, leaning on the counter and looking up from the newspaper he was reading. When David didn't move, he sighed and folded the paper. 'Give me a second, will you?'

Jack raised an eyebrow, but David simply shrugged, the epaulettes on his shoulders bobbing with the movement. Strictly speaking they weren't supposed to borrow money from each other, particularly from a senior officer. It was one of the chief's many codes of conduct, and David knew that. It was a risk speaking about it in the police station itself, but apparently David was not concerned. He smiled at Jack just as William returned.

He sat down heavily at the desk and let out a sigh. 'Can you wait for it, David? You know I'm good for it.'

'What's the problem? Spent it all again?' David was smiling, joking, but William didn't seem to notice.

'It's this blasted money.' He put a few of the new German coins on the desk, turning them over trying to see what they were. He reached for his glasses that hung around his neck, perching them on his wide nose before going in for another look. 'What am I supposed to do with it? I don't understand. Why couldn't we just keep what we had?'

'Pounds and shillings are the property of the British crown, William. In case you hadn't noticed, they're not in charge anymore.' He attempted a smile, but William just scowled at him.

'It's a pain in the backside, that's what it is. If they wanted to keep us onside, the least they could do is keep things the same.'

Jack laughed. 'Maybe you should be the attorney general,' he said. 'Tell him to sort it out. Ask him for a loan while you're at it.'

David snorted, but William just collected up his coins with a glare and placed them in his trouser pocket.

'As if they'd ever listen. I'm just a bumbling old man. Not like you, young men, the vision of the future.' He jabbed a finger into Jack's chest. William was only a few years older than Jack, but he acted like a man of more advanced years. As for the future, who knew what it held? It was better to take each day as it came. 'Speaking of the future, hadn't you two best be off on duty? Don't make me a party to your laziness.'

'Hey—' David started, but Jack stopped him with a hand on his arm.

'We should be on our way. Good morning, William.'

*

'William's right,' David spoke up when they were along by the Weighbridge, away from the police station. Apparently he had been thinking about it since they left. 'It's the blasted clock changes.'

He waved vaguely in the direction of the town hall clock. 'If British Summer Time wasn't bad enough already, they have to go and change it again. Now we've got nippy mornings, and it doesn't get warm until the afternoon.'

Jack nodded absent-mindedly. He looked up at the clock tower at the end of the street. The time was wrong anyway, stuck at a few minutes to seven. It hadn't moved an inch since the Germans had bombed the harbour and its mechanism had been damaged. He didn't know how long it would stay like that, but he didn't think anyone was in a hurry to fix it.

'There are always rules we have to obey,' Jack said.

'Oh, I get that there need to be rules. I just don't see why we need to have the same time as Berlin. It's miles away, and it's not like their great Führer is going to visit and they're worried he might lose track of time.'

'Shhhh,' Jack said, putting a finger to his lips.

'Tish, Jack. What are they going to do to me? Half of them don't understand English, and the rest wouldn't demean themselves listening to the likes of me. Unless, you're going to report me?' He flashed a grin, but Jack sensed something there, a wariness that David wasn't quite ready to discuss.

'Not unless you do something really stupid. I'm just telling you to be careful. They've only been here five minutes, and we don't yet know how they're going to treat us. We have to be careful.'

David stayed silent for a long moment. 'You see,' he said, eventually. 'That's your problem ... you're too cautious.'

Jack opened his mouth to object, but David talked over him.

'You're never going to get what you want, if you're always too cautious. Sometimes you have to fight for something; sometimes you have to just do it and worry about the consequences later.'

'If only it were that easy.'

'It can be, if you want it to be.'

'We're policemen, we can't just do what we want. As the chief inspector says, we have a duty to the island.'

'What does the old man know about our island? He's English, almost as foreign as the Germans.'

Jack stared at him for a minute, waiting for the penny to drop. After a few seconds David's eyes widened and he took a step forward. 'Oh,' he said. 'That's not what I meant. Sorry! I don't think of *you* as a foreigner. Anyway, it's just a job like any other.'

'It's more than just a job. I've got my family to think about – so do you. Without our jobs they'll starve.'

'I get that, but maybe sometimes there's more to life than a job. You'll know what I mean when it comes to it.' He looked at his wristwatch and placed a hand on Jack's shoulder. 'We can always find other work, but I don't want to argue with you. We need to stick together. We'd best be getting on. These streets aren't going to walk themselves.'

Jack nodded, uncertain of himself. If David thought it would be easy to find other work, he was more naive than Jack thought. If they defied the Germans they would lose more than just their jobs. If someone had overheard what they were saying, they could easily get in trouble, not just with the inspector, but the German army. David turned and walked back the way he had come, and Jack fell in a moment later. The island may be occupied, but the Guernsey Police still had a job to do.

*

There was a furious knocking at the door. Three bangs, every few seconds. Jack hadn't been expecting a visitor, but he jumped out of bed and threw on some clothes. What if the Germans had discovered Johanna's presence on the island? As he stepped down the stairs, he noticed his mother standing by the bottom banister staring at the front door. She looked up at him, her eyes wide.

'It's okay,' he said quietly as he reached the bottom step and placed a hand on her shoulder. 'I'll see who it is and send them away. Go back to the living room and I'll be there in a minute.'

Her head bobbed in a shallow nod, and she disappeared into

the house. Jack took a deep breath and wrenched open the front door as the next knock was about to fall. The door creaked on its hinges and a figure almost fell on him, with a raised fist, but caught themselves before they crossed the threshold.

'Nicholas?' Jack said. Nicholas had a large frame and thick, curly ginger hair. The fluffy growths of a beard were breaking out on his chin, irregular and patchy, as if he was trying to look older but failing spectacularly. By comparison, Jack's own beard grew thick and black if he didn't shave it off regularly for work.

'Jack,' Nicholas replied, breathing heavily as he leant on the doorframe for support. His face was flushed as if he had been running for miles, but then his pale skin always made him look flushed. 'You'd better come quick.'

He turned to leave, but Jack caught hold of his arm. It was thick and Jack's hand barely encompassed his whole bicep. 'What's going on?' he asked. Nicholas had been in the same school as Jack, but a couple of years behind him. He only lived at the other end of their road. Jack could tell this was something serious.

'I don't have time to explain. Just come. Quick. Please.' He shook off Jack's arm and Jack only hesitated for a moment. He grabbed his long coat from the hook by the door and threw it around his shoulders, before stepping back towards the living room.

'Nicholas needs my help,' he called for his mother's benefit. Her moods grew worse every time he left, more so if he didn't tell her. 'I'm going out for a bit. I'll be back soon.'

With that he closed the door and followed Nicholas down the road. The younger man, only just out of his teens, walked slightly ahead of Jack, urging him on, and every time Jack tried to match his stride, he pulled ahead again.

'They're trying to take our house, Jack,' he said over his shoulder.

'Who?'

'The Germans, they say they need it for a billet. For their soldiers.'

'Why your house? Aren't there other empty buildings?'

'It's because it's nearest to the town. They won't listen to us. I told 'em we've got nowhere else to go. You've got to help. Tell them you're a policeman.'

Jack wasn't sure what he could do. The police had become nothing more than an arm of the German Military Authority. If they had decided they needed something, then you could be sure that they would get it. Jack had already seen plenty of other examples, but this was the first time he had heard of them throwing people out of their home.

*

A German officer was standing outside the house, with his hands on his hips. His uniform was pristine, as they all were, boots polished to an impeccable shine. But this man had gone to another level. There was an almost sycophantic observance to this man's uniform as if it was the most important thing to him, an outward show of his status, and under normal circumstances Jack wouldn't dare confront him.

As Jack marched up to the officer, puffing his chest out as much for his own confidence as anyone else's, he flashed his warrant card. The officer swivelled his clean-shaven head in Jack's direction.

'May I have a word, sir?' Jack stepped to one side, indicating the German officer should join him. Jack's heart thumped in his chest, and he was already regretting his decision. Why did Nicholas have to drag him into this? 'I was just wondering if this was a good idea, sir?'

'What? Who are you?' The man's English was not as perfect as his uniform and he called one of his subordinates over to help.

'I'm a policeman, sir. Island Police. And well, I don't pretend to speak for the kommandant, but as far as I'm aware he rather wants the occupation to go as smoothly as possible.' He was

80

bluffing and he hoped that the soldier wouldn't notice. So much could be lost in translation. 'This family have nowhere else to go, and they will resent being moved.'

The soldier put a hand to his jawline and looked back over at the house.

'What you say makes sense,' he said. 'I do not wish to upset the kommandant's plans. But my men, they need somewhere to live on this island.'

He turned to Jack, giving him an appraising stare. Jack was aware of his casual civilian clothes and the lack of an air of authority they gave him.

'Where do you propose that my men should live, *Constable*,' the German continued, enunciating the last word as if it left a distasteful flavour in his mouth. 'Do you have a house we may use? One that is as convenient to our needs as this one?'

He pointed towards the house and the family that were still standing by the front door, observing in silence. Jack thought for a minute, and then something occurred to him. All of the soldiers had left, leaving empty rooms or homes behind, and a number of the Guernsey militia had gone with them to sign up for the British army. Others had simply left for the mainland, preferring to try their luck in England than to risk life under the Germans.

One of Jack's old schoolmates, Henry, had lived a bit further up the road, closer to St Peter Port. The house was down a side street, easy to miss from the main road, especially if you didn't know the area well. It was quite likely that the German officer had driven straight past it.

Henry had been a member of the Guernsey militia and when they had been disbanded, he had gone to England on the boats to sign up with the British army. Jack often wondered where he was now, and how his parents were coping. Since then they had moved out of their family home and into a smaller cottage up in The Vale, probably to escape from the occupying forces. As a result their old home was put up for sale and left empty.

'There's an empty house along the road that may suit your purposes. If you'll permit me to show you, sir.'

'Very well. You may show me. However, if it is not fit for our needs then I will return here and station my men in this house.' With that he gave a pointed look towards the family, then turned, clicking his heels together. 'We shall take my automobile.'

He indicated that Jack should head towards the driver's seat, and within a few minutes he had manoeuvred the heavy car down The Grange. As he turned the corner, Jack thought he saw a head pop up from behind a wall. He recognised the face, a grin that he knew couldn't be real, the unmistakable warm eyes of a friend he hadn't had time to miss, but as he looked back over his shoulder the head was gone, as if there had been no one there at all. He put it down to exhaustion and stress, and focused on leading the German soldier to where they were going.

He showed the German officer Henry's parents' house, the house that they were no longer using. From the drive they could see that its grey slate roof was missing a few tiles, and that some of the windows were in dire need of resealing, but at least it had a roof and four walls. He wasn't sure whether Henry's parents would mind or not, but he felt that they would understand. The gravel drive clicked as the men walked towards the house, the German pulling ahead to inspect it.

'It needs a bit of work,' he said, looking on as the officer flicked a piece of peeling white paint from the wall and then wiped his finger with a handkerchief.

'It does.'

'But maybe your soldiers can work on it in their downtime? Make it into something they can be proud of and call home?'

'You think the soldiers of the Third Reich are mere builders?' Jack stuttered, but the officer headed him off.

'No,' he continued. 'We will make use of the local labourers, support local business. That is, until the Operation Todt labourers arrive.'

There was a nasty glint in his eye that made Jack uneasy. He didn't know who they were, and he didn't have an opportunity to ask as the officer and his men stalked off into the house. One of them jerked his head at Jack to indicate that he was no longer needed.

It was clear that the Germans were going to take over the whole island in time. They had even turned the local Woolworths into a shop purely for German customers. The truly crazy thing was that the shop still needed local staff to run it, even though they themselves were not permitted to shop in there. He was sure that this wasn't the last of the illogical rules that the Germans would put in place, but what could he and the others really do about it?

Chapter 8

9 July 1940

The summer sun was glaring down on the island, almost making it seem like all his troubles were far away. Jack had decided to do something about the back garden that his grandfather had once taken care of, before he had grown too frail. Jack had been down on his knees pulling the weeds from the grass, but the sun had become too hot overhead. He had given up and was sitting in the corner, in as much shade as he could find. It was an idyllic escape from the world. If he could he would spend all his time here, but his duty and honour would not allow him. He wished Johanna was there, but she had found work as a nurse up at the Emergency Hospital in Castel and was doing even longer shifts than he did in the police. At least, he thought, she was safe up there surrounded by doctors and other nurses. He wondered if work would always keep them apart, but he understood her need to keep occupied. Even here away from the outside world his mind couldn't help but wander back to the occupation.

He heard a sound from the other side of the hedge, like an animal scrabbling in the dirt for something to eat. A familiar face appeared through the greenery a moment later. 'Jack?' it whispered.

'What the hell are you doing here?' Jack asked, embarrassed by the shock in his voice. His old school friend, Henry, was supposed to have gone to England. Jack hadn't really ever expected to see the man again, especially not while the Germans were still occupying Guernsey. He had no idea what on earth a British soldier was doing on the island, but he knew immediately that it was dangerous. He caught hold of Henry's arm and hauled him inside the house, not caring whether he hurt him. The mere fact he was here could cause untold trouble for Jack and his family, and he hoped that no one had seen the other man in his garden. He repeated himself, for emphasis, 'What the hell are you doing here?'

He looked almost as Jack remembered him, a tall, thin man, with a mess of curly brown hair. But he had grown trim, presumably from his training, and the army had cut his hair shorter. There was still a slight grin on his lips that had always been there when they were children, and at times was so constant it almost irritated Jack. It was a grin he felt he had seen recently. He had never before been able to be annoyed with one of his oldest friends, one of the few children who hadn't mocked him for being born off the island.

'Shhh. Be quiet! You'll wake the dead carrying on like that.'

Jack paced the hallway, trying to compose his thoughts. His grandmother shuffled into view, through the narrowly opened door to their room. 'Jacky?' she called, her voice shrill, but still warm. 'Jack? Is that you?'

A moment later his grandfather called out something, followed by a violent, racking cough that seemed to linger in the air.

'Yes, dear. I'll ask him,' she responded then looked towards the kitchen. Jack's heart thumped in his chest, even though he trusted his grandmother without question. Things were no longer that simple. 'Jacky, your grandfather wants a cup of tea,' she continued, looking past Jack to where Henry stood. 'Oh, hello young Mr Le Page. My how you've grown!'

He nodded in reply, before Jack took her by the arm and led

her gently back to her room. 'I'll bring you both tea in a few minutes, Nan. Let me take care of it.'

'Thank you, dear.'

She shuffled back into her room, a smile on her face. Jack didn't want to neglect her, but he needed to speak to Henry privately. Thankfully his mother was upstairs, otherwise he would have to try to explain what was going on. She would be far more suspicious.

'It feels strange being back,' Henry said when Jack reappeared.

'I thought I'd never see you again, least of all here,' Jack replied, his voice taking an edge as he turned on Henry. 'I have my family to think about.'

'Look, old pal,' Henry replied, raising his hands. 'I can explain, if you just give me a minute.'

A thought occurred to Jack, a fleeting image from a few days ago. 'Wait a second,' he said, pacing again. 'I thought I saw you the other day. I thought I was hallucinating at the time, but it *was* you hiding in the bushes behind a wall.'

Henry flashed that smile of his again, but it only served to make Jack angrier. 'You still haven't explained why you're here,' he said.

'Right, okay. One thing at a time, eh? I'll start at the beginning.'

Jack nodded, then sat down at the kitchen table. The shock still hadn't worn off.

'Well, as you know myself and the others went to sign up for the British army. We'd all been split up and sent wherever it was we were needed. Then we heard that the War Office were looking for soldiers who had lived here, or at least knew the island.

'I volunteered right away when they said there was a chance I could come back here and help in the war effort. Anyone would have jumped at it. That's why we came.'

'"We"? Why do you keep saying "we"?' Jack asked. 'They wanted you to scout out the island?'

'In a manner of speaking. We? Well.' Henry leant closer to Jack and lowered his voice. They sent me here as a spy, although I don't think anyone actually used that word. They hadn't given me any training. But as far as the War Office was concerned I knew the island and that was enough. The rest I've had to learn "on the job" as it were.'

'What's the point of them sending you here?' Jack asked. 'It's not like you can get rid of the Germans.'

'Too true, old pal.' He put his elbow on one crossed arm and stroked his chin. 'Not yet at least. No, the idea is to find out what the Germans are doing and report back. That's why I've come to you. As a policeman, I hoped you'd be able to tell me.'

Jack was struggling not to feel annoyed. He still couldn't believe the British had walked out on them, only to return and act like nothing had changed. Now it seemed as if they were playing games with their lives. 'Why? The War Office doesn't care about the islands.'

'That's not fair, see. I know it hurt when we all left, but what were we supposed to do? The army didn't have the numbers to defend the island. The fact we're back shows that we care.'

'Isn't it too late for that?' Jack knew his voice had risen, but he no longer cared. 'The Germans are here now.'

Henry leant against the wall behind the door, as if he had already developed an instinct for hiding. 'I know how it sounds, but we have to play the long game here. You've heard the stories about the first war. If we can slow them down, annoy and harry them, then their supplies will run out. Eventually they'll have to retreat. This is all part of that plan – why I'm here, to feed back info for the raids.'

'The what?' Jack stood up, now almost shouting. But Henry waved him back down.

'That's where the "we" come in.' Jack was too shocked to respond, so Henry continued. 'The British have arranged some kind of raid. I'm not sure what they're going to do; they wouldn't tell me in case I was captured. I could really do with some help.'

'What do you want from me? I can't hide you. Not here.'

'Information. That's all I need. What can you tell me about the Jerries? What forces do they have on the island? What are they up to?'

Jack hesitated for a moment, and then made a decision. What difference did it make if he told Henry everything that the Germans had done? If they found out he had been helping a spy he was done for anyway. At least this way he may do some good. Perhaps they could change the course of the occupation before Johanna or anyone else he loved got hurt.

He told Henry about the kommandant, how they had taken over the hotels, commandeered all the cars, how the police were the Germans' tools, and how powerless they all were to do anything about it.

Henry sat and listened intently to every detail as if he was memorising it. Jack wouldn't have been surprised if he pulled out a notepad and pencil, but then writing anything down was dangerous. He just listened until Jack mentioned Henry's parents' house. It was his turn to look shocked.

'I see,' he said, at length. 'That was what you were doing with that German the other day. I'm sure you had good reason.'

Jack couldn't tell whether Henry was annoyed with him. They had been friends since they were children and Henry had always looked after him like an older brother, even though they were almost the same age. But there had been times when he had been short with Jack, or had criticised him unnecessarily. As a child, Jack had been put off by it, and it had only been as an adult that he had realised Henry had been trying to look after him, in his own way.

'I was alerted by a neighbour to a German officer trying to take over a house along the road.'

'The bastard!' Amazingly Henry managed to shout without raising his voice.

'He was trying to commandeer the house for his troops. They hadn't any billets, and apparently the kommandant hadn't arranged anything either, so it they had decided to put a roof over their heads by turning others out.'

Henry clenched his fists and paced around as Jack continued his story. 'I arrived just as the officer was on the doorstep about to remove the family by force.'

'So what did you do?' Henry sat down on another chair and laid his head on his hands as he had often done when they were children. When Jack had finished telling the story Henry was silent for a moment. Eventually he gave a long sigh. 'I'm not sure my dad is going to like that. He was born in that house. The idea of the Germans shacking up there will make him mad. It makes me pretty angry too.' He put up a hand to silence Jack. 'I understand your reasoning. But the house doesn't belong to them. What right do they have to take it?'

'Everything belongs to them now.'

Henry sighed again, closing his eyes. 'Churchill won't let them do this for much longer – you just wait. We'll make them pay somehow.'

After a long moment he wrenched his eyes open again, looking straight at Jack. 'Look, I've been here long enough. Thank you. I just wanted to see you, warn you that we were here, but I shouldn't stay in one place too long. I was going to go and see my parents.' He paused for a moment, scratching his chin again. 'The thing is, I don't want to get them involved. You live nearer to the landing point; I *knew* I could get here without being seen. Thank you for giving me that information.'

Jack shrugged, not sure if what he had told Henry was really any help at all. 'The island's theirs now,' he said. 'There isn't much we can do. The war's over for the islands.'

'Is it? Is it really? Do you really believe that, Jack? I thought better of you. They can come here with their guns and take over the place, but can't you see? This is exactly why we must fight them. It starts with taking our homes. What does it end with?'

Jack didn't have a good answer for him; he had thought the same, but what was he supposed to do? It was all right for Henry who had escaped the island and was now swanning back in here to tell them all what they should be doing, but he hadn't experienced the occupation. He didn't really know what it was like. He had some romantic view of right and wrong and had picked a side with ease. Jack struggled to keep himself from telling Henry exactly what he thought of his spying, but he held his tongue, took a deep breath and let the anger go.

'We can't do much. They're always watching us, and who knows what they'll do to us if they catch us. Especially those of us in the police. We're supposed to enforce their laws.'

Henry walked back over to Jack and patted his shoulder. 'That's why I'm here. Why we're doing what we can.'

'And what is that, exactly?'

Henry was quiet for a moment, looking deep into Jack's eyes as if trying to come to a decision. 'The raid is next week.' Back to the conspiratorial voice he had begun the conversation with. 'That's all I know. Don't tell anyone, understand? I'll be heading back to England by then, but it's not safe for the rest of you to know.'

Jack wanted to scream at him, tell him that this was no game, that lives were at stake, but he just nodded. They were in this together now, whether Jack liked it or not, co-conspirators. History told him that that never ended well.

'Look, it's about time you went,' he said, standing and moving to the door so that Henry would follow. 'I'm supposed to be starting my night shift soon.'

The other man nodded, still completely calm. How could he stay so still when they were in such danger? 'Please, for our sake, don't be here when I come back. If the Germans find you—'

'It's all right,' Henry said. 'I'm going. I won't push you any further. I appreciate how difficult it must be and I'd do the same if I were you. We have different paths, you and I, and neither of us have been given much in the way of choice.' He paused to sigh heavily, before standing up and offering a hand. 'Thanks for not running straight to the Germans when you saw me. Not many others would have done that.'

Jack shook the other man's hand. A part of him really wanted to do something to help, and it gnawed at his resolve.

'We'll meet again, Jack, before this is all out. You can be sure of that.'

*

That evening he met Johanna who was coming home from work while he was on his way to start his own night shift. Her hair was in a mess, and her brow was creased with a deep frown. They hadn't arranged to meet, but Jack had made sure that he was near the hospital when she was due to finish. A few minutes out of his cycle patrol wouldn't be a problem.

She smiled at him when he jumped off his bike nearby, but there was a weariness that hadn't been there before. In the few weeks that she had been working as a nurse, he had noticed her change, her vibrancy and humour lessening with each day. Although he suspected that the work wasn't the only reason.

'You're exhausted,' he said, reaching out for her. She fell willingly into his arms.

'I am, but it warms my heart to see you.' Her head fell against his chest and his heart rate increased, as it always did when he was around her. 'It's been a long day.'

She pulled back, placing a hand either side of his head and pulling it down so that she could see into his eyes.

'Do you remember when we first met?' she asked. 'It was an evening like this, warm and dry.'

'Almost two years now,' he said, fondly. She had just come to the island to work as a nanny for a wealthy family, putting her skills as a nurse to good use before the family had returned to

England at the outbreak of war, leaving her here. 'You caught my eye right away.'

She laughed. 'Bah!' she said. 'If I remember correctly you bumped into me on your bicycle because you weren't looking where you were going!'

'Well, as soon as I saw you then.' He looked into her eyes, remembering the day as if it were only yesterday.

'It was a good thing I wasn't hurt, otherwise I would never have come to love you.' There was a wicked look in her eye. 'Although offering to buy me tea as an apology certainly helped.'

She pulled away from him and walked to the side of the road, looking out over the sea. Jack followed.

'I came here to get away from it all,' she said, her voice now a low whisper. 'To somehow build a new life, and I got so much more. Even if the states locked me up as an enemy. This is now my home; you are my home. If only my family could be here to see me now.'

She turned back to him. Jack wanted so much to ask her what had happened in Germany. He knew only whispers of how the Jews were oppressed, but never more. He didn't know what to think. Her brown eyes looked into his and he was mesmerised.

'Why do you never speak of your family?' he asked. 'I would love to hear about them.'

She stared at him, still, transfixing him with those deep eyes. 'I can't. It's too horrible. You wouldn't believe me if I told you, not yet. One day, when the time is right I will tell you all about it, but it's still too raw, too painful. I want to tell you, but the words will not come, the story is too heartbreaking. Just remember that the other Germans can't be trusted, no matter what. They cannot know that I'm a Jew – it's too dangerous.'

With that she broke their gaze and flicked her hair aside as if remembering herself.

'Go, go now and do your work,' she continued. 'The island needs you as much as I do.'

Again she smiled, but it didn't reach her eyes. She kissed him on the cheek, then unlocked her own bicycle from the rail by the hospital gates. He whispered goodnight, but she left without another word.

Chapter 9

17 July 1940

Jack and the other policemen were ordered to assemble at the police station at five in the morning. The past week had been relatively uneventful, which was unusual given everything that had been going on. The old man stormed into the office as early morning light trickled in through the windows, aided by the orange glow of the kerosene lamps.

'At ten a.m. on Monday morning,' the chief started without so much as a welcome, 'German soldiers in the south of the island found a barricade across the Jerbourg Road near the tavern. The road was blocked with large granite boulders, which must have taken considerable effort to place there. They also found a soldier's haversack and some other supplies littered around the area.'

There was a stony silence from the assembled policemen. Jack's heart sank into his stomach. He had to be careful not to give anything away. It was possible that Henry had visited other policemen on the island, but he thought it unlikely.

'The German Military Authority consider this evidence that British soldiers are operating on the island. The kommandant demands to know who was responsible for building the barricade and leaving the supplies.'

Jack's heart skipped a beat. They could put him in front of a firing squad, and then what would happen to Johanna and to his family? He would just have to keep quiet and go about his duty as normal.

The old man cleared his throat. 'It falls on us to investigate and report back to the Germans.'

There were one or two grumblings of resentment, but the chief silenced them with a pointed look.

'That's why I've called you all here. I want you in teams with the special constables.' He indicated the group hovering at the back of the room. Most of the policemen didn't think of them as real policemen, but in times like this their help was indispensable. 'PCs Godwin and Roussel, you'll take three specials and comb the area between La Corbière and Le Crieux Mahié caves.'

The old man nodded, dismissing them to their duties. Jack hurried to follow David and the others as they left the police station. He knew where the soldiers had been, but he wasn't about to tell the others. Things had got out of hand very quickly, and he would have to be calm and careful to make sure everything fell back into place. He picked up his bicycle from the station park, as the police car drove around the front of the building to collect the inspector. The whole force would be out doing the Germans' work for them.

*

A group of German soldiers in green uniforms were standing across the Jerbourg Road when the police cycled past. They were guarding the place in the road where the barricade had been made from heavy stones. There were more soldiers dotted along the road. Jack and David reached their section. He took a foot from a pedal, dismounted and leant the bicycle against a garden wall. There were a number of houses, but a lot of the land had been taken over as farms, ample ground for the soldiers to hide in. Jack didn't know how long it would take to find them. He didn't know if he even wanted to, it could put him and his family in danger, but as always he had a duty to do.

Jack marched up to the German soldiers to present himself. As he drew near he threw a salute and introduced himself. After a moment of awkward shuffling between the soldiers one of them stepped forward. He was over six feet tall and made even Jack feel short. He shook hands with Jack.

'*Leutnant* Henrik Bäcker, *Feldgendarmerie*. Pleased to meet you, Constable.' Henrik looked very much like many of the other Germans, a strong face with a faint hint of blond stubble, sea blue eyes looking out from between the field grey of his uniform. He was what they would describe as a true Aryan. There was a warmth to his smile that was equal parts reassuring and unsettling. He gestured to a man beside him. 'This is *unterfeldwebel* … *Sergeant* Gerhart Hofmann, my second.' Gerhart smiled with a kindness Jack hadn't expected. He was a stocky man, with a pugilist's nose, but the grin suited him. Jack was becoming increasingly familiar with the smiles of his enemies, and he didn't like it.

'This is PC David Roussel,' he said, feeling he should continue the introductions, as David joined them. Everyone exchanged nods.

'Your inspector has informed you of what happened?' Henrik asked.

Jack and David nodded. 'We were briefed this morning,' Jack said, not wanting to give away too much.

'Good.' The *leutnant* didn't seem concerned. 'Why don't you two check on the houses over there. I'm sure the locals would rather see you on their doorstep than us. And we will continue checking the nearby lands for any clues.'

'We'll report back here when we're finished,' Jack said as he turned, pulling David after him. Together they went to the first house in the row, the one furthest from where the barricade had been constructed, but there was no answer. Whoever lived there must have been at work. Jack moved along to the next house while David peered in through the windows.

'Hello. What's that?' David kicked a bit of metal and it slid a few feet in Jack's direction. It was unmistakable to anyone who had spent any time around the British army, or the Guernsey militia. It was a magazine from a rifle.

David whistled. 'Ooh, the British have been here all right. What on earth were they up to? Better keep that to show the old man.'

Jack nodded and pocketed it. Whether he would report it or not was another matter, but he didn't intend to tell David that. Jack liked to weigh up his options. They tried the rest of the cottages in the lane, but had no luck. Eventually they walked to the cottage at the end farthest away from the area the Germans had been searching and Jack rapped three times on the door then, as usual, waited patiently a step or two away from the doorstep.

'Oh, hullo, Arthur,' Jack said as the door opened and Arthur Parr looked out.

'Hello, Jack. What brings you here?' Arthur was one of the farmers who worked on the nearby lands, and Jack knew him in passing.

'We've got reason to believe there are some British soldiers operating in the area. You wouldn't happen to know anything about that would you?'

Arthur shook his head. 'Sorry, not me. I wouldn't even know what they look like. Good luck though.'

Jack nodded, remembering vaguely that Arthur had spent some time in the army himself. It was entirely likely that the soldiers had turned to him when their raid had failed. Ditching their equipment had been foolish, but perhaps they had had no choice, perhaps thinking it would distract the Germans enough to give the soldiers time to hide. Maybe, as the equipment had been left by the edge of the trees, they had wanted them to think the soldiers had gone off into the woods.

Jack adjusted his stance to get a look around Arthur and into the house. He could see the dining table upon which sat four cups and saucers, as well as a pot of tea. 'Why then, are there four cups of tea on your table? Who are they for?'

'Oh, them? They're for me and my mum. I've just washed them up. I'd invite you in, but I'm sure you don't have the time.'

Arthur let the door close by an extra inch, as if they were done. It was clear from his reaction that he hadn't expected the police to knock on his door. Inside Jack could just make out a hallway door gliding open, before being hauled back. It happened in a flash, but Jack was certain he had seen a khaki sleeve. Jack had seen enough. He wouldn't push the issue now, but he would have to tell the old man when he got back to the station. Let the chief decide what to do with the information.

'You'll let us know if you see anything, won't you?'

'Sure, Jack. Whatever you say.' Arthur smiled in a way that said he had no intention of doing anything of the sort, then shut the door a little too quickly.

David and Jack retreated back up the lane, while he wondered what he would tell the old man. When they had regrouped with the Germans, the two groups checked the area, including some local caves, for another hour or so. Occasionally they found the odd piece of military equipment, but no sign of the soldiers who had left them. The telephone wires in the area had been cut, but apart from that they had left no visible signs of sabotage.

Back at the station, they had come to no real conclusion as to what had happened to the soldiers, but Jack suspected that he knew where at least some of them were.

'What did you find, PC Godwin?' the inspector asked as he came downstairs to check on the investigation. Other policemen had gone out on their regular beats. Jack weighed up his options. He would never tell the chief that he had seen Henry, but he would tell him about the soldiers. It was the best way to make sure that he was above suspicion.

'We didn't find much, sir. Apart from this.' He handed over the magazine. 'But I have a feeling that some of the soldiers may be hiding out in the cottage at La Corbière.'

'What makes you say that?'

He recounted what had happened, telling the inspector of how Arthur had responded, the tea set he had seen, and the khaki uniform.

'Don't do anything until I've checked with the bailiff.'

The inspector left the police station immediately, leaving Jack to finish his entry in the occurrence book. Even with the Germans on the island, the bailiff was still in charge of legal matters and he would advise the old man what they should do, or whether they should just leave the Germans to it. Jack waited, wondering whether he should find other duties, but he couldn't stop staring at the clock. It was almost ten minutes later when the inspector returned and marched back into the office, his face red.

'Ah, Constable,' he said. 'I've spoken to the bailiff and let's just say that he "blew his top" at the suggestion a citizen was harbouring the British. He told me that if the soldiers weren't handed over to the Germans immediately then you and PC Roussel would be arrested.'

'Arrested, sir?' Jack's heart thumped, and he wondered what the bailiff would do. The inspector held up a hand to wave away Jack's panic.

'It's an idle threat, but if you can make contact with the soldiers and advise them to surrender to the Germans, then I think we can solve this little problem.'

'Yes, sir!' Jack saluted. He daren't think what would happen if he couldn't convince the soldiers to turn themselves in. He hoped that Henry wasn't with them, but then his friend was supposed to have left the island by now.

*

When Jack knocked on the door of the cottage again, after a frantic cycle from the police station, it took a minute or so to open. Jack was thankful as it gave him a chance to catch his breath and try and come up with something to say. It wasn't Arthur who wrenched the door back on its hinges, but a soldier Jack recognised. It was the sergeant he had spoken to during the evacuation.

'It's okay, I know him,' he shouted back over his shoulder into the room. He hadn't seen the man since the army had evacuated from St Peter Port. 'Quick, get inside, son.'

The soldier led him into the kitchen where three other soldiers sat at the round wooden table. They quietly sipped tea from fine china mugs and eyed Jack warily. Arthur stood in the corner with his arms crossed. His face showed he was deep in thought. The sergeant introduced Jack to the men. 'We suspected you'd be back,' he said.

They looked at Jack as if he were their enemy, and he felt a great sense of unease building, as if he were on trial. All he could think about was that he was glad Henry wasn't there. His friend must have made it off the island after all.

'I'm not here to arrest you,' Jack said. He realised he sounded like a schoolteacher. 'But you need to hand yourself in. You can't just hide out here waiting for the war to finish. Even if you ditch all your khaki and equipment the Germans will know who you are.'

The soldiers stared gloomily at him, the tea forgotten. 'They've introduced ID papers,' Jack continued. 'And anyone caught without one can be locked up. If they find you in hiding, it'll be bad for anyone who helped you.'

He looked over at Arthur, who nodded, then looked over at the soldiers. 'You're right. And to be honest we've been having the same discussion here. It's taken us all morning, but they've come to a decision.'

'The raid was a complete bust,' one of the soldiers added, with a thick accent Jack thought might have been Scottish. 'We couldn't do any significant damage, not even to the telephone masts. This little island is more resilient than we thought. We've got to take the consequences of that.'

'What will you do?' Jack asked, relieved that his argument seemed to have worked. Their faces were downcast but resolute.

'I'll go and see the attorney general,' Arthur replied. 'Appeal to his good nature and see if he'll smooth things over with the Germans.'

'Then we'll all go and turn ourselves in,' the sergeant took over. 'Put our uniforms on so they don't think we're spies. They'll have to treat us as POWs. Then? Who knows ...'

The sergeant left the rest unspoken, but every man in that room could feel the tension. He held out a hand for Jack to shake, gripping it firmly. 'Thank you, son.'

'For what?' Jack asked. He felt a small pang of shame.

'For not coming in here and rounding us all up. For making us see sense. You don't know how much you've done. Thank you for helping us realise we've made the right decision. I knew there was something about you when I first met you. Good luck, son.'

When the soldiers turned themselves in to the police station later that day, it was the last time Jack ever saw the sergeant. He knew then that Johanna hadn't been exaggerating when she had told him not to trust the Germans. He would have to be careful.

Chapter 10

1 August 1940

He hated going to see the Germans more than he hated anything else about this sorry affair. If he had his way, he would keep as far away from them as possible. Jack had been waiting for a few minutes, but then he had always thought it was a good idea to be early, even when attending on the Germans. The fewer reasons they had to be unhappy with him, the better. He enjoyed his work, but recently it had seemed as if they were no longer doing the work they were supposed to be doing. Today was a good example. The chief was trying to impress to their new German occupiers, and he was using Jack to do it. The old man had assigned Jack to head down to the Royal Hotel with the car and collect the German Kommandant, then to drive him to the states offices. Then he was to escort the man inside, wait for him to finish, then take them back to the Royal Hotel. Today was the first time the States of Guernsey had met since the occupation had begun, and the German Kommandant and his associates were attending the meeting. It was far from what Jack expected his police duties to be, but he could hardly refuse.

Jack sat in his car outside the hotel waiting. The kommandant's timing was usually impeccable. He prided himself on the efficiency of his forces and their timekeeping was no different. Jack thought that maybe there was something they could all learn from the Germans. But if the price of efficiency was being ruled by a foreign army, then maybe it wasn't worth it after all. Jack checked his wristwatch, the watch that had belonged to his father; he was two minutes early.

As soon as he looked up, the kommandant and his interpreter marched out of the hotel. Jack barely had time to open the car door before the kommandant jumped into the back seat. The Wolseley Salon de Ville was used to having criminals in the back, but now all motor vehicles were to be used by the German authorities or with their permission. The kommandant had even gone as far as attaching Nazi emblems, which waved like pennants on the wings of the car, as if the Islanders weren't already aware that everything belonged to them.

Jack wondered why the kommandant hadn't imported his own car for use while he was here. Only the very best German engineering for the representative of the Reich in the Channel Islands. Jack fought a smirk as he drove the car up to the states offices, the sound of its engine reverberating off the surrounding stone buildings. It was like the burr of an aircraft engine, rich and warm, and Jack found it reassuring. He didn't get the opportunity to drive much, and was at least thankful for that simple pleasure that so many others had been denied.

When they arrived at the states offices, which was only a short walk away, he rushed to open the rear passenger door. He was faintly aware of a camera flash going off beside him, but he paid no attention to the reporters who were here for the occasion. The kommandant stepped out of the car, pulling the shirt of his uniform straight. The German walked around the back of the car and up the steps of the offices all without acknowledging Jack. So much for manners, Jack thought, before hastily shutting the door and moving around to follow the men inside. He was supposed to be an escort, but the Germans obviously had no intention of allowing him to be. The chief wouldn't be happy with him if Jack didn't do his job, no matter what the Germans thought. The two Germans walked along the corridor, politely working their way past the civil servants and other staff, before pushing through a set of double doors and into the main meeting chamber.

Jack didn't follow after them, instead taking a position outside the door where he could see the room and also be ready to leave when needed. No one had told him to attend the meeting, but equally no one had told him that he couldn't. He was curious what would happen now that the Germans were in attendance, and his role as a policeman gave him a unique opportunity to observe, after all, as security. Not that the Germans needed it, as they were the only ones with any weapons. At least, they were supposed to be. Jack had heard rumours that there were still a few weapons in the possession of civilians and farmers around the island.

Jack couldn't see the entire chamber from where he stood, but he would be able to hear almost everything.

The German Kommandant sat himself on the main chair in the chamber, directly beneath the sigil of the States of Guernsey. The seat would normally be reserved for the attorney general, but the thin man sat in another chair at the side of the conference table. The attorney general should have been leading the meeting, but he had decided to show deference to the Germans. Although, Jack wondered whether the man had really had any choice. The attorney general welcomed the Germans and started with a speech.

'I have frequently over the past few weeks been perplexed and baffled by the problems that have arisen,' he said. 'I wished that I might have been doing the type of work to which I was accustomed. I certainly never realised how little I know about anything.'

Jack winced as the attorney general sat down. He had little dealing with the man before, having seen him in the trials, but it seemed now as if he was doing everything he could to show that he was unfit to govern. What the Islanders really wanted was someone to be strong, to stand up to the Germans and show that, even though they occupied the islands, the Islanders wouldn't be pushed around. He was playing into their hands. What hope did the rest of the Islanders have in resisting the Germans if the man in charge behaved like this?

'Jack? What are you doing here?' a voice whispered from behind him and he turned. Beth stood, holding a pile of papers to her chest. She pursed her lips and frowned. She was dressed in a neat grey matching woollen blouse and skirt, more smart than Jack had ever seen her wear before. When they were kids their group had gone off into the woods together, roaming and exploring, and Beth had always been the one to tell Jack off for getting stuck in a bush, or rolling down a hill.

'I err, escorted the kommandant here,' he said, sounding like a scolded schoolboy. Beth was only three years older than him, but every time she spoke to him he still felt like a child. Her age had always made her like the mother of their friendship group, and she had revelled in it.

'I know that,' she replied, shifting the papers as if she was crossing her arms. 'But what are you doing *inside*? This is a private area.'

'It is? I was … Er … Told to wait inside for the kommandant.' It wasn't a complete lie at least. He didn't expect the German commander would care where he was as long as he was ready to leave at the end. As a matter of fact, it wouldn't be a good idea to keep him waiting, even if he was capable of opening his own door.

'It's a good thing I know you, Jack Godwin. Otherwise I would have to report you.'

A faint smile played at the corners of her lips.

'I had no idea that you worked here,' he said, trying to shift the focus away from him. His voice was a whisper, careful not to be heard by the other people in the room.

'I got a job as a clerk, just before the occupation. I wanted to be useful. I had ambitions to work my way off this island. Little chance of that now.'

'You never know what'll happen.' He looked through the crack in the door to the chamber, trying to keep an eye on the kommandant and his interpreter in case he was needed. He didn't want any reports of slackness to make their way back to the inspector.

'Still the optimist, Jack?' She smiled knowingly at him. At one time Beth and he had been good friends, but their lives had moved apart. Before he had a chance to reply, a group of German men walked in through the front door. They held themselves in a way that suggested they were looking down on everything, and the tailoring of their clothes was a level above anything the Islanders could afford.

'Who are they?' Jack asked once they had gone into the chamber.

'Plain-clothes policemen, I believe. They've been coming and going from here the past few days.'

'Gestapo?'

She thought for a moment. 'I don't really know. Their organisations are confusing. I've been doing some research, but it's impossible to keep up with it all. I think they might be another type of secret police.'

'What are they doing here?' Jack tried to keep the question casual. He wanted to keep an eye on everything that was going on. For all their sakes. 'What do they want?'

'What do you think they want? They want the island.' She shook her head in response to his confused look. 'What I mean is they want control. It's one thing having a police force like yours to command, but we know that's how they do things. You've heard the rumours about what the Gestapo do. Why would they not do the same thing here?'

Jack looked over Beth's shoulder at the men she had been talking about. They didn't look that sinister, not compared to the

Germans in uniform, but perhaps that was the point. To make you drop your guard and say something incriminating.

'Be careful what you say around them, Beth,' he said, nodding towards the Germans to emphasise his point as they disappeared from view into the various offices at the other end of the corridor. 'It would be a mistake to trust them. Even a little bit.'

'I know,' she replied, a heartbeat later. 'On that note, I'd better get back to work. I've already been gone too long, and you shouldn't be here, Jack Godwin.'

She accented the last few words with a wagging finger like a disappointed schoolteacher and Jack felt himself blush. Then she left him, returning to whatever office it was she worked in here. Jack took another look in the direction the group of Germans had walked. If there were secret police on the island then they would have to be careful. He thought of Johanna, of the rumours from other occupied territories. She was at an even greater risk than the rest of them. He decided then that he would have to be careful that none of the German police saw them together. It was the only way he could protect her.

Later that night, sleep would not come. It had been a long day, attending to the Germans. The worst part of it was the look on the faces of his fellow Islanders as he opened the car door, as if he had been conquered along with the island. He didn't know how he would protect Johanna, his mother, and his grandparents. He tossed and turned, running the scenarios through his head, unable to shift the faces of the German police from his troubled nightmares.

*

A few days later Jack was cycling past the airstrip on his beat when he heard the noise, a deep rumbling sound steadily varying in pitch. It reminded him of a day not so long ago, a day which now seemed like it had happened in another world, another lifetime.

He looked up and immediately saw hundreds of black shapes in the sky, like spots of dark black cloud. Only, they weren't clouds but hundreds of German bombers. Jack had seen them before, but never as many as this. It was as if the sky was full of aircraft, all heading north. He felt for the people on the mainland, for that number of munitions would cause untold damage. He wondered if there was a way to warn them, but it was already too late. Perhaps if the spies were still here, they could have done something.

A moment later further engine noise added to the sound from nearby. Jack glanced over in the direction of the airstrip to see the German Messerschmitt fighters rising up in the air one by one, off to escort the bombers to Britain. The RAF was in for a serious fight. He couldn't imagine the Germans invading Britain, but it was clear that was their intention. If they had already taken France and the Channel Islands, then what, other than the RAF, was stopping them from taking the mainland? Soon the whole world would be living under the Nazi jackboot.

He watched the planes for a while longer, as the steady stream of bombers seemed without end, then continued on with his patrol. It was beginning to look as if they wouldn't have been any safer in England even if Johanna had been allowed and they had decided to evacuate the island. Where were all the people who had gone to England? Were they safe?

A Messerschmitt flew low over the road, almost deafening Jack. For the Germans, the islands were only a stepping stone to further conquests.

Chapter 11

7 September 1940

'Jack, old pal, I need your help.'

Jack recognised the voice straight away. It had been echoing around his head since the soldiers had turned themselves in to the Germans, and he wasn't sure if he was hallucinating or whether it was real. Jack was hardly surprised. It was as if he had been expecting the man to appear at any moment, even if he had been telling himself that Henry had already left the island. Somehow he had known it wasn't the end of it. Perhaps it was a foregone conclusion that the British Government would keep sending spies to the island, that they would use men who had grown up there. It was exactly what Jack would have done, had he been in their shoes, rather than tending to his grandfather's garden again.

'Jack? Are you listening?'

Jack smiled, relishing the familiar voice. He treated it like a welcome memory, recollecting a time before the Germans, before it spoke again, forcing him to accept reality.

'Hullo, Henry,' he replied, turning to take in his old friend. He stood with his shoulders hunched and his hands interlaced. Even with the smile plastered across his face there was a hesitation. Jack could sense it in Henry's body language, as if he feared what Jack might do. It brought a pang of sadness to Jack's heart. His friend should have known that Jack wasn't about to turn him in; no matter what happened he would never do that to a friend. So Jack grinned back, hoping to ease the tension, passing an unspoken commitment between them. 'It's good to see you.'

Henry relaxed, then laughed. It was a wonderful sound, and Jack couldn't remember the last time he had heard a laugh like it. The other man stepped closer and pulled Jack into a giant bear hug. 'It's so good to see you too, old friend,' he said. 'I told you we'd see each other again. Let's hope next time it's under better circumstances.' He pulled away. 'I'm afraid I'm in a bit of a pickle.'

Jack pulled the other man inside the house. He wondered whether his grandmother would show her face again, but the kitchen was thankfully empty.

'What's wrong?' Jack asked. 'I didn't think you'd be back, but I should have known. Start from the beginning so we can work out what's to be done.'

'Right you are, old pal. They'll make a detective of you yet.' He leant against the back door in case someone came through it. 'I was supposed to meet up with the Royal Navy last night. A boat was going to come into the beach and pick me up. But I waited and waited, and it never came. I must have been there an hour and a half, but I saw no sign, not a soul.

'I didn't make a noise, nor use my torch for fear the Germans would find me. We'd heard what happened to the last lot, so there is a chance they could have missed me. But that wasn't part of the plan – they should have been there. It went swimmingly the first time ...'

Jack wished that Henry hadn't mentioned the soldiers. It brought a wave a feeling that he could only describe as guilt for his part in their capture. He couldn't bring himself to admit his shame and his friend was rambling, his nervousness shining through. Jack couldn't imagine what it would have been like for him. Sure, the army had left the islands and abandoned the

110

Islanders to the prospect of a German invasion, but it wasn't the same. They hadn't given the Islanders any hope of rescue, but Henry had been completely on his own and he had been promised he would be retrieved. Here on the island he was far from safe, and if he was found as a spy he would be shot. Those concerns would no doubt be playing through Henry's mind, but it was clear he was trying to put a brave face on it, as a soldier should. His voice didn't waver, only the haste of his speech gave him away.

Jack needed to do something for his friend, to focus his mind on the task at hand.

'What happened to them, do you think? Will they attempt a pick-up again?'

'To tell you the truth, I don't have the foggiest. I had thought about going down to the beach again tonight, but that would only increase the chances of the Germans finding me. And what am I to do in the meantime? I can't stay here.'

There was a hopefulness in his voice that made Jack's heart thump in his chest.

'No. You can't stay,' he replied, thinking. 'If they find you here then it's not only you that'll get it, but you'll drag my family down with you as well. It's too much of a risk. I'm sorry.'

'I had a feeling you might say that,' he said, a glumness settling upon him, a further sign of the changes he had been through since their carefree childhood. He stalked over to the kitchen table and pulled out a chair to sit down on. His body almost slumped onto the table, then he held himself up straight, training shining through.

Jack sighed, releasing some of the pent-up anguish he was feeling. He did want to help his friend, but the Germans had introduced identification and there was no way Henry would be able to go unnoticed. Not unless he stayed out of sight permanently, but that was impractical. It broke his heart, but he couldn't protect everyone.

'As much as I hate to say it, you need to turn yourself in,

Henry.' Jack had decided that only way to deal with this situation was to be direct. They were adults now, and they had to make difficult decisions. He remembered giving the same advice to the group of soldiers who had found themselves on the island, and he wished he knew more about what had happened to them to give him some confidence that Henry handing himself in was the right thing to do. He felt it was. If they took him to a prisoner of war camp they would be obliged to look after him, but if he stayed on the island then it would be dangerous for all of them. 'There's no way we can get you any ID before the Germans work out who you are. There's no way to hide you. I can't hide you here and if I do and they find you then we'll both be up before a firing squad.'

Henry nodded, but refused to look Jack in the eye. After a moment he spoke. 'I'm not ashamed to admit it, but I'm … well, I'm a little bit afraid of what might happen.'

'I know. But you must have known the risk you were taking coming here?'

'Truth is, my old mate, it didn't occur to me for a second that the British wouldn't come for me. It worked so well the first time. They arrived just when they said they would, and I thought, what's the harm in going in a second time? After all. I'm doing something for the war effort. Who'd have thought they'd just leave me? I'm a fool.'

Jack felt a pang of guilt, but then the British had abandoned him too, along with all the other residents of the Channel Islands.

'Maybe something got in the way of the retrieval? There could be a U-boat operating in the area or anything. We just don't know.'

His grandfather had told him of the German U-boats and the havoc they had caused in the last war. It had been one of the few times he had talked about it, without running the risk of mentioning Jack's father.

'You should go and speak to the attorney general,' Jack said, moving to stand across from Henry. 'He'll know what to do. He helped the soldiers the British sent, made sure that they were treated as a POWs and not spies. He can help you too.'

'*We* sent,' Henry murmured, through the hands that covered his face.

'What?' Jack asked.

'The other men that *we* sent, Jack.' Henry looked up at him, taking his hands away. His eyes were bloodshot and wide. 'I'm worried about whose side you're on. You refer to the British, but what are we if not British? The Germans may have taken over the islands, but they won't have them forever, and we can't forget who we really are. You of all people should recognise that. You weren't born here after all.'

Jack felt his face redden, but he knew that Henry wasn't trying to make him angry. He knew the other man too well for that. Jack was British. Whether the other Islanders identified as British or not, Jack should, and Henry was right: he needed to remember that.

'You're right. But what am I supposed to do?'

He stood, as if he was about to make a great speech. 'Resist. In any way you can.'

'If only it were that easy.'

Henry didn't reply. He paced for a few seconds, then stopped again. His eyes fixed on Jack with a look that he had never seen before in his friend. It was somewhere between compassion and concern; the boyish charm was completely gone now. Henry stood before him, a man. 'No one ever said this was going to be easy,' he said. 'Even before the Germans came, we had an idea of what it would mean for us. That's why we joined the army.'

Jack opened his mouth to object, but Henry held up a hand.

'You had your reasons for staying,' Henry continued. 'And I don't judge you for that. Not all of us could go, and not all of us could stay.'

Jack stayed silent. He realised that Henry needed to vent and get some of his anger out.

'You're right. I'll go and see the attorney general and ask him for his help before turning myself in. What other choice do I have? But before I do that I need to go and see my parents. Even if it's for the last time.'

Jack nodded. He didn't need to tell Henry the danger that would put his parents in.

'Do you have their new address?'

Jack scribbled it on a piece of paper and handed it to his friend. 'Burn that.'

'You've been a good friend,' Henry said, staring at the address. 'I'm going to miss you. You have a way of making one feel better.' He held out a hand for Jack to shake and then pulled him into a bear hug. 'Don't let the bastards grind you down. Fight them every step of the way, no matter what it is.' He left the way he had come, leaving the back door open for Jack to close behind him. Jack stayed there for a few minutes, before he sighed and closed the door. The inside of the house was quiet, and for once he liked it like that.

*

Jack trudged across the muddy path in the rain, his boots sucking up the dirt. He had come to help at the farm on his day off. On an island where everyone knew each other, it was not unusual for people to help each other out. The farms needed all the hands they could get, particularly now that many of the workers had evacuated to the mainland. Jack had volunteered by accident, when a few careless words to Frederic had given the farmer an idea. Jack had arrived in the roughest clothes he could find, knowing just how dirty they would get. Silently, he hoped that Johanna didn't see him like this. The smell of manure was almost unbearable.

At first he had been asked to carry things from one part of the farm to another, including rotten tomatoes that had been left to go that way as they were no longer exported to the mainland.

Then he had heard the farmer calling his name from the field. His voice was raised and desperate and Jack put down the box he had been carrying and ran towards him. The older man was kneeling down in the pigsty, holding on to one of the sows.

'Help me, will you? She's birthing.' Jack didn't know what to do, but he moved closer out of the rain so that Frederic could show him. Before Jack could do any more there was another shout.

Jack looked towards the path and saw a German sergeant jump over the fence and walk over to them. His mouth broke into a wide smile as he approached. '*Hallo! Guten Morgen!*' he called. Jack stared back, the rain dripping down his face. What could the sergeant possibly want? When the sergeant drew nearer he gave Jack's hand an enthusiastic shake that almost pulled him off his feet. As Jack regained his balance the German held out his hand for Frederic. The older men stared down at it, but did not move. He kept his arms pinned at his sides. Jack knew Frederic's thoughts on the Germans, and that he wouldn't do anything to accommodate them. Frederic had fought in the Great War, and it had affected him deeply. He only ever talked about it after a few drinks, and even then he said very little. Shaking the German's hand was, to him, an admission of defeat, and one he was far from willing to make.

The German's smile didn't drop, but he did take his hand away. 'You don't like me, yes?' he said. He looked the farmer up and down, clearly noticing the way Frederic held himself. He stood to attention even when he otherwise appeared to be relaxed. Frederic had scars that weren't from farming, and the wind and rain made them stand out even more. 'You were in the first war?'

'Yes, I was,' Frederic replied. It was clear to anyone who looked at him, but there was no malice in his voice. It was a simple statement, as little as he could get away with, without being openly antagonistic.

'You would like to shoot me, then? If you had the chance?' The rain beat down but none of them seemed to notice. There was a look of intensity in the German's eyes, as if he was on the edge of something. How could someone appear so friendly, yet say the things he was saying? It was all an act, and the fact that he could maintain it for so long struck Jack as a kind of metaphor for the entire German personality. They all appeared to be hiding something more sinister under the surface, if only you took the time to look for it.

'Yes, I would.'

Jack tensed, sensing the situation growing out of hand. He was shocked by Frederic's reply, but not really surprised. Neither was the German. He simply laughed, unclasped his pistol from the holster at his waist, cocked and proffered the gun to Frederic. He held it there in his hand and they locked eyes for a long moment. 'You would no more shoot me, than I would shoot you,' the German said.

There was an arrogance to everything the German did, as if he was in charge and everyone else conformed to his will. He *knew* that Frederic would not dare shoot him. Not just because of the trouble he would find himself in with the German authorities, but because a man of honour would not shoot an unarmed man. But behind it all Jack could also feel an uneasiness, as if the man was not as sure of himself as he was trying to appear. It was as if he was trying to prove a point to himself as well as Frederic.

'So,' he continued, raising his arms in a gesture of surrender, palms facing out above his head. 'Shoot!'

Frederic looked down at the weapon in his hands, and Jack could only guess at the emotions running through his head as he pointed the pistol at the German's forehead. Jack didn't know what was going to happen next, but all he could think about was Frederic pulling the trigger. Would Jack be labelled an accomplice and punished? He wouldn't be able to protect Johanna, and that thought filled him with dread. It would no doubt mean a firing squad for both of them. Apparently coming to the same conclusion, Frederic sighed a deep sigh and handed the weapon back to the German. The air changed as if a storm had suddenly cleared, and Jack realised he had been holding his breath.

'You see,' the German said, wiping the rain from his face. The arrogance dropped from him like the water from the sky, his point made. 'You do not want to shoot me, nor do I want to shoot you.'

He returned his pistol to its holster, taking care to make sure that it was safe, then held out his hand again for Frederic. 'I don't want to be here,' he admitted. 'I am a farmer, like you. I would rather be back on my own land than here on your island.'

Frederic shook his hand, albeit reluctantly. They would all have to get used to the changes.

'Let me help you with the swine.' The German rolled up the sleeves of his uniform and knelt in the dirt where Frederic had been before. It was the first time that Jack had seen any of them abuse their uniform like that.

They set to helping the sow together, spending the next hour or so in silence. They had done enough talking for one day and it was as if they had said everything they could possibly say. It was awkward at first, at least for Jack, but after a while he returned to what he had been doing before, leaving them to handle the birth of the piglets.

When everything was finished, Jack caught the German washing his arms. 'You will have to register the birth with the authorities,' he said to Frederic. 'I can do that for you.'

The implication was clear: there would be no way that the farmer could lie about the number of pigs that he had. The Germans would know everything. Again Jack thought of Henry, wondering where he was on the island. By now the game would be up, and he should have handed himself in, but Jack had a feeling Henry would spend as much time with his parents as possible before leaving. Jack hoped that his friend would be all right, but he knew it would be hopeless.

Chapter 12

21 October 1940

'What have you got there?' Jack asked as he pushed his way into the small room. There was a faint smell of damp in Johanna's small flat above a shop on the High Street, and the windows had picked up dirty condensation again. He had often thought about Johanna moving into his home, but neither she nor his mother would hear anything of it, and he had yet to find a satisfactory solution. Whatever happened, Johanna couldn't go on living like this. She was holding a metal tin between her hands, with the Niederegger Marzipan logo stencilled across it. As he looked on, she pushed it under the frame of her bed, then looked up at him with a smile.

'Just a collection of memories. Some photos of my family,' she said. 'You startled me.'

He wondered what it was that she appeared to be hiding from him, but he respected her enough to leave it be. If it was important, she would tell him in time.

'I didn't know you were coming.'

'I thought I would surprise you,' he replied, reaching down to unlace his boots. Despite the poorness of the room, he knew that she didn't like people entering with their shoes on and walking more dirt into the place. He placed them outside the door and closed it, leaving the two of them alone in the flat. It wasn't appropriate for them to be alone, but he didn't care. 'I wanted to see you.'

She moved along to the head of the bed so that he could sit next to her.

'They've ordered all German citizens to report to the authorities,' she said. Her voice was hollow.

'I know,' he replied, feeling stupid that he didn't have anything else to say. 'It's why I came.'

'They intend to do away with us, Jack. They hate us.' Her body rocked with a sob, but she immediately regained her composure. Jack sighed, letting out a breath he didn't know he had been holding. He wanted to reach out to her.

'It's just a record – all they want is for you to register. It doesn't mean you will come to any harm. They can't just "do away" with you. We wouldn't let them.'

She placed a hand against his cheek, turning to look into his eyes. He could see the fierce intelligence burning there, part of what had attracted him to her in the first place.

'You're so naive, Jack,' she said and even the burr of the way she said his name did not comfort him. 'I don't mean that unkindly. Would that I could live in your world, to have no fear. It's not registering as German that I'm afraid of, but them finding out I am Jewish.'

She took her hand away and his cheek felt suddenly cold. 'I am not like you. Since I was a child my life has been filled with fear. From the day I understood what death meant I knew with certainty that it would come for me one day. What am I going to do?'

He had been thinking about that question on the way over to her flat. He wanted to help, but he also didn't want to give her false hope. Only Johanna knew with any certainty what the Nazis were capable of. 'If they ask, tell them you're a Christian'

Her head shot up. 'I should lie?'

'Not a lie. You're not exactly practising, but saying you are Christian may help alleviate any suspicion. We can make it look true. And if a lie keeps them away from you, then why not? And it might be best to keep your distance from Susanne, for the sake of both of you.'

He liked lying even less than she did, but for once it was worth it.

'I suppose you're right,' she said. 'But in the long run, I don't think it will be enough. What if they look into my background, my parents?'

'We'll cross that bridge when we come to it. Germany is a long way away; information like that may never make its way here.'

She dropped her head into her hands. 'I'll think about it,' she said. 'For now I have to go to work.'

It was his turn to put his hand to her cheek and she placed her hand over it. 'Be careful,' he said. 'Do what you need to do to be safe.'

*

They left the flat together, hand in hand because they couldn't bear to be apart, not even for a moment. Eventually Johanna had to walk one way and Jack another. They reluctantly let go of each other's hands. They had decided it was best to keep apart until Johanna had registered.

As he passed a doorway a man stepped out in front of him. Jack sidestepped to walk around him, putting a thumb and forefinger to his hat in apology, but the other man stepped into his path.

'Excuse me,' Jack said and tried again, but the other man wouldn't be moved.

'Wait,' he said, in a clipped manner.

Jack looked at the man properly for the first time, wondering if they had shared a conversation before. He was vaguely familiar as one of the German cohort that had come over to Guernsey and worked in the kommandant's offices. Jack had seen him at various meetings, but had never spoken to him. He didn't even know his name. It was clear that the German wanted something from him, but his body language was not threatening. He stood with both hands in his pockets, and a slight smile played across his face. He was tall like many of the Germans and had closely cropped light brown hair. It was unusual to see one of them out of uniform, and it struck Jack that this man looked totally at ease in civilian clothes, and somehow normal. It was sobering to acknowledge that, beneath all the bluster, the regimentation and everything else, these men were human just like Jack and the other Islanders.

'That woman,' he said. 'The German nurse from the hospital.' It was somewhere between a question and a statement. His English was good, better than most of the Germans. It lacked the usual harsh consonants, as if he had tried to work on his pronunciation.

'The two of you are close?' he asked, nodding as though he had answered his own question.

It wasn't a secret that he and Johanna were a couple, but even in these modern times it was not considered appropriate for a man and woman to be seen together unless they had made some formal arrangement. Who knew what the Germans thought of such things? Given how they were about everything else, Jack suspected that they wouldn't be any more tolerant of young love.

'That depends on how you mean,' Jack said, already regretting his choice of words. His casual attempt to deflect the issue may well backfire. The German watched him through narrowed eyes. It was clearly not what he had been expecting Jack to say.

'We're a long way from my home,' he said, ignoring Jack's response. 'But that does not mean we are any safer here.'

*

'The Germans want the Royal Court to register a new law.' The chief looked at the paper, adjusting his glasses and wiggling his nose as he read. Apparently he needed new glasses. 'The new law would require … blast it,' he said, raising his voice for the first time in the conversation. He took his glasses from his nose and looked at them from the other side as if that would help his ability to see. 'These damned things.'

He handed the sheet of paper to a sergeant. 'You read it. I lost my good pair last week, and my optician evacuated with the others.'

The other man hesitated, looking between the brief in his hand and the chief. 'Err, sir, it says that they are introducing a law in all German-occupied territories, to bring it in line with the Reich.'

'To do what?'

He hesitated again. 'They say that all Jewish shops must be clearly identified as such in English, German, and French.'

'How can they ask us to do that? What's it got to do with us?'

'The kommandant is keen to uphold the laws of the Reich. They will come down on us just as hard as the civilians if we're found not to be following their new laws. It says here that he is keen on better integration between our peoples.'

'How is this better integration?' Sergeant Honfleur asked.

No one had an answer. The chief looked at them all. 'That's enough of that talkback,' he said. 'They expect us to enforce these laws and make sure that they are followed. They have also asked whether we have a list of Jews on the island?'

Jack's heart dropped when he heard those words, and he clenched his fists to stop himself from making it obvious.

'No, sir,' someone answered. Jack didn't catch who. 'But we can see about making one.'

'All right,' the chief said, scratching his temple. 'Make a list and then I will personally see what their situation is. Better than letting the Germans do it. PC Godwin, I want you to attend Grange Lodge; they've asked for someone. Everyone else, back to work.'

Jack was suddenly thankful for the chance of some fresh air. He wanted to be as far away from them as possible, to keep Johanna safe, but no matter what he did he kept ending up under the Germans' watchful gaze. He inwardly cursed his luck.

When he attended to them at Grange Lodge, the soldier on duty pushed a ledger in his direction without so much as a hello. He told Jack to take down all the details of the German residents who were in attendance and then left him to it. It was a responsibility he didn't want, but what else could he do? He knew Johanna would be there, and he didn't know whether to acknowledge her presence or treat her like any of the others. His thoughts raced, and as the German residents of the island queued up in front of him, he listened only enough to note down what was needed, even when Susanne passed by him, and went on to the next.

Then came a face he recognised well, and his heart raced. Johanna stood there, the faint approximation of a smile on her face that he knew was put on. He wouldn't show outwardly that he knew her, or treat her any different, but he hoped she heeded his earlier warning. She pushed the recognition from her face as she took the pen and muttered a 'thank you' in that accent of hers that had originally drawn him to her. In her long flowing script she wrote her name on the register. She glanced up at him before she filled out the rest of the details, and he gave her a shallow nod, hoping that no one would notice. Next to her name she wrote the word 'Christian'.

*

'These are the names of people we think are Jewish. Once the inspector has it, he will conduct interviews with them.'

William passed Jack the list of names, and his heart dropped into his stomach. He had no idea that the island's records were so thorough. People generally came and went freely and before the occupation the harbour had been awash with activity, fishing, import and export. He supposed it only stood to reason that someone would keep a record of everything that was coming or going. It wasn't much of a leap to go from that to keeping a check on all the people living on the island. He knew the government took a census from time to time, but that was kept in London and they had no way of accessing it now. Jack wondered why the States of Guernsey had agreed to help with this, but they must not have had much choice – none of them did.

He carried the file over to a desk, took a deep breath, then flicked through the list. He was looking for one name, only one name. It wasn't long until he found it: 'BRASCH, JOHANNA'. He stopped and almost pushed the sheet aside. He couldn't bear it. This was his chance to do something. Jack looked around to see if he was truly alone. William had gone back to his own paperwork and the only other policemen in the office were busy themselves. It would go badly for him if he was caught. He couldn't trust them any more than he could trust the Germans. Not as far as Johanna was concerned.

He slipped a piece of paper out of the file and lay it next to a blank one. In the few years he had been in the police force he had seen almost every piece of handwriting and could make a decent copy of the clerk sergeant's lazy scribble. Without a pause, he set to copying out the list of names, making sure that one was missing. Susanne's name was also on the list and he thought about striking her out as well, but the more he changed the more dangerous it would be for Johanna and him. He then crumpled the paper into his pocket, safe in the knowledge that he had at least slowed things down. He would burn that list later.

The inspector stormed into the office, and Jack hastily thrust his copied sheet back into the folder. He was followed by Sergeant Honfleur pulling a prisoner. For the second time in as many hours, Jack had to clench his jaw to control his emotions. Henry was wearing a khaki uniform, but it was unmistakably him. Jack tried to make eye contact, but his friend was smart enough to avoid it.

The inspector turned to William. 'Make a note in the occurrence book. British POW has surrendered to Guernsey Police. Will be processed and placed in the prison for the German authorities.'

Chapter 13

11 November 1940

'How well do you know Henry Le Page, Mr Godwin?'

The question came again. The German police had rounded up all of Henry's family and friends, placing them in prison. Jack had initially thought that his time was up, but then the questions had come again and again and he had started to realise how little the Germans knew. The outside storm racked the building, giving the proceedings an oppressive air.

'That's Constable Godwin,' he replied, trying to inject some steel into his own voice and show that he was not afraid. They had been questioning him for a few days now. Each time a different German officer had spoken to him, asking the same questions, and getting the same replies. The man sitting opposite Jack was one of the German secret police officers he had seen at the states offices when he had been speaking to Beth. He sat up straight in his chair, angular jaw jutting out. He had tried to be stern with Jack, continuing to stare at him until he answered. Jack hesitated, but not for long enough to make the German suspicious.

'We went to school together,' he said, trying to be as general as possible. He had said this all before and it would be on record. There was nothing new to tell them. The Germans knew that everyone practically knew everyone else, and if they were the same age then they very likely would have gone to school together, but that didn't mean that they were friends. The German looked at his notes and hummed to himself.

'But how well do you *know*, Mr Le Page?' he asked again, determined to get a more thorough answer from Jack. As a policeman Jack was familiar with the technique.

'No better than I know anyone on the island,' he said. 'As a policeman I meet most of them at least once a week, as I'm sure you can understand. He and I socialised in different circles, if that's what you mean? He had his interests and I have mine.'

At least that much was true. The two of them were still good friends, but they had drifted further apart as adults. Henry had joined the Guernsey militia, while Jack kept away from it. As a policeman, he didn't want a conflict of interests.

'So you would say that you had no idea that Mr Le Page was back on the island?'

This time Jack didn't hesitate. 'No, absolutely not. If I had known, then I would have reported it to my superiors in the police force.'

'And you have not seen Mr Le Page since he stepped foot back on the island? You are certain.'

Jack stared at the officer, wondering how many times they would go through the same questions, with Jack giving the same answers. They had no way of knowing whether he had seen Henry or not, and nothing they could charge him with.

'I'm certain,' he said. 'I haven't seen Henry since before the British forces evacuated the island. I had no idea he was back, and I had no way of knowing.'

The officer sighed, matching the cadence of the storm, then shuffled the papers in front of him. It was not the first time that the interrogation had gone like this, but the German's manner had changed. He slouched in his seat and his eyes looked as weary as Jack felt. He ran a hand through his hair and gave Jack another long look. 'All right, enough,' the German eventually said. 'Enough of this. I believe you.' He sighed and stood up, stretched and went to the door. He opened it and spoke to the officer outside. 'I'm satisfied that he is either stupid, or knows nothing.' He spoke in English, apparently for Jack's benefit.

Jack stayed silent, not sure whether this was just another trick in the interrogator's arsenal.

'You're free to go.' The German stood and opened the door, leaving it ajar for Jack to leave. Jack didn't hesitate. Outside, the sun hurt his eyes, but at least he was free. He had only been in that room for a few days, but it had felt much longer. He breathed in the salty sea air of St Peter Port and closed his eyes. If that was how they treated prisoners of war, then what did they have in mind for the Islanders and the Jews? He didn't know it then, but he had been one of the lucky ones.

*

Later on, Jack was by Vazon Bay to the north-west of the island. He was enjoying the air and the smell of the freedom. He had asked for specifically cycle duties after all the contact he'd had recently with the Germans, and luckily the inspector had agreed. His night shift beat had led him to the area, but it had been uneventful and it was time to go home.

Waves slapped against the cliffs, throwing up white foam. It was always like this in the autumn during the tail end of a storm, as the cold took over and brought the risk of ice, but there was something even colder about this year. Jack couldn't tell whether it was the temperature, or something about the island itself. Probably both. He wouldn't be surprised to find bits of ice floating by the shoreline, like cold winter jewels. If he had any way of making them last, he would collect them for Johanna.

Jack was on his way home, and he went to pick up his bicycle from the wall he had propped it against, when a change in the sound of the waves caught his attention. There was a boat out in the spray, its prow pointed directly at the beach. It was unusual to see a boat so close to the north of the island, so Jack watched on, mesmerised.

The boat crashed against the sand as it ran aground on the beach. Jack hesitated as he took a step towards the vessel. He wondered whether the occupants had become lost, landing on the beach by accident, or whether it was another intended raid by the British. He didn't think they would attack during the day, but given what happened with the previous raids, he wouldn't put it past them to try a different method. A few other people nearby looked up at the sound, including a couple of German soldiers who were on patrol. They glanced between each other, before they too marched towards the beach to see what was going on.

Now the men were standing by the boat waving at their new-found audience. There were smiles on their faces as their arms waved back and forth enthusiastically. They shouted, but at first it was lost on the wind. As Jack instinctively moved closer the words became clearer, they were singing the Marseillaise.

'Hullo!' one of them shouted over the singing in a heavy French accent. *'C'est Anglais?'*

The two soldiers pushed past Jack, leaving him on the road to look after them. As they marched down the beach they raised their rifles at the men by the boat whose waves were slowing. They quickly stopped waving and started shouting in French. They moved about the boat trying to get it going again, pushing against the hull, trying to dislodge it from the sand, but it was no good. He couldn't move it on his own.

A German shouted *'Halt!'* as the crack of a rifle rang out. The round hit the water by the boat, missing its occupants by a few feet. It had been a warning shot, but it was clear that the next one wouldn't be. The Frenchmen's hands went into the air as they signalled their surrender. The resignation was clear in their eyes. He could only imagine what it must be like to escape one

129

occupation only to find themselves in another. Sailing to England was treacherous, but in the recent storm, it was a miracle they had survived. They must have lost their way to end up so far off course. They hadn't really got that far at all.

The Germans shepherded them into a group at the end of their rifles, never once letting the weapons drop. It took a minute or two before they were all standing together on the beach, their hands on their heads. Jack couldn't help but watch, his gaze fixed on the poor men as they were marched up the beach, a completely different welcome than the one they were expecting. The Germans would take them to their headquarters and interrogate them. As a policeman he may even be called in to help find out what they were doing there, but he thought that was clear: they were trying to flee occupied France. If Jack tried to help them, he too could be arrested. As the soldiers walked back past him, he sighed, taking one last look at them, before going on his way.

*

Jack was busy clearing leaves with a rake from the garden at the back of the house, collecting them into a hessian sack. He hadn't had time to tend to the garden for a few weeks and the autumnal fall of leaves had piled up. They had been blown around by the storms and it was a difficult task to collect them all, so he stopped and went to get himself a drink.

There was a knock on the front door. Three hits, evenly spaced and equally weighted.

Jack had to take a breath to calm his nerves before he opened the door. 'Good afternoon,' the German said, bringing his feet together in attention. He waited outside, but it was clear he wanted to be granted entrance. He stank of gun grease and leather polish. Jack wouldn't let the man in until he knew what he wanted. No German soldier had ever set foot in this house.

'How can I help you?' he asked, trying to feign politeness. He had got quite a lot of practice as a policeman.

'I'm afraid I am here to confiscate your wireless machine. We are attending to each house in the area and making sure that all wireless sets have been collected.'

The man's English was stuttering and overly formal, but Jack understood him well enough.

'Why?' was the only word that escaped his lips.

'On orders of the kommandant. The wirelesses are too easily used for sedition.'

Jack scoffed without thinking, tutting as his mother emerged in the doorway to the front room.

'They are my orders, sir. I cannot leave until I have fulfilled them. If you would assist—'

'Yes, yes. I know.' Jack waved a hand in frustration. 'If you'll give me a minute.'

He shut the door as the German started speaking again, not caring what else he had to say. They had been expecting this order to come, but he had at least hoped for some warning. He followed his mother into the living room and walked over to the wireless set to unplug it. It was heavy, but he wouldn't ask the soldier to help carry it. His mother's eyes followed the wireless from its stand to the door. When the door was open again, he dropped it into the soldier's waiting arms and smiled inwardly as the man struggled under the weight. Jack slammed the door shut again, chuckling at his own small act of defiance.

'What do we do now?' his mother asked on his return, as he sat down on the chair next to hers.

'We could talk?' He flashed a smile, but her face clouded over as she leant back in her chair. She closed her eyes and took a deep breath.

'What's wrong?' Jack asked.

'I was just thinking of your father.' She opened her eyes again, but they were distant. 'He would have been proud of you and the man you've become. Sometimes you look just like him. And other times you remind me of myself.

'Of course, there were no such things as wireless sets back then, but your father would have loved it. "New technology!" he would have said. He loved how technology opened up new options.'

She drifted off into quietness, looking into the fire. A log cracked in the heat, filling the silence between them. Despite his mother's mood, Jack thought he would try his luck.

'Why is it that you never talk about Dad? What happened between you two?'

She looked at him, then placed her hand on his chin. There were tears in her eyes.

She sighed heavily, the movement racking her fragile body. 'It's too difficult to talk about him. Even thinking about him makes my heart ache. Sometimes even looking at you reminds me of him and breaks my heart all over again.'

At her words Jack pulled back from her hand. The implication that his very existence brought her pain hurt him deeply and he didn't know how to respond.

'I'm sorry,' she said, her voice wavering. 'I didn't mean … It's not your fault. I'm proud of you, so very proud.' She paused. 'But what happened to your father broke me, almost completely. When they took him it was only my shock and the support of your grandparents that got me through.'

'You don't need to say any more, Mum. We've all been through a lot recently.'

She smiled through her tears. 'I do,' she said. 'You deserve to know. But I can't tell you everything. Not yet. War killed him, and I'm worried that it will be the death of you too. Especially consorting with that woman!'

He had never really understood her dislike for Johanna, but it was starting to become clearer. She was worried that he would come to harm by being with Johanna, because she was a Jew.

'Mum, I'm safer here than I would be if I was involved in the

132

war.' He wanted to reassure her. 'It isn't like the last one. There's no fight left for us. I'll just keep doing my job and staying out of their way.'

He had to be careful, because she was already on the edge of a mood that could take her for days. When they came on it was like a black cloud settling as sadness permeated her soul. But he carried on, feeling that the time was right.

'And I really wish you wouldn't be so mean about Johanna,' he said. 'She's a good person, a nurse, and you would like her if you got to know her.'

'Hmphh,' was the only response he got. It was the first time he had tried getting through to her about Johanna, and for once she appeared satisfied in a way with his words. Rather than undoing his work he changed tack.

'If you would tell me what happened to Dad, then I could make sure I avoided it.'

'I can't. I just can't. I will tell you what happened another time. Please.' Her appeal was desperate.

He knew that if he pushed her now then it could be dangerous. She had tried things before. As it was, he would have to keep an eye on her for the next few days anyway. It wasn't that he didn't trust her, but he had experience of how she usually reacted to these moments in their lives.

The loss of the wireless had hit her hard. He supposed that it was a sort of escapism for her, or that the regular messages from the BBC gave her a sense of routine, and a sense of hope. He would have to help her find another coping mechanism now.

This was just the start, the first of many intimidations by the German authorities. So far they had been doing it subtly, but in time there would be harsher rules to make sure the Islanders knew exactly who was in charge.

There was a storm coming, and this time it wasn't just the weather.

Chapter 14

24 December 1940

The wind buffeted and pushed Jack as he walked towards the house. The grey skies pressed down, throwing the islands into a gloom he wasn't sure they would ever get out of. The storm that had been threatening for the last few days had finally hit them. He wrenched the front door of the house open and it strained against him in the wind. His long coat whipped over his shoulders and then back again. The rain stung his face. He wrestled the door shut behind him, blocking out the roar of the wind. It was far from the snowy, white Christmas Eve that everyone always seemed to wish for.

Pools of dirty water formed around his boots, but he would only be here for a moment, before heading back out into the storm. He pulled his long coat off and hung it up on the metal hanger by the door where it could drip and add to the puddles by the door. The coat's wax was aged and cracked, and the rain had got through in parts to drench his underclothes. He shuddered and rearranged his trousers, peeling them away from his sodden legs. He would have to see about getting some new waterproof clothes if this weather kept up, especially if he was required to patrol in it. No doubt the Germans had already bought up every last piece of waterproof clothing. They had bought everything else. He put a hand against the package in his coat pocket to check that it was still there, then went through to the living room.

His mother sat next to the fire in her usual chair, reading a newspaper. As he entered, she looked up at him and a smile broke out on her face, bringing a light to her eyes that he didn't see as often as he liked.

'You look like a drowned rat,' she said, laughing.

He couldn't help but laugh back as he ruffled his hair, dislodging another pool of water from his head and shrugging apologetically at his mother. 'It's a bit wet out there,' he said.

'If you start shaking it off like some kind of dog, then I will spank you. I don't care how big you are!' She smiled, like she used to when he was a child. Maybe it was the festive spirit, or he had just caught her in a good moment. 'Be careful though, you'll catch a cold if you carry on like that.'

'I should probably put some dry clothes on.'

He headed for the stairs, but before he made it two steps she spoke again, 'You may want to read this first,' she said.

As he looked back she proffered him the newspaper. He trudged across the living room, dripping more water on the floor, but for once she didn't seem to mind as he reached for the folded paper in her hand. It was the familiar *Guernsey Star* and the front page, as they often did now, contained a letter from one of the Germans, a Colonel Schumacher from the German *Feldkommandantur* in Jersey. Jack had never met the man, but their office was responsible for the running of the occupation in the islands and it would no doubt be serious. He read on.

He held his breath as he realised it was about Henry Le Page and his family. Jack and the other Islanders had been waiting to find out what had become of his friend, the man the Germans had arrested as a soldier, only to later work out that he was a spy. And then, despite promises to the contrary, round up his family and close friends as co-conspirators. Jack had been lucky to avoid being implicated, either by his position as a policeman, or because of the lies he had told, he wasn't sure, but he felt an equal measure of relief and guilt that he hadn't been sent off to prison in France with the others. The colonel went on to say that they had proven the guilt of all the prisoners without doubt. That they were spies and collaborators all.

'Oh no,' he said, the words escaping his lips before he could stop himself. He sat down on the arm of the chair, not trusting his legs to support him. He wondered what they would do to Henry and his family now. There was quite a bit of detail on what the Germans thought Henry had got up to when he had returned to the island. No doubt they would charge them with treason or whatever they called fighting against the Reich and go for the most severe of punishments. He felt another wave of guilt in the pit of his stomach and looked up at his mother to see her reaction. Oddly, she smiled at him.

'Keep reading,' she said and nodded at the newspaper.

It took him a few seconds to find his place through the blurriness that pulled at the corners of his eyes. The next line made him stop again. The sentences for all of those in German custody had been commuted. They weren't going to be punished!

'That's great news,' he said, jumping up and walking across the room. 'Great news. They're sending Henry to a POW camp, but that's better than we expected. At least they should look after him there and he can see out the war without getting into trouble again.'

He looked at his mother and finally understood her good mood. Occasionally a piece of good news could bring her out of one of her darker moments, even if it was good news for someone else. It seemed to give her some sort of hope for the world, as if everything was going to be all right after all. 'They're going to let the others come home. The attorney general, Henry's family, all of them. Isn't it great?'

There was a look of genuine happiness on her face that warmed

Jack's heart. He simply nodded, not wanting to shatter that rare moment. He wondered whether the French sailors would be sent to POW camps as well, but there had been no news.

'A wonderful Christmas present for the island,' she continued. 'They're also going to give all the wireless sets back.'

They'd be able to listen to the BBC again, and with luck they may even get a chance to listen to the king's speech tomorrow. A knocking sound came from the direction of the front door. It was so faint that at first Jack wasn't sure if he hadn't imagined it. He hesitated, torn between going to see who it was and enjoying his mother's happiness. Who could that be, he wondered, fearing the worst. 'Who is it?' he asked his mother who was busy smiling to herself and had resumed reading the newspaper. 'Who would we be expecting on Christmas Eve, apart from Father Christmas?'

'Why don't you answer it and find out?' his mother replied, still smiling.

He gave her what he hoped was a suspicious look and went to the door. The weather still battered about and he kept a firm hold of the handle as he opened it to make sure that it didn't catch on the wind. There was a figure outside, just as sodden as he had been only minutes earlier. They pushed past him into the hall without saying a word and he shrugged, shutting the door behind him. He would have to get used to people calling unannounced, and he couldn't very well leave them on the doorstep in that weather. He turned to the figure, wondering who they were, but too polite to ask. Peeling a wet hood of a coat from their head a mass of curly red-brown hair became visible. His heartbeat raced in his chest. Sudden recognition dawned.

'Johanna? What are you doing here?' he asked, taking her coat by instinct and hanging it on the hook next to his own, without taking his eyes from her. He then moved around her to the living room door, to see if his mother had noticed Johanna's arrival. He glanced in at his mother and noticed that she was still reading. 'I'm pleased to see you, of course, but my mother—'

'Actually,' Johanna replied, shaking her head at him while a faint smile played across her lips. A faint mist of water fell from her clothes. 'It was your mother who invited me here.'

Jack wasn't sure whether he was more shocked that his mother had asked Johanna here, or that Johanna had accepted the invitation. The two of them had not exactly seen eye to eye before, and the thought of them being civil to one another, let alone friendly, was not something he had expected.

'Your mother, she sent me a letter,' she continued. 'She said that she had come to a realisation that she was never going to change your mind about me, and that since I was working as a nurse, I "couldn't be all bad".'

She smiled at him and unwrapped some more of her wet clothes. Her shoulders bunched up as if she was unsure what to do next. Then, noticing him, she put her hands on his shoulders to give him a kiss on his cheek. She stood back quickly, and threw a guilty glance towards the living room. He wasn't sure if he liked the thought of them conspiring together, then realised that if even if they were, only good would come of it.

'I'm glad you're here,' he said, meaning it more than words could express. Then he smiled, finally letting his happiness show. 'I guess I don't need to come and see you then.'

His light mood and easy manner made her smile too, and her shoulders visibly relaxed. 'Come in,' he said, leading her to the living room. 'Come in and make yourself at home.'

He led her by her hand to a chair by the window, letting go before his mother looked up. She was still reading the newspaper, but he knew it was simply a show for their benefit.

'How's that?' he asked. 'Can I get you anything? A drink perhaps?'

She looked back at him with wide eyes, then swallowed. 'No, thank you,' she said. She was imitating his tone and inwardly he cursed himself for being so formal. He needed to relax and put her at ease so that they could just act like this was normal. 'Well, just say if you change your mind.'

'Look, Mother,' he said, raising his voice slightly. 'Johanna is here.'

There was a couple of seconds of silence as his mother made a show of finishing a paragraph, then she looked up and over the rim of her glasses. 'Oh yes,' she said. 'Hello, dear. Do make yourself at home. We must share what we have in these times, after all.'

There was a faint hint of a smile in her words, more like a smirk. Jack suspected that his mother was pleased to have company, especially that of another woman, despite her previous objections. If they could get along then it was one less thing for him to worry about.

'Thank you, Mrs Tabell,' Johanna replied, shifting in the seat. Jack was pleased that Johanna had remembered his mother's maiden name. He reached for Johanna's hand, which was resting on the arm of the chair and gently placed the pads of his fingers on the back of it. Then he looked down at his clothes, remembering how wet they were and that he was soaked through. Johanna had seemed to have remained dry.

'I had better change out of these before I catch a chill. My waterproofs are no good, it seems. Will you be all right here for a few minutes?' he asked, looking sideways at his mother.

Johanna nodded shallowly. She beamed up at him. 'Don't be long,' she mouthed through the smile.

*

Jack came back downstairs only a few minutes later. He had dressed in fresh, dry clothes and immediately felt better for it. He realised he had left Johanna alone with his mother for the first time, and almost ran down the stairs to make sure that she was all right. He knew how deep his mother's words could cut if they were unsheathed.

'That's better,' he said, entering the room to silence. Both women continued staring into the fire. A smile played around

Johanna's lips, which suggested to Jack that they had been talking about him. He didn't dare ask how they had been getting on. Instead he asked if Johanna was warm enough after having come in from the storm. She nodded, thanking him, but the smile dropped from her face.

'Have you heard about Mr Le Page?' she asked. 'It was in all the papers.'

'I have,' he replied, sitting down on the only other spare seat in the room. A chair that had been there since he was little and had not worn well. The sharp wooden frame dug into his side. 'Isn't it great? They're letting them go.'

'They don't print everything in the newspaper,' she continued, staring into the flames.

'What do you mean?'

'I work in the hospital. There are plenty of rumours going around that place. Apparently they found Henry's father. Shortly after they had decided to commute the sentences. It's too horrible to say, really.'

Jack took hold of her hand. His mother didn't seem to notice, she was on the edge of her seat waiting for Johanna to continue.

'He was dead. The poor man.'

There was a shocked silence before Johanna continued.

'When they found him, he had cut his wrists on something.'

'How on earth did he get a knife in prison?'

'That's just it, they have no idea. Of course, the family don't believe it. But can you imagine what it's like to get the news that your family is returning, only to find out just before he was due to come home that he had died?'

Jack swallowed. He thought about what Henry had been like as a child growing up, how many times he had been there for Jack over the years. What it must have been like for the rest of the family, to have that moment of hope snatched away from them. The worst thing was that he didn't think it would be the last time something like that happened to the Islanders before the war was over. And what would the Germans do with them if they won?

His mother sunk back into her chair, closed her eyes and breathed deeply. Jack had a thought to change the mood and rushed upstairs. 'Just a minute,' he said to a confused Johanna. He returned a moment later with small parcel wrapped in brown paper, and knelt down next to the chair Johanna was sitting in.

'I know you don't celebrate Christmas,' he said. 'I was going to come round later and give this to you then. But as you're here now.'

He passed her the brown paper parcel and her eyes widened. 'A gift.'

He couldn't help but smile at the look on her face.

'You shouldn't have.' She started carefully unwrapping each side of the paper, taking her time, and Jack laughed.

'Come on,' he said. 'Rip it open, enjoy the moment.'

'I am enjoying the moment.'

She laughed too as she continued unfolding the paper. Even his mother chuckled softly from her chair. A minute later the brown paper was neatly folded on her lap and she held a wooden shape in her hands.

'It's a …' she breathed. 'A horse. It's wonderful.'

'Frederic showed me how to whittle it when I was helping him on the farm. I know it's not much, but it's yours.'

'It's beautiful.' She couldn't take her eyes off it, and Jack thought he saw her wipe away a tear. 'I'll cherish it.' She pulled it to her heart and closed her eyes.

'There's something else,' he said. 'They've relaxed the curfew so that people can go to midnight mass tonight. I think we should go.'

He wanted to tell her that he had removed her name from the record of suspected Jews on the island. He had had a number of opportunities, but he didn't want to drag her any further into his deceit. If it was discovered what he had done, then she could claim ignorance.

'I didn't think you were religious?' She frowned.

'I think it would be a good idea, for the time being at least, if you were to go along with it. Come to midnight mass with me and then the Germans will see you there.'

She nodded. 'A Jew wouldn't go to midnight mass.'

'It's for your safety. I'm sure God would understand.'

'It feels like a betrayal though. A betrayal of my beliefs and my parents' beliefs.'

'If it's what you need to do to survive then I'm sure they would understand.'

'Okay, I'll go. As long as I'm with you.' She looked across at him and smiled.

*

There were a number of Germans in the church, in their neatly pressed grey uniforms sitting up straight in the pews. Thankfully there were none there that Jack knew, otherwise he may have had to make conversation. Johanna pulled at him, moving them as far from the Germans as possible, but she kept silent.

As the mass started, neither Jack nor Johanna knew what they were supposed to do. Jack's mother hadn't taken him to church since he was little and his grandfather had stopped attending. They did their best to follow along. As the church was crowded, allowing the Islanders to be out after dark for the first time in months, the pair of them were not alone. When it was done, Jack stood to leave, but was interrupted by a faint noise from the back of the church. At first he had taken it for chanting, but when the rest of the congregation stopped to pay attention, he realised that the German soldiers at the back were singing together. With closed eyes they sung the calming tones of 'Silent Night' in their native tongue. Jack sat down again, taken aback by the sweeping noise as more Germans joined in.

'It's beautiful,' Johanna said, although it was barely a whisper. 'How can beings of such evil create such beauty?'

Jack closed his eyes and listened to the sound of music. It

reverberated in the church, filling the stone chamber with pleasing noise. It had a calm sorrow to it that Jack would never have expected.

'It reminds me of home,' she breathed.

He wondered again what had happened at home to force Johanna to leave, to abandon her language and faith. Despite everything he felt himself wanting to join in with their song.

*

There was a knock at the door. Two gentle knocks and then a pause. It was Christmas Day and every member of the family was already crammed into their small front room for Christmas dinner. Even Jack's grandparents had joined them. The aroma of roasted meat still filled the house. Usually his grandparents spent all their time on their own in their part of the house. Occasionally he or his mother would pop in to make sure that they were all right, or take them something like a cup of tea or some food, but they never left their home. As far as Jack knew, they had no idea at all what was going on in the outside world, except for what they read in the newspaper.

That morning, he had helped his grandmother through, by holding her arm and gently directing her even though she kept reminding him that she knew exactly where she was going. His grandad came behind, grumbling the whole time that he didn't care for Christmas anymore, that he was too old for it.

Now, as usual, Jack was the one to open the door. He had expected to see another soldier, but instead he was greeted with the beaming face of one of the men he knew from the Civil Transport Department.

'Afternoon,' he said. 'Here's your wireless set. At least I think it's yours; it says Tabell.'

'What?' Jack blinked in surprise. 'Yes, right. Thank you. That's my grandfather's surname.'

Jack took the set back inside, closing the door behind him with his heel. The hinges squealed as it slammed and he winced, knowing that his grandfather would have something to say about that. But, they were shocked into silence just as he had been, so he carefully placed the wireless back where it had stood before, noticing the line of dust around its feet as he plugged it in.

'I should go,' Johanna said, pursing her lips. 'This is a moment for family.'

Jack's mother's head tilted in Johanna's direction. 'You have family here,' she said. 'If you'll have us.'

Johanna smiled for a moment and a tear ran down her cheek. Jack leant over and switched the big dial of the set. There was a click and then white noise blared through the speaker. It was strangely reassuring, a reminder that there was something out there. With a practised hand he tuned the dial until the calm tones of the BBC broadcast filled the room.

Those registered tones, that calm speech of the BBC presenter, was like hearing the long-lost voice of a family member and picking up as if they had never left. It warmed Jack's heart to feel part of Britain again, only separated by the Channel. He hadn't realised until that moment just how isolated he had felt. Hearing German spoken officially and living through the changes they had brought to the island, had affected them in ways he was only just beginning to understand.

'Almost in time for the king's speech.' His mother's voice dragged him from his reverie. It was best to concentrate on the matters at hand, on Johanna and his mother. They both sat there smiling at the sound of the wireless set. His mother had her eyes closed, concentrating on the words filling her ears.

Johanna reached out a hand and laid it on top of his. 'It's wonderful,' she said.

It truly was, and the most wonderful thing was that she was here. He would not have imagined even the day before that his mother would have allowed Johanna into the house, let alone to stay for Christmas. The Christmas spirit had helped his mother to change her mind about Johanna and it was the best present he could ever have expected.

It would soon be a new year, and the war couldn't last forever. Jack at long last felt some hope for the future, and no matter what happened he would always have Johanna.

1941

Chapter 15

January 1941

The new year didn't bring as much hope as it was traditionally supposed to. The island was grey and miserable, and the storms that had battered it still came and went as they pleased, bringing further misery to compound the Islanders' already sour moods. The gloom of the season only seemed to make things feel darker, especially after a barren and almost joyless Christmas. The lack of any sign of the war ending and the constant presence of the German armed forces only seemed to make things worse. Jack tried to find something to cling on to that would brighten his mood in such a dark winter, but he failed. The only thing that managed to brighten his mood was that Johanna and his mother were now on speaking terms. He wanted to see Johanna, but that would have to wait – he had a day of work to get through first. Despite living so close to each other and being stuck on the island, they never got to see each other as much as he wanted.

'It's like living in another country, now,' David said as they sat at their desks in the police station. 'These Germans are everywhere, speaking their language, with their own shops and their own theatres. We may as well not even call it Guernsey anymore. What do the Germans call it anyway? Something strange I expect.'

David was, as usual when they were not on a beat, sitting with his feet on a desk and waxing lyrical about the way the world used to be. Jack smiled, he never had the heart to tell the man that his view of the world was slightly skewed and naive. William paced over to them, took a sideways look at David's feet on the table and spoke to Jack.

'We've just received new orders from the Germans,' he said. 'Here.'

He handed over the sheet, and Jack quickly scanned it, a list written in the official German way, everything ordered and bureaucratic. They had provided a list of groups that were now banned from meeting on the island, mainly those who wore uniforms.

'The Salvation Army?' Jack asked, louder than he had meant to.

The sergeant made a movement somewhere between a nod and a shrug, before leaving Jack and David to their discussion.

'What have the Sallies got to do with any of this?' Jack asked. 'They're harmless.'

'Must be the uniform.' David's legs fell back to earth. 'For some reason they love and hate uniforms at the same time. The strange contrary nature of the German Reich. I wonder if they ever really know their own minds, or they just do what they're told.'

He laughed, but the humour didn't reach his eyes. There were many things the Germans had banned since taking over the island. Some of them the police had managed avoid enforcing, but this would be difficult as wearing a uniform was obvious to anyone who saw it. If anyone was stupid enough to don their Salvation Army uniform, then the police would be forced to arrest them. He hoped that he was nowhere near when anything like that happened.

'I wonder how long it will be before they ban us.' David laughed again, still forcing it. Jack knew that behind the humour there was an even greater sense of worry. Jack felt it too.

'They need us,' he said. 'For now, at least. Who knows what

happens when the war is over? Will they incorporate us fully into the Reich?'

David's laughter stopped abruptly. 'You really think that?' His tone was hard, as if he felt betrayed. 'You think this is going to turn out in their favour and we'll be brushed aside for their own people?'

'I hadn't really thought about it, to be honest; there's too much other stuff going on.' He was getting good at telling half-truths and wasn't proud of it. He was more concerned about what might happen to Johanna than what might happen to the police force. 'But if you think about it, if the war ends with things as they are, then we won't really be swept aside for their own, we will *be* their own. We'll be a part of Germany, German people.'

David didn't have an answer to that. His eyes narrowed as he looked away in thought. Jack knew that his friend hadn't really considered that until now. It was a good nine hundred years since the islands had last been conquered. What was to say that they wouldn't spend the next nine hundred years under German rule? It was a sobering thought.

As was often the case in the evening shift, partly thanks to the curfew, there was nothing to do in the station apart from talk. Jack had taken to reading, but David seemed determined to stop him at any opportunity. His friend didn't appreciate the moments of quiet reflection as Jack did. He had just fallen into a rare moment of silence when there was banging from outside the station.

'What the hell?' David asked.

He, Jack, and William were up in a heartbeat, rushing to the door. As soon as Jack's eyes adjusted to the dark he spotted a German soldier riding a bicycle down La Marchant Street. Only, he recognised the bicycle as belonging to the sergeant.

'Hey!' William called, realising that the German had taken off on his bicycle. 'That's mine!'

The three of them ran after the cyclist. It didn't take them long to catch him up as only gravity had taken him down to the bottom of the street and eventually toppled him over and out of his seat. Rolling on the ground, the soldier brought up his pistol. Without thinking, Jack clasped the soldier's wrist and yanked the gun to the side, away from the policemen, then planted his knee on the man's chest. '*Nichts!*' the German slurred. '*Nichts!*'

Jack could see from close up that the man's eyes were bloodshot, and his breath stank of alcohol. He shook the pistol from the soldier's hand and David caught it. The German grunted as Jack pulled him to his feet. Despite being a lithe man, he weighed more than Jack had expected. They hauled him and the bicycle back to the police station to report the theft to the German authorities. It would be up to them to punish the man, but if the last few months were anything to go by, then the police would hear no more of it after tonight.

*

The next day, on their beat, David came to a stop at the corner of the High Street, looking up and down its length. There were a few people wandering from one shop to another, even a queue around the corner of Smith Street. People had become unwilling to leave their homes, but they still needed food. The queues had become common on the island. Surprisingly there were fewer German soldiers than normal. When they had arrived they had taken to the shops, impressed by the wares that were apparently unavailable back in the Reich, but it seemed that now as things were running out they were less interested. Either that, or their orders to patrol had been more readily enforced.

Some of the shops now had boards on their windows, not to protect them from any further bombing, but to signal to the public that they no longer had anything to sell.

'Wait here a minute,' David said, coming back to where he stood, then taking a detour towards the pub on the other side of the road. Jack suspected where he was going and would rather not have to deal with the consequences.

'Oh, really?' he asked, already exasperated. 'Now?'

They often had occasion to break the chief's code of conduct, but Jack didn't have to like it. He wasn't "chapel" like some of the others who completely abhorred alcohol, but he didn't want to do anything that may get back to the chief and jeopardise his career. Thankfully, David stopped in his tracks. 'It's all right. Carry on the beat if you want to. I'm just going in for a chat. Nothing to worry about. I'll be as sober as a priest when I come back, scout's honour.'

David smiled at his own words, enjoying the irony that scouts were now forbidden on the island. Jack didn't return the smile. He knew David liked a drink, but they were strictly forbidden from drinking on duty. He couldn't believe his friend would be stupid enough to break one of the chief's rules.

'I'll see you back at the station,' he said, turning to leave. It was David's career he was ruining and Jack wouldn't let him drag him down as well.

The Boys

The boys were playing around the corners of the buildings, rushing up and down the winding alleys of St Peter Port, away from the High Street and the prying eyes of adults. All except Henrik's, as he sat on a set of stone steps writing in his small notebook. He had been trying to get to know the Islanders better since he had been posted to the island, finding time off duty to sit and watch, to see how they interacted with one another. Beth had helped him to understand their way of life, but he wanted to know more and to see it for himself. He had become adept at watching without being seen, but Gerhart had laughed at him.

'Why concern yourself with them?' he had asked, but he simply did not understand. Like many of the others, Gerhart had thought they were being posted to England. Henrik had known better.

The boys were chasing each other, unsure what they were really doing but playing all the same. Henrik knew there was little else for the boys to do on the island other than to run and to enjoy the feeling of running. One of the boys came back again, sweeping around a corner, laughing in sheer joy and then stopped dead. The shadow of a man loomed over him, one of the Wehrmacht officers.

The boy, who Henrik had heard the others call Francis, looked up to see a shortish man, with broad shoulders and wearing the grey of the Wehrmacht. The German grinned at him. It was wolf-life, off-putting, and the boy turned to go as his friends ran around the corner, stopping their laughter as they caught up with him and saw that something was wrong.

'Wha—?' one of them asked, but was interrupted by the harsh bark of the German.

'*Kommen Sie her!*' he shouted at them, beckoning with the slab of a hand. Still he smiled that smile. The boys didn't understand the language, but as he barked the words again, '*Kommen Sie her!*' they got the gist of what he was trying to say. They shuffled closer to the German soldier as he beamed down at them.

'Good good,' the German said, switching to English with a heavy accent. 'You are English schoolboys, yes?' He nodded at them, apparently trying to be friendly. The boys didn't bother to correct him about their nationality. It was clear from their nervous shuffling that Francis and the other boys simply wanted to be as far away from there as possible. An afternoon of fun had quickly turned into something altogether more worrying. Henrik wondered whether he should intervene, but something stalled him. The other officer would not take kindly to being watched, and Henrik could do without another enemy on the island.

'Yes, sir,' they murmured in unison, clearly unsure of what else to say. The German nodded and reached into the inside pocket of his tunic. He produced a long metal cylinder, something like a cigar case and the boys flinched.

'*Gut!*' the soldier said, unscrewing the cap. 'Hold out your hands.'

He held out the palm of his hand, demonstrating what he wanted the boys to do. At first they hesitated, but as he gestured again, the boys put their hands out as he had shown them, small palms up, grubby with the dirt of playing. With a tap of his index finger on the tube he deposited a small circular disc on each of their hands. It was a kind of gummy sweet much like the *gummibärchen* Haribo produced back in Germany. None of the boys moved, staring blankly at their hands and the curious gestures of the German soldier.

'Eat!' he insisted, moving his own hand to his mouth as if they were stupid. No doubt the boys had been told by their parents never to accept anything from foreigners on the island, especially not from Germans. They were unsure what to do; if they refused then what would the German do? Would he get angry with them? One by one the boys placed the gummies in their mouths, careful not to chew and break the surface of the sweet.

'*Ist es gut?*' the German soldier asked, smiling at them again. The boys nodded, still desperate to get away. The soldier patted one of them on the head with a leather-gloved hand. 'Go!' he said, not unkindly.

Without hesitation the boys turned and ran back around the corner from where they had come, trying to put as much distance between them and the German as possible. As soon as they thought they were out of sight, they each spat out the sweet. Henrik could see their relief from where he sat, because in their imaginations there could have been anything in that gummy. They would rather get in trouble than be poisoned. The boys chatted amongst themselves while Henrik still watched on. They decided then to go home, no doubt planning to be more careful in future.

Henrik knew that they had a long way to go if they were going to convince the Islanders that they were working in their best interests, even if women like Beth were willing to put aside their differences.

Chapter 16

3 February 1941

Jack let the day's issue of the *Guernsey Post* drop to the table in front of him and put his head in his hands. The story of the Frenchmen arriving on the islands had been going around Guernsey for weeks now. Even those who hadn't been there on the day were talking about it, adding their own rumours. The column about them was hidden amongst the other news in a small-print section of the newspaper, presumably to try to keep it as quiet as possible. But Jack had been looking for news about them ever since he had first seen them. Now the news had come he wished it had never arrived. The trial would take place today and the Frenchmen would be tried for their crimes against the German Reich. From the wording alone it was pretty clear what the Germans intended to do with the men, but Jack tried to hold on to a small sliver of hope that the island's lawyers may be able to do something for them. All they had wanted to do was get away from the occupation and they had ended up here by accident.

Jack pushed the newspaper aside and tried to eat his breakfast, but he wasn't hungry anymore. The rich Guernsey milk made him feel sick. He would be hungry later, but he had too much playing on his mind to eat. He managed to force some bread down while mulling over his thoughts, trying to ignore the bland flavour. He heard his mother offer to cook him some bacon, but he just grunted a negative and she continued preparing her own breakfast. Within seconds the smell filled his nostrils and he regretted his decision. Their rationed portion of bacon wouldn't go far, so he would save his share for another day.

He couldn't stop staring at the *Guernsey Daily Post*, the various news items wrestling for space in his mind. The one thing that kept coming to the forefront was the trial.

As a witness he would be ordered to attend, should they need him to speak. It was far from the first time he had attended a trial, but for many reasons this one felt different. However, when he had asked he had been told that the Germans were handling things themselves and that his services would not be required. The Frenchmen had been moved to Jersey for a military trial and no witnesses would be required. Jack couldn't help but feel a sense of incompleteness about the whole thing. He didn't know the men, indeed he had only even seen them for a few minutes, but he felt something for them.

They weren't criminals. As far as he was concerned, the only thing they had done wrong was to mess up their navigation and end up in Guernsey rather than England. He couldn't imagine the horror they must have felt as their freedom slipped through their fingers when they saw the German soldiers.

In a way Jack was glad that he had not been asked to attend the trial. There was nothing he could do for the men and witnessing their demise would only hurt him further. He felt a pang of guilt, but people were dying all over Europe and he didn't know any of them. He had to focus on those he could protect. He had to force his emotions to comply, steel his heart.

He tried another bite of bread, but it was dry in his mouth. Food had lost all flavour since the Germans had arrived in Guernsey.

*

Jack had spent the day filing records at the police station. When he had arrived there had been a small queue of civilians leading up to the front door. They had been told to hand in any weapons they may have at home, including the souvenirs they were allowed to keep when the Germans had first made the order about weapons. They had handed over all sorts of things, from some kind of musket, a barrelled rifle which was missing its trigger to various long knives that were no use in the kitchen. There was a collection of swords and daggers, even Zulu assegais and a bow and arrow. Jack wondered where they had got them all from, but the backgrounds of the Islanders were diverse and obscure, much like his own. Now the station had its own little armoury, but it would be no good against the Germans.

Afterwards, he was ready to spend some time with Johanna away from the troubles of his work. He tapped on the front door and waited for a minute, but there was no reply. He knocked again, louder this time, in case Johanna hadn't heard him. Jack spent a few minutes shuffling from foot to foot and wondering where she had got to, then let himself into the apartment, using the key she had given him. Johanna's apartment was tidier than when he had last seen it, but there was still the lived-in look that allayed his fears that she had packed up and moved away. He thought about looking under her bed for whatever she had been hiding, but he couldn't betray her trust like that. Whatever it was she would tell him when she was ready. Instead he looked for some sign of where she might be, or something to occupy himself while he waited for her to return. The curfew was fast approaching, and she wouldn't be far away by now.

He hadn't really spent much time in the apartment, and he noticed for the first time that from the window one could see almost all the way down the road outside. It was quite a view, with the sea just about visible in the distance. In the twilight gloom he could just about make out a shape heading down the road in the direction of the apartment. It was Johanna, the curl of her hair and pattern of her stride unmistakable. He smiled to himself at the image of her and relaxed. She was walking at quite a pace, somewhere between a purposeful stride and a jog, and she would be at the flat in a matter of seconds. Crossing the road, she disappeared as she walked under the sill of the window, then shortly afterwards Jack heard the sound of footsteps on the staircase. He opened the door wide so that she could see him, but still she jumped when he held his arms out for her.

'What's wrong?' he asked, the smile slipping from his face. She eased past into the flat. Jack turned to her, but a moment later there were more footsteps on the staircase. These were heavier and somehow disjointed as if one leg was longer than the other. Jack wondered who it could be as he stepped towards the sound.

A German stood in the doorway, staring directly at Jack, the smell of schnapps coming off him in waves. It was one of the soldiers who had arrested the Frenchmen, Jack was sure. Neither man moved, squaring off like two dogs over a bone. Jack knew that he was the David to the German's Goliath, as the drunk was a much bigger man and could beat him if it came to a fight, but he wouldn't leave Johanna. The soldier's eyes were bloodshot. The drunk was about to do something, Jack didn't know what, but he would stand his ground. He didn't dare break his gaze, but holding that stare was growing increasingly difficult. Jack wished that he had worn his uniform – the navy blue had proved an effective deterrent before. He thought about asking the man what he wanted, but there was no guarantee he spoke even a word of English, and Jack wasn't sure he would like the answer even if he could.

The German took a step forward, almost crossing the threshold, but Jack used the opportunity to stand up taller. '*Nein!*' the soldier said, then shook his head. His foot stretched back and Jack thought that he was going to fall, but instead he turned on the spot and guided himself down the stairs. Jack could hear him muttering the word '*nein*' to himself the whole way, and then he was gone.

Johanna rushed to the door and locked it, then leant with her aback against the wood. She sighed and her shoulders relaxed. 'Thank God you were here. I don't know how long he was following me, but I could sense him there, getting closer.' She shuddered. 'I thought … I thought he …'

'Are you all right?' He didn't move closer to her. He didn't want to crowd her. She was right – it was a good job he had been there. It wasn't clear what the soldier intended, but Jack was sure it wouldn't have ended well.

'I'm all right, really. I'm fine. It's not the first time something like this has happened,' she said, shuddering again. 'Last week I was working, minding my own business, when a brute of a German put his arms around me from behind. I almost punched him on the nose, had to struggle out of his grip. By then he had got the idea.'

'You should report the man to somebody.' Jack could feel his anger rising. 'He shouldn't get away with it, especially at work. The hospital should do something about it.'

Jack didn't know who could do anything about it, without knowing who the German was. Putting it in the occurrences book would only draw official attention to Johanna's name, but he would mention it to the other policemen. They would keep an eye out for him when they responded to other situations like this. There had been cases of serious assault by German soldiers on the island, but the police were never told whether the German Military Authority had done anything about it. If it happened again, they would just have to deal with it themselves.

'What good would reporting him do? They would never believe me over a German soldier. It's best just to avoid them. The hospital are doing everything they can, but they're so busy.'

'This is why I always worry about you being on your own. We all need to stay away from the Germans as much as possible. As soon as we start to think like them, then it's all over.'

She took his head in her hands. 'I pray that you never think like them, Jack,' she said, a frown crossing her brow. 'They are evil. The things they do to us. We are beneath them, like animals.'

'They're not all evil. Some of them are in as difficult a position as us.'

'What does it matter? The rest of them stand around and do nothing. They behave like beasts, treat us like animals. None of them did anything in the beginning and that was how the Party gained power. They didn't oppose them, and those of us who did were too few. By then there was nothing we could do.'

He pulled her closer into an embrace, noticing the way she shook as the anger flowed through her. 'You can't be here on your own,' he said. 'Why don't you come and live with me?'

'Jack. You're such a romantic.' She touched his cheek with the palm of her hand. 'I would love to, more than anything, but we're not married. People would talk, which would only draw more attention to us. The last thing we want.'

Then there was only one solution. He didn't know why he hadn't thought about it before. It wasn't just that his mother hadn't approved. But now she had had a change of heart.

'Let's get married!' he said, kissing her forehead.

She laughed, and it was like a dagger in Jack's heart. They hadn't really known each other that long. What was two years really?

'We can't. You know that. Not while our countries are at war! No one will marry us – it's against the law.'

Jack dropped into a chair, and the padding was not much of a relief. His grand plan had come crashing down around him with the simple application of facts. He warred with the horrible thought that Johanna didn't actually want to marry him after all and was just humouring him, trying to ease the pain. At the same time, he reminded himself of the look in her eyes when she had said they couldn't marry. It had hurt her as much as it had hurt him. He had to believe that.

She knelt down at the base of the chair and took his head in her hands again. As she pressed her forehead against his, he could feel the warmth of her breath on his face. 'I would marry you in a heartbeat,' she said. 'If they would let us.'

Then she pulled him closer and kissed him. Her lips were warm on his and he closed his eyes, breathing her in, savouring the moment. Jack would find a solution to their living apart. His mother now would understand well enough to let them, but then he would need to convince Johanna. He hoped he could keep her safe from a distance until that opportunity arose.

Chapter 17

March 1941

The Lyric Cinema was in the centre of St Peter Port, just on New Street a little walk up the hill from the police station. While the Germans had taken away or censored most of their films, they had at least permitted them to continue having live performances on the island. In fact, such performances had grown even more popular since the Germans had occupied the island, and not a day went by without Jack hearing of some new theatre company or performer asking for a licence to perform in the island's few theatres and venues, or advertising their next show. Johanna had shown some interest in going to the theatre, even before the Germans had come, and since then he had been determined to take her to help take her mind off the occupation.

Johanna was wearing a pretty, light blue dress and her auburn hair had been further curled for her by one of the other nurses at the hospital. Not that Jack thought her hair needed it. He himself had dressed up as best he could with the clothes available to him, complete with jumper to keep away the cold. The cinema itself, being used as a theatre for this performance, sat around five hundred people, and tonight every seat in the house was occupied. It smelt of cigarette smoke and sweat in the dim light. They all needed something to take their minds off the occupation and it seemed that the theatre was the perfect thing. With the curfew and the other new rules, there was really very little else to do on the island, and Johanna wasn't the only one to complain to Jack about it. It was a wonder there hadn't been more open displays of dissent, but people were scared.

The performance they were attending was being conducted by the Lyric No.1 Company, established by the owner of the cinema. The repertoire consisted of a variety of acts, some better than others, and all drawn from the local population. Some of them had experience of the show halls and would sing their bawdy song right under the eyes of the German censors, while others played the piano.

It was during a performance of 'Pack up Your Troubles', that Johanna shifted uncomfortably next to him, and he let go of her hand. He looked at her to see what was wrong and she scowled back, before taking hold of his hand again. 'Don't let go,' she whispered. Her eyes were wide as if she had seen something that terrified her, and her grip on his hand was firm.

'What's wrong?' he asked, no longer caring if he disrupted the performance for the nearby audience members. A German had returned to his seat, but rather than returning to where he had sat, he was now sitting closer to Johanna. He nodded at Jack in a friendly manner, but Jack felt Johanna shift again beside him.

'Let's go. Come on,' he said. He no longer cared about the performance. He stood, pushing his way along the row of seats. It was awkward in the dim light of the theatre, and he was sure that he stood on more than one toe. In the aisle Jack put his arm around Johanna and led her from the auditorium and through a heavy curtain. Back in the corridor the air was cooler and fresher, and he could feel Johanna taking deep lungfuls of air. He reassured her with a squeeze and after a few seconds she steadied her breathing. Jack found the nearest exit, pushing through a pair of heavy doors that took them out onto the quiet street.

'That's better,' Johanna said, raising her face to feel the cool evening air.

A couple of the performers stood by the stage door smoking, and they eyed Jack and Johanna warily. 'Everything all right?' one of them asked, a younger woman wearing a bright blue dress with her blonde hair curled around her face. She was known around the island for her singing voice, but Jack had never spoken to her. The other had been playing the piano earlier on in the performance. He nodded at Jack in recognition, taking a drag on his cigarette.

Johanna's eyes widened. 'Oh,' she said. 'Everything is fine. The performance was lovely. Just too many Germ— We just needed some fresh air. It was too hot in there.'

'You should try being on stage,' the girl replied, flashing Johanna a smile before throwing her cigarette on the ground and grinding it out with a heel.

'Oh yes, maybe one day in the future,' Johanna said, apparently misunderstanding the other woman's words. The smile only got wider. It was warm and genuine. She held out her hand to shake Johanna's.

'Pleasure to meet you,' she said, swapping from Johanna to Jack. 'I'm Annie.'

Jack didn't need to introduce himself.

'Say,' Annie said. 'If you don't like that audience, I may know something better suited. We're having a get-together at the hotel later, after the performance is over. There will be a few people, a little singing, and fewer Germ— Much less hot in there.' She winked at Johanna, who somehow went an even brighter shade of pink. Jack knew the hotel well; it was near the beach that the French refugees had landed on.

'You'd both be very welcome. Just pop by and ask for Annie.'

'I'd love to,' Johanna replied, before Jack had a chance to think about it. He smiled knowing that he was beaten. He wasn't going to take this opportunity away from Johanna, even if the thought of a party filled him with dread. It wasn't that he didn't welcome the company, but it was another way to put Johanna and himself in harm's way. If the Germans found out about it, they may look into Johanna's background.

'Great,' Annie replied, clapping her hands together. 'We'd better get back to the company. But we'll see you later?'

With that Annie and the silent pianist were gone.

*

Jack and Johanna stood in the hotel reception and listened to the sound of music coming from the lounge. He had never been invited to a party before, at least nothing like this. The senior officers often had parties and social gatherings, and they were usually reserved for the island's upper classes. Those who owned the hotels or businesses, who always seemed intent on spending their money on gatherings rather than paying their employees. Parties were not the social currency of a lowly police constable such as Jack. No, their place was the pub with friends, and that was usually good enough for him. Except, Johanna would never come to the pub with him and here she was on his arm.

Likewise, he had never had any reason to make use of a hotel before, nor the money to afford one. He could imagine gentlemen sitting in the lounge, sipping drinks and smoking cigars. Only now the gentlemen had either evacuated the island, or found more private locations in which to conduct their drinking. The hotel's business must be struggling under the Germans, but then they all were. It wasn't just food that was becoming scarce.

He had hoped that the theatre would cheer Johanna up, but it had only upset her more. Perhaps the party would be better. They were running a risk with the curfew, and Jack was anxious about Johanna. But she had been adamant that she wanted to go. She did not have many friends on the island.

The sound of the party drifted out to them, and Johanna

pulled him towards it. There was piano and singing coming from the back lounge. As he opened the door, everyone in the room stopped what they were doing and stared at him. It was like a scene from a nightmare, and he could feel the sweat break out on his brow. There was silence. He knew some of the people in the room and in turn they knew he was a policeman. They must have thought that he had come to stop the party. Either that, or it was because he wasn't born on the island.

There were a few awkward moments and Jack stood there with Johanna next to him, not knowing what to do. He wanted to turn and walk away, but that would be admitting defeat.

'Johanna! Jack!' Annie rushed towards them from behind a group of partiers. She took them by the arm and led them into the room. 'These are a couple of friends that I invited along. Say hello, everyone.'

The room suddenly burst with noise again as they welcomed the newcomers and someone even said, 'Hello, everyone.' There was a round of shaking hands and Jack's fears were put at ease as everyone smiled at him and the pair of them were invited to have a drink.

'Now where were we?' Annie said as she sat down at the piano. 'Oh yes of course!'

She started playing the keyboard and everyone joined in a rendition of 'We're gonna hang out your washing on the Siegfried line!'

Jack didn't consider himself a singer, but Annie and the others belted out the words with such enjoyment that it was hard not to at least mumble along. Even Johanna was singing by the time they returned to the chorus, and she didn't know the words. She reached for his hand and their fingers clasped. The room was filled with people of around their own age, including other couples, and it felt good to be amongst them, no longer hiding. Some of them put their fingers above their mouths like a moustache and marched across the room in an exaggerated goose step.

Everyone laughed. It felt good to laugh, to be surrounded by friends.

Jack heard the sound of a door opening and he spun to face the room. Once again the music stopped and everyone stared at a newcomer. The German stood on the edge of the room in the same way Jack had before, uncertain of the partygoers. The song they had been singing would no doubt have upset the man, and Jack could see the disappointment in his eyes. The room had gone silent. Everyone was waiting to see what would happen, to see if the soldier would report them. Jack could hear his own heartbeat. He knew this had been a bad idea, but he had so much wanted to be a part of something, to bring Johanna and himself closer, to have some fun in the monotony of the occupied island. He should have known better. He and Johanna had tried to stay away from the attention of the Germans, but now they had been caught in the firing line.

He looked over to Johanna at the other side of the piano. She was almost shaking where she stood and he tried to get her attention, to reassure her. After a second or two of staring at the German she inclined her head slightly towards Jack. He could see the look in her eyes and his heartbeat increased further. He could feel her edging away from the gathering, so he tried to shake his head without the soldier noticing.

The German still hadn't said anything, but a smile broke out on his face, washing away the disappointment Jack thought he had seen there before. 'Good, good,' he said in heavily accented English, closer to the German word '*gut*'. He crossed the room towards the piano and everyone tensed. 'Please. Explain to me how to play it.'

He sat down at the piano next to Annie and tested a few of the keys. Apparently satisfied he played a few notes of a tune Jack recognised, but he couldn't remember where he had heard it before. As soon as it lodged in his memory the German stopped playing. The smile was still wide on his face as he gestured for Annie to show him the song.

'Please,' he said again, perhaps struggling with the language. 'I would like to learn your song.'

Annie played the piano again, this time it was less fluent than before. She played slowly, hitting the odd wrong note as she showed the German the tune. When she sang her voice cracked is if she were on the verge of tears, but the soldier encouraged her with a smile. When she was done, he clapped and looked to the rest of the group to join in. 'Perhaps now I will show you a German song, yes?' he said, placing his slender fingers on the keyboard.

Jack felt a tugging at his sleeve. 'We have to go. Now,' Johanna whispered in his ear. He didn't ask why. He placed the glass he had been holding on a table, before carefully following Johanna from the room.

*

He wasn't sure what he had expected from the party, but it hadn't been that. These sorts of things were organised deliberately to avoid the prying eyes of the Germans. But Jack was in that strange position, a type of purgatory between being one of the Islanders and, as a policeman, essentially working for the German civil authorities. His fellow Islanders had already decided that he was a lackey for the Germans. He should have known better, but then it was always difficult to see yourself how others saw you. It would take time to convince them that he was on their side, that he was still a good person. If the party was anything to go by, he couldn't force it, he would just have to take his time. Now that the Germans knew of the party, he didn't think they would risk going again, but that was up to Johanna.

He held her hand tight as they walked down the street, keeping to the side and out of the way. If they were spotted by any German patrols, he could talk his way out of it, say that he was escorting Johanna to the hospital because she had been taken ill or something else. He practised the lie in his head over and over again, as they walked beside each other in silence. Johanna hadn't said anything, but he knew what she was thinking. They had come close to danger, closer than they had expected. They would have to be more careful in future, to keep a greater distance between themselves and the Germans. He looked at her as she trudged along beside him, still wearing the dress she had put on especially for their night at the theatre. Her eyes were downcast, not because she was concentrating on her steps, but because her thoughts and worries played on her mind. He stopped for a second, jerking her back a step as their arms extended.

'What?' she asked, turning to face him. Her wide eyes looked up to his, bright even in the evening darkness. He could fall into them forever, but he wanted to take away the pain he saw there, give her reason to smile again.

'Everything will be all right. I promise you.' He pulled her to him, putting his arms around her back.

'Oh, Jack. You're sweet, but how can you possibly know that? So much has changed in the past few months. The other Islanders are already accepting the occupiers as their friends. Things will only get worse.'

'I won't let anything happen to you. I promise. Whatever happens, I will protect you. Even if it means sacrificing myself for you.'

'I don't want you to do that.' Tears formed at the corners of her eyes, bulging before spilling down her cheeks.

'I don't care,' he said, placing a hand behind her head and pulling her closer still. She didn't resist as he kissed her and it felt good to finally take charge of the situation. He had wanted to feel the warmth of her lips all evening. He never wanted it to end. They were safe there in that single grain of time, lost together in the moment.

There was the roar of an engine as a car came around the corner, and Jack stilled. He could only make out the car by the reflection of the moon. It took an age to reach them as the pitch of the engine rose. The dimmed headlamps bounced around as the surface of the road took the vehicle over bumps and it progressed up the hill. Jack practised his story internally as he readied himself to tell the soldiers what they were doing out after curfew. He fingered his police identification in his pocket as the car finally reached where they stood by the road, but rather than slowing down it sped up past them, forcing them to fall back into the gutter.

Jack lay there on the ground, muddied and bruised, laughing at their luck at not being seen, while Johanna cursed. She had landed on top of him, so had at least missed the mud. His laughter subsided as they helped each other up. They wouldn't be as lucky next time.

Chapter 18

16 March 1941

A few days later, Jack had only managed to see Johanna once since the evening of the party. She was still disappointed at how it had ended, a rare moment to spend time with friends. Jack had suggested they try again, but since then she had been busy with work. He had invited her to the cinema, but she had flatout refused. Jack had decided he would see what it was like for himself, which is why he found himself approaching the Gaumont Theatre, on St Julian's Avenue. He had a rare night shift off while Johanna was busy working, so it made sense to use the time. At first she had told him not to go, but when he had explained that he just wanted to see it with his own eyes, she had relented.

The Gaumont, a typical whitewashed building, was now decked out in all the signs of the German occupation. Red flags hung down above the main entrance with the German Hooked Cross in pride of place, and a large golden eagle was stationed over the entrance. The signage had been changed from English to German, including the name of the film currently being shown. *Jud Süß. Süss the Jew.*

The occupying Germans had made sure that the cinema was a spectacle, to remind the Islanders that Guernsey was part of the Führer's Reich. Jack doubted they would continue to get access to films from the mainland. Every film that was played had to be certified by the German culture representative, to make sure that there was nothing anti-German in the films. Some of Jack's favourites had been excluded for what seemed like officious reasons. They had even at one point banned the Islanders from booing the films, but had changed their minds when they had stopped attending the cinemas. Now they were permitted to clap and applaud.

When he got to the cinema he had to find the correct entrance, not just because of his ticket, but because the German audiences and native audiences had been split to prevent unrest. The Germans sat on one side, with exclusive access to the balcony, and the Islanders sat on the other. To enter through the wrong entrance would only cause trouble he didn't want. He didn't even really want to be seen there at all.

Just as he was checking the flyer to see where he should go, he bumped into a grey shape and turned immediately to say his apologies.

'Jack?' the shape asked, as Jack recognised Henrik's voice and felt a wave of relief that it was at least a German he knew, and one he was partially friendly with. Since they had first met, when they were searching for British soldiers, they had met again a few times. Through their conversations they had come to know each other a little better.

'Hallo, Henrik,' Jack replied, feeling on show. Henrik was not alone.

'I believe you know, Beth?' Henrik asked, nodding towards the woman who was holding on to his arm. Beth was wearing a light grey evening dress that sparkled in the lights of the theatre entrance. It looked more expensive than she could have afforded. Her cheeks turned a bright shade of red, which was visible even below her rouge.

He nodded, and they fell into an awkward silence.

'I did not expect to see you here,' Henrik continued, oblivious to their discomfort. 'I did not think of it as your kind of thing.'

Jack shrugged, then realised that wouldn't be enough of an explanation for Henrik. 'It's not really, I have to admit. But I thought I should come and see what it was like. See what the fuss is all about.'

Henrik made a *hmmm* noise, apparently unsatisfied with Jack's explanation. 'There is not much here that would change your opinion of us, Jack,' he said, lowering his voice to a whisper. 'If you were anyone else I would advise you not to take any of this seriously.'

With that he swept a well-manicured hand at the regalia. 'However,' he continued, 'I know that you are more intelligent than that. You had seen through the drama and the glory before the first time we had met. You will not like what you see tonight, but I will not say any more than that.'

He gestured for Jack to continue towards the cinema. He lowered his voice a fraction. 'If I were to say any more, it would be dangerous. You must make up your own mind. You are your own man, as am I.' Jack thought he suspected a faint smile at Henrik's words, but he couldn't be sure. 'I am here because it is required of me, but you have a choice, Jack. There is always a choice.'

Henrik nodded to Jack and indicated the way to Beth, as they walked over to the ever-smiling Gerhart. As they walked away Beth looked over her shoulder at Jack, her face still red. Jack walked the other way into the cinema, refusing to acknowledge her. She had made her decision and the consequences were her own.

Inside the lobby, they had placed a portrait of the Führer above the doors to the auditorium. From there Adolf Hitler looked down on them. Jack felt that the man was trying to act like some kind of monarch, but he didn't have the look to pass it off. Of course, voicing that sentiment would not be wise. The Germans were fanatical, showing almost religious observance to their Führer. They treated him more like a god than a political leader. Jack had read a bit of the man's book *Mein Kampf*, but had thrown it away after a few pages. There was something about his self-importance. Not to mention the war he had started.

There was a smell of stale sweat, which reminded Jack very much of the inner workings of the police station. Soldiers, grease, and firearms. Even when they had dressed up, the smell was unavoidable. A German greeted his fellow officers under the Führer's portrait. Once Jack had got his ticket, he was shown to the right-hand side and up a set of stairs to the double doors that led to the seating. Jack was surprised to see around a hundred or so other locals already sitting there awaiting the showing. He found a seat near the side, as far away from the Germans as he could get. The cushioned seat was somehow comforting and he sank back into it, as if it would protect him from being seen. He didn't know what he was doing there. As he looked over at the Germans he made eye contact with Beth just as the lights dimmed and a fanfare indicated the start of the film. At first they were shown a news reel prepared by the German authorities. The black and white images of other parts of the Reich flickered across the screen, followed by a recording of a speech by the Führer.

The film reel stretched and there was a faint squeal as the projector was changed over to the main feature. The opening of the film was impressive in its style. People lined the streets of what he assumed was a nineteenth-century German city, awaiting the coronation of some duke. He hadn't seen so many actors in a film before and the production had clearly done their work. He sat up in his chair. Jack couldn't understand what was being said, even though he recognised the odd word. But due to the production of the film, he could follow what was happening. The plot involved the duke making an agreement with a Jewish jewel trader called Süss. As far as Jack could tell Süss was using his power over the duke to change the rules for Jews in the city, and to pursue a woman who apparently had no interest in him. Jack tried to follow this for some time. At one point, the duke died and the Jew was arrested and shown to be a despicable human, perverting the minds of the duke and his followers.

Jack couldn't believe what he was seeing and he looked around the other cinemagoers. *What is this?* he thought, watching on in horror. His horror was not directed at the film, which was crude and obvious, but the other audience members. They sat there enraptured by it, some even clapped when Süss was arrested. *How could anyone fall for this?* The argument wasn't even compelling; it was bordering on farce. Jack thought of Johanna and knew that the reality couldn't be further from what he was seeing in this film. She was beautiful, not just in appearance, but in character. Yet still people were enamoured, there was cheering and whooping as Süss got what they felt he deserved. There was a euphoria attached to the downfall of this 'beast', and Jack could only think one thing: compassion was dead.

Finally he understood some of what Johanna felt when he thought of these people. They would never see her as anything more than subhuman. There was a sickness at the heart of the Reich, and it wasn't the Jews.

He wanted to leave, but he felt trapped. He had a sudden feeling of what it must have been like for Johanna, what she must have gone through. Sweat poured down his temples, but it wasn't from the heat inside the cinema. He shuffled in his seat, suddenly uncomfortable. He couldn't move, couldn't go anywhere. He was trapped.

*

17 March 1941

Jack's spoon hit the plate as the clock tolled eight-fifteen in the morning. The time had come, and Jack could think of nothing else. Somewhere in Jersey a shot rang out in the garden. Another member of the resistance against the Nazi Reich drew their last breath, preceded by the words, '*Viva dieu. Viva la France!*'

Jack wasn't around to hear it, safe in his own home, but it still cut through his heart like a knife. The knowledge of the execution was enough to scar his soul. He was growing tired of being unable to do anything to stop what was happening, and each time the anger grew within him. Every time he thought about Henry and the soldiers, wondering what had happened to them, Jack's heart sank. Feeling sorry for themselves was a luxury those men no longer had. Had they suffered the same fate as the French Resistance? Sooner or later Jack would have to make a difference or suffer the same fate as François Scornet, a man whose only crime was landing on the wrong beach. He had to keep Johanna as far away from harm as possible. Something had changed in Jack, but he didn't yet know what it was.

Chapter 19

20 April 1941

'Jack? Come quick.' His mother's voice was somewhere between a shrill scream and desperation. Even in her darkest moments, he hadn't heard her speaking like that. He let the front door shut behind him, eliciting its usual squeal.

'What's wrong?' he called, heading from the corridor in the direction of her voice. His mind rushed with the possibilities, each one worse than the last. His stomach was in his mouth and he found it difficult to talk. Had she hurt herself somehow? Would he be able to help? She was speaking, so there was that at least. He forced himself to think happy thoughts, but her voice came from his grandparents' room. The door was wide open when he reached it, which was unusual in and of itself, but weirder still was the fact that his mother knelt by the bed, almost leaning over it. Jack stumbled across the doorway.

His grandfather's breathing was shallow, his skin pale and clammy. The skin around his eyes was red, almost like a rash. His eyes were closed, as if he was asleep, but Jack could tell he was in great pain. His mother held his hand in hers, and Jack thought then how small it looked.

'Grandpa? I'll telephone for a doctor,' Jack said, turning to leave the room. If he wasn't in there, then it couldn't be happening.

'No,' his mother whispered, stopping him dead in his tracks. 'There's no need.'

He knelt on the floor close to her and took hold of both of their hands. 'What do you mean?' he asked, speaking softly, so as not to wake his grandfather.

'It's too late.' She spoke with a sudden calm, as if she was resigned to it. His grandfather's chest was no longer rising with breath. He had stopped breathing. Jack felt for a pulse on his wrist, but there was nothing. A single tear dropped down his mother's cheek, onto the bedsheets. 'He's gone,' she said, her voice a detached monotone.

There was a sigh from across the bed where his grandmother lay next to her husband. Her body shook as she sobbed to herself, words failing to form on her mouth as she sat closer to the man she had been with all these years. Jack searched for something to say, but the words wouldn't come. What could he possibly say to console these two women who had lost the most important man in their lives?

Jack wondered if perhaps his mother had expected this to happen, even when Jack had no idea. He had known that his grandfather had been ill, but they hadn't really spoken about it these past few months. They had been told by the doctor that it wouldn't really affect his day-to-day life, but now that seemed like a lie. All the while the cough had been getting worse, but since the occupation Jack had been too absorbed in himself, too busy to pay much attention to his family. He felt no small amount of guilt for that.

'I'm sorry,' he said, searching for the right words. 'I had no idea. I should have taken him to the doctor sooner.'

His mother took a firmer grip of his hand, and shook her head. He knew that before long she would sink back into herself again.

'There was nothing you could have done,' she said. The tone of her voice had shifted again, back to the way she had spoken to him when he was a child. 'It's everything that's happened. It was too much for him. He wasn't eating; he wanted to make sure that we all had enough. It would have happened sooner or later.'

She looked up at him for the first time and her eyes were red with tears. 'You can go and telephone the doctor now; they'll need to know. I'll see to Grandma.'

She let go of his hand and wiped the back of it across her face. All the movement did was release more tears from her eyes and they made the rouge on her cheeks run in clogged streams. She tried to force a smile, but it was more of a grimace. The smile dropped as she walked around the bed and took the smaller woman up in her arms. They sat together, gently rocking in their grief. For some reason Jack felt completely detached, as if he was merely an observer looking on without permission. He wanted to reach out to them, but thought it was best to let them come to terms with it on their own. He would talk to Johanna about it. She would know what to say, would provide him some comfort.

He took a long look at the man lying on the bed, the man who had been a sort of father figure to him, told him stories in an attempt to help Jack understand the world. In death he looked different, smaller certainly, but as if he had never lived at all, as if he was some kind of myth. He realised then that the man's strength had left him years ago. Jack tried to find a mental image of a younger grandfather, one full of life as he had been when Jack was little, but Jack couldn't manage it. His grandpa had been declining for a long time, and the German occupation had taken that final spark from him. Jack cried then, realising what it was that he had lost. He had never really had many men in his life, and he had finally lost the one who had meant something to him.

He left the room in silence, not sure whether his mother and grandmother saw him go. He didn't know what he was going to tell the doctor, but it had to be done. Jack would have to go along the road to the only house with a telephone, the house that Nicholas lived in, and ask to use it. His legs took him there automatically and as the door opened he heard himself explain what had happened as if from a great distance. Nicholas's mother was like a phantom, as she led him to the telephone. He picked up the receiver and placed it to his ear. He suppressed a sob before the tone told him that it was connecting to the operator.

*

He wanted to be anywhere, anywhere but the house. A cloud hung over it now and it would never be the same. His legs took him to the only place he could bear to be, down into the High Street of St Peter Port and up the stairs he had come to know so well. He didn't see the people he passed, ghosts, pale spectres in his peripheral vision. The door was locked this time, and somewhere deep inside himself he was glad of that fact. She was safe at least.

He knocked and waited. A few moments later Johanna answered the door. 'Jack?'

She looked surprised to see him. Again, he couldn't find the words.

'My grandfather died today,' he said, cringing about how abrupt it sounded. Johanna looked as if she had been punched, but then Jack supposed that must have been how he had looked when he had seen his grandfather pass.

'What happened?' she asked, a hand over her mouth, tears welling in her eyes.

So he told her, recounting how he had arrived at the house and what he had found there. 'Doctor Abbott said he had pneumonia in his lungs. That there was nothing we could have done.'

'Oh, that's awful, I am so sorry.' She rushed to him, putting her arms around him and pulling him closer. She kissed him on the cheek and he closed his eyes. He wanted to kiss her back, but it didn't feel appropriate in the moment, not with what had happened. She pulled away, sensing his reluctance.

'I'm all right,' he said, not really meaning it, but not knowing how else to articulate his feelings. He had thought it would be easier with Johanna. He didn't want to overload her, nor did he want her to feel sorry for him. If anything, he just wanted things to be normal.

'I only met him that one time at Christmas,' Johanna said, filling the silence between them. 'But he was a lovely, sweet man. How is your mother coping? Your grandmother?'

'I don't know,' he replied, honestly. 'Mum doted on her father even though they had drifted apart these past few years. But I don't know, she was different.'

'Different?'

'Yes.' He pulled away so that he could look at her while he was talking. 'She seemed more focused than I had seen her in years, as if caring for someone else gave her something to concentrate on, something to live for.'

'But what about now? Is she not upset?'

'Yes, of course. When I left the house it was clear she had been crying. She was sitting in their room with my grandmother. Neither of them were talking.'

'As you would expect,' she added, nodding.

'Yes, but not quite. My mum was quiet, but not in her usual way. It was like she was being reflective, keeping an eye on her mother and thinking about her father. I could understand how she was feeling for once.'

Once again, Jack wondered what had happened to Johanna's family and the brother she had once mentioned, but it was not the time to ask.

'I'm sorry,' he said. 'I shouldn't have dropped this on you like that. I know you suffered with your own family. I wasn't thinking.'

'Jack Godwin.' She had almost picked up the Guernsey accent in the way she said his name. She reached out and put her hands either side of his head and looked him in the eye. He was used to being the one to comfort and reassure her, but her presence was more than welcome. 'Don't be silly,' she said. 'You can always speak to me, always be honest with me. I'll never judge. I love you.'

He tried to repeat the words back to her, but in that moment he was incapable. For some reason it felt like a betrayal. He didn't see the expression on her face as they held each other, fighting against the darkness threatening to overwhelm them.

Chapter 20

22 June 1941

It had been another long shift and Jack was ready to go home, but David had insisted that the pair of them meet for a drink, as he wanted to cheer Jack up. Jack's grandfather's funeral had been a small affair. He had few friends left on the island, so Jack, his mother, and grandmother had sat on their own at the front of the chapel as the vicar read out the service. Jack and his mother had sat there in stony silence while his grandmother had broken down. He wanted to have a pint in memory of his grandfather, who had, before he became ill, loved a drink and a story as much as any man.

Their usual was The Prince of Wales, across the road from the police station and as convenient as any other. Some might have thought that it was a policemen's pub, but that really wasn't the case. It was frequented by locals from all walks of life, from dock-hands to shop workers. That was before the Germans restricted the sale of spirits, and implemented the curfew.

Jack crossed the dark road and headed straight for the pub. The door swung open as he pushed, the squeak of the hinges lost in the noise of the bar. The smell of sweat and old beer hit him immediately, bringing back fond memories. The place was almost full of men, deep in conversation, forgetting the outside world if only for a brief time. He hated that feeling of walking into a busy pub, when everyone looked at you as your eyes adjusted to the gloom, wondered what on earth it was you wanted and why you were alone.

He pushed past the two men at the table nearest to the door, who nodded at him, and went through a cloud of smoke to the bar. Jack would have liked to have brought Johanna here, but she wouldn't step foot in the place. She would rather be outdoors than cooped up in a cramped and smelly pub, and at times he could understand why.

He ordered a pint of Randall's then headed towards the back of the room. Even from the front Jack could hear David's jovial voice, repeating some anecdote he had probably already told them a hundred times before. It brought a smile to Jack's face as he pushed his way deeper into the crowd.

'Ahh, Jack!' David stood up and beamed at him, before pulling him close in a bear hug that almost took the breath out of him. Most men would have simply nodded at Jack and welcomed him to the table, but David wasn't most men. They had worked together for years now, and since Jack had started David had treated him like a brother, like the brother neither of them had ever had. He let go of Jack, and Jack took a deep breath of air to refill his lungs, hoping that David didn't notice. David gestured for Jack to sit.

There were three other men at the table, one of whom he only just recognised. The other two Jack knew well from school. Nicholas patted Jack on the back as he sat down next to him and nodded as he played a hand through his short ginger hair. There was a smile on his young face, apparently in good humour from whatever anecdote David had been telling. To his right was Peter, a skinny man, who was an old school friend, and then the man Jack didn't know.

'Glad you could join us,' David said, before leaning to the side so he could speak only to Jack. 'Listen, about the other day when I disappeared—'

'It's fine. No one found out. Let's just keep it that way, all right? I don't want to know what you're up to.'

Nicholas leant over his pint. 'Say, have you seen the Germans try and play cricket?' he asked, repeating a joke he'd clearly got from David. 'They don't know their stump from a crease.' Everyone laughed, except for the man Jack didn't know, who watched for Jack's reaction.

In a way, the man reminded Jack of the pictures of the Führer he had seen. He never seemed to smile, the faint movement of his lips more like a scowl. His eyes were deep set and gave him a considered look, as if he was always appraising from a distance. He was prone to staring, and it immediately made Jack feel uneasy.

'You work with them?' he said, scrunching his eyes and looking from Jack to David and back again.

'Come on, Clive,' David responded. 'You know that we do.'

'Not exactly,' Jack responded, lowering his voice to something only fractionally above a murmur. 'It's not like that.'

'Oh? What is it like then?'

'Careful, Clive. Jack's lady friend is German too, and she's all right!'

Jack winced, closing his eyes. At first he had wondered why Clive seemed to be singling him out, but now he knew why. Not for the first time he wished David had kept his mouth shut.

'You're consorting with them too?'

'Now, hold on,' David jumped in, trying to come to the rescue, but only drawing the attention of the drinkers at the tables around them with his booming voice.

Jack held up a hand to placate him. 'Everything works exactly the same way it did ... before.' He hesitated, thinking that to invoke the name of the British might only make things worse. 'Anything to do with the Germans is referred to them and then they have to deal with it.'

187

'But you still arrest Guernseymen for them?' Flecks of spittle formed at the corner of the man's mouth as his face reddened and his voice became a growl.

'I thought we had come here for a drink, Clive?' David asked, smiling at each of them and hoping to lighten the mood. 'Not for a debate.'

He opened a battered carton of cigarettes and handed them around the table. Clive refused, and Jack thought about accepting just to spite him, but in the end David didn't even offer. 'What were you saying about the cricket, Nicholas?'

'What do you care?' Clive continued, ignoring David's attempts to calm things down. 'You're not even an Islander, not really.'

'What are you talking about? I'm as much of an Islander as you are.'

Clive stood, and his stool fell over behind him. 'But you weren't born here were you, Jack? You're English really. And so was your father. Your lot left us to the whims of the Germans, and I'll never forgive them for that.'

David stood too, facing off against Clive. 'You've had too much to drink. Calm down.'

'I wouldn't expect him to understand. He's not one of us.' He turned back to Jack. 'You're as much an outsider as they are.'

Jack had heard it all before, but this was the first time anyone had shown this level of anger towards him. There was something else behind those words. Jack decided to leave. He didn't want the trouble, and he thought if he wasn't there then David and the others could get back to the drink.

'You haven't got any fight in you – you only care about yourself.'

Jack couldn't help himself. 'What are you talking about?' he asked as his own stool flew back.

'Your cowardly English father. They're all the same.'

Jack almost didn't notice as the man twisted and swung a fist at him, but his police training took over. Alcohol had made the other man slow, and it allowed Jack to take the punch in the palm of his hand, and grip, locking the man's fist there. Using Clive's momentum he pulled him around and locked his arm behind his back. Now facing the other way, there was no way that he could attack. He struggled to free himself, kicking out, but Jack was in control.

Jack bunched his right fist and was about to swing when he heard the door to the pub open. There was a sudden silence and Jack could sense eyes watching him. There was a clink of an empty glass as someone put it down on the table. Jack let go of Clive, who loosened his shoulders and stormed off.

No one else moved as a uniformed soldier entered the room, holding open the door behind him. Jack wondered how much the German had heard of the conversation, but the man simply nodded at the room and headed to the bar. As the soldier cleared the doorway another man entered. He wasn't in uniform like his companion, but he certainly wasn't from the island. He had a distinctly German look, reminding Jack of the secret police he had seen at the states offices, but there was something more to him. He had small, calculating eyes, and Jack could feel the man quietly assessing him. For what, Jack wasn't sure, but there was an analytical mind behind those eyes. A smile broke out on the German's lips, but it didn't reach his eyes. It was like a predator that had caught sight of his prey and realised there was nothing the poor creature could do to defend itself. He said nothing as he walked past Jack, following in the wake of the soldier.

Jack turned to the room as everyone went back to their drinks. Clive had gone, his anger with him, but Jack knew it wouldn't be the last of it. With tensions running high under occupation, it was hardly surprising that someone had taken it upon themselves to make a point of it, even if it was the alcohol talking. He had a feeling that next time he saw Clive they would both act as if nothing had happened.

Jack noticed that the short German was still looking at him over the top of his untouched drink while the soldier talked to him. The man had the enquiring gaze of a detective, beady eyes that were always looking for information, even if there was a smile underneath them. That smile was false, put on like some kind of act to make Jack feel more at ease, but all it did was make his skin crawl. It was snake-like. The man had to be one of the Gestapo, and the thought made him feel decidedly uneasy. Even though they were supposed to be secret police there was something so obvious about the man, conspicuous in his entire manner.

Not for the first time, he wondered if it would be worth trying to learn the language. If he remembered next time he passed a bookshop he would see if he could pick up a book on German. By now the military authority would have censored the books and imported their own.

He couldn't shake the feeling of those eyes following him, and every time Jack looked up there he was. The man nodded next time he looked, and took a sip of his beer. Jack was frozen, unsure how to respond, but after an awkward moment he nodded back. Whatever was going on, Jack couldn't concentrate. He nudged David, who was nursing his own pint, in the ribs. He twisted towards Jack in shock. 'Hmm?' he asked, not really paying attention.

'I think it's time we left, David.'

The other man looked at the dregs of his pint and shrugged. He put the glass back on the table and it made a hollow banging sound.

'All right,' David said. 'I wasn't having much fun anyway. And I've finished my drink. If I leave now, at least I won't have to crawl home.'

He turned to Jack with a big grin, hoping that he would react, but Jack simply shook his head.

'I'm not carrying you. I couldn't bend over for days after the last time!'

As they left, Jack could still feel the man's eyes boring into his back. He felt an enormous sense of relief as the door shut behind him, putting some distance between them. He wouldn't put it past the German to follow him, but as they got further down the road there was no sign of him. Jack kept looking back over his shoulder as the two of them walked in silence. There was also the possibility that Clive could be following him, looking for revenge, but Jack hoped he had learnt his lesson. David would normally be talking his head off, but he was unusually quiet. The only noise was his footfalls as he stumbled along the road. He had clearly had more to drink than Jack had realised, and Jack wondered whether he had too.

'Just a minute. I need to pop in somewhere.'

'But you've already had your lotion.' Jack shrugged, letting his hands play out by his sides. 'Where are you going?'

David didn't answer but stumbled off into the dark. Jack thought about following, but he couldn't bring himself to. David had a mind of his own, and no matter how much Jack tried to keep him in line, it never worked.

Jack stood on the corner, keeping an eye out and waiting for David to come back. He was more concerned about the Germans and he still couldn't shake the thought of that member of the secret police watching him. *Hurry up,* he said to himself. After a few minutes he saw David coming down the road. Jack reprimanded himself for being so stupid. He had to stop jumping at shadows.

'Where did you go?' Jack asked, his voice barely above a whisper but cutting through the darkness all the same.

'I went to check on Clive,' David replied, slurring his words. Somehow Jack knew he was lying, but before he could say anything, David pulled him into a big hug.

'You're a good friend,' he said, almost in Jack's ear. There was a package under David's arm and it pressed into Jack's ribs. 'I love you.'

Jack could hear the drunken smile on David's lips. David was his best friend, but he knew it was the alcohol talking. He just nodded in agreement.

'Have you heard the news?' David continued. 'It's all over. The Germans have invaded Russia!'

Defiance

Susanne was clearing a table in a lounge of the Imperial Hotel when she saw a Wehrmacht officer stand up, pull the hem of his field grey tunic back down to his waist, then walk over to an elderly couple that were sitting by the window. The couple had been sitting there for a number of hours; they often came into the hotel to gaze out of the long window at the sea in the distance. Susanne wasn't sure what they were really looking at or thinking, or whether they were simply just *being*, but they spent hours by that window. Sometimes she wished she could do the same, but she had to work. As a foreigner to the island she had to earn her keep somehow.

The soldier had stood abruptly, and Susanne couldn't tell from his manner what he was doing; they all walked in that same self-confident way, something close to goose-stepping, but less officious. She had been wary of that look since it had first shown up in her home country, but here so far from Germany she had never expected to see it. He marched to the elderly couple and stood over them, clenching and unclenching his hands. After a minute, the officer spoke.

'That brooch,' he said, with a faltering accent. 'Please remove it immediately. It is offensive.'

There was silence for a moment as the woman looked down at

the brooch she had attached to her blouse. Susanne could make out the shape of a pair of sapphire wings, similar to the wings worn by the RAF pilots that had been stationed on the island. It was just like her countrymen to take offence at something like that.

The woman's eyes widened in shock. 'No!' she replied, rather forcibly without moving in her seat. 'I am proud to wear it!'

Susanne could feel the tension in the other woman from where she was standing and watching, wanting desperately to help. It was dangerous for her to intervene, not just as a German, but as a Jew. She wanted to melt away into the shadows.

'I will not! My son …' The woman hesitated. 'My son gave it to me when he earned his wings, and I wear it to remember him.'

Susanne put down her tray of teapots and cups. She had no authority in this situation, despite working in the hotel. Her mind raced with possibilities. She had already seen someone hauled off to the cells recently, and she couldn't bear to see it happen again. It had been when that Swiss Nazi had shouted, '*Heil Hitler!*' and the woman had replied with the stupid remark, '*To Hell with Hitler!*' It had been awful, awful and stupid, but this was different. The poor old couple were being intimidated. Why couldn't he leave them alone? What did a silly old brooch matter to him? The Nazis had enough of their own symbols and colours around the place; why couldn't the Islanders have something of their own for once? Susanne wanted to go over there and tell him as much.

Before she could do anything the woman's husband had stood and pulled himself up to his full height in front of the officer, but he only came up to the soldier's nose. Susanne had to think fast. It was clear that they weren't going to let this go. Without turning she pushed open the door to the kitchen. 'Maggie. Get the police on the telephone – there's a soldier in here spoiling for a fight.'

She didn't know whether the serving girl heard her or not, but she was too busy watching the scene unfold to find out. The soldier was looking down at the elderly man. 'If the lady does not remove this badge right now,' he said, his voice calm, but

194

his body language anything but, 'I will tear it from her myself.'

'If you do any such thing, I will knock you down where you stand!' The husband's voice carried across the lounge. The veins on his forehead stood out, red as a Nazi flag.

The officer took one step back and lifted his pistol. Pointing it at the husband, the soldier reached his other hand down and pulled the brooch from the woman's blouse. There was a tearing sound as it came free. The husband stared at the barrel of the pistol and his wife clasped her hands to her mouth. Neither of them moved as the officer stalked back to his own table, brooch in hand. As soon as he was gone the husband turned to his wife to console her, but it was no good. She shook where she was sitting, her hands still across her face and tears falling down her cheeks.

Susanne stood in shock. She decided to get them another pot of tea, a small gesture that might calm their spirits. Before she could leave the lounge to fetch the drink a couple of German soldiers marched into the room. Susanne recognised them instantly as Feldgendarmerie. They didn't come up to her to ask what had happened; instead they spoke to the German patrons of the hotel, but Susanne couldn't hear their muttered conversations. Eventually they made their way to the window. They exchanged a few words with the couple, who were shaking their heads through the entire conversation. One of the field police shrugged and then led the husband away. He looked back over his shoulder at his wife and told her that everything was going to be all right, but his eyes told a different story.

As they passed Susanne she wanted to scream, *'No! You've got the wrong person! The German sitting over there is the one you want.'* But the words would not come.

When they had gone, she finally peeled herself away from the spot she had been standing in the entire time to get that pot of tea. The manager wouldn't be happy, but she didn't care about him. She only had thoughts for the dear old woman sitting in the window.

Chapter 21

2 July 1941

The first year of the occupation had gone quicker than any of them could have imagined, and it was far from over. Jack couldn't believe that the Germans had been in charge of the islands for a year. Gone was any hope of the occupation being over soon. The Germans had settled in and the islands felt more like theirs than they had ever done. He had heard that they were even starting to teach German in the schools. On his way to work he wondered how long it would be before the German authorities insisted that the local police should learn it. Having a passing knowledge of French was already a desirable skill, but many would refuse the new language.

Jack heard the sound of a car engine coming along the road, breaking his reverie. Even now, almost a year later, he fought the urge to duck for cover. Most of the vehicles on the island were used by the Germans, meaning that Jack paid them little heed. But this time it was heading straight towards him on the wrong side of the road. There had been rumours of them deciding to change the rules to the German side of the road, but he hadn't thought they would be that stupid. He pulled his bicycle to the side, to try to avoid the oncoming car, as a truck appeared behind him. A squeal of protesting brakes came from the truck as it spotted the car on the wrong side of the road and tried to avert disaster. There was a screech of rending metal as the truck skidded, narrowly avoiding Jack as he fell from his bicycle. It knocked a lamppost over as it came to rest against a building. From where he lay, Jack saw the car careen to the side, before it too came to an abrupt halt.

Jack picked himself up and dusted himself off as the German driver of his car shouted at the truck driver from the open window. 'You idiot!' he screamed. 'Drive on the right!' Without waiting for a response, the German revved the engine and pulled off down the road, apparently in a hurry. Seeing Jack, the truck driver didn't wait around either. He put the truck back into gear and carried along the road.

*

Back at the station, the office was boiling as the light glared in through the windows. Jack was lucky that he was manning the cells as it kept him out of the sun. A cell door opened and Sergeant Honfleur came out. He nodded at Jack and left the station, presumably to resume his beat. Jack turned to leave the cellblock, but Honfleur returned leading another man by the arm. 'Got another one for you, Jack,' he said, nodding towards his captive. Jack tried to hide his shock; it was Charles, the man Jack had carried to the hospital during the invasion. The man had spent time recovering from his injuries and Jack hadn't seen him since. He didn't say anything to Charles, but there was a knowing look in his eye.

'What's he in for?' Jack asked. He was required to enter the name of every prisoner in the inspector's book for their records.

'Caught him red-handed scrawling a 'V' on one of the German signposts. Seemed almost proud of it. But the Germans want them punished.'

Jack suppressed a smile and sighed loudly for effect. He looked around him at the block of cells. As far as he could remember, there was only one left. He lifted the heavy key chain hanging at his waist and picked out the right one. The cells had been filling up recently. It wasn't that Guernsey had much in the way of criminals, otherwise their little police force would be overwhelmed, it was that times had changed and the Islanders were starting to see resistance as a source of great pride. The more serious criminals were moved to the prison and other available cells on the island. Jack sympathised with them, but as a policeman he would never say so. Getting yourself arrested wasn't the best way to 'stick it to Jerry'. He unlocked the door to the last empty cell and the man entered. The police would let him stew in there overnight, and then let him go. So much for resistance.

David spotted Jack and walked over to him. He clutched a newspaper in his hand, which was somewhat unusual.

'Have you seen these 'V for victory' symbols popping up around the place?' Jack asked as David flicked over the page of the newspaper.

'They're everywhere,' David replied. 'The Germans aren't going to like it. They'll take our wireless sets again.'

'There's already one of the vandals in the cells.'

'That's exactly what I wish to talk to you all about, Constable.' The chief had snuck up behind them and was peering at them over his glasses. It appeared that he had been listening to their conversation. 'Fall in, men. I have some news about the symbols appearing across the island.'

The policemen in attendance stopped their conversations and filing as they heard the chief's voice and turned to listen to what he had to say. 'As I'm sure you agree, these overt showings of dissent don't help. The Germans have treated us well, and it would only cause trouble if we continue in this manner. If only the BBC had known what they were causing when they put out that suggestion.'

Some of the assembled policemen nodded, but it was half-hearted. The inspector didn't seem to notice as he gave them their orders for the day. He beckoned Jack over. 'Godwin, I want you to find out who is responsible. We'll have the men keep an eye out, but I want you to take a more … proactive approach. You're a clever lad, I'm sure you can work out something.'

'Sir? If I may ask. Whose orders are these?' Jack asked, already knowing the answer. It had to have come down from higher up. 'The kommandant's, of course,' the chief replied. 'He's understandably upset.' The chief didn't appear as upset as he claimed the kommandant was, and Jack thought he even noticed a slight rolling of the eyes, but the old man would never admit to it.

'The kommandant has promised £25 to the person who finds the ringleader.'

There was an intake of breath from several of the policemen. Each of them would like to get their hands on that kind of money, especially with the way the island was going and the constant refusal of the police committee to raise their wages. The Germans really didn't like being undermined, but the more they punished it the more likely it was to happen. Better to leave it be, Jack thought, and the culprits would soon get bored.

Using the local police was another mistake. There was no way that the old man would put any serious effort into finding the dissenters. Nor would he put his best man on the job. Jack would do his job and follow orders, but he was still only a constable, and he wasn't about to put his unhappy compatriots in jail if he could help it.

The chief wasn't done. 'I want you to go out on patrol with your German counterpart and keep an eye out for anyone vandalising property like this.'

*

About half an hour later Jack was patrolling through the centre of St Peter Port, past The Pollet and down Smith Street. He had collected his German counterpart, who had turned out to be none other than Henrik Bäcker. The two of them had fallen into easy conversation as they searched for any information about the vandalism, and thankfully Henrik had not yet asked about the film. Jack turned the corner and stopped dead in his tracks. There, plain as day, was a letter 'V' scrawled large across the wall in white chalk. He looked around, but the pair were alone on the road. He thought that he should probably report it, or even wash it off, but what was the point? It wasn't really causing any harm.

'Doesn't look like whoever did this is still around,' he said to Henrik, who nodded in way of reply. Jack made a note of the location in his notepad and carried on, assuming that Henrik would follow him.

Further on there was an even bigger 'V'. This time on one of the German shop signs, informing them in German, English, and French that it was a German shop for German customers only. Someone had painted over the sign in thick white paint, the kind of paint usually reserved for the outside of a house. That one wouldn't go unpunished, Jack thought as he passed. It was too obvious and too large for someone not to have noticed, and Jack would have to report it. Jack thought about asking the shopkeepers whether they had seen anything but decided against it. They wouldn't tell him even if they had.

Someone had also written the word '*unter*' over a German sign that read: *Deutschland Uber Alles.*

'What does it really mean?' he asked, turning to Henrik for the answer.

Henrik stopped and regarded Jack. There was a wry look on his face. 'Can it be that even after a year of us being here you still do not speak a word of German?' he asked, laughing. 'Are the British all so bad at other languages?'

Jack shrugged. Even though he had thought about it, learning German wasn't high on his list of priorities.

'I will tell you,' Henrik continued. 'It means, "Germany over all". Except, someone had decided to write the German word for "under" across it. It is crude, but the sentiment is clear.'

Henrik looked thoughtful. It was obvious for anyone to see that the majority of the Islanders didn't want them here. Jack had his own experience of that. Some locals were more accommodating than others, but they couldn't avoid the fact that they were being occupied. Jack liked Henrik. Unlike many of the other Germans he had met he was calm and considerate. There was something he had been wanting to ask for a couple of weeks, and he might not have a better opportunity.

'What do you think about the invasion of Russia?' Jack knew he was pushing his luck.

'A mistake. They like us even less than you do.' Jack was taken aback, and Henrik smiled across at him. 'We should go. It is unlikely that we will find whoever did this now.'

Jack nodded, he really shouldn't have asked the question. He was putting Henrik in a difficult position.

'We'll just have to keep an eye out, I suppose.'

*

A few weeks had passed since the symbols had been spotted, and for a while everything had been calm. Jack and David were due to go on night shift, and no doubt it would be uneventful. Even before the Germans had arrived there was very little crime on the island, and since the curfew there had been even less. They were really there to make sure that the curfew was adhered to, but most of the police just warned people to get back inside before the Germans spotted them. David had disappeared again. Jack would have to do something about it soon – it was going to get them into trouble – but as usual David came back a few minutes later.

'Here. Help me with this will you?' David appeared, carrying a heavy container in Jack's direction. It dragged along the ground as he struggled with its weight.

'What the hell is it?' Despite himself Jack moved to assist him.

'Not so loud, will you?' He looked like a naughty schoolboy.

Jack stopped dead as he took the other handle of the container that looked like something between a milk urn and a paint tin. The contents stank of tar and oil, and Jack had to turn his head so that he didn't breathe it in.

'It's bitumen. What the hell are you doing with bitumen?'

'Quiet,' David said as he dragged the container a little further to the middle of the road. 'I got it from the states depot. They won't miss it.'

'It's stealing,' Jack whispered this time, knowing that he was now an accessory. 'What are you going to do with it?'

David stopped dragging the bitumen and stood up straight so that he could look Jack in the eye. 'It's not as if they're going to miss it. They've got loads of the stuff and there's not much money to work on the roads at the moment.' A faint smile played around his lips. 'We're going to have a bit of fun with it.'

It didn't take Jack's imagination long to work out what David was referring to. Before Jack had a chance to ask, David pulled out a metal rod that he had secreted in the back of his trousers and dipped it into the container of bitumen. He pulled the rod, now covered in the thick tarry substance, out of the container and started to draw a line on the road. In the darkening night it was difficult to see what David was drawing, but after a few minutes the "V" was clearly visible.

David came back over to the container and beamed at Jack, who didn't return the smile. It wasn't to say that he didn't want to show the Germans what they thought of them, but he wasn't sure what good could come of it.

'What now? Now you've had your little rebellion?'

David looked down at the now-empty canister, then kicked it so that it rolled with a clatter into the gutter at the side of the road and down the hill.

'Now,' he replied. 'We scarper!'

*

202

If David had thought that their act of rebellion would go unpunished then he was mistaken. It didn't take long for the Germans to find the defaced road and for their anger to trickle down to the local police force. The inspector stormed into the office.

'They've decided to punish the parish unless someone owns up to it.'

Jack wasn't sure whether the trickle of sweat that ran down his own temple was from guilt or from the summer heat. David looked over at Jack. There was a slight shake of his head and Jack closed his eyes.

'Men from the parish will need to wash all of the marks from the signs as best they can, and then will be required to guard the sign in pairs until a time that the German Military Authority decides. It falls on us to ensure that those men are doing their duty. If anyone here should know anything about this, then they should come forward.'

The chief paused again, this time looking at each of them in turn. Every policeman in the building stared back stony-faced. Jack and David were safe for now, but thanks to their act of rebellion the people of that small parish in the north of the island would suffer.

Chapter 22

As soon as Jack arrived at the police station he had his first order. He was to collect the car, drive it around to the Royal Hotel and pick up the kommandant, then take him to the states offices. As he was given the order, he felt warmer, his uniform tighter around his neck. Had the Germans found out that he had helped David? Or that he had struck Johanna's name from the list? He drove all the way there on edge, flinching at other vehicles, gripping the steering wheel. Thankfully the kommandant and his interpreter sat silently in the back as he drove. Jack followed them up the stairs and into the building, keeping his distance like a scolded child.

Beth was coming out as he entered. She stopped and grinned at him. 'Trespassing again, Constable?'

Jack hadn't seen her since the film and there was an awkwardness to her glance that told him she was thinking the same thing. He thought of something tactful to say. A question came out first.

'What are you thinking?' he asked, his tone biting, thankful there was no one else around to hear the conversation. 'He's the enemy.'

'I wasn't thinking, Jack,' she said, closing her eyes and taking a deep breath. 'We don't get to decide who we fall in love with.'

They fell silent. Love? He hadn't expected her to say that.

Many of the women who were hanging around with the German soldiers wanted only to improve their lives, but this seemed to be different. He hadn't really expected to fall in love with Johanna, but it had happened nevertheless. She had enthralled him in a way he couldn't possibly explain. But Johanna wasn't the enemy. Yes, she was German, but she had left the country before the war started, exactly because she hadn't been able to stand and watch while the Führer ran roughshod over her country. But what had Henrik done to stop them? He was not only culpable; he was a soldier in the Führer's army. Worse than that, he was one of their policemen, bringing their version of order to the towns and cities they occupied. But even Jack had to admit to himself that he liked the man.

'I … I had no idea,' he said, feeling just as stupid as he sounded.

'Yes,' she replied, quiet as a whisper. He could tell that she was crying. 'I tried to tell myself I didn't, but the more time I spent with him …'

He no longer felt like a child in her presence. It was as if he had matured in a way that she had not, that somehow falling in love had made her more vulnerable. It softened her and Jack felt more empathy towards her than he had before.

There were tears in Beth's eyes, and Jack knew it would not be easy for her. Others on the island would be even less forgiving than Jack when they found out that Beth was consorting with the enemy. Jack had already witnessed first-hand what it could be like.

'What are you going to do?' he asked as tactfully as he could manage. He wanted to be a friend despite everything. The locals needed to stick together.

'I don't know. They call me "Jerrybag". Some spit at me. My father would throw me out of the house if he knew.'

Jack felt that heat again, as if he were responsible. He should have kept his mouth shut and allowed Beth to go about her day as normal. 'The others don't understand,' he said. 'I'm sure they will in time. Henrik is a good man … despite being a German.'

He smiled at her and she gave a faint chuckle.

'You are too, Jack Godwin,' she replied. 'Despite being a policeman.'

It was his turn to laugh. Perhaps it was the shared circumstances that had smoothed things over, or maybe friendship could never really be beaten, no matter what fought it. He hoped that it was the latter; perhaps then the Islanders would have a way of seeing it out after all.

*

'You shouldn't have gone to see the film,' Johanna said, exasperated when Jack had told her about his conversation with Beth earlier that day. 'It wasn't your smartest idea, Jack.'

He couldn't disagree with her there, but he didn't want to admit it. No one enjoyed having their decisions questioned.

'I wanted to go to,' he said, weakly. 'I needed to see what it was really about. What they really thought of the Jews.'

'It was just some disgusting propaganda, written by Goebbels. They all are. They're perverted and malicious.'

'I know, but how can I be critical of them, if I've never seen them?'

She was quiet for a moment, then nodded. 'I've seen too much of it. I've seen people act in real life the way they do in those films. Full of hatred.' Her tone changed to something more sympathetic. 'For you it's different. You've only ever seen things from this island, from a distance. I was there in the beginning when the Nazis took power. And they did take power. They made anyone who opposed them disappear, filled the people with fear and hate. Made my people a scapegoat for the nation's woes. My people are sick and they are not getting better.'

'They're not all bad. I've spoken to some of them, worked with some of them. They don't want to be here.'

'That's how the Party gets you, Jack.' Johanna was in full flow now. To say she was angry would be an understatement. She was furious with the world, with what her people were doing to it. 'They befriend you, treat you like you're one of them, and all the while they are trying to undermine you, to lull you into a false sense of security. They promise you the world. Then when they can't deliver, it's someone else's fault, scapegoat an entire race of people if need be.

'I saw it happen. Even in my hometown, Lübeck, miles from Berlin. I was there, and there was nothing I could do.' There were tears in her eyes now, but he didn't move to console her. He knew that she needed to say this, needed him to hear so that he might finally understand what she had been through. 'They promised to make Germany great again, to cast off the shackles of the first war, to repair the damage. Some people thought they were mad, but so many others believed them. Apathy and hate won Germany for them, and now look where we are.'

The passionate fury in her voice had diminished slightly as she had been speaking; now she just sounded tired. She paced a little, but then sat in her heavy reading armchair. 'The only choice I had was to leave, to find another place, a better place, and now the Nazis are here too.

'They're doing the same thing here now,' she said. 'On the island. Soon the people here will agree with them. I can see it happening again. My family were ripped apart by them. My father's business, a business he had built from the ground, destroyed because he was a Jew. Who cared what happened to us, as long as the Aryans were happy? They put my father in a camp.'

Jack opened his mouth, then shut it again, before eventually managing to formulate some words. 'Why didn't you tell me this before?' he asked, slightly hurt. He would have listened, and he might have understood. Now he knew he longed to do something about it.

'How could I? It all sounds crazy,' Johanna asked. Her voice was faint, close to a whisper. She looked into her hands, wrung so tightly in front of her that they had become ever paler. 'How could I possibly make you understand? Before now, before seeing the Nazis for yourself, then you would have thought I was over-reacting. You might still think that.'

He knelt down and gently lifted Johanna's chin to look her in the eyes. 'I don't think you're over-reacting,' he said, lowering the volume of his voice to match hers. 'I have known you long enough now, long enough to see when you are truly upset or angry.'

He tried to smile. 'I believe you,' he said. 'I have always believed you.'

Johanna broke into tears. They streamed down her cheeks, turning her eyes red. A sob racked her body and Jack pulled her closer. He allowed her to weep for a few minutes while he held her tight. Something in the back of his mind told him that she needed a release more than anything right now. After a while he could hear her trying to form words through her tears.

'Thank you,' she said eventually, each word punctuated by a tear.

'For what?'

'For believing me. No one else ever has.'

Those words cut him to the bone. How could anyone have thought she was lying? There was nothing about Johanna that made her a liar. The darkness and the horror she had seen were clear in the depths of her eyes.

Chapter 23

November 1941

The Kriegsmarine carefully guided the big troop ship into the harbour, as Jack watched on. The ship was very similar to the mail boats that used to service the island – a wide hull, low on the water – but bigger. The mariners patrolled the deck in their navy-blue uniforms, clutching submachine guns. There were a few harsh barks from officers as the ship bumped against the pier, before its mooring ropes were hauled overboard. It was not the first such ship to arrive in the harbour, and Jack was far from the only Islander who had been curious about them. For what seemed like days now thousands of people had come to the island, and Jack had never seen anything like it. It was as if they were preparing for an invasion, but they had already occupied the island. It was like the army evacuation, but in reverse. Only it seemed like there were far more men squeezed into this ship than there had been on the ships leaving. They were crammed in every available space, and it can't have been happy sailing over from the continent.

The gangways came down like hammers against the deck of the pier, and the guards stalked along them, carrying their guns. The first ships to arrive had mostly contained civilian labourers, of various nationalities. Those men had now taken up the empty houses across the island. Presumably to help out on the farms and with other manual labour, but there were more of them than there had ever been before the war.

This ship was different. As with those that preceded them, the passengers wore civilian clothes, but many of them were dishevelled and dirty, clothed only in basic cloth rags that covered their torsos, their limbs open to the elements. Some were barefoot as they stumbled down the gangway, and others had simple shoes or wooden sabots. They looked like prisoners or slaves, not caring about their new surroundings. Their gaze was fixed on the floor in front of them as if the effort of taking each step was going to sap the last of their energy. Some were little older than children, young men who could have been in school rather than here. Jack couldn't tell how he knew, but they all looked like they hadn't eaten in days.

The Germans kept a close eye on them as they were handed over to the OT officers. One man, hunch-backed and sickly pale gestured to Jack for a cigarette. The others around him took up the sign, placing thumb and forefinger together and placing it against their lips, but Jack had to decline. He would have given them a cigarette if he had them.

'Back!' one of the soldiers barked in Jack's direction, but it wasn't clear who he was shouting at. 'Back! *Schnell!*'

The labourers shrunk away from him, like chastised pets. The smell was overbearing, like cattle but much worse. These men had not washed in days, and as a collective that stench had only grown, permeating the very air around them. He wanted to hold his nose. Even the smell of the ships in the harbour, the fishing equipment and oil, couldn't break through.

Jack strode up to one of the soldiers nearby who wasn't involved with shepherding the labourers to their camp. 'What are they for?' he asked. The soldier must have recognised Jack as a policeman, as he didn't order him to move. 'Surely you don't intend to build factories on the island? It wouldn't be worth it. Where will they all go?'

'Do not worry, Organisation Todt workers will be housed in camps, and kept away from the general population,' the soldier replied, apparently misunderstanding Jack's question. 'The Führer has ordered that the islands be fortified. It is for your own good. We will not desert you, not as the British did.'

Those words hit Jack like a hammer. What could the German know of how it had felt to be abandoned by the British army? Worse than that was the thought of the island being fortified. The British had been correct – it wouldn't keep bombs out, and it wouldn't make the island any more defensible. Using these poor slaves as labour was an appalling abuse of the Germans' power. The Islanders had fallen on hard times with limited rations and the Germans controlling everything that came into the island, but the labourers looked much, much worse. They were a sorry example of the possible future for the Islanders, and a wave of fear rose up as Jack watched them go.

The soldiers formed them into lines and marched them from the boats. Rather than directing them through the centre of town, they led them down the coastal road, to wherever it was they were going to set up camp.

*

A few days later Jack had spotted a German as he caught young Francis vandalising a signpost. The boy had fled along the road and ducked into a side street. Jack, giving chase, stopped dead as he turned a corner, hot on the German's heels. The soldier raised his pistol and pointed it at the young Islander. He swore in German, harsh and guttural. The pistol was one of the angular Lugers they all seemed to have, and Jack was sure that it was loaded. The German's eyes bulged and his cheeks were red. Jack didn't want to provoke the soldier, but he could see him visibly trembling. Jack wanted to wrench the gun out of the German's hand, but he knew that it would only go badly for all of them. He took a step closer to the German, who glanced at him without moving his head.

'What are you doing?' he enquired with that thick-accented English that was now so familiar.

'Easy,' Jack said, his voice lower, as calm as he could force it to be in the situation. 'Easy.'

Normally in situations like this he would talk to the culprit calmly, as if they were a child, but he had never before encountered an angry German with a gun. He had no idea how this man would react. The slogan Francis had been in the process of scribbling had certainly not helped matters, when the "V" he had already drawn was offensive enough to the Germans. He almost whimpered where he stood, holding up his hands either side of his head.

'Step away, this does not concern you,' the German said, without looking at Jack. 'I will deal with it myself.'

'I'm sorry, sir, but I can't allow you to do that. This is a civil matter. The military shouldn't be getting involved.'

For the first time the German soldier looked at him. 'Do you want to get involved here?' he asked, frowning at Jack. 'You would be better to walk away.'

'You could get a court-martial for this.' Jack wasn't sure if that was true or not, but it sounded believable enough. The soldier's gun wavered for the first time. 'And if they find out that I was here and did nothing, then I would get in trouble too. It would be better for you to walk away and leave this to me.'

The German soldier held Jack's gaze and there was something in those grey eyes that Jack couldn't put his finger on. At first he thought it was hate, but the more they stared at each other, the more he realised that it was fear. 'Leave it to me,' Jack said again, pressing the point. The pistol trembled in the soldier's hand, and his finger edged closer to the trigger. Jack felt a bead of sweat trickle down between his shoulders. He wondered what else the German soldier had gone through to bring him to this point. Shooting a teenager for insulting the Reich was crazy even for the Nazis.

The pistol dropped back to the soldier's side and both men let out a breath. 'I want him punished,' the soldier said as he clipped the pistol back into its holster at his waist and pointed with his other hand.

'Of course,' Jack replied, words tumbling from his mouth in relief. Jack fully expected this soldier to follow it up and even come into the station. He knew Jack's face, and if he made enquiries it would become difficult for Jack. It may even bring up what David had got up to on the road those few months ago. No, there would be another young man occupying a cell in Guernsey that night, and Jack would be the one to put him there.

Chapter 24

The bicycle's makeshift tyres clattered over the road, slipping as the rainwater greased the surface. The station office had received a desperate call from a woman on the other side of the island and due to the car being already in use by another PC, Jack had been dispatched to investigate. He rode as hard as he could, but the irregular surface and the hosepipe he was now using for tyres only made things more and more uncomfortable. Just when he was getting used to it another bump would come along and unsettle him again. He pulled into the narrow lane that led to the woman's house. It led up the hill to a cottage, with perfect views over the Channel. From there he could smell the salt of the sea and hear the gentle crash of the waves against the cliffs.

His first sight was a group of labourers marching up the lane, led by one of the Operation Todt officers. Jack cycled past them, through the narrow gap by the side of the lane. Some of them watched him go with hollow eyes. There were a few soldiers by the front gate to the house, and as Jack pulled up he noticed that two of them were almost physically holding back the owner of the house.

Unsurprisingly, Henrik was already there. It seemed his

German counterpart was everywhere he went these days, but on the island that was hardly surprising. He smiled and shook his head as he saw Jack.

'I should have known they'd send you,' he said.

'What's going on?' Jack asked, without returning the smile. He marched through the gate, past Henrik and up to the house. Jack heard Henrik sigh and fall into step.

'The OT workers are up here to build a gun emplacement. There on the hill.' He pointed past the house to a grassy bit of land that stuck out. This was only the latest in a series of development works for the island. It was now clad in concrete, vast grey shapes that were designed to keep the enemy out, like a fortress, but it felt to the Islanders much more like the walls of a prison. They ran for miles along the coast, turning the glowing green grass to dreary grey.

'But that'll be next to the house. They can't build there – there'll be soldiers traipsing all over the land, and the owner of that house will hear nothing but guns.'

Henrik shrugged, as if he simply didn't care.

'Is there anything you can do?'

'I wish I could. But I have orders just like the rest of you.' He sighed again, and Jack felt it in his bones. Henrik stepped around so that Jack was between him and the others. 'I wish I could just walk away,' he continued. 'But in a way I'm trapped on this island too. I do what they say, otherwise …'

Henrik drifted off into silence. Jack had never really thought about it like that. He was used to taking orders in the police force, but at least he could resign. These soldiers had no choice. It didn't matter that they were posted here and away from the war front; they were still trapped.

'Is there nothing that can be done?' he asked, already making a mental note to question his superiors about it.

'I am afraid not, Jack. These orders come from the very top, the Führer himself.'

Henrik's voice changed when he said that name, and Jack shook his head.

'The bloody Führer,' he said, as loudly as he dared. 'You all treat him like some kind of god.'

Henrik's eyes widened. 'I am not a National Socialist, Jack,' he said. 'Never think of me as being like them. I am not a card-carrying member of the Party, but as much as I want to, I can't stand in the way of his orders. Even discussing them is dangerous.'

Jack felt a pang of guilt at the look in Henrik's eyes. It reminded him of Johanna.

'I'm sorry,' he said. 'This is all frustrating. Our lives are decided for us now. The police can do nothing.'

'I know, but I cannot speak of it anymore, not here.' He wheeled around again, so that Jack was closer to the gate. 'Please, go,' he said. 'We will deal with this as best we can. Perhaps we can convince the Todt officers to move the site further away. But you must go.'

As he left, Jack took one last look at the woman who owned the house. He didn't know her, but he knew now exactly how she felt as she argued with the Germans who had arrived on her doorstep.

*

That Christmas would be no better than the last, but then he hadn't expected it to be. He supposed that they should hold on to what they had and take joy in all the little things. There was no telling how much worse it would get. His grandmother's health was declining, and Doctor Abbott had been to see her a few times already in the last few months. According to the doctor, her heart was failing, but Jack didn't know the full details. He had known that his grandmother had been struggling to cope without her husband, and it seemed likely that she was dying of a broken heart.

They had a small affair, sitting around his grandmother's bed, sharing what food they'd saved up for the Christmas meal. He and Johanna sat one side of the bed, talking softly to each other as his mother knitted and his grandmother rested. Sometime in the evening there was a gasp from the other side of the bed and Jack stood. His mother was leaning over the bed, her head moving between resting on the older woman's chest and looking into her eyes. 'Help me,' she cried. 'She's not waking.'

Jack moved to the bed and took up his grandmother's arm. It was frail and limp in his grip as he checked for a pulse. He waited for a minute, but the only sound in the room was his mother's soft sobbing as she held her mother close. Jack walked around to her and gently pulled her from the bed, putting his arms around her and making soft comforting sounds. Johanna's practised hands were checking over his grandmother, and she nodded to him as he looked on.

'She's gone,' he said, hearing the words as if they had been spoken by someone else. His mother's sobs filled the room again, like waves against a cliff. At that point he knew that Christmas would never be the same again, for any of them.

*

'Someone's been shot, Jack.' William slammed the telephone down on its cradle as he turned from the clerk's desk. Jack had been dreading the New Year's Eve night shift, not just because of the relaxed curfew, but because of the number of drunk German soldiers they would no doubt have to deal with. However, he hadn't expected anyone to utter those words. 'That was the St John Ambulance. Get yourself down to Mahaut Gardens and find out what the hell is going on.'

Jack grabbed his helmet on the way out. He wasn't sure if it would do him any good against a deranged gunman, but he would rather have it than not, and if the old man saw him without it he would be fined for improper conduct. His bicycle leant where he always left it, its hosepipe tyres making it look like some kind of toy.

It only took Jack a few minutes to cycle up the hill to the block. He leant his bike against the first block, occupied by Germans who were still partying at quarter past midnight, and ran around to the rear. There was a group of people standing outside the building near a St John Ambulance. One of them, a young man whom Jack had seen in a shop on the High Street, beckoned him to their door. Jack ran through it, nodding a 'thank you' to the man. He easily found the paramedics inside the building; the smell of iron was thick in the air. They were kneeling over a man who was spread out on the floor. The man was groaning faintly as they tried to stop him bleeding. One of them pulled back on some gauze to replace it, and Jack could easily see the hole through the man's chest.

'What happened here?' he asked the nearest medic, as commanding as he could possibly be. The island police didn't have much experience in dealing with shootings, and Jack had not seen someone wounded like this before. A female voice answered from the other side of the room.

'A German soldier pushed his way in here,' she said. She stood cross-armed, worry etched deep into her face as an older version of her sat on a chair crying into a handkerchief. 'I'm Ruth Martel. He's my father, Richard.'

She held out a hand so that he could shake it, but it was limp in his grasp and she broke his eye contact almost immediately. Jack knew Richard Martel; he used to run the Guernsey lifeboat before the Germans had come.

'You're the one who telephoned?' Jack asked, flipping to a fresh page in his notepad. The chief would want extensive notes if this was going to be brought to a prosecution. The Germans quite often ignored their reports involving German soldiers, but they would find it difficult to ignore this. Jack wished that Ruth had not mentioned the word 'German', but there was nothing he could do about that now. He would have to deal with it.

'I telephoned for the ambulance first and then they telephoned you.' She motioned at the men working on her father. 'I wasn't sure what to do. My father … We already lost my brother on the lifeboat …'

Those words brought a fresh stream of sobs from the woman on the chair, and a tear trickled down Ruth's cheek.

'I understand,' Jack replied softly. 'You did the right thing. Now, if you don't mind just talking me through the details of what happened while they're fresh in your memory. For my report.'

She nodded, although her eyes were fixed firmly on her father. They were distant, blurred by alcohol. Jack wondered if what had happened had been an accident caused by drunkenness. It wasn't going to be a 'Happy New Year' for the man sprawled on the ground with a bullet hole through his chest.

'Of course,' she stuttered. 'We were having a do, you know? Then a group of Germans came in – I think there were six of them. One of them had had too much to drink and got into an argument with Sarah. Then he went to the back door and started firing his revolver into the air. My father, he used to work the lifeboats and he doesn't like people putting others in danger. He tried to stop him and the German …' Again her voice broke. 'He shot my dad!'

'Thank you. That'll do for now.'

He thanked her with a nod, then turned back to see how the paramedics were getting on. They had stopped the bleeding, but Richard's face was pale and his eyes were no longer open.

'Here, Constable,' one of the paramedics said. 'Help us get him into the ambulance.'

Jack shoved his notebook into a pocket and grabbed Mr Martel's legs. It was a far cry from trying to guide a drunk into the police car. Walking backwards, Jack helped the paramedics as one of them held the dressing to Mr Martel's chest and the other carried him under the shoulders. The ambulance was on the road and it took them a minute or two to manoeuvre the man into the back. 'We'll take him up to the emergency hospital in Castel.' Without ceremony they closed the doors to the ambulance and its engine roared into life as they eased up the road.

Jack would have to report immediately to the German police, even if it was the early hours of the morning. Thankfully, Grange Lodge, the German police headquarters, was only a short bicycle ride away. As he arrived at the Feldgendarmerie headquarters it was clear that some kind of party was taking place. There was singing coming from one open window, the thick German consonants intermingled with laughs and the clinking of glasses. Jack marched in through the front door.

A big German grinned when he saw Jack and slouched over to him. '*Willkommen!*' he slurred, and tried to pass a small glass to Jack. Schnapps or some other light spirit sloshed around inside. Jack shook his head and made to move past the man, but he stumbled to intercept him.

'*Nein, nein.* Drink!'

'I'm looking for your senior officer. *Senior* officer.' Finally the man realised and shouted back into the lodge. The shout was repeated until an officer appeared, scowling. Jack had expected to find Henrik, but he must have been somewhere celebrating the end of the year with Beth. He frowned and mentally wished them all the best.

'Yes, I am Major Obertz. What do you want, Constable? As you can see we are in the middle of a … gathering.'

The major was a short but stocky man. His uniform was cut wider than that of most of the German soldiers. There was a seriousness on his face that should have sobered up even the most drunk subordinate, but the other men continued their celebrations, oblivious. Jack told the man what had happened, and the major's face turned a deep shade of red. He turned to the room and barked out an order in German.

'You take us.' He pointed towards the German car outside.

Jack didn't have to be asked twice. The Germans had already

had too much to drink to drive, and the thought of driving that powerful engine gave Jack a rush he hadn't expected. He pushed himself into the driver's seat as the major and another German accompanied him in the back.

Jack showed the major the scene at the house. The family were no longer there, having gone to the hospital, but as soon as he had seen what had happened the major spoke only eleven words, his face as hard as stone. 'We will arrest the man. He will be tried and executed.'

*

'Richard Martel died in the hospital.' The old man took a solemn pause. 'Which now makes this a case of murder.'

In normal times those words might have brought about a rush in the police station, a guilty excitement that they would be able to work on the case, but now all it brought was shame and guilt. The man had died needlessly, and it would be up to the Germans to prosecute the killer. Jack and the others were impotent, as if their very purpose for being had been taken away from them. There was no other way to describe it.

Nineteen forty-two had not started in the way that Jack had hoped, but at least he still had his life, which was more than could be said for poor Richard Martel. Jack couldn't imagine what it would have been like to see your father die in front of your eyes. Later that night Jack crawled into bed, thankful for its warmth, and fell asleep to troubled dreams.

1942

Chapter 25

January 1942

Jack's stomach rumbled like the sound of an aircraft engine, distracting him from the practised steps of his well-trodden beat. He longed for the end of his night shift, but even then he wasn't sure that he would be able to sate his hunger. He was due to collect their rations in the morning, but how long would they last? With the war raging on they were growing desperately short of food. He passed some of the greenhouses that people kept behind their houses, and he wondered what delights were inside, but he knew he couldn't succumb to temptation. Those vegetables belonged to the people who were growing them.

Even the Germans on the island appeared thinner than they had before. The Islanders weren't the only ones who were suffering. But Jack had to remind himself that this was all their own doing, that it was their desire to conquer that had caused this. He had heard that the German's Eastern Front wasn't going particularly well. Just like the last war things were getting worse, and there was talk that the army had overextended themselves. He didn't know much, but it felt like history repeating itself. Only, last time the Germans hadn't got anywhere near their little island.

Jack wasn't sure when he'd last had a good meal, but he had always made sure that his grandparents and mother got everything they needed. When he eventually finished traipsing around the quiet night-time streets of St Peter Port he reported to the station to inform the day shift that nothing had happened, relishing the relative warmth of the office, and then went straight to claim their rations. The sooner he got in the queue, the better. His stomach rumbled at the thought.

On the High Street, Creasey's department store was almost empty of stock, a shell of its former splendour. Several windows were boarded up, like many of the other shops in St Peter Port, unable to import stock. There was already a queue outside the shop, even at this early hour of the morning. There had been trouble on occasions before, as those waiting grew impatient and arguments turned into scuffles. Today, they were simply queuing, the thin, worn-out residents resigned to the state of the world. Jack knew exactly how they felt. In this act of gathering food for himself and his mother, he was a civilian just like the rest of them with the same needs and weaknesses. He had to come early to make sure that he could get all the rations they needed.

About ten minutes later, he was finally close enough to enter the shop. The person leaving didn't hold the door for him, and it almost hit him in the side. He threw a frown in their direction, but they simply hadn't noticed him. People turned their gaze inwards when they were desperate.

When he was queuing inside, Jack felt something brush against him and turned, expecting to see a small child. Instead, he saw a woman, hunched over and standing far too close to him. She looked worse than the rest of them, wearing a dirty beige coat wrapped around a threadbare woollen jumper. He half expected her to smile at him and apologise, but she just grimaced at him with blackened teeth as she passed. He thought he recognised her from somewhere, but he couldn't be sure. She looked like the woman who had been working in the department store when he had popped in and spoken to Maddy. No one looked the same as they had done before the occupation had started. Maybe he had seen her as one of the people begging around St Peter Port and was mixing them up. As usual with these poor people, no one else seemed to notice her.

The cashier stepped away from the till to gather something for the customer they were serving, who in a bored fashion, looked around the shop and its wares. Meanwhile the beggar woman looked at Jack, then reached a hand over the till and cupped whatever she could get before making her way out of the shop as quickly as possible. Jack stood in shock. He had never seen such brazen disregard for the law before, not least directly in front of a policeman. She can't have known who he was, but if she was truly that desperate maybe she would have. She could have only got away with a few coins and with the current conditions and the nature of the German currency it wouldn't be worth very much. It might get her something warm to eat, or a roof over her head for one night. Jack was still battling with his conscience when he heard the cashier's voice speaking to him.

'Sir?' she asked. Her voice had risen in pitch and volume since the last customer. 'How may I help you? Sir?'

It was too late. He turned to her, trying to remember what it was that he had come for. Handing his ration card to the cashier, he flashed her a smile. 'In a world of my own,' he said, not entirely lying. He then recited the list of items he wanted from the shop as he had practised on the way there. He had wanted to make sure that he didn't forget anything. The shopkeeper gave him a look that spoke of her frustration. 'Only four ounces of meat,' she said, with a tone of voice that suggested it wasn't the first time she had said those words today. 'I can only give you four ounces once every two weeks. Same as everyone else.'

Something about her reprimanding tone made him feel small,

like a child. He could have sworn that he didn't collect any meat last week. The humiliation threw him and all he could manage to say was, 'Oh, right. Thanks.'

'I'll get your items,' she replied.

He thanked her and reached for his ration card. Looking down at the desk he realised there was very little there worth stealing. The shop itself had nothing. They didn't even think it was worth locking away. Reporting the thief would do no good now, and she had only got away with a few coins. He was supposed to write things like that down in the occurrence book, but he would keep an eye out for her and if he saw her he'd impose on her the need to never do anything like that again, lest the Germans get their hands on her. If he was being dishonest, at least he was saving the poor woman from that fate.

Jack realised for the first time that only a couple of years ago this event would have played out very differently. Back then he cared a lot more about right and wrong, or rather the extremes seemed clearer. Now, he realised, it was more of a spectrum.

The cashier returned with his three ounces of sugar, seven ounces of flour, five pounds of potatoes and some acorns for making coffee, then wrapped them into a pathetically small parcel of newspaper. There wasn't even any string to hold it together, so he placed it under one arm to make sure it didn't fall apart and said his goodbyes.

*

Frederic had brought around some pork, which technically they weren't supposed to have. How the farmer had got away without registering the death with the authorities, Jack didn't dare ask, but the meat would make a nice change to their potato-peel pies. He pushed the newspaper parcel across the kitchen table.

'It's not much,' he said to his mother. 'But it will do.'

'Thank you,' she said, and pulled the package across the table to check its contents. Unlike Jack, she didn't leave the house these days. Whereas his response was to stay away as much as possible. Especially now that both his grandparents had gone. 'I'll divide it up.'

Jack nodded. 'Is there anything you need me to do?' He was conscious of how his mother was coping since the death of her parents. It hadn't seemed to have affected her yet, and that was worrying him the most. He felt as if she should be more distraught than she was.

'No, you do enough. I'll take care of this. Let me know if you want anything now.'

'I'm fine,' he said, turning to leave the kitchen. 'I managed to grab a bit to eat at the station earlier.'

'Jack?' his mother called after him. As he turned back to her, she placed the rations down on the table in front of her and stared at him.

'What?'

'I just wanted to say,' she started and then stopped. 'Listen, sit down, this is important.'

Jack gave her what he thought was a quizzical look and then pulled out one of the chairs from the table. It felt partly as if she was about to tell him off, but his mother had never been one to punish him like that.

'If I die ...' she continued, once he had sat down.

'Mum. We'll be all right,' he said, trying to stop her. He moved to stand up again, but she shot him a look that was somewhere between pleading and a warning. He had seldom seen her look so focused.

'I'm serious, Jack. We need to talk about this. If I die, I don't want any fuss. I can't go through another funeral like my dad's whether I'm there or not. I can't imagine anything worse than you sat there moping and miserable.'

'I know.' Jack tried to swallow but his throat was dry. 'You've said before. We don't need to talk about this now.'

'But it needs saying again, Jack. Promise me, you won't let that happen.'

'I won't—'

'Promise me, Jack!'

Jack couldn't tell whether the tears were in his mother's eyes or his own, as his vision became cloudy. 'All right,' he said, trying to make it stop. His mind raged, masking his thoughts. 'I promise. Of course, I'll do what you wish. I just don't want to talk about it.'

He put his head in his hands, thinking back to how his grandparents had passed away and unsure he would be able to cope if it happened to his mother. Then he looked up at her, trying to focus on her through wet eyes, to form the image in his mind. He wanted her to put her arms around him and tell him that it would be all right. All she could manage was a hand on top of his as it lay on the table. They stayed there for some minutes in silence before Jack managed to compose himself. Before he realised his mother had put a chunk of mouldy bread and a sliver of butter on a plate in front of him.

Chapter 26

March 1942

'Bah, it's all bad news! Written by the Nazis,' Johanna said as she threw the copy of the *Guernsey Post* on the table in her flat. Jack looked down at it.

'What's it say?' he asked, not really interested, but wanting to talk to her all the same. The sound of her voice was always a comfort to him.

'The despicable Royal Air Force have bombed Lübeck.' She mocked the voice of a BBC news reporter. 'It was an unprovoked and dastardly attack.'

She pointed a finger at the newspaper. 'It's propaganda, of course. And your journalists have to go along with it. The only thing they get to write themselves these days are articles about the greenhouses. And I bet even those are censored, as the authorities don't want the Islanders to know how little food there is for everyone.'

She slumped into a chair as her anger left her, and Jack pulled out another chair to sit on. They looked at each other across the table, a distance between them.

'Lübeck was my home,' she said, tears welling in her eyes.

'I remember,' Jack replied. 'Does it mention the damage? Your family?'

'My family are no longer in Lübeck, Jack. They were arrested before I left. That's *why* I left.' She shook as each word left her mouth. 'First they put my father in a camp for daring to try and run a Jewish business. Then when the rest of the family struggled they came for us. They wanted to put us all in camps. I had to hide and escape, change my identity to get away from the Nazis. Brasch is my grandmother's maiden name. She was not Jewish.'

'Oh.' Jack reached out a hand for hers. 'Why didn't you tell me before?'

'It didn't seem right until now, I'm sorry.' She clasped his hand, intertwining their fingers. 'The less you knew the less danger there was for you, but we're all in danger now. It gets worse.'

'How? What else has happened?'

'They've put a notice in the newspaper. It lists all those who are to be considered Jews, how far away you must be from Jewish ancestors to be safe. They require all Jews to register again, giving their full details.'

Jack thought of the lists the police had been ordered to compile. The Germans must have put them to use after all. He was glad he had removed Johanna's name.

'You told them you're Christian, remember?'

Johanna ignored him, still clasping his hand. The lie had not sat easily with her, but it had been necessary.

'But what about the others? They did the same thing in Germany. Before I managed to get out of Lübeck and work my way here. First they made us register as Jews, and then people started to disappear. You wouldn't notice it at first – everything seemed normal – but then someone you had seen every day on their way to work would disappear. First you would think, "maybe they're ill," or "maybe I'm late and I missed them". On the second day you would wonder if it was a coincidence. On the third day you started to get suspicious. Then someone else you knew well would disappear. I was lucky to get out when I did.

'You wouldn't hear much about it here; they kept it quiet. Even we only knew what we heard via word of mouth. There was no way the Party were going to let their dirty little secret become public knowledge.'

'We're a long way from Berlin here though,' he said. 'They will find it more difficult to enforce. We're still the police of the island. We won't let them just disappear people.'

'Can you speak for the rest of the police?'

Jack hesitated. Before the occupation he would have said yes without thinking about it, but now, he wasn't so sure. For the most part the police were good men, just trying to do a difficult job, but there were perhaps one or two he wasn't sure about. He didn't know every man as well as he might, and there were some who would want to increase their standing with the occupying Germans. Some people on the island expected them to be here for a long time, and if you can't beat them …

'No,' he said, simply. 'You're right. I don't know if I can trust all of them. But none of them know you are Jewish. I haven't spoken to any of them about it, not even David.'

'Be careful,' she said, squeezing his hand. 'Not just for me, but for you. I can't lose anyone else.'

It was the first time she had said that to him, and his voice caught in his throat. All he could do was hold on to her hand and trust that she knew how he felt. He had come to understand that sometimes actions were more important than words. The simple act of being together was all they ever wanted, and Jack would fight for that with every breath.

*

The man scrabbling through the hedge was one of the workers from the German labour camps. If it wasn't for his threadbare clothing, ripped and in tatters, then the unshaven and decrepit state of the man was enough of a clue. He hadn't yet spotted Jack watching him, and Jack pushed himself further into the crook of the wall to avoid detection. They had received reports of thefts by the Todt workers, but this was the first time Jack had stumbled upon one of the men on their own. He was curious what the labourer was doing. They were allowed to leave the camps, but as none of them had any money they didn't get up to much. There was nowhere for them to run. The police had received reports of thefts from the Islanders, some of them even being conducted by German soldiers, and so they had been told to keep an eye out.

The Todt labourer disappeared out of sight and Jack had to leave his hiding place to keep an eye on the man. He detached himself from the shadows and walked slowly around the building as if he was stalking a criminal. He didn't want to give the game away, but he wondered whether it was unfair on the man to follow him. His superiors would have wanted him to find out what was happening, but he asked himself whether he should be doing something now, rather than just following.

He pulled one plant out, exposing the roots before moving to another. At first it looked like a random act of vandalism, but then the man picked up a carrot, putting it into his mouth. He had to chew for a few seconds on the raw carrot before he could swallow, but his hunger was obvious, as he moved about and took more of the vegetables. He didn't discard any of them, bundling some together and placing them into a pocket in his threadbare coat. They bulged out adding to his crooked frame, giving him the appearance of some sort of creature in the winter gloom.

Jack watched, unsure whether to intervene. He felt sorry for the hungry man, and he was most likely going to take the vegetables to the others at the camp. But this garden belonged to someone, and they too would go hungry. Jack had a decision to make: whose hunger was worthier?

He was beaten to it, by the sound of someone shouting, '*Halt!*'

A German soldier appeared from the other side of the garden. The labourer started, stumbling into the dirt. He struggled to get up, but the German covered the ground between them easily. Jack saw candlelight appear at the back door to the house, but he waved it away. 'Get back inside,' he hissed, hoping the German didn't hear. All the same, he edged closer to the vegetable patch himself.

The German shouted something and lifted his rifle above his head as a threat. The worker tried to get up, but struggled. The soldier swore and brought his rifle down. With a sickening crack it smashed the man's head aside and he fell back to the ground. It was like the sound of a dog being beaten. The man cried out in pain, pleading in whatever language he spoke. Even though Jack couldn't understand it he knew exactly what the man was saying. Pain and fear were the same in any language. The German didn't seem to feel pity as he put the rifle back on his shoulder and lifted the man up by the collar of his shirt. The labourer, weakened, fell down again, and this only served to make the soldier angrier.

Jack took a step forward. He wanted to do something to help, anything, but he felt a hand on his shoulder. 'Leave him,' came the familiar voice of Henrik from by his ear. It was a whisper. Jack knew he wouldn't take a step further, but every fibre of his being wanted to.

'Henrik?' he asked, out of disbelief that the man was there.

'It's me,' he replied, appearing at Jack's shoulder. 'We received a report of a foreigner acting suspiciously as well. Why don't we let the OT man deal with this one, eh?'

He turned and put an arm in front of Jack to guide him away, but Jack stood where he was, staring at the soldier abusing the labourer. The beating would be etched in his memory forever. 'How can you let them do this?' he asked as he exhaled the breath he had been holding. 'Don't you care?'

Henrik sighed and his head dropped. He put a hand on each of Jack's arms and looked him in the eyes.

'You think we are all evil, Jack.' As usual Henrik's English was impeccable and spoken with a surety that many native speakers lacked. 'But I am not even sure what that word means anymore. How do you think I have managed to last this far? By staying out of trouble. If I tried to stop all the evil in this world, I would not get very far.'

He let go and put a finely wrapped white cigarette to his lips, took a drag, letting the blue smoke play around his nostrils, then leant back and closed his eyes. He had stopped offering one to Jack, as he knew he wouldn't accept.

'You think I am like them? But I tell you, I am not! We must pick our battles, make sure we survive this, so that there are still good people in the world. Otherwise, we have failed.'

Jack stared at Henrik, unwilling to commit. Henrik had got used to Jack being evasive and so simply nodded and took another drag of his cigarette. 'Evil isn't really a word I'm familiar with. At least, in a theological sense,' Jack said.

Other men might ridicule Jack for trying to be clever, but Henrik just looked at him with those cool blue eyes, considering his point. It was one of the reasons that, despite everything, he liked him. He was never quick to judge, and he always gave Jack time to speak his mind.

'It is not a word I would throw around lightly.' The OT officer had dragged the labourer away out of their sight, leaving Henrik and Jack to talk unobserved. 'Most of these men are misguided; some are desperate. Maybe our Führer is evil, but I have never met him. He surrounds himself with greedy jealous people, but are they evil? I do not know. All I know is that they would kill me as soon as they heard me speak this way. Because of that, we can never have this conversation again. You understand?' He took another long pull on the cigarette, then dropped it under the heel of his boot.

Jack watched the embers die, thinking of all those who had lost their lives in this war.

'I understand,' Jack replied, feeling for the first time that he recognised the danger they were all in. Jack, Johanna, and even Henrik, were a fine line away from being like that labourer, broken down, beaten, and put to work. 'I understand,' he repeated, knowing that in order to keep them all safe he would have to stay away from Henrik as much as possible.

Chapter 27

20 April 1942

Jack stopped as he was leaving the station. A woman stood in the entrance, clutching her handbag as if she was about to apologise for something. He looked around for William, but the desk sergeant was nowhere to be seen. Like all his colleagues, William had a habit of disappearing just when he was needed.

'Can I help you, madam?' he asked, walking up to the woman. The chief had told them to always be polite, but Jack didn't need to try where this woman was concerned. The look she gave him was enough to break even the coldest of hearts. Her face was downturned and she wouldn't meet his eyes.

She spoke, but there was a catch in her throat. Throwing him an apologetic look, she cleared her throat with two polite coughs. 'I'm here,' she said, her accent reminding Jack of Johanna. 'To have my identity card stamped. As a Jew.'

Jack blinked. None of them had expected the Jews to turn up and identify themselves. The inspector had a list somewhere, and he had expected that to be enough, but here she was. Now he understood the concern on her face, but what was she doing? She should be hiding, like Johanna, like Susanne, keeping away from the authorities as much as possible. But then maybe she hadn't been in Germany. She didn't know the fear, couldn't take what was happening at any more than face value. She must have lived on the island a long time, dismissed the rumours as fear mongering, as the rest of them had.

Without a word he escorted her into the station, found a chair and went to find the inspector. The old man could deal with the records. It was a task Jack didn't relish, a task that he absolutely wouldn't do. He made sure he was far away from the police station before any more Jews turned up. If he didn't have to see their forlorn faces, then maybe he could pretend it wasn't happening. Perhaps he could process the guilt then.

*

'I just need to stop off somewhere,' David said, gesturing vaguely in the direction of the High Street. 'I won't be long. Wait for me outside?'

Jack left David to it. His excursions had become more common, particularly on the night shift, and Jack had given up trying to stop him. Other policemen would have dived into the recessed entrance of Boots the Chemist to smoke a cheeky fag, but not Jack. Still, he realised that standing aimlessly in the middle of the road was not going to look good if a German patrol came past.

David came back a few minutes later and walked straight past Jack without really seeing him. Jack shrugged and moved to match his colleague's step. They walked for a time in silence, patrolling St Peter Port and nodded at any civilians they passed. David's habitual smile had left his face, and Jack couldn't help but feel that something was wrong.

'Everything all right?' he asked as he touched to brim of his hat to a passing woman who didn't seem to notice him any more than his partner did. She hurried off down a back alley and Jack watched her for a few moments, wondering where she was going in such a hurry.

He quickened his step to catch up with the other policeman. David had always been a large man, larger than Jack, but with the dire situation on the island, their lack of food, he had lost weight. His sallow skin hung loosely from his jowls and the bottom of his arms, and his uniform desperately needed taking in. As Jack got nearer he noticed a bulge in one of David's pockets, as if he had stuffed a packet in there. David fingered it absent-mindedly as he walked, appearing not to notice what he was doing.

Jack looked sideways at him, and decided that it was no good, he would have to ask. Part of him didn't want to know, but the other part, the part that thought it was better to know and then be able to deal with it, won out.

'What have you got there?' he asked, nodding in the direction of David's jacket pocket.

'What?' At first he gave Jack a look of confusion, then he looked down at his hand and realised what he had been doing. 'Oh,' he said. 'This? Oh … oh, it's nothing. Just something for my wife.'

Jack didn't really mind what David was getting up to. All he was concerned about was whether it would affect him or not. He had his mother and Johanna to think about and he couldn't risk losing his job. He pulled David aside, noticing how skinny his arm had become.

'Listen,' he said. 'I don't care what you're up to. But I don't want anything to do with it, okay?'

'I don't know what you're talking about.' David moved to shake off Jack's hand, but his grip was firm. David wouldn't look at him.

'David. You don't have to tell me anything. In fact, I'd rather you didn't tell me anything about whatever it is you're up to. The bitumen incident was enough for my liking. Just make sure that you don't drag me down with you. Keep their attention away from Johanna.'

'Of course, whatever you say.' He succeeded in displacing Jack's hand and stormed off. 'Don't we have work to do?'

Jack looked at David for a minute as he walked away, then

followed him. He wasn't sure how their friendship would survive the occupation, but he would try to make sure that it did.

*

'You can't do this!' Jack was sure that his voice could be heard in the rest of the office, but he didn't care. David stopped in his tracks and his head slumped. As if their night shift hadn't been enough to rattle their friendship, this was something else. Jack could see that his friend's eyes were closed and he was breathing deeply.

'Don't do this,' he said again, as if David hadn't heard him the first time.

'You think I want to?' David's voice was quieter than Jack's, barely above a whisper. He opened his eyes and turned them to Jack. There was a steel there. 'This is our job.'

The deportation order had come down from the Germans, but like so many of their orders they relied on the police to enforce them. As far as Jack was concerned this was a step too far. From what Johanna had told him about the camps, deporting the Jews from Guernsey was akin to a death sentence. If they sent those women to the camps, then how long would it be before they found out about Johanna?

'Is it?' he asked, his voice rising. 'Is it really? Why can't the Germans tell those poor women themselves? When did we become executioners as well?'

'What are you talking about?'

'You're on your way to tell three Jewish women that they have to pack up all their belongings and leave! That's what I'm talking about.' He thought of Susanne, and how he should have done more to protect her, but Johanna was always his priority. He didn't dare think about her, lest she end up on the list as well. 'Where will they be sent?'

'I don't know! I don't want to know.' David sighed. His gaunt face was far from the jovial man he had been. 'We all have our part to play. It's just a job. And I need it to support my own family.'

'You can refuse. You've heard the rumours.'

David laughed. It was bitter and short. 'When has the old man ever let us refuse an order? What's the use? If I don't do it then someone else will. It doesn't make a difference.'

'But. What if we all refuse?'

'See you later.' David pushed past Jack and out of the police station. The doors flicked back and forth in defiance at his parting. Jack didn't want to follow too soon in David's footsteps, but he didn't want to go back into the office either, so he stood there, his eyes shut, wondering what on earth he could do to fix things. He had joined the police to help people, but the Germans had turned them into something else. If he had any other options then he would have quit then, but an image of his mother being thrown out of their home came to him. He couldn't give up, not just yet.

*

Jack arrived at Johanna's flat around half an hour later. He wasn't sure whether she was supposed to be working at the hospital, so he was pleasantly surprised when she opened the door. She took one look at him and asked him what was wrong, so he told her. He told her about everything that had happened recently, about how his and David's friendship was at breaking point, and about the deportation order for the Jewish women. Rather than expressing sympathy, she was rightfully angry.

'How could you go along with that?' she asked, pulling away from him.

'I didn't, not really. I tried to stop him. He didn't want to go but he had to.'

'And he just went? To tell those women that they were no longer welcome? Think of Susanne – you know her! And Hilde, she works in Creasey's. They're living, breathing people, who don't deserve to be treated like cattle. Can you not imagine what it must have been like for them? To be told they're no longer welcome in the place they've come to call home?'

'I told him not to go, to refuse. But he wouldn't. He had his orders and if he didn't follow them then he would lose his job. What else was he supposed to do?'

'He should have refused. I know it's not easy, but there's always a choice; there's always something else you can do. The Guernsey police shouldn't blindly follow the Nazis' orders. You're supposed to protect people. Not hand them over to the Nazis. Too many people are just doing their jobs. But that makes them complicit.'

'I know,' he said, voice cracking. He sat down heavily in a chair that creaked with his weight, and put his head in his hands. He could hear his heartbeat thumping in his ears, and he took a few deep breaths. He hated arguing with Johanna. 'But maybe we're just scared? Surely you can understand that? They're watching our every move. David is scared for himself and his family; I'm scared for you and my mum. Since they came here I've been trying to find a way, a different path or something. But so far nothing has presented itself. Every time I think I've regained control of the situation something changes.'

'It seems like you and David understand each other after all.' She attempted a faint smile. 'What happens when they come for me? It's only a matter of time now.'

There was a hesitancy in her tone. She coughed as if the grief was making her ill, but it gave Jack an idea.

'I know someone who can help,' Jack said, in a hurry.

He was thinking quickly and as he did so he stood up and began to pace around the room. Johanna's eyes followed him. He stopped in the middle of the room and turned to face her. For some reason he was suddenly worried that if he went to her, that if he got closer, then something would happen to drag them apart. He didn't want to tempt fate. The Germans could arrive at any moment, and the thought terrified him. She looked up at him from where she was sitting, worry in her brown eyes.

'Who could possibly help?' she asked, her voice low. 'Telling someone else is dangerous.'

'There's a doctor up at the hospital,' he replied, pacing again. 'You must know Doctor Abbott. I've helped him out a few times and come to know him quite well, in a professional sense. He's the doctor I got to know when the harbour was bombed.'

His duties had taken him up to the hospital several times in the last eighteen months, and when he was there he had always made a point first to check in with Johanna, then to see Doctor Abbott and enquire whether he needed any help. Jack had come to admire the older man.

She nodded. 'I know him – he's a good man. But what can he do about … about my situation?'

'He's done things like this before. We can ask him to give you some medical reason for staying on the island.'

'It won't be enough. I'm *untermensch*. Medical reasons mean nothing to them if you are subhuman.'

'Then he can change your details. Make it official so that anyone who needs to can see the proof that you're Christian. Make it look like you've been on the island for some time, whatever it takes. We have to build a lie – it's the only way. If you do that then they will have no reason to evacuate you.'

'Fine, I will ask him. But if he is not comfortable with it then I won't force him.'

Finally Jack sat. He had to hope that Doctor Abbott would go along with it. They had built up a relationship since Jack had helped in the hospital during the invasion. The doctor *was* a good man, but would he be willing to risk his livelihood? If he did, then they might just be able to keep her safe. It was risky, but it was the only choice they had. He looked over at the woman he loved, noticing the way her hair curled around her ears and the intense look in her eyes. He would do anything for her, risk anything for her, and it would all be worth it.

Chapter 28

The police station was quiet, and there was no one on the front desk. Jack leant on the surface and peered into the room behind to see if anyone was there, but it was deserted. He had found William in the office sorting through some paperwork. He looked up as Jack entered and put the papers down.

'Oh. Hullo,' he said. 'Doing the night shift again?'

William knew full well who was on each shift, but he liked to have something to say, anything to start a conversation. It was why he was the desk sergeant, his easy manner and habit for talking.

'I'm on call. Harry and Bob are on shift.' He decided to throw William a lifeline. 'What's that you're doing?' He pointed at the table.

William's wide face seemed shocked that Jack would even bother to ask. 'Oh, just some paperwork for the inspector. Nothing exciting. What about you?'

Jack walked past William, whose head tilted to observe him, and sat down on a chair at the back of the office. 'I was hoping to keep out of the way for a while, to be honest with you. And maybe read this book.' He pulled the book out of his jacket pocket and waved it for William to see. He knew that the sergeant was keen on reading.

'H.G. Wells? Where did you get hold of that?' He almost stood up to come and get a better look at it. 'You know the Germans have banned his books, right?'

'I'd heard. According to my mother it belonged to my father. He was a great reader, and I wanted to see what the Germans had against Mr Wells. What exactly is anti-German about a book?'

'Who knows! Don't let me interrupt you then.' William beamed at Jack before returning to his work. The pair of them settled into a working silence, William shuffling papers and occasionally tutting to himself, before licking his finger and scribbling a note on the page, and Jack staring intently at *The War of the Worlds* and trying to concentrate. The station clock ticked to itself on the other side of the room.

An hour or so later, the office door opened and David entered. He didn't look over at either Jack or William, but carried on as if he expected no one to be there. David pulled a chair from one of the desks over to the wall, then stood on it to take down one of the keys. From where Jack was seated he could see that it was the key to the market gate, but what would David want with that? As he stepped down from the chair he looked straight at Jack and stopped. A grin flashed across his face, as if he had only just noticed them.

'Don't say anything,' David whispered, with a wink.

Jack stared back with a straight face. What would he tell anyone? He wasn't even sure he knew what David was doing. David nodded at William, who Jack knew owed him a favour. There was no way he would say anything either.

'Look, it's every man for himself,' David said. 'We're just doing what we need to do to survive.'

The one thing they had all got better at was guarding their words. A careless conversation could see them in trouble if the wrong people heard it, even if the intent had been perfectly innocent. Apparently, David was an exception to that rule. But he had always spoken his thoughts aloud. It was a wonder he had made it this far.

'What do you mean by that?' he asked, angry with himself for getting drawn into a conversation. Whatever David was up to he was better off out it.

'Well …' David hesitated in his answer. It was clear his mind was catching up with the danger of his words. 'Times are hard,' he continued. 'That's all I meant. Why don't both of you just forget you saw me, okay?'

It was the first thing David had said that he agreed with, and he nodded, pointedly returning his gaze to the book in his hands. David shrugged and left the police station without another word. Jack stared at the door as it closed behind him, wondering whether he should go after his friend and stop him. It felt like there was a cloud hanging over their friendship. Jack wouldn't push the issue, but he would keep an eye on David's behaviour.

William looked over at where Jack was sitting, his mouth opened a few times as if he wanted to say something. Jack buried himself in the book, forcing William to stay silent. He didn't want to discuss what had happened. He didn't want to discuss anything; he just wanted to escape into another world and forget that anything was happening at all.

*

The shift continued in silence for the rest of the night, each man concentrating on their own task. After a few hours William had finished his paperwork and pushed his chair back. He pulled a newspaper out from somewhere and stuck the end of a pencil in his mouth as he considered the crossword. David did not return to the police station, but as the morning drew on more policemen arrived. Daylight took over from the faint light of the candles. Eventually William got up and left, finishing his shift, but due to being short-staffed Jack was on until midday. He struggled to stay awake as he drifted in and out of the book he had been reading. When the inspector came into the office, quietly inspecting them, Jack hid the book back in his jacket pocket. After only saying a few words, the old man proceeded upstairs to his office.

It had gone eleven when the door slammed open and a German officer wearing the uniform of the Feldgendarmerie entered. He looked around at the half dozen policemen, then clicked his heels together.

'Where is your senior officer?' he barked as if on a parade ground.

Sergeant Honfleur was the first to respond, jumping up out of his chair, his face red.

'What on earth do you want? You can't just barge in here like—'

'Do you know who I am, Sergeant?' He pushed past the sergeant to stand in the middle of the station office. 'I suggest you do not push me. I am a member of the German Feldgendarmerie and I am here to place you all under arrest for thefts.'

'What? You can't—'

'I suggest you do as I say and find the inspector immediately!'

*

Jack had never seen the old man so furious, as he paced up and down the office. Typically a man of few words, he muttered to himself before turning to the German policeman. His skin was red and splotchy as if he had been holding his breath. He looked up at the assembled policemen as if noticing them for the first time. His eyes played around the room, then he shook his head in defeat. He opened his mouth to speak then closed it abruptly. He did so again a few times, which made him look like a fish struggling for air.

'What do you want me to do?' the chief eventually said, looking smaller and older than he had done before. They called him the old man, but it had only been a joke. Now he truly looked his age.

'You are to close the police station and everyone present is to come with me,' the German shouted, apparently for everyone's benefit.

'Where are we going?' This time it was Sergeant Honfleur. 'What do you want with us?'

'You will follow me to the Feldgendarmerie Headquarters at Grange Lodge and submit yourself for questioning. Immediately. The police station will remain closed.'

'You can't just close the police station. What if someone needs help?'

'I have men outside. If you do not come willingly then we will take you by force. One of them will stay here to take charge of the police station.'

'Force will not be necessary.' The inspector had found his voice at last. Some of the old steel had returned to it as he held his head up high and looked the German in the eyes. 'We will come and answer these accusations against my police force. Lead the way.'

They all stepped out of the building, leaving it empty for the first time since it had opened. Not even the bombing of the White Rock had left the station unmanned, nor at any other time during the occupation. There was a group of half a dozen soldiers outside the station, all carrying rifles. Two of them raised them as the policemen appeared, but their officer waved them away and muttered something in German.

For the roughly ten minutes it took to walk up La Grange to Grange Lodge the Germans flanked them, never taking their eyes from the policemen. The locals stared at them, confusion and anger writ large upon their faces. It was as if they were already convicted criminals.

*

Jack could feel the sweat building under his uniform as he sat there awaiting judgement. The policemen had been separated, and Jack had been taken into one of the upstairs rooms and left there.

For a long time there was a silence behind the locked wooden door, a silence that meant they were on their way. His time would come. He wasn't sure if there was anything special about these doors, whether the Germans had installed something to silence their interrogations. He had heard horror stories of intimidation techniques and worse. At first he hadn't believed them, but the older he got and the more the occupation went on, the more he shed his naivety like a snake shed its skin. Some of the policemen on the island were apparently no more trustworthy than the Germans, and he had seen some of the methods they used. He expected the Germans to be worse.

He wondered whether this was a test, to see how long he would be able to keep his silence before his guilt ate away at him completely and he broke down.

There was a thump that sounded like a butcher slamming his blade down on a slab of meat, then silence.

He wanted to get up and try the door, but he didn't know what would happen if he did. It was part of the deliberate fear, forcing him to sit there on that uncomfortable chair, waiting for something to happen.

Whoever was in the room next door sounded as if he was in trouble. It could have been David, but it was hard to tell. As far as Jack was aware David had stolen, and no matter how desperate he was a policeman should not steal. He had every right to be in trouble, but that didn't mean he deserved what was happening to him. Jack was not above suspicion either; as a friend of David's it wouldn't be much of a leap to assume he had something to do with it. If he stopped sitting there and tried to open the door, would that show his guilt? But if he did nothing, would that not also make him seem guilty? He stood and walked to the threshold.

There was a further series of thumps through the wall, then

the sound of metal being drawn against metal. Jack reached out a hand for the cold steel handle, but stopped just shy of his fingertips touching it. The scraping sound stopped with the rattle of hollow metal, as a chair fell over. Then silence again.

There was a click as the door handle turned a fraction of an inch, then stopped. It seemed to take an age before it moved again, Jack watching it the entire time as if doing so would put off the inevitable. The door wheeled open and a face appeared through the crack.

'Henrik?' Jack asked as his voice cracked from thirst. Henrik nodded and placed his index finger across his lips.

'I heard what they were doing,' he said. 'And had to check if you were here.'

'Can you tell me what's going on?' Jack tried to keep his voice as low as possible.

'I cannot tell you more than I have seen first-hand. I am not involved in this investigation, perhaps for obvious reasons. Those who are interrogating your friends … Well, they are not good people. They will get what they want, even if they have to beat it out of them.'

'And what do they want?'

'Signed confessions of the thefts from German stores.' He paused, looking out of the door to see if there was anyone in the corridor. 'Do you have anything in your home you should not?

'No! Of course not.' He thought of the H.G. Wells book, but that was at the station where he left it. 'I have no idea what the others have been up to.'

Henrik let out a long sigh. 'Good,' he said. 'If you have nothing to hide then you shall be fine. I should go, before they return.'

He closed the door with a slight click. Jack wanted to call after him. Henrik had done the only thing he could, and that was to check on Jack. He didn't know whether Henrik would have gone to his house to hide anything that he shouldn't have had, but then it occurred to him. What if Henrik was part of their plan as well? What if they had expected him to confess to Henrik that he had been involved in the thefts?

Jack pushed the thought from his mind. The isolation was driving him crazy and his thoughts were going around in circles. Instead, he settled back into his rhythm of watching the door handle. If he cleared his mind, he could settle into a sort of absent-minded trance that he used when he was posted on guard duty. But no matter how hard he tried he couldn't stop thinking about Johanna. He had to make sure he got out, for her sake.

He didn't know how many hours had passed when the door opened again and Major Obertz stepped in. Jack had lost count of how many times they questioned him, going over and over the same points, looking for a weakness. He no longer knew what time it was or how long it had been since he had last eaten. All of their questions had led nowhere. Jack knew nothing about what his colleagues had been up to, and even if he did he wouldn't tell the major.

'PC Godwin,' he said, looking at Jack as he sat on his chair.

The German's clenched knuckles were covered in dried blood, but he didn't appear to notice. The colour matched the hue of his cheeks as he looked as if he had run a marathon. His eyes were black in the dim light of the corridor, and they appeared to be staring into the middle distance. He cleared his throat.

'We found no stolen goods in your possession, and therefore you are free to go.'

Was that it? Jack's mind raged at the needlessness of it all. He wondered whether they were testing him, but they could keep him locked up if they so desired. This was something else. They trusted him, thought he was on their side, and the thought made him sick.

'If, however, we find evidence that demonstrates you helped your colleagues in their thefts then we will arrest you again. Be warned. Now go.'

Jack stood up on unsteady legs. He didn't know how long he

had been sitting, but it had been long enough for his thighs to cramp at the unusual movement. He followed the major out of the room as quickly as he dared, wary that he was walking into a trap.

He smelled the stink of iron as he passed the door to the next room. Someone had left it open and Jack could see right in. What he saw made him stop on the threshold. David sat on a steel chair in the middle of his cell. His chin was resting on his chest as if he had fallen asleep, but his face was covered in red splotches and bruises that were already turning purple. He had one black eye and blood had stained his uniform shirt brown. Jack stared at his friend, wanting to run to his aid, but knowing that he couldn't.

He tore his eyes away from the injured man. They had left him there as a warning to Jack. 'Steal from us and this is what happens,' it said. So, he followed the major, on his unsteady legs, eager to be away from that hell as quickly as possible.

*

The air at the station had changed, but Jack couldn't put his finger on how. The few remaining policemen had gathered to find out what happened next, as the inspector's deputy addressed them. None of them dared look him in the eye, lost in their own private despair. Amongst them were a few special constables who had been promoted to acting constables.

'I am replacing the inspector for now as acting inspector,' the deputy said, his accent demonstrating the quality of his education. 'And the Guernsey Police Force will for the foreseeable future come under the purview of the Occupation Force's Kommandant, and 515 Feldkommandantur. All our reports will be forwarded to them for review, so make sure that everything is above board. They will be looking for mistakes, gentlemen. Don't give them one.'

That was it then. The old man had been arrested and imprisoned with the others. If things hadn't been hard before, then they would be now. The police force had carried on almost as normal since the occupation, but now things would be different. If he thought they were being watched before, then it would be even worse now. They would all have to be more careful. If not, then Jack could find himself behind bars, and that mistake could lead them to Johanna.

Later on, during his beat through the harbour, Jack spotted a small vessel making its way under power from one of the piers. It was the wrong time of day for a fishing boat, and it didn't fit the shape. He couldn't see from where he walked, but as he looked out over the White Rock he wondered whether the three Jewish women who were being deported were on board. If they were, then it was only a short journey to France, then on to wherever they were being taken.

He wondered whether they would end up in the camps that Johanna had spoken of. There could only be one reason to take people away from their homes and that was to imprison them. If it had been within his power he would have stopped it from happening. Maybe after the war they would be allowed their freedom again, but somehow Jack doubted that. It didn't seem like the war was going to end. They still saw the aircraft flying over every day, on their way to drop death on their enemies. How many more would be punished before those bombs stopped falling?

The Islanders just had to hope. Hope and wait.

Chapter 29

3 May 1942

Stones clacked their way down the hill as Jack scrambled along the dirt path, trying to keep his footing. The shingle slid every time he adjusted his weight and it was no wonder that very few people came down here. He couldn't remember if he had ever been here before, but he wouldn't be trying again. He had responded to reports of a boat launching from the area. At first he hadn't wanted to go, but he had relented when he had been warned of the potentially dangerous tides in the area. Anyone who knew what they were doing with a boat would not have risked launching. The best they could hope for was washing up on a sandbank.

Sure enough, when Jack had climbed down close enough to see, there was a boat listing in the water. The waves smashed against the hull and spray covered the men on board. They were all young men, around Jack's age or younger. The shallow wooden hull would never make the journey to the mainland, and he had no idea what they were thinking.

From there he could just about make out their shouts of alarm. The three men were speaking in the language of the island. Although Jack hadn't heard Guernesiais in some time, he recognised it instantly. The local language wasn't spoken by everyone, but most knew enough to understand the basics. Jack was perhaps more familiar with it than some. His grandfather had taught him, when he had been well, and right now the French-like parlance was clear as day. From what Jack could hear, the men didn't want anyone to overhear them and even if some Germans stumbled across them, they wouldn't understand what was being said. It didn't matter whether the Germans heard them or not, what they were doing was stupid. If the Germans saw them then they wouldn't ask questions, they would shoot.

Part of him wanted to leave them alone to give them a chance to escape, but another part knew that he had to stop them.

Jack's foot slipped and a pebble came away, cracking as it bounced down the hill, hitting other stones in its irregular path. The slip caused him to stand fully, using his legs to regain balance. One of the men looked over from the boat and made eye contact with him. The scene seemed to freeze for a long moment as the other men stopped what they were doing and spotted his uniform.

Before Jack could shout, a wave dipped the boat forward, then flung the stern up in the air. The men disappeared from view, but he thought he saw a shape slip overboard. The boat rocked as the wind caught it. It wasn't designed for this kind of weather, and it was stupid to think that it would be safe. The rising tide was causing problems itself. The boat dipped below a wave and then swung heavily to one side. Some of the contents spilled over the side splashing into the dark water. The men onboard struggled to control it, shouting through the wind. Their words were lost, drowned out by the gale. The boat moved again, edging ever closer to the beach.

'Oh, God! Nick!' he heard one of the men shout as he leant over the rail, scanning the water for someone. The man looked over at Jack who had just made it to the beach. 'For God's sake, man,' he shouted. 'Do something. Help!'

Jack took a step closer to the water, but a wave splashed up over the sand coating him. He took another step, but it was no good. If he got any closer then he too would be dragged out to sea. The waves were too strong, the currents shifting and rippling, spreading out into the bay, then crashing back again. He looked around, searching for something, anything that he could use to help, but the small beach was deserted.

The boat crashed back up onto the beach as a wave took hold of it, depositing it on the sand like an unwanted toy. It stuck, tilting to one side. Jack moved around to get a better look, wary that at any minute it could fall. The hull was empty except for a few puddles of water that pooled between wooden joists.

One of the men had jumped overboard then slipped as a wave brought the heavy wooden boat into him, knocking him over. He cursed as he went knee-deep in the water and scrabbled to right himself. His shipmate had landed spread-eagled on the sand, apparently thrown free from the boat as it landed. He leant up on his elbows as Jack ran over to him. He coughed water over the beach, groaning to himself. Jack reached down to check the man was all right, but he pushed him away with an arm and coughed up more water, bile mingling with the liquid on the sand. The other man was trying to work his way out into the water, but was being forced back by the waves. He fell to his knees.

'Oh, Nick,' he said, shaking where he knelt. 'Nick, Nick.'

It became a kind of mantra, a memorial for his lost friend. Jack felt sick. Why hadn't he been able to help? He had frozen, been trapped by fear. He would always blame himself for the man's death, as no doubt the two survivors would too. Something occurred to Jack. 'Nicholas Le Roux?' he asked, already dreading the answer.

The man nodded as he shook his head in shame, pounding his fists against the sand. Jack felt the shock overcome him. He too dropped to his knees, remembering the young lad who had been his neighbour and friend. What had caused him to attempt a dangerous escape in the middle of a tide like this? Why hadn't

Jack been able to save him? It was another needless death in the name of the Third Reich. Jack helped the other man up, his body heavy with shock, and escorted them inland. He wouldn't take them to the police station; it would be their responsibility to turn themselves in and report Nicholas's death. He wasn't doing the Germans' dirty work for them anymore.

*

'Mum?' Jack called over his shoulder from just inside the front door. He wasn't sure whether she would respond. He turned and headed back into the house proper. 'There's a card here for you.'

As he looked at the postcard, he was unable to keep the surprise from his voice, and when he walked into the kitchen his mother gave him a confused look. He handed the card to her; it had been addressed to her. It wasn't his place to be nosy about his mother's post, even if it was unusual for her to receive anything. He couldn't remember the last time any of them had received any letters. Not since the Germans had come and they had been cut off from the mainland.

'What's this?' his mother asked, looking at the card. Jack waited for her to answer her own question. He was still reeling from Nicholas's death, but he wanted to try to forget it, at least for now.

While she read, he made himself a small cup of tea and took a sip. He almost spat it out. The flavour was awful. He didn't think he would ever get used to carrot tea, but regular tea was long gone from the island. It almost stung his gums. How did his mother drink the stuff? While he poured it away he wondered if he would be able to get a proper cup of coffee at work later, maybe from the Germans, but then realised that would no doubt be the fake, ersatz coffee as well.

His mother sat as she was reading. 'It's from the Red Cross Bureau in Market Square,' she said, a moment later. Jack turned to her.

'What do they want?' he asked. The Red Cross had been instrumental in bridging contact between those who had evacuated and those still on the island, managing to bring letters through neutral Switzerland. A number of parents had received a coded letter from their children in England. The letters were still censored by the German authorities, but it was better than nothing.

His mother clamped her palm to her mouth and then spoke through her fingers. 'It's from your grandparents,' she said.

'What ...? I don't understand ...' He too sat at the table.

'Your father's parents,' she said, handing him the card. 'Here, look.'

His eyes scanned straight to the signature at the bottom of the letter, showing two names he didn't recognise.

'It's the first time they have ever written to me. The first time they have spoken to me since your father died.' She stifled a small sob at those words. 'I didn't think they even acknowledged my existence.

'They even asked after me and you. Do you think I should write back?'

'Yes!' Jack responded immediately, then attempted to hide his haste. 'Yes, I think you should. It would be good for you, for both of us, for you to write to them.'

'You're right.' She smiled at him, and it was one of the most pleasing things he had seen in a while. His mother didn't smile much, but when she did she meant it. 'I'll have to think what to say.'

'I'm sure you'll think of something. Tell them about how beautiful the island is.'

Jack stared at the postcard. He had no doubt that it would become one of his prized possessions. If his mother would allow it, he was going to keep that letter on him at all times. Jack had never imagined getting to know his father's side of the family in England. But perhaps one day he and Johanna could go and see them; perhaps there was a little bit of hope in the world after all.

Chapter 30

1 June 1942

Jack hadn't wanted to attend the hearing, but Johanna had insisted. 'It would show your support for David,' she had said. 'You don't know how much he needs a friendly face right now.' So, as always, he had relented. Jack didn't know if his was the friendly face David wanted to see, but he would at least try.

He wasn't the only one who had come to see the trial – there was a group of friends and family as well as some well-wishers and those who just wanted to see the police get what they deserved. They had even formed a sort of queue outside the Police Court awaiting the accused. Eventually two coaches arrived, and the men were led out, all eighteen of them, almost half the strength of the police force on the island.

As they were led off the coaches, some of the bruises were still visible, but they looked in a far better shape than they had done when they had been interrogated. They all wore civilian clothes that had been taken to their cells in Fort George. A few people in the crowd gave the police thumbs up, or the 'V' symbol as the policeman sloped past. Someone even shouted, 'Keep your chins up.'

David came towards the back of the group, his gaze focused on the floor until he looked up and made eye contact with Jack. In a moment of defiance Jack put up his index and second fingers in a 'V', which brought forth a smirk from David, who nodded his head. Jack expected his friend was remembering the night they had vandalised the road together. Once the police had taken their place in the court, the public gallery filled up with the friends and family. There were even members of the local press there.

The accused sat on wooden chairs facing the Royal Coat of Arms, which now had a massive swastika draped over it. Along a bench underneath the Nazi symbol were the gathered Germans who were going to decide the fate of the policemen, and the bailiff of the court. At their head was the kommandant. Jack thought it was odd that the man who was about to be in charge of the police was also the one to pass judgement. How could he be impartial? The defence for the men was the attorney general, but Jack had heard rumours in the station office that he had decided there was no point trying to defend them.

A clerk read out the charges, and it was an impressive list. The main offence was larceny, with some being accused of thefts from German military foodstuffs, and even wood from a military timber yard. The initial stages of the trial took a long time, and Jack struggled to pay attention as the policemen were questioned about their backgrounds, families, military and police service records and their ownership of property.

As the prepared pleas and statements for each man were read out for the court, each policeman's eyes widened as they listened. The statements had been translated from German and it was becoming clear that the men had no idea what they had admitted to. There were cries of shock from the gallery, those family members who knew better shouting that they were lies, but immediately the kommandant ordered silence.

The attorney general stood to give his case for the defence. 'Had I been the prosecutor of this case, I might have asked for sentences perhaps not differing from those suggested by the

German prosecutor. The Guernsey police have betrayed the trust reposed in them as guardians of the public.' There was a stunned silence around the room.

'However, I must insist that, based on the statements of all the charged, that PC Baker be acquitted as not being present for any of the aforementioned crimes.' He continued to give the reasons why Baker should be excluded from the charges. Jack looked over at his family and saw their anticipation there. While the others were damned, he was being offered hope. The attorney general had sacrificed the defence of the group for the one who he thought most capable of getting off. Jack almost sympathised, but then his eyes played across David's wife and children. She held a struggling toddler in her arms as she closed her eyes to listen to her husband's demise. Jack should have done something to stop his friend committing the crimes of which he was now clearly guilty.

The kommandant nodded along with every word. It was as if he had prepared the statement himself. After many hours of statements and charges, he called for an end to proceedings for the day. It was clear that it was going to take longer than one sitting. Jack stood up as soon as they were dismissed, wanting to avoid the families of his colleagues who would no doubt see him as complicit in their punishment.

*

The trial continued for three days, but Jack was unable to attend due to his duties. It was probably for the best as the guilt of letting David down was weighing heavily on him. He had been made an acting sergeant by the acting inspector as one of the only experienced men left. At one point in his life the new stripes that he had been allowed to apply to the left arm of his uniform would have given him an immense sense of pride, but now they only felt hollow. There was a strand of guilt threaded through them.

Yet again the Germans were determined to stamp their order

on the islands, and Jack had just finished processing paperwork about them taking away the wireless sets again. They had written in the newspapers that it wasn't a punishment, but he knew better. He had always wondered how long it would take them to remove the Islanders' link with the BBC, especially after what had happened with the 'V' for victory symbols. No doubt they would now expect the local police to enforce the rule.

On the last day of the trial Jack appealed to the acting inspector to allow him time to attend and support the men. He wasn't best pleased, but allowed him all the same. Jack arrived at the court just in time to hear some of the pleas from the accused.

He recognised Sergeant Honfleur's voice right away. 'We were taking from those who didn't need it and giving to those who did.' There was a silence before he continued. Jack sat down on the bench and turned to listen. 'The Germans have everything they could ever want and we are all starving without basic needs.'

One of the members of the tribunal looked at the sergeant over the top of his glasses. 'That as may be,' he said. 'However, I very much doubt that you were operating on purely altruistic motivations. In fact there is very little evidence of you providing any of the items which you stole to those who …' he paused to emphasise his words '… those who you claim need it. On the contrary all the evidence points to you keeping it all for yourselves. You even stole from your fellow Islanders. Those Islanders who you were sworn to protect.'

Honfleur sat down, deflated. Apparently he had pinned all his hopes on that defence, but the tribunal were having none of it. Stealing from the Germans had been stupid, but stealing from the local stores was unforgivable.

David was invited to stand next, but unlike the sergeant he refused to meet the eyes of the tribunal. He stared at the floor as he spoke. His voice was broken and small. 'I know nothing about it though I have made a confession. I cannot tell the court anything.'

What he said would not help him. The bailiff of the court agreed when he tutted and said, 'I have never heard such an unsatisfactory case before the court. Not even the first inclination to speak the truth or anything to do with it. You may be seated.'

David stood where he was. 'I would like to make a statement now, sir,' he said. David would only damn himself by saying anything more.

'No, certainly not.'

David stared for a moment longer, before collapsing back into the chair. The bailiff turned to the rest of the tribunal and they nodded at his words. He then announced to the court that they would take a recess while they deliberated on the sentences. A couple of the accused policemen looked on the verge of saying something, but the tribunal left through a side door. Jack jumped up and headed downstairs from the gallery, not wanting to be alone with the families.

Downstairs he bumped into Acting Constable Robins. The man had been one of the special constables before being promoted to take the place of the arrested men. He wandered over to Jack when he saw him. 'Didn't expect to see you here, sir.'

'Nor you,' Jack replied, then spotted the men he had been accompanying. 'They're the men from the boat. The ones who tried to escape.'

Robins looked around as if unsure who Jack meant. 'Aye, apparently someone turned them in.' He checked his notepad like a good acting policeman. 'A Mrs Fletcher. They're awaiting their trial now.'

Jack sighed, a name he hadn't heard in a while and hoped he wouldn't again. Mrs Fletcher was a menace on the local community, but he had thought she was harmless in her own way. Mistaking Jack's sigh for a sign of exasperation that an Islander would turn in another, Robins continued.

'It's worse,' he said. 'Apparently she's the mother of one of them.'

Jack shook his head. Only part of him was shocked by that.

'Oh, looks like you're going back in,' Robins said, nodding in the direction of the court.

Jack nodded his thanks and rushed up to the gallery. The families were all still there, holding on to each other for support, so he sat at the back to keep out of their way. He didn't want to invade their private grief. He sat down just in time to hear the tribunal give their verdict.

'After careful deliberation with my colleagues, we acquit PC Frank Baker of all charges, and pronounce all other parties as guilty of the charges that have been brought before them.'

Tears broke out as the families heard their husbands' and fathers' sentences, no longer able to hold the emotions at bay.

'No appeal will be considered, and all men will serve their prison sentences in France.'

Some of the men collapsed into their seats, resigned to their fate, but David looked up and round at the gallery. His eyes didn't fall on his family, but on Jack, wide and pleading. Jack would remember that look for the rest of his days.

*

'We've received reports of a black wireless at a property down in the forest.' William handed Jack an address card. 'Apparently a soldier overheard the bells during a news broadcast.'

Jack had known that at some point he would be called in to arrest locals who had not obeyed the command. There had been other cases already, and the Germans were handing out prison sentences for disobeying, but so far Jack had not been required to be the arresting officer. Within half an hour he had arrived on the road in the forest, where Henrik was already waiting for him.

Jack supposed he would have to get used to working more and more with the German police as time went on. It was now required for them to work with the Feldgendarmerie on these cases. Apparently the local police couldn't be trusted. It would only be a matter of time before the local police force was wound up completely and their duties handed over to the German authorities.

Henrik simply nodded as Jack arrived and tied up his bicycle, then led Jack between the houses on the Villiaze Road. He must have been aware what Jack was thinking. Everyone on the island would have heard about the trial of the policemen by now, and Henrik was keeping quiet.

'This is the house,' Henrik said as he knocked on a front door. As they waited for the occupant to answer, Jack wondered what they would do if they found a wireless set in the house. They would be required to take the owner into custody, but Jack would let Henrik do that. It was his country's rule. He was only there to make sure that the homeowner was treated as fairly as possible.

A few seconds later the door opened, and a middle-aged man came out. His clothes were tattered, torn in some places, and his eyes stared at a place between Henrik and Jack's shoulders. Henrik opened his mouth to explain why they were there, but Jack beat him to it. He didn't want the German to unduly scare the man. 'We're just here to check you don't have any wireless sets in the house,' he said. 'It won't take us long.'

The man walked back into his house, nodding a couple of times as Henrik and Jack stepped over the threshold. The building smelled of boiled cabbage. When the man disappeared into his living room, Henrik stopped Jack with an outstretched palm.

'Do you see a wireless set?' he asked, leaning aside to show the opened door.

Jack could barely see in the door, let alone see the owner's possessions. He wondered if Henrik was testing him, checking his loyalty. Jack had long since decided that you couldn't trust the Germans. At one point he had thought that Henrik might be better, but now he was no longer sure.

'No,' he said, the upward inflection of his voice indicating that it was part question, and that he was unsure what was really being asked.

'No more do I,' Henrik replied, guiding Jack back to the front door. He thanked the owner and closed the door behind him once they were outside. Jack couldn't help himself.

'What the hell was that?' he asked as they headed back towards where Jack had left his bike.

Henrik laughed. It was a short bark. 'That man is no master criminal, or resistance leader. I did not think there was much use in wasting our time.' He marched a few steps more, then seemed to consider something. 'Jack, I am sorry for your friend.'

Jack stopped dead. 'What the hell does it matter to you?' he asked.

'If there was anything I could have done ...'

'You could have stayed in Germany.'

Henrik looked down at his shoes. 'Yes, you are right,' he said. His voice had lost its Prussian steel. 'If it helps then I have a feeling that I may not be here for much longer.'

It was Jack's turn to consider his words. Something in him had changed. The thought of Henrik leaving hit him hard. 'What do you mean?'

'There are rumours that a number of us are going to be redeployed. Do not tell anyone, but things are not going as well as they say in the war.

'The fighting is far from over.'

Chapter 31

There was a knock on the door, quick and regular. It was the kind of knock Jack would often tap on a door when he was on duty. He hesitated in the kitchen, halfway between bites of a mouldy slice of bread. His stomach rumbled, but the front door drew his attention as there was another knock. Part of him was always expecting the secret knock used by the small group of Guernsey resistance on the island, but it never came. The signal was three short raps then a long one, the opening of Beethoven's *Fifth Symphony*, or 'V', the same music used at the beginning of BBC broadcasts. It was clever, but one day the Germans would work out what it meant.

It was clear that whoever it was, they were not going to go away. Sighing, he dropped the bread back on his plate, hoping no one would steal it while he was out of the kitchen. Then he stood up and headed towards the door. 'I'll get it,' he called up the stairs, just loud enough to be heard, but not loud enough to wake his mother if she was sleeping. The knock came again, more insistent this time. Jack had been there many times before and he wondered who it could be. Fear rushed through him as he reached out for the door handle. Had the German authorities finally come for him? Had they realised that he had been harbouring a Jew and taken Johanna into custody? Every possibility ran through his head. He almost took his hand back, unwilling to open the door, but it was no good.

He wrenched the door open, determined to meet his fate with as much power as he could muster. The hinges squealed as it swung open, revealing the bright summer sunshine and the figure at his door.

'Henrik?' Jack asked, surprised. The German had never come to his house before; Jack had no idea he knew where Jack lived. It was unusual to see the man out of his uniform, and he wore a simple, dark grey, linen suit.

'Jack!' he replied, flashing that familiar smile of his. 'I thought I had the wrong house. I'm glad to see you.'

'What are you doing here?' Jack poked his head out of the door to see whether there was anyone else on the road. He had a hard enough time as it was with people considering a policeman to be complicit with the Germans without one of them actually being on his doorstep. Even if he had come to consider this man to be a friend.

'I want to show you something,' Henrik said, his eagerness drawing the words together, making them less familiar in a foreign tongue. 'But you must come quickly.'

'Where?'

'Come, come. People will see.' Apparently he too had realised the danger they were in. Jack's thoughts again ran away with him. Living under German occupation had made him doubt everyone, question everything.

'Wait a second.' Jack closed the door and leant against it. He closed his eyes, asking himself what he was doing, and reached for his jacket. Others would say he was mad, including his mother, but he had always been this way.

'Come with me.' Henrik beckoned to Jack. 'Come on,' he repeated. 'Quick. We do not have the entire night.'

He was right – the curfew would be starting soon, and Jack

had spent too many nights out after curfew already, sneaking home after dark hoping that he wouldn't be seen.

'What is it?' he asked, looking over his shoulder. 'Why do I have to go?'

'It will be worth it. Permit me this one indulgence.'

*

A few minutes later they had walked further into the town, and Henrik had stopped in front of a house. 'This is where I live,' he said with a smile. But there was a look behind his eyes, the same one he had seen when they'd argued. He entered the front door without saying another word.

Jack, intrigued more than anything, followed shortly behind, walking into the relative gloom of the house. It was like many of the other houses in St Peter Port. A corridor led to stairs with rooms leading from the sides. Many residents had given their spare rooms over to German soldiers and many of the houses now were more German than local. Jack had never stepped foot in the house before and he didn't know Henrik's landlady other than what the German had told him about her. According to him she was accommodating and welcoming. Jack wondered whether she was simply intimidated by the Germans. However, she was nowhere to be seen in the house. She must have been out, or had already taken herself to her room for the evening.

Jack followed Henrik up the stairs. As he reached the top banister, he heard a key turning a lock and light spilled into the darkened landing. Jack walked tentatively forward, and the light blinded him for a moment.

'Come in, come in,' he heard Henrik whisper from the doorway. Again, Jack followed, but he kept a safe distance behind.

Henrik walked to the window and pulled the curtains shut. He mumbled something to himself in German, and Jack recognised something to do with privacy. 'Close the door,' he bid Jack as he looked around for something. Jack did as he was told, and the room descended into darkness. He tensed, not knowing what was going to happen next. The smell of boot polish was overpowering.

There was the satisfying click and then the fizz of a match being lit. The room filled with shadows. Jack could see Henrik reaching for a candle and touching the match to the wick as he tried to coax it to life. Henrik only lit the one, relying on it to provide all the light they needed. Other sources of light were now scarce on the island since the fuel had run out. They had become used to living by candlelight, much like their grandparents and great-grandparents would have done. It was a strange light, throwing flickering shadows around the room, and Jack's eyes never quite adjusted to it. It was as if there was a fuzzy blur over his vision, coloured slightly by the flame of the candles.

The room was small, but Henrik had tried to make it a home. There were a few pictures of smiling family on a desk in the corner and a couple of books neatly piled by their side. As Jack had expected, there was no swastika to be seen.

Henrik placed the candle on the desk, then went to his bed and knelt down beside it. He reached under the frame with both hands and then hauled a box out, before placing it on the desk with the candle.

'What is it?' Jack asked, uncertain. The shape was wrapped in a sheet of cloth.

'Ahh, just a moment.' Henrik was clearly enjoying the suspense, building Jack's expectations. His mind raced, wondering whether Henrik had managed to get hold of some extra rations, or had somehow looted the German stores and was willing to share it with Jack. Whatever it was, there was a sense of danger that Jack couldn't quite shift. He felt he had been in this situation before.

A second later Henrik pulled the cloth from the shape, flapping it in front of him like a magician performing a trick. Underneath the cloth was a metal device with a couple of dials and needle meters. The candlelight reflected back from it.

'What do you think?' Henrik asked, the excitement clear on his face as he beamed up at Jack from where he knelt.

'What is it?' Jack replied, asking the same question again.

'A wireless set! A basic one, of course, but it works. Listen.' He plugged the device into the mains electric then turned one of the dials to switch it on. White noise spilled into the room before he adjusted the volume control. Jack hadn't realised, but he had taken a step closer, eager to hear the wireless. He heard the familiar four notes that signalled the beginning of a BBC broadcast and realised how much he missed them. 'This is London calling …'

Jack closed his eyes, breathing in the sounds of the broadcast, the familiar British voice that he felt like he hadn't heard in years and the faint crackle of interference. After a few seconds he opened his eyes again. 'Quick, turn it off,' he said, regretting the words. 'Before someone reports you.'

Henrik did as he was told, clicking the dial into the off position. 'Where did you get it?'

'It is best not to ask that, I think. It saves me having to lie to you. Gerhart helped me get it, but the important thing is that I got it. It is a secret between us, yes?'

Jack nodded quickly. He certainly wasn't going to tell anyone. It took a special kind of stupidity to inform on the German soldiers themselves, not to mention a special kind of cruelty. Jack liked to think he wasn't that stupid, stupid enough to draw attention to himself. So, he said nothing, leaving his silence as confirmation he would do whatever Henrik asked of him. It had become a sort of unspoken agreement between the two of them. Jack had another question though.

'Why did you show it to me?' he asked. 'Why haven't you kept it secret?'

Henrik sighed and pushed the wireless under the bed. Then sat on the end. He looked smaller than before, somehow deflated, a thousand miles from the tall imposing German police officer he was to the outside world.

'I've been ordered to the Eastern Front.' He said it matter-of-factly, monotone. There wasn't even a hint of emotion in his voice, and Jack thought that itself was strange. Jack opened his mouth to say something, but Henrik headed him off.

'I wanted to show you this before I had to leave. Gerhart is coming too, otherwise he would have taken it. If you think you can hide it, then you may have it when I am gone. But be careful. You remember what happened to your colleagues.'

Jack wasn't sure he'd ever forget. He didn't know if David would ever return from prison in France.

'When do you leave?' He was sorry that the man was leaving the island, and that was as close to friendship he would allow himself to feel.

'In a few days, I should think. I will be sorry to say goodbye to the island.' He dropped his head into his hands. It looked as if he was praying.

'What's wrong?' Jack asked, suspecting he knew anyway.

'I am sorry. I should not lay this burden on your shoulders.' He looked up again, his bright blue eyes boring into Jack's. 'But it is a death sentence, in all except name. I do not know anyone who has been sent to the Eastern Front who has not lost their life.'

News on the island was limited to the German channels, which had no doubt been censored and sanitised so as not to cause any problems. Even the local newspapers had to get their material from the same sources, but none of them had been able to truly spin the news coming from the Eastern Front into anything positive. By all accounts the German army had taken on too much by attacking Russia and with the harsh eastern winter closing in they were getting bogged down by the troubling terrain. Many of the superior officers still said that victory was only a matter of time, but the regular soldiers knew the situation was far more complex than that.

'I wanted you to know, before I go. That I consider you to be a friend. That is why I brought you here, where we could talk in private.'

Jack was taken aback and touched. It was a difficult friendship between them, when they were really enemies. But it showed that even enemies could find a common ground. He was one German who Jack wished well.

'I will be sorry to see you go.'

That was all he could bring himself to say.

'Thank you and good luck.'

'Good luck,' Jack replied, reaching out to shake Henrik's hand.

The Eastern Front

His conversation with Jack had gone well, and he was glad that
they had managed to build something of a friendship. He didn't
want to leave the island without him knowing that Henrik considered him to be a friend. Now, however, he had to see to another
friend. Neither of them had received the news about being posted
to the Eastern Front well, but he knew that Gerhart had already
lost a brother there.

Henrik knocked on the door, then waited. It was not unusual
for the man to take his time, and Henrik had always believed that
one of the strongest traits of his own personality was his patience.

'Gerhart? Are you there? I have news.' There was no reply,
but the door rattled slightly in its frame as if the window in
the room was open. He knocked again and waited. Perhaps
Gerhart had been sleeping, but even that was unusual during
the day. He had been known to sleep off a hangover, but as far
as he knew Gerhart had not been drinking the night before.

He tried the handle and it turned in his grip. The lock clicked
back as the door swung open. There was no sign of him, but there
was a strong metallic smell: iron. He walked through the door
and turned to look for Gerhart. He stopped dead in his tracks.

Blood coated the white bed sheets and splattered across the

wall beyond. The red-brown stains would never completely come out. A Radom pistol lay the other side of the body, fallen as the shot was fired. There was a faint black stain around the pistol. The smell of cordite still hung heavy in the air, despite the open window with its white net curtains blowing softly in the breeze.

Henrik didn't step any further into the room; it was already dangerous him just being here. It was bad enough that the man had committed suicide, but if Henrik was found near the body, there would no doubt be questions. Suicide may be hard to prove, and Henrik would become a suspect. Gerhart was a soldier, and the Wehrmacht hierarchy would be interested in why one of their soldiers had taken his own life. Henrik did not wish to be caught up in all that, but what could he do?

He would have to report the death; it would be better that way. However, he couldn't leave his friend like that, sprawled out in that dingy bedsit. He deserved better. He was a good man, a caring man, even if life had proven too much for him. He stared long and hard at the body of his friend, trying to remember him in life. Henrik had lost many friends since the war had started, but this one seemed to cut the deepest.

He turned and left the room. He couldn't shift the image from his mind, but he was a soldier. He had seen death before, countless times, but this was different. He went to find the housekeeper to see if he could use her telephone, but there was no one else to be found in the building. That would explain why no one had heard the gunshot. Perhaps it was better if he left Gerhart for someone else to find. It felt callous, but even as a military policeman, Henrik was not above suspicion. In the Reich, and even here on this island far from the administration of the Reich, it was best to avoid suspicion at all costs.

*

276

'Ahh, *Leutnant*. There you are.'

Henrik had only just entered Grange Lodge when the Hauptmann spotted him. He clicked his heels together and Heil Hitlered in response to the Hauptmann's attention. There was a slight slip as he incorrectly saluted in his haste, but he hoped his senior officer wouldn't notice. Hauptmann Hofmann was a Party man, constantly trying to find ways to elevate himself above the other soldiers. Naturally he was suspicious of everyone, including Henrik, but unusually he was also capable of reason.

'*Ja, ja. Heil Hitler*. Where have you been? No matter. I have some news for you.'

'News, *Herr Hauptmann*?'

'*Ja*. The notification you received detailing your reposting to the Russian front was delivered in error. You are part of the vital troops needed for the occupation of this island.'

Henrik almost collapsed, but years of Prussian heritage kept him upright. *Damn them all,* he thought. *I didn't ask for this.* He forced himself to respond. '*Danke, Hauptmann.*'

'Thank you? What for? One would expect every man to want to represent his Fatherland in the war, *Leutnant*. Remember that, these orders can change at any time. Glory awaits on the front line, glory in the name of the Reich!'

Henrik hadn't forgotten that the Hauptmann considered him to be a true Aryan, one of the so-called master race of the German people. But his ancestors would be rolling in their graves at the state of the German nation. Henrik just wanted to see the war out and return to his home.

'Of course, sir. I merely wanted to thank you for keeping me informed.'

The Hauptmann looked at Henrik with narrowed eyes, then nodded and returned to his work.

'*Gut*. Then you'll have work to do I expect. Report to your station immediately.'

Henrik was glad for the respite, even if that was all it was.

The situation on the Eastern Front could change rapidly. He considered telling the Hauptmann about Gerhart, but changed his mind instantly. Someone else would find his friend. Henrik didn't want to end up on the Eastern Front after all. He clicked his heels together saluted and left. He had some thinking to do while he attempted to work. The only thought that kept him going was the possibility of seeing Beth. He would need a strong drink to calm his nerves.

Chapter 32

Jack had responded to reports of strange noises coming from one of the boat huts by the beach in Grand Havre. In peacetime it wasn't unusual for the bay to be used for fishing boats, but these days, as the Germans had stopped overnight fishing, there were only a few boats left. The locals jumped at anything in the quiet waters, suspecting foul play. Early on in the occupation there had been sightings of mysterious U-boats that had never materialised. Jack didn't give the call much weight, but it was still his duty to investigate.

He found the hut in question with ease. It sat next to three fishing boats of various sizes, pulled up onto the sands. The wood of both the hut and the boats was green and rotting in places, but they still looked seaworthy. Jack tried the thick iron padlock that held the hut's door shut, but it was locked. There was a waxed sheet covering a small storage space around the back. He presumed that was where the sounds had come from.

Jack pulled the sheet aside, not knowing what he would see. It took his eyes a second to adjust to the gloom, but before they did a shape huddled back into the crevice, eliciting a low moan much like that of a trapped animal. Jack could see that it wasn't an animal, but an adult man curled up on the floor in the hole.

He was dishevelled, his pale skin blackened and bruised in parts, and his bones poked through his flesh, giving him the appearance of a skeleton. There was a smell somewhere between that of the public urinals in Market Street and a compost heap, and Jack had to resist closing his nostrils with his fingers. If Jack hadn't seen him move, then he would have wondered whether the man was alive at all. His eyes were sunken in their sockets, but wide with fear. Jack didn't know how he had got there, but he must have been one of the Operation Todt men who had come to the island, and had been hoping to sneak aboard one of the fishing boats when it set sail. Unfortunately it wouldn't have got him very far.

Jack reached out a hand to help the man, but he recoiled further into the hole. He rolled into a foetal shape but kept his hands free so that he could repel the intruder if needed. Jack felt a wave of something wash over him and he pulled his hands back, raising the palms to show he meant no harm.

'Whoa, whoa,' he said, forcing softness into his voice as if talking to a disturbed horse, or frightened dog. 'Let me help you out.'

Jack wasn't sure whether the other man understood him, but his eyes bored into Jack's, white dots in the dark hole. He looked away from that gaze, hoping it would make him feel more at ease. The smell grew more pungent the longer Jack stayed there squatting down near the man. He wanted to recoil, to breathe some fresh air and get as far away as possible, but something deep inside him told him that he had to help this man, no matter what. Whoever he was, Jack could not leave him in this state.

He thought about what had happened to Henry and his family, to the French sailors and the rest. He remembered David's face in court and the way his wife had looked as he was taken away. Jack had vowed that he would never shy away from helping someone in need again. He had forgotten why he had signed up for the police force in the first place. Because of his father's death, he had wanted to help others.

He thought of the only way he could communicate with the man. *'Ich helfe dir,' I want to help you,* he said in broken German, with as best an approximation of the accent. *'Bitte. Ist ordnung.' Please, it's okay.* It sounded ridiculous, and it didn't help at all as the man started to shake where he lay, rocking back and forth.

'*Ne Nemetskiy*,' he replied in his own language, but Jack didn't understand.

'Sorry,' Jack said, switching back to English. He doubted that he would understand the only other language Jack spoke, the Guernesiais of the island. He pointed to himself, 'Jack,' he said a few times, emphasising the point with a jab of his finger. The man blinked, and Jack wondered if it was a show of understanding.

'British,' Jack said in the same calm tone, but still the man stared. He changed his tack, opting for something that might make more sense. 'English.' Again he pointed to himself. 'English.'

This time the other man nodded. It was shallow, apparently all the energy he could muster in his rotten state. He had stopped shaking, but he still pushed himself into the hole. Jack hoped he realised he wasn't a threat. It occurred to Jack that he hadn't checked to see if anyone had spotted him, but it was too late for that now. If he was caught not returning the man then he could perhaps claim that he had only just spotted him and he was trying to work out what he was doing here, but he couldn't leave him now. His duty was to help people, all people, no matter who they were. This man may have committed some crime in the Reich, but now he was a human in need.

'I want to help,' he said, using both hands to gently beckon the man towards him. 'Help.'

The man just looked from Jack's hands to his face. His lethargic gaze swept back and forth a few times before he reached out a hand. Jack thought that the man was going to push him away again, but he grabbed hold of Jack's hand with a strength that he never would have imagined. He nodded to Jack. It only took a moment of hesitation before Jack remembered himself and pulled the man out from the hole. They scrabbled together as they had to work the man out of the awkward space and Jack almost slipped over. The smell was worse now that he was closer, but he tried to push it from his thoughts.

Eventually he came free. As the man uncurled, Jack could see that he was tall, over half a head taller than Jack, had he been able to straighten his back. Jack couldn't tell whether the curve of the man's spine was from being trapped in the hiding hole, or the hard work he had been forced to do as one of the Todt workers. Despite the hunch, the man's large eyes still looked into Jack's, filled with a sadness that Jack could never appreciate.

Jack turned to lead the man away, to where he wasn't yet sure, but he had to get him away from here and as far from the Germans as possible. The figure behind him didn't move, and Jack looked over his shoulder to see why. He stood by the hole, his lips moved as if trying to form words. When Jack stared blankly back, the other man gave an almost imperceptible shake of his head and then screwed his eyes shut. Jack felt an odd sense of relief that he was no longer under scrutiny. The man took a deep breath, then mumbled something that sounded vaguely familiar. It was like an electric light going on in Jack's mind.

'Help,' the man mumbled, remembering the word that Jack had used. He said the word again, and then pointed a long, bony finger back to the hole.

Jack thought quickly. The man couldn't have any possessions. 'The hole?' he said, moving back to the man. 'What are you trying to show me?'

Jack stopped dead. There was another shadow inside. It moved as he got closer, as the man had done before. Jack rushed closer and found a younger man inside, barely older than a boy, curled at the back. Jack hadn't realised that such young men were being used as part of the workforce on the island, although it was difficult to guess his age. He was severely malnourished and dirty, his ribs poking through his skin and his cheeks sunken and hollow. It gave the youth an ageless quality that placed him anywhere between adolescence and death, and Jack thought he wasn't far from the latter. He was struggling to pull himself out of the hole. Jack knelt down again and reached out a hand to steady him. Like the older man, the youth pulled back, uncertain, but took less time to come to terms with the idea that Jack was trying to help him.

He allowed Jack to gently drag him out of the hole. Jack expected it to be like dragging a sack of potatoes, but as the young man weighed very little at all, it was much more like lifting a small dog or a cat. Once the youth was on his feet he swayed, unsteady, as if standing on the deck of a ship.

Jack had no idea what he was going to do with them. He couldn't hand them over to the Germans. He could take them home, but then it was more likely that they would be found. If they were in his home, then there would be no doubt about who was responsible for giving them shelter and not returning them straight to the German authorities.

Jack needed help, and there was only one person left on the island he could turn to.

'I know just the place,' he said, hoping the sound of his voice would calm the men. 'An old farm up in the Vale. No one would find you there.'

Thankfully the Vale wasn't far, but they would have to walk. The safest route was over the fields away from the roads. That way they could try and avoid any German patrols that might be in the area. They didn't have time to lose and he started giving them directions. He was gentle with them, but the longer they took the more likely they would be caught.

Jack didn't know how Frederic would react when he saw them. Perhaps it was better not to tell him, keep him away from any blame should the Germans find them. He could hide them in one of the barns that was no longer used, but Jack trusted the man implicitly. Frederic hated the Germans more than anyone, and he would keep these men safe even if it cost him his life.

Chapter 33

19 August 1942
Peter's bicycle squeaked along the road, the tyres long since worn down or traded for something else. Like Jack's own bicycle it must have been uncomfortable, but what else could they do? The Germans had taken all the cars and it was still preferable to walking. Jack waved as Peter cycled past, but rather than continuing his journey he reined in next to Jack. He sighed heavily and checked the makeshift tyre of his bike to make sure that nothing was wrong with it.

'Why do you look so glum?' Jack asked, trying to inject some humour into his voice and apparently failing.

'Haven't you heard the news?' Jack knew that Peter was one of the men who printed the *Guernsey Underground News Service*, but neither of them would talk about that in public. Peter had contacts in all the major services on the island, and Jack supposed that he was Peter's police contact, though he had never willingly told the man anything.

'What's happened?'

'Another sorry excuse for a raid. This one was in Dieppe and the British have only gone and buggered it up again. You'd think by now they'd know what they were doing, but clearly not.'

Peter waved an apology at Jack.

'How do you know about that? Surely the BBC—'

'No, they didn't mention it,' Peter cut Jack off. It was the way they all talked on the island now, in clipped sentences just long enough for each other to know the meaning, but not enough to give anything away. 'Except in some kind of passing cypher, but they wouldn't talk about it anyway. It was a complete disaster.'

'Then, how do you know?'

'You know better than to ask questions like that. How do you think I know? Keep your ear to the ground and you'll find out things. But the less you know the better, right?'

Jack nodded. If the Germans caught them talking about British operations they would be taken in for questioning by the secret police. The less they knew, the more difficult it would be for the secret police to get anything out of them. Jack had already been questioned more times than he liked. He wasn't eager to end up in a locked room again.

'Have you heard the rest?' Peter asked, tilting his head in a way that was almost condescending.

'Go on then. We haven't got all day.'

'They're deporting the English. Well, they call it "evacuating", but you know full well what they mean. Only the English, mind. They're doing it as retaliation for someone killing some German prisoners in Turkey or something. The Germans are making lists of all the people who weren't born on the island now. No word on exactly who's going, but I thought you'd like to know.'

Jack nodded, the only reaction he could muster as he weighed up Peter's words. Jack's father was English, and he had not been born on the island; as far as he knew that put him on the Germans' list. He wondered about his family in England, and what they were like but, apart from the letter they had received, his mother had never told him about them. If the Germans sent him to Germany, then what would happen to Johanna?

Jack wasn't sure what to do, but the first thing he thought of was speaking to the inspector. He was the person best placed to help Jack. He thanked Peter, sending him on his way, and went to fetch his own bicycle. The rubber hosepipe he'd used for a tyre was perishing, but he needed to get to the station quickly.

*

He climbed the stairs outside the police station, practising the words he was going to say to the acting inspector every step of the way. When he got to the new chief's office, silently noting the way the electric lighting no longer worked upstairs, he knocked politely and waited.

A moment later the chief called 'come' through the door, and Jack turned the handle to enter. The room smelled of polish as if he had been polishing his immaculate uniform, and the candlelight cast everything in an orange hue. The new inspector was taking just as much pride in his position as the old man. Jack closed the door behind him and stood to attention the other side of the chief's desk. He threw a salute as the old man would have expected and waited until he was invited to speak. The Guernsey police force wasn't like the military, but they had their own code of practice. The new chief was a patient man, and he expected the same of his officers, as long as they were doing their jobs and not drawing the attention of the Germans. They couldn't allow that to happen again. Jack silently chastised himself for acting as if the old man was dead. There was still a chance he could return to lead the police force.

All these thoughts rushed through Jack's head while he waited for the chief to finish what he was doing. Eventually he pushed some paperwork to one side into a neat orderly pile.

'What can I do for you, Sergeant?' he asked, looking up at Jack. He was a younger man than the old inspector, but that also meant that he was less experienced. Unlike the old man, he had not spent any time at Scotland Yard, and his entire service record was in the Guernsey police.

'Well, sir,' he said, still standing to attention and holding his helmet in front of him in both hands. 'It's about the evacuations, sir.'

'Hmmm?' The inspector shifted a pair of reading glasses on the table in front of him, first moving them one way and then another. He then linked the fingers of each hand, leaning on his elbows, and looked Jack straight in the eye. 'I am aware of them, Sergeant. Our German counterparts tell me that they have decided to limit the influence of the English on the island. I can't say that we've had any trouble so far to warrant such a course of action but, well, they make the rules.'

'The thing is, sir.' Even though he had been practising what he wanted to say, it was still hard to get the words out. 'The thing is, my father was English. I was born in England, and my mother brought me back to the island a few months after I was born.'

The inspector stood up, walked around his desk and leant against it. It was as if it was an action designed to put Jack at ease. It didn't. Jack stayed where he was, still standing to attention, breathing deeply. He wanted to make a good impression, and he didn't know how the new inspector would react to his request. He was starting to second-guess his decision in coming here.

'And you're worried that you'll be on the list?'

'Yes, sir.' Jack nodded as he spoke, glad that the chief was quick on the uptake.

'I see. Yes, I can understand why that might be playing on your mind. It cannot have escaped your attention, Sergeant, that a number of the local police force are English born. They are just as likely to be on the Germans' list as you are. It's a concern, indeed.'

'Yes, sir.' Most of the other English members of the police force were now in a prison somewhere in France, and Jack had no intention of joining them. Of course, he had no way of knowing what the chief's opinion of the English was. Not everyone on the island had forgiven the British for abandoning them to the Germans. A wave of something rippled through Jack, turning his stomach upside down. 'My family—' he started.

The inspector lifted a hand to stall Jack and nodded his head in what he apparently thought was a consoling way. 'Let's keep it professional,' he said, turning back to his desk. 'I will have to see what I can do. I certainly can't imagine losing one of my best officers to such a derisory order from the German hierarchy. I will not allow them to evacuate any of my men to a prisoner of war camp. There are precious few of you left as it is. I will speak to my German counterpart and ensure that this matter is settled.'

Jack almost collapsed as air rushed into his body. He didn't realise how long he had been holding his breath. 'Thank you, sir.' The words spilled out of his mouth in a tumble, in between deep breaths. The chief didn't seem to notice.

'And I'll hear no more of it, Sergeant. This conversation is strictly confidential, you understand?'

'Of course, sir. Thank you, sir.'

'Thank me by doing your duty to the best of your ability, Sergeant, and keeping the Germans off our backs. I trust that will be all?'

'Yes, sir.' Jack threw another salute and wrenched the door open. Despite his relief, he couldn't have taken himself out of that room any quicker. It was another crisis averted, but how long would it be before the next one? The Germans were getting closer and closer to him and Johanna, and Jack knew that the occupation was only ever going to end up one way.

They had all been fooling themselves that the Germans would come and go. But an occupation was exactly that, the Germans wanted the islands for themselves, and it was only ever going to end in one way. They were here to stay, and they would get rid of the Islanders sooner or later.

Chapter 34

25 December 1942

Christmas under German occupation had long since stopped being something to look forward to and the third was no better than the previous two. Jack thought about getting a present for Johanna, but there was nothing left on the island that was worth buying. He had tried to barter some extra food from his colleagues in exchange for taking on more shifts, but understandably no one had been interested. He felt guilty that he couldn't provide for his family, and idly wondered what it must be like for those with children.

He had stopped at Johanna's flat on his way home from work, as he often did. She had got better at pretending to celebrate Christmas over the last couple of years and had even put some decorations in her windows, made from small bits of spare paper cut into patterns of holly and various other shapes. She had kissed him on the lips when he had got there, holding the moment for as long as possible, before she rushed back into the room.

'Here,' she said, passing him a large matchbox. Jack was just as surprised as his voice sounded.

'What is it?' he asked, turning it around in his hands and trying to guess.

'Something in return for your gift two years ago.' She kept the small wooden horse he had given her on her person at all times, and he wondered if anyone ever asked questions about it. 'Open it and see.'

He slid the compartment out of the matchbox. Inside was a small circuit with a couple of cables sticking out. 'What is it?' he asked again, feeling his face pulled into a confused frown.

She took it from him and adjusted the cables. 'It's a crystal radio set,' she said. 'It's not very powerful but on good days you should be able to hear the BBC broadcasts. I thought that your mother might like it.'

'It's wonderful, but how did you—?'

'One of the workers at the hospital showed me how. Speaking of which.' She fetched another package from the table. 'I asked around and managed to get a few extra rations. For you know who.'

Jack had told Johanna about the two Operation Todt workers he had rescued. He had expected her to be angry, but she had told him how proud she was of him. They didn't have much food to go around for themselves, so it was a great help to be given something to support those even less fortunate.

'Thank you,' he said. He would take it up to them later that day.

Jack wrapped up the few items in some newspaper, first folding them one way then another, trying to make it appear as if he wasn't carrying anything like food. Too many questions would be asked if anyone saw him with a mysterious package. After the police thefts people would wonder where he had got it from. He said goodbye to Johanna, returning her long kiss from before. She had been asked to work at the hospital over Christmas so that others could see their families. He would see her again when Christmas was over.

*

He walked up to his house as he had done many times before, but for some reason he stopped at the front door. It was closed, but it felt different, as if there was a dark cloud hanging over the place. He put it down to his imagination playing tricks on him, making him think the worst.

He pushed open the door and inside the house was dark. Perhaps that was what had caused his unease. He couldn't remember a time there hadn't been some kind of light in the house, either in his grandparents' room or the living room where his mother would usually be sitting, knitting or reading the newspaper. He had half expected to hear the sound of the wireless blaring out for all to hear as if his mother was deaf. Something about the volume of it gave her comfort; it was company when he wasn't there. Even still, she often carried on listening to it at volume even when he had come home, absorbed by whatever was being broadcast. But that was impossible now, at least until he gave her Johanna's gift.

There was no sound from the living room, not even her breathing or humming to herself. He thought about calling for her but maybe she had gone to bed with a headache or something. He turned the corner, peered through the doorway. A shape was slumped against the foot of the chair, sprawled across the floor.

'What have you done?' The words escaped his lips without him knowing. His mother had tried things before, but they had only been half-hearted efforts, a cry for attention or a moment of darkest despair. He rushed to where she was lying against the chair and fell to his knees. He placed a hand against her cheek, but there was no movement. She wasn't breathing. There wasn't even a shallow motion of her chest as he had seen many times before when he had checked just to make sure. There was no movement at all. A feeling of panic welled up inside him, but he pushed it away, trying to force his training to the forefront of his brain. He had to be objective. Follow his training. What would he do if it was someone else? He checked her airway to see if there was anything blocking it. There was nothing there.

She had taken something, something that had slowed her breathing and caused this. He didn't care where she had got it from, only that he had to stop it. He pulled her arm up and clamped his fingers against her wrist, feeling for a pulse. A bottle rolled away from her hand and under the chair. No matter how hard he pressed, there was nothing there. He pulled her closer, willing her to take a breath and the smell of her was strong in his mouth. It had been a reassuring scent that he had known since he was little, the smell of cleaning soap and love. She hung limply in his arms and he realised for the first time that tears were running down his cheeks. The only noise he made was a faint pleading sound that he had no control over. He thought about phoning the doctor, but it was too late, and he couldn't leave her.

He had always known that it would catch up with her one day. He had just hoped he could put it off as long as possible. She had never really talked about death, and like all children he had hoped that his mother was invulnerable. She had always been there, through school, through growing up and becoming a policeman, and then the war. Now she was gone and he couldn't think of anything else. The thought that he would never be able to speak to her again brought another wave of tears. He knelt there for some time, the only sound his own ragged breathing.

He knew he was in shock, but that was the only thing that made sense in his cluttered mind as it went from one thought to the other. He clutched at his mother as if holding her would make everything all right again. There had to be some kind of help, something someone could do, but how could they? He was too late, always too late. His mind warred with itself as guilt and anger fought for control.

He heard a gasp from the door. It could only have been Johanna. He must have forgotten something at her apartment.

It was strange that he could think so clearly about such mundane things at a time like this, yet when he tried to …

She scrambled to her knees beside him, but he didn't really register anything other than noise. He knew that she was talking to him, but none of the words made sense. She reached for his mother's arm. He was limp and numb, completely without control. She threw her arms around him, making soothing sounds as she did so. The corner of his mind that was still functioning realised that he would need Johanna now more than ever. She was the island he had built his life on.

*

27 December 1942
The evacuees arrived at the Gaumont cinema each with a small suitcase of whatever belongings they still possessed, forming lines and small pockets of people standing together, waiting for the inevitable. It struck Jack that but for a small incident of fate he too would be part of the massed gathering.

When the time came, he watched them heading down to the harbour past the White Rock and towards the merchant boat that rocked in the swell of the water. Wind whipped around the harbour, making it difficult for many to walk against the headwind. The German soldiers who waited by the pier checked each bag with a cursory look, throwing some of the belongings aside into piles that other Islanders would no doubt collect later, then ordered the men, women, and children to board. Jack heard one soldier apologise to a couple who were clutching each other as if trying to keep warm. As he watched, all he wished for was that there was something he could do to help them, something he could do to prevent eight hundred and fifty English residents of the island from being shipped to the continent.

The Germans didn't use their own Kriegsmarine ships, relying on merchant shipping to do their deeds for them, just as they relied on the local police. The mail boats and coal ships were moored up at the end of the pier in the White Rock, and the evacuees were marched down to them in narrow lines.

Jack wasn't the only one there to see the evacuees off. Islanders had come to the harbour, in ones or twos at first, then in larger groups. Many of them helped the evacuees with their bags, or provided them with support against the wind, where others sang songs of solidarity. Some of the German soldiers looked embarrassed at what they were doing, where others looked angry that their work was being interrupted. Should any of them choose to make trouble with the Islanders Jack was ready to step in, but so far they had simply glared from their posts.

Jack stood there by himself. He was numb, the events of the past few years finally taking their toll on him. He thought he should have been in the line of evacuees, maybe then he could do something to protect them, but so far fate had chosen that he should only pay witness to their suffering.

One of the soldiers marched over to Jack, a frown clearly visible under the line of his steel helmet. 'What do you want?' he asked in perfectly good English, singling Jack out from the crowd.

'I'm a policeman,' he said, showing his identification. 'I'm just making sure there's no trouble.' It was a lie, but only a small one. He couldn't exactly describe himself as being curious – that wasn't true either – but a part of him wanted to see what was happening with his own eyes. He knew it was part of the grieving process, forcing himself to witness pain, to see if he could still feel anything.

'Well, you're not needed. Go find some drunks to round up.'

'I have orders.' Jack's voice was pathetic, and he cringed as he heard it.

'Do you want to end up on the boat with them?' The soldier gestured over his shoulder with a thumb. Jack shook his head, without taking his eyes off the evacuees. In truth he had no idea where they were going, but none of the stories about the camps were particularly encouraging. His stomach lurched every time he thought of the possibilities, proving that indeed he could still feel something for these people. Only a few had ever returned to the island from captivity in Europe and even they were irrevocably changed. None of them had talked about their struggles, but they all had a haunted look deep in their eyes.

'Go on,' the German prompted again. 'Get lost!'

Jack turned and spotted a woman in the crowd carrying a small child in her arms. Her blonde hair was recognisable even though her habitual smile was pulled down into a deep frown. 'Maddy?' Jack called after her as she headed towards the row of people boarding the boats. 'Madeleine!'

She turned at the sound of his voice and a smile faltered on her face. 'Jack Godwin, are you a sight for sore eyes.'

He felt guilty that he hadn't seen her since that day in the department store over two years ago now; he had never plucked up the courage to go back and buy the shoes for Johanna, and life had got in the way. That was the way of things in this strange world.

Maddy had changed as much as they all had in the past years, her face lined, thinner and older now. The babe in her arms must have been about eighteen months old.

'What are you doing here?' he asked, reaching out for her.

She looked down at her child, then back up at Jack. 'My parents were English' she said, gesturing at the older couple ahead of her. 'And they don't want us here anymore.'

'Your daughter?' Jack asked. 'They can't.'

'Her father was English too. He was a soldier, remember? For some reason we're a problem to them.'

The soldier had caught up with Jack. He growled something at him in German, then switched to English. 'I told you to get lost,' he barked.

Maddy held out a hand for Jack and the tips of their fingers brushed against each other. 'Stay safe, Jack Godwin,' she said as the soldiers dragged her onto the ship. Jack held his hands up to the German, signalling he meant no harm, and backed off. From a safe distance he watched those boats as they sailed off into the horizon, wondering what would happen to the civilian prisoners on board.

1943

Chapter 35

January 1943

To say the winter was harsh would be to understate it. It wasn't just because of the weather, which came and went, providing at least some variation to daily life. It was the increasingly desperate situation. Under more than two years of German occupation life on the island had steadily declined. They had been rationing for some time now, but even that had become difficult. Even those who grew their own food were struggling. Jack had no such option; he relied on the rations like everyone else. At least now, there was only him to think about at home.

That was the other problem. He had never felt so alone in his entire life. He sat in the living room of what was now his house, looking out of the window. Occasionally he would glance at his mother's empty chair, but he didn't dare sit in it. He wanted to keep things as normal as possible, to deny the change. He had asked Johanna to move in with him and she had agreed. Whether it was just so she could keep an eye on him or not he wasn't sure, but the house did not yet feel like she lived there. When she was at work he spent his time sitting there in a daze, wondering what life could have been like if the Germans hadn't come.

Outside his house, it was quieter than usual. Either people's work had dried up, or they were too scared to go out with the Germans around. Jack knew how they felt. He did not want to see what had become of the island, but neither did he want to stay inside in the empty house. So he stayed in a sort of limbo near the window, looking out at the world and trying to avoid looking back into the emptiness. He knew he had responsibilities, but they drifted at the edge of his consciousness, never quite realised.

Every so often he saw someone walk past and he stared after them. He longed to talk to them but couldn't bring himself to run out and speak to them. What would he say? He had no words for what was happening, only the constant drone of his mind trying to process his feelings.

The clock on the other side of the room clicked and clicked, filling his mind with the infernal passage of time. Because it had belonged to his grandfather, he had not yet broken it up for firewood, but as the ticking continued he strongly considered it. With it would go a connection to his grandfather and he wasn't yet prepared to take that step. Eventually it dinged, signalling the hour. He was due to start the day shift soon and he would need to make his way to the police station.

A wave of relief hit him, knowing that he would be able to throw himself into his work and use it to forget about how his life had crumbled apart. He hadn't forgotten that he would need to visit the Todt workers at some point and take them some of his rations, but for now he could be allowed his indulgence.

Jack dragged himself up the stairs, past his mother's room with its permanently locked door and into his own. It was a mess, but then he didn't care. Clothes were left where he had taken them off and his bed sheets were draped half on the floor. Johanna had her own room next door and that gave a space of her own to keep tidy. The one semblance of order in the room was his uniform that hung next to the wardrobe. It was the last piece of pride he had left, and he took great care as he lifted it from the hanger to get dressed. When he left his house he looked a different man, no longer the scruffy heap he was before but beaming in his dark blue police uniform. Even though it was an act, it was one he relished. He had to put on the act to get through. For Johanna, if nothing else, life was still worth living. He had to prove that to himself.

*

He had been assigned to file paperwork in the station office. It had probably been decided as some sort of light duty for him, but he would much rather have been outside somewhere, possibly as far away from St Peter Port as possible. He had thought about asking for a different posting as he would have done before the war, but there was likely no chance of that now. He also didn't feel like going anywhere near the inspector's office, lest he ask Jack how he was.

William had taken it upon himself to assist Jack, even though, as far as he knew, Jack had not indicated in any way that he needed help. At least the old desk sergeant was a familiar face, a feature of the island that Jack thought would never change.

'Where do you think they're going?' William asked.

'Hmmm?'

'I said, "Where do you think they're taking the evacuees?"'

Jack knew that William was trying to distract him, but it wasn't a particularly great choice of alternative subject. 'I've no idea,' he said. 'Can we at least describe them as they really are? They've been deported, not "evacuated", and we've all heard the rumours of the camps. They'll end up there, then who knows?'

'Aye. Who knows indeed? How many have gone now? And we've heard nothing from them. Too many. At least we hear from the evacuees in England, thanks to the Red Cross. But the ones going the other way? I guess we'll find out if this damned war ever comes to an end.'

'There are new rumours you know?'

301

'There's always rumours. What else is there to do on the island apart from tell stories and spread rumours? I guess it helps some people get by.'

'No, these are serious. Not just idle gossip.'

'Go on, then.' Jack wasn't really sure why he was growing impatient. He knew he should be thankful for the conversation, but he would rather talk about the weather or something more mundane.

'They've built camps on Alderney. They say that the SS are holding people there.'

'Who's they?'

'I don't know really. The Germans?'

Jack scoffed. He had hoped that his work would distract him, but unfortunately it was proving to be one of those quiet days when they were left with nothing but conversation. He supposed it was strange to wish for something to happen to drag him from this reverie. But at least he wasn't locked up in a camp somewhere.

'Isn't it your mother's memorial today?'

Jack nodded. He hadn't been expecting William to bring it up.

'I was so sorry to hear about it. I'm sure if you asked the inspector would give you some compassionate leave.'

Jack nodded. It was his way of thanking William. He couldn't bear to open his mouth and utter something he would regret. For the first time in what seemed like hours William stood up and left him alone, but as he did so he turned to Jack. 'Let me know if you ever need anything. Anything at all.'

Nodding and gripping the pen in his hand as tight as possible was all Jack could do to stop the tears from flowing, as William disappeared from view.

*

Jack had asked Frederic to do something to honour Jack's mother, and he had agreed readily. It was the least he could do for Jack's help with the farm. When Jack saw what the man had created he felt a tightness in his chest, and reached out to grab Johanna's arm. She wrapped an arm around him, steadying him against her body. He nodded to her to indicate that he was all right. He wondered if he would always stay bottled up, just as his mother had closed off her feelings and thoughts from him. He would force himself at a later date to tell Johanna how much he loved his mother, and how much he loved her.

Johanna knelt, bunching up the hem of her dress around her ankles, and lay some camellias next to the memorial. The pink flowers were pretty against the little wooden bench in which Frederic had whittled Jack's mother's name. He wasn't sure where Johanna had got them from, but they were his mother's favourite, and he had no idea that Johanna had known that. The two of them had become closer than he realised, and he was quietly glad of that fact. He knew now that his mother approved of Jack and Johanna's relationship.

Johanna pulled out a letter from the pocket of her coat and handed it to Jack. 'Your mother left you something at the house. I thought now would be the best time to read it.'

It was a letter written in his mother's handwriting, the pretty scrawl he always had difficulty reading. Even after all these years, he still struggled with the way she wrote. Now the tears in his eyes obscured the letters even more and it took him several attempts to discern any meaning from it. It started with an apology, an apology for not being able to go on. He almost couldn't read any more as his throat constricted, but he pushed himself on.

She couldn't cope with the war anymore, and she had always known that she would not make it through. His mother didn't want him to blame himself, but how could he not? There must have been something he could have done. The letter told him a little of his father, as she had once promised him she would. He was not a soldier, as she had always said he was, but he had been a good man. He had been born in London and had objected to

303

the war, and that had eventually killed him. He had refused to fight, but still they had sent him to the front as a stretcher bearer, where he had died. His name had been James Godwin, and Jack's mother had loved him almost as much as she loved her son. She had done everything in her power to discourage Jack from following in his footsteps.

The day that he died, she said, was the day that she had also died. Something had changed in her that she had never been able to describe. That was why she had never been able to talk about Jack's father. Bringing him up in conversation broke her heart all over again, and while she wanted to forget him, she never could. Jack was very much like him, and James would have been proud of his son, and proud that he had found himself a good woman like Johanna, no matter what she had originally thought of her. She had been too scared to lose him, as she had lost his father.

The letter was signed with a loving kiss and a final message that Jack could now live his life without worrying about her, and live it fully. He pushed it inside the pocket of his jacket with the other letters that he kept there.

It struck him that now that his mother was … gone … he no longer had any reason to stay on the island. Maybe he and Johanna could find a way to escape to the mainland. They could live their lives together in England as his mother and father should have done, before the war had taken him away from her. He held Johanna's hand as he closed his eyes, thinking what it would be like for them to live together in peace.

Chapter 36

February 1943

'Sarge! Jack! There you are.' William was almost out of breath as he cycled up to Jack, and the words spilled from his mouth in one quick burst. His breath turned to steam in the cold. 'I've been looking all over for you.'

'What is it? Calm down.'

The desk sergeant doubled over, putting his hands on his knees and taking wrenching lungfuls of breath. It was another minute or so before he spoke again, still desperately trying to get the words out between breaths. Jack wasn't exactly hiding from the world, but he had deliberately cycled out to the west of the island to get some fresh air. He had spent too long moping in his house.

'The Germans,' he said, and Jack felt his heart rate rising. 'They know!'

'Wait,' Jack said, losing control and raising his voice. He put his hands on the other man's upper arms and shook him. Jack wasn't normally prone to manhandling people, but he needed to know. 'What? What do they know?'

'They know that Frederic has been hiding Todt workers. They're on their way there now.'

Jack pulled away. He thought about lying, but knew it was too late for that. 'How?' he breathed. It was all he could manage.

'They know how many are missing, and the rest wasn't much of a leap of imagination.'

'But how? How could they know who was hiding them?'

'Come on, Jack. They've got their eye on everything! They watch our every move, and they've been checking our rations, totalling everything up. Frederic had been claiming rations for family that had passed away, and the markets had been helping him. He didn't report the deaths of some of his livestock. It's only surprising it took the Germans so long to work out what was happening. They've been searching for them for months.'

Jack cursed. He had known all along that it was stupid. But after what had happened to Henry and David, he couldn't sit by and watch the workers suffer too. They had thought they were playing the system, that no one would notice, but he should have been more careful. A part of him had always known the day would come; the Germans had a way of catching up with everything like a schoolmaster you had thought you had outsmarted, but really knew what you were up to all along. He would head up to the farm and help Frederic to move them somewhere else, then he would have to find Johanna. The time had come for them to get away from here, and he would think about how on his way to the farm. He should have done something earlier, but maybe he wasn't strong enough after all.

He grabbed his bicycle from the wall and threw himself over the saddle. If asked later he could just say that he had been responding to a call and ask William to cover for him. He had already put himself at risk by coming to find Jack, and Jack was sure that he wouldn't mind going a step further.

Right now, that was far from his thoughts. He rode so hard up Vale Road, his legs pumping, that the bicycle started to wobble on its makeshift tyre. He sped up past a group of German soldiers marching the opposite direction along the road, and as he went, there was a bang like the crack of a rifle. He tipped forward from the bicycle as the front tyre collapsed, spinning the handlebars, landing in the gutter next to the road. The bicycle spun over itself and landed about a metre away. He breathed heavily, winded, as he looked back the way he had come. Two Gewehr rifles pointed in his direction as the German soldiers leered at him. They couldn't have known where he was going, even if he had been riding unusually hard.

He sat up in the gutter and checked himself over. He was unharmed, but maybe a little bruised. One of the rifles lowered, but the other stayed pointed at him. Jack's heart was racing. He raised his hands slowly, so that the Germans did not think he was reaching for anything. As soon as his hands were in the air the soldier with his rifle raised burst out laughing and let the rifle drop to his side. It dawned on Jack what had happened then. He pulled himself out of the gutter, grumbling at his bruises and patting himself down. The hosepipe that he had wrapped around the front wheel of his bicycle had come loose; the clip that held it in place had snapped off. At speed the clip had caused the sound of a gunshot.

The Germans, still laughing, turned and continued on their march back into town. With a grimace, Jack knelt down to reattach the hosepipe to his bike. It was looser than it had been before, but it should last until he got to the farm. When he was there, he would try to find another method. This time he cycled more carefully, avoiding potholes in the roads, and keeping his speed to a safe level. The minutes dragged interminably on, the wheels turning like the hands of a clock.

Eventually the gate to the farmlands came into view at the end of the road. It was a welcome sight, like coming home after a hard day's work. By the time he reached the gates his bike had finally given out, and he threw it to the ground as he continued the rest of the journey on foot. The old barn behind the farm-house was abandoned. It was so far from the main road, that

Jack suspected that even the Germans didn't really know of its existence. From the look of the place it would need a lot of work to get it up and running again, and it had been enough to keep them from it. Until now.

'Bobby?' Jack used the name that they had given the refugee. He didn't know if anyone was listening, and he had become used to it. It had seemed like a good joke at the time, 'Bobby' for the nickname people gave policemen, but right now he didn't feel like laughing. They hadn't given Bobby's son a name, but the young man had not yet found his voice and spent the majority of his time hiding in the basement underneath the farmhouse. Eventually they had managed to work out that the two men were Russian refugees, captured and sent here from the Eastern Front. They could have gone into town. Frederic had managed to find Bobby some fake papers, but they didn't risk it very often and he doubted they would have done so on a cold day like this.

'Frederic?' Jack called as he moved out to the where the field joined the farmhouse. The field was empty and eerily silent. Jack searched around the house for the farmer, but he couldn't find him. There was a half-eaten meal on the kitchen table and Jack's stomach rumbled at the sight of the food, but he didn't have time for that now.

Turning, he ran back out to the driveway. He hadn't noticed it before in his exhaustion, but there were deep grooves in the mud that led up to the building. They were wet, dark brown and fresh. A car or truck had driven up here in the last few hours, then it had gone away again. The only people allowed to use cars on the island were the Germans, or the police who drove for them. If either one had been here then that was it for Bobby and his son. It was all over. They would return to the camps and then there was nothing Jack would be able to do help them.

If the Germans knew who had put them there, then Jack would be in serious trouble. He looked around the farm for evidence that he had been there, rushing from the barn to the main house, but the only visible sign were his boot prints in the mud. He reasoned that they could be from anyone. There was no way anyone could know he had been there unless they had seen him, and the fields around the farm were empty.

He had to find Johanna and warn her what had happened, then they could try and find a way off the island. There had to be someone with a boat they could use. He thought of the fishermen he knew, but he wasn't sure who he could trust. He looked at his father's wristwatch. Johanna would be arriving home by now.

He fetched Frederic's bike, abandoned by the side of the house, and rode back out onto the lane, making sure to cycle through the grooves that had been scored in the mud by the Germans' vehicle. He wasn't sure if they would bother to track him, but it wasn't worth adding any more risk.

The bicycle rocked as he pedalled along the road, the thought of Johanna the only thing driving him on. His front wheel was struggling to stay centred and he had to keep wrestling the handlebars back to the middle. He kept going, even though his lungs screamed at him to give up. He wouldn't. He would never give up on Johanna.

The chimneys of St Peter Port were just coming into view as the tyre of his bike gave out again, throwing him to the road. As he stood up he saw that the hosepipe was ripped into shreds. It would never wrap around the bike again and the wheel was almost bent in half. He would have to make the rest of the way on foot. He could hear Johanna's voice on the wind, calling him closer.

*

12 February 1943

He didn't think he would have much breath left when he got home. The sun was lowering towards the horizon and it had taken him far longer than he would have liked as he opened the front door to the house and it squealed on its hinges. As he had done at the farmhouse, he searched for Johanna, but she was nowhere to be seen. There was a note on the kitchen table written in Johanna's handwriting.

Jack
They didn't give me much time to write this. They have come for me. Deporting me with the next group of English. I love you with all my heart. Johanna xx

Jack almost collapsed into the chair in front of him, but something forced him out and back into the world. Why had he left her on her own? She had always been his priority. The Germans had learnt their lesson from giving the evacuees time to prepare. Now all sense of law and order had been taken from the island. Why had he not gone to her first rather than the farm? All their plans, everything they had been through and Doctor Abbott's help had been for naught.

A few seconds later Jack's boots pounded on the dry earth as he sprinted up the path, thumping with each footfall. It had been a terrible mistake and he wouldn't make it in time …

Chapter 37

All he could see was the faint light of a lantern illuminating the boat as it rose and fell in the water, moving away from the harbour. There were a few silhouettes on board, some wearing the distinctive steel helmet of the Wehrmacht. He could just about make out a shape in between them, scrabbling towards the back of the boat. Was it a woman? A hand reached out to the shore, then disappeared into the darkness.

A few moments later he faintly heard the slapping of boots as they ran along the pier. The sound was like a memory to him, a faint echo at the edge of his thoughts. All he could perceive was the darkness that surrounded him, drawing in with every passing second.

He lay there staring out to sea, ignoring his physical pain as the other pain was overbearing. Johanna had gone. The Germans had taken her and he had been too slow, too self-absorbed to save her. He could imagine her, fighting against the hold of the Wehrmacht soldiers, desperately trying to claw her way back to land. They would overpower her, as they had overpowered everything else. His face was wet, whether from the spray or from the redness that was building at his eyes, he couldn't tell.

Strong hands grabbed him under his shoulders and hauled him

to his feet, as pain flared in his side. He could feel something sharp rubbing and it almost made him pass out. Dizziness racked him and he vomited across the floor. The nearest man said something in German, but the intent was clear. The big German was angry, and he pulled Jack up the pier, muttering under his breath. All Jack's strength was gone, and his feet dragged along behind him as they carried him to his fate. He wanted them to leave him to die on the pier, leave him with his guilt. The soldier's MP40 strapped around his neck banged against Jack, the metal stock adding to his bruises. On another day Jack could have grabbed it from him, but he didn't have the strength. What good would it do anyway? It wouldn't bring her back.

At the end of the pier a group of Germans waited and his captors stopped him in front of an Oberleutnant he recognised. The man was atypically friendly for the Germans, but as he threw a cursory glance over Jack a scowl crossed his features. In that moment Jack knew that this man was his enemy. Since the beginning he had been wary of the Germans. Their ideals and motivations were so very different from his, but for the first time in the past couple of years it actually struck him. They were his enemy and they could no longer live together.

*

The cell was dank and cold. In his time as a policeman he was no stranger to prison cells, but he had never expected to be on this side of the door. Once was bad enough, and that had only been a locked room. A flash of sympathy burned in his mind as he thought of those he had put in this cell and others like it. He wasn't like his captors. While he too had been upholding the law, his law was a *good* law, not a law that segregated people, manipulated them and treated them like animals. He could never treat people as they treated the Jews and the Todt workers, like some kind of subspecies, expendable and inhuman. Only an evil mind could countenance such behaviour. They were sick, even though some of them put up a facade. He couldn't bring himself to think that they all believed the same things, but he had seen enough evidence of it. For things to have come to this, they must do.

He had too much time to think, he told himself. He wouldn't be surprised if he went mad with only these four walls for company. They had left him overnight and he hadn't slept. He didn't know how anyone slept in these cells.

If he had possession of his diary, he would have written to himself, tried to articulate his feelings. It was even more difficult trapped in his own mind where the emotions crashed against the part of his consciousness that told him he had to fight, to understand what was happening to him. There was a feeling deep in his stomach that he couldn't explain to anyone else. It was a sickness, but even that wasn't close enough. He had no common reference for it. It was the strongest feeling he had ever had, yet it was as abstract as anything. It was similar to how he had felt when he had first met her. There was that sense that something profound was happening, a tickling at the back of his mind telling him that there was something special about this person, mixed with a feeling of joy. Every time he thought of that moment, his stomach lurched and the sickness took him further and further into himself, deeper and deeper to a darker place he never knew existed until now. Sometimes it manifested as a longing, like a hunger in his chest telling him he needed something desperately in order to live, but stronger, more visceral.

He knew it as love but saying that word, even in the confines of his mind, seemed somehow inadequate, somehow crass and unfeeling. There didn't exist a word in the English language to explain this.

He thought of his mother. At least she wouldn't be at home wondering where he had got to. There would be food spoiling in the house, precious rations. His stomach rumbled at the thought. He had no way of knowing what time it was, but he had been in that cell long enough now to realise he had nothing left on the island to stay for. As every second ticked by Johanna was being taken further away from him.

He had known for a long time that this day would come, but he had tried to deny it to himself, to everyone around him. In the depths of his mind he had always feared it. He wasn't meant to be happy. Despite all that he had and all that he had tried to do for others, to be a good person, to help those in need and have a kind word. Perhaps it was because of something he had done, mistakes he had made as a child, and maybe they stuck with a person, maybe God was counting. Some people just ended up that way, alone and unhappy. He thought then of his mother. She had been the same. Could it be something in their family line?

Wallowing made him feel better in an obscure way, as if by making it all his own fault he could understand it better, take responsibility for it and in a way control it. He knew if he said that to anyone else then they would think him mad, but it made a certain abstract sense to him. It didn't do him much good languishing in this cell, but at least he managed to keep his thoughts from the images of horrors that lingered behind his closed eyelids.

*

The heavy steel door opened with a creak of rusty hinges. When he had been on the other side, it had an entirely different meaning for him. Now it brought only fear. A couple of Germans entered the room, clear from the Wehrmacht uniforms of the Feldgendarmerie. Neither of them were men Jack recognised, but they had the same air of authority that all Germans on the island had, the tight lips and gaze that suggested they were in charge and that the world was a better place for it. Jack could tell they were judging him without them even opening their mouths. The true Aryan race looking down on all others and deeming them unworthy. They had been brought up that way, and they did it without even thinking. For even if he wasn't unworthy naturally, he had fallen in love with a Jew, and that was anathema to them, impure, dirty. It was all there in their look, the purity of hatred.

Was Henrik the same? Would he hate Jack now, after everything that had happened? He knew the man was different. But he had done nothing to stop these men from destroying the island, from deporting the Jews and those who thought differently. He blamed Henrik just as much as he blamed all the others. They should have resisted.

The two Germans lifted Jack up from where he slouched against the floor, carrying him out of the cell. His feet were sore from running. He realised then how a poor diet and lack of nourishment had affected his body. Jack was weak and failing, both in body and mind. They placed him on a chair in what looked like an interrogation room and left him there without locking the door. They must have known he was incapable of running. There was no escape for him.

A few minutes later a familiar face appeared in the doorway. The man was taller than Jack remembered him, more imposing than the first time they had met.

'Henrik?' Jack tried to say through broken and parched lips. The word came out more as a groan than the man's name.

'Yes,' he replied, his voice loud in the confines of the room. 'I thought you may be surprised to see me. It took a lot to convince the guard to let me in.'

He walked around the perimeter of the room, glancing between Jack and the walls that contained him. His steps were calm and confident as they always were, and his pressed green uniform was a stark contrast to the dirty, mouldy grey-brown of the walls. It struck Jack that this must have been how Henrik conducted his interrogations. With an effort of will Jack forced himself up into a sitting position, if only to stop Henrik from looking down at him, as the rest of his countrymen did.

'What the hell are you doing here?' He almost had to stop between each word, the effort croaking and painful. He didn't want to talk any more than he wanted to be in that cell. Henrik stopped in front of him and regarded him for a time, his breathing faintly rising his chest.

'I had to see you,' he said, eventually, after what seemed like hours. 'To see what had become of you.'

'And?' Jack asked, unexpected venom in his voice. He had never spoken an angry word to Henrik before, but now he knew what the man was really like, it felt good. Henrik had been playing him all along, had been no better than his countrymen and the way they treated people. 'Are you happy?'

'You have every reason to be angry. I understand, but I did not do this to you. I told you something once, something that if heard by the wrong people could see me exactly where you are now. We are only enemies because of a war neither of us wanted, a war neither of us wished to take part in.'

'Why are you here?' Jack asked again. This time he felt less angry.

'To get you out of here.'

*

Jack knew the shock was showing on his face, but he didn't have the energy to hide it anymore. 'Why?' he asked.

'If I can do some good in this war, then it is this. I owe it to you, I owe it to these islands. I see what my people are doing, I've seen what they are doing to the Fatherland and I despair. But I am outnumbered, and they are as dangerous to me as they are to you.' He suddenly jerked his head towards the cell door as if he had heard movement from outside. 'I've said too much.'

Jack felt a pang of sympathy for the man in that moment. He had forgotten that not all of the Germans were the same, not all of them were Nazis. Although he still didn't really understand how any of them could have allowed the Nazis to take over. Maybe it was easier to find one's objection after the fact. He could certainly say that was the case as far as he was concerned. He had been too much of a coward to do anything before, and now it was too late.

Henrik placed a hand on Jack's shoulder. It was unexpectedly warm and comforting. 'We have to go,' the German whispered. 'Now.'

'No. I don't want your help.' It was the first solid decision he had made in some time, and it was the correct one.

'Jack?' Henrik protested, but Jack stopped him with a shake of his head.

'No. I can't just run away. They've taken Johanna. I have to go after her. I couldn't live with myself if I escaped and somehow made it to England if she was somewhere else. My life is nothing without her.'

Henrik nodded and pursed his lips. 'I don't know how to help you,' he said, a frown crossing his brow.

'Just make sure they send me with the other evacuees.'

'We will see each other again,' Henrik responded. 'I am certain, although I do not know when. After the war, when the world is a different place.'

'After the war?' Jack asked. 'How can you be so sure?'

'It is coming. I don't know how long it will take, but things are changing in Berlin. Things are not going as well as they pretend. The Eastern Front has cost the Fatherland dearly. The Russians will soon be in Germany, I am sure. Then Hitler will have no choice but to surrender.'

Jack felt a small glimmer of hope, but then became angry with himself. There was no hope here. The Nazis had ruined everything, ruined the island and taken the woman he loved. It didn't matter what happened with the war. His only hope was to get off the island and to find another path. He wanted to fight them, wanted to make them feel his pain. Even Henrik was not completely free from his anger, despite his help, for he had been an accomplice.

'I hope you're right,' was all Jack could think to say. It was all he could do to control his anger and stop himself from shouting. He switched from rage to despair in a heartbeat and back again. The German held his hand out for Jack, a faint smile playing across his lips that Jack knew neither of them truly felt. Their roles had been reversed, and somehow it wasn't fair. Henrik should have been the one on that boat.

'I wish you all the best, Jack Godwin,' he said, shaking Jack's hand in a way that conveyed more meaning than either of them could say. Despite everything they were friends and no war could alter that. 'I will be eternally sorry for what has happened to your people and that I could do nothing to prevent it. This is not what I wanted.'

Jack could feel a tear pulling at his eye. It was easier to be angry with them than to allow himself to understand that many of the Germans were suffering just as much as the Islanders were. He wished the German would go before he broke down completely.

'Thank you,' he said as his friend left the room. He would need that hope to get him through until the end. If soldiers like Henrik thought that the war was close to ending, then maybe there was some hope in that. He would hold on to Henrik's words even in the darkness that was sure to come.

*

They came for him an hour or so later, without ceremony, carrying him from the cells as if he was a dangerous criminal and prone to run at any moment. 'Mr Godwin,' the major had said. Jack didn't have the energy to correct Obertz that he should address him as sergeant. 'As you are English you will be put on the next boat to France. It is better this way, better than dragging it through the courts and extending your sentence. Harbouring a

318

Jewess and assisting in the escape of OT members is a serious crime. You should have known that we would be able to track a German citizen's history, to discover their dark past, no matter how much you try and misdirect us. As for the labourers, your trust was misplaced. Your friend, the farmer, told us everything under interrogation. You are lucky that your service record is exemplary, otherwise your punishment would be more severe.'

In a way, Jack was fortunate that the Germans were still deporting others from the islands. A ship waited for them, one that looked very much like the mail ships that used to service the island. It was moored at the end of the pier where every previous evacuation had taken place.

They marched him down to the boat, his hands bound behind him, cutting into his thin wrists. He remembered that Hitler had ordered all prisoners to be bound after some German soldiers had been killed during an escape attempt. The shackles pulled against his skin, but it was a small price to pay in exchange for being free from that cell. He closed his eyes and breathed in the salty sea air of St Peter Port, relishing the scent of his home. He wasn't sure when he would smell it again, if he ever would, and he wanted to store the memory. Whatever happened he would know that his home was still there, somewhere across the sea, waiting for him to return.

The soldiers he had come to be so familiar with walked him up the gangway like a criminal. He was used to being the one doing the marching, and he felt a strange sense of empathy with all the people he had ever arrested. Had they felt as thoroughly rotten as he did now? He turned to follow another group into the hull, but a rifle butt struck him in the stomach. He doubled over, breathing heavily, trying to will away the tears of shock that dripped from his eyes.

'No,' the soldier said simply. Perhaps the only English word he knew. Before Jack had a chance to regain his composure and clear his eyes the man pushed him down into the hull. They were separating men and women on either side. A small group of soldiers stood between them, making sure there was no way they could be overpowered, holding their weapons out in front of them. None of the evacuees dared move closer to them and there was a clear line of delineation in the middle of the ship. Jack was one of the last men to be taken on board and the soldiers shouted orders to each other, ending the chain of commands with the Kriegsmarine who were operating the vessel.

He had only been on a ship a few times, despite living on the island almost his entire life. And even then it had only been a small fishing boat or dinghy. He remembered then that he didn't really have the legs for it. The swell and buck of the ship knocked him sick, and he did his best not to throw up. He tried to shuffle towards the gunwale, but as soon as he moved a soldier shouted at him in German and gestured with his submachine gun. He held his breath and swallowed slowly in an attempt to bring the sensation under control. He had often wondered about visiting France and taking a holiday on the continent, but he had never had the money or means before now. The fates had a strange sense of humour and he was starting to suspect that they were not fond of him. The northern coast of France was a blur against the horizon. It would be a long trip.

The hour had now come to leave the island. He fingered the letters in his pocket, the only possessions he had been allowed to take from home. There was nothing left there for him.

HMS *Limbourne*

October 1943

There were shapes floating in the water. At first they looked like logs, but then with a sick feeling Henrik realised what they were. Hundreds of bodies floating there as if they had gone for a swim and forgotten to stop. Nearby, one of them was rocking against the sand as the tide deposited it on the beach. Its navy uniform almost blended in with the water, pale flesh the only thing standing out against the blue.

They had heard the sounds of gunfire in the seas to the west of the island, but it must have been a terrible engagement to bring about such destruction. Bodies had occasionally washed up before but never more than one at a time.

'*Mein Gott.*' There were no words to describe what they were seeing. He had never seen so many bodies before. The war had never really come to the island, but now it felt like it was finally here.

Those who saw the spectacle rushed down to the beach to collect the bodies, hoping against hope that they would be able to do something. The bodies were badly decomposed, far beyond help. Their caps and identification tags identified them as the crews of the HMS *Limbourne* and HMS *Charybdis*. The fact that

321

two Royal Navy ships had been sunk would not sit easily with the Islanders. It wouldn't have been the same had they been Germans.

The thought of the British coming to their rescue now seemed further away than ever, and his compatriots on the island would take this as yet another victory. The Islanders wept over the dead as if they were their own children, lost at sea in this great, terrible war. Henrik felt only sympathy in that moment. No one deserved to die like that.

1944

Chapter 38

March 1944

It was the first time Jack had ever seen a train that wasn't a picture or a model. As a child some of his friends had been interested in trains, but he had never really understood it. They were something odd and alien to him, as the islands didn't have their own railway until the Germans had built a narrow gauge to move supplies up to the building sites for the fortifications. He had what he approximately described as a year in a small camp in France. There had been some other Guernsey folk there, but he had withdrawn into himself, refusing to talk to them. They reminded him too much of a life before. But now he was being moved, he wondered where they were, what had happened to them.

His mother had once told him about the time when after his father had died, the two of them had caught the train south to Weymouth to get the ferry to Guernsey. That had been the only time before now when Jack had travelled by train and he had been too young to remember it. He wasn't sure how he felt about the steam-fuelled beast. It was loud and something about it seemed on the verge of exploding any minute. He wondered whether if he understood better how they worked he might feel a little less apprehensive about them, but the most disconcerting thing was

325

not knowing where they were taking him. Like everything else, the train was run-down and barely operating. Those who seemed to know how to fix it had disappeared. It gave Jack no comfort that the situation in occupied France was no better than it was in the islands.

He hugged his knees closer to his body, trying to force some warmth into them. It was cold in the cattle cart they were moving him in, colder than anything he had experienced before, even the cold island winters. His new uniform chafed more than his police uniform ever had, and not just because he was forced to wear it. He knew what he was doing was right this time, that he had finally chosen the correct path. He still hoped to find Johanna here somewhere in the camps. He couldn't give up that hope. Even if they were imprisoned, they would be together. They had to fight against the Nazis, fight them every step of the way to stop what they were doing to the world. He would never forget and never forgive them for what they had done to his home, and to Johanna. He had thought he would find David out here, or someone else, but that had proven a false hope. He felt a pang in his stomach then, a deep sickly feeling that quickly turned to anger.

Jack wondered what could have happened to him had the Germans not started the war. Would he and Johanna have got married, had children? Would they have just been allowed to be happy together? On the other hand, he would never have met Johanna and come what may he would always be glad for that.

A few soldiers came and closed the door to the box carriage he was sitting in and the press of bodies pushed against him. His sense of smell had numbed, but he still gagged at the scent of humanity, that raw unwashed stench that covered them all. He couldn't remember the last time he had washed.

He could have gone with the Guernsey militia in the beginning, gone to join the army, but then his relationship with Johanna would never have progressed as far as it had. She may have been sent to the camps earlier, and his mother and grandparents would still have died. No, in that way this was better than having a rifle in his hand. He had known since the initial evacuation of the island that he had made the right decision not to join the army. Even though he had now seen first-hand what the Germans were capable of, had now seen the labour camps, the so-called evacuations, he knew he was right. He couldn't run away. He would fight the Germans on his own terms, by finding Johanna and surviving. The Germans wanted to change the world and rebuild it in their image.

His mind rocked as the steam train chugged away from their camp, taking them further into the Reich. The thousand-year Reich. In his mind he was fighting an idea, not a nation.

*

Jack pushed himself through the new camp, like a fish through water. Everywhere he turned there was another person pushing back against the tide. He had been moved through a number of camps now, passed from one livestock carriage to another. At first they had been refugee camps, small and temporary, but this place felt more *permanent*. Its walls were taller, the look of its inhabitants more sullen. It had the air of a small town, the solidity of purpose. They were somewhere in the north of Germany, and here he hoped he would find Johanna.

He looked through the crowd of faces to see if there was anyone he recognised, anyone he could cling on to. There were faces of people he recognised, but as he drew closer to them they were either swept away by the crowd, or his mind realised his eyes had been deceiving him. He searched and searched until he finally had to accept that he was on his own. He had been assigned to a hut, but he would not go in there. He couldn't bring himself to believe that even amongst all these evacuees there were none of the people who had been taken from Guernsey.

He looked at the other inmates and wondered whether he

looked as they did. He put his hands to his thick black beard and felt the lice wriggling underneath. His clothes were no better than the ones he had been wearing when he had arrived in France, thin and threadbare. He had the postcard his mother had received in his pocket. It was dog-eared and well read. He kept it there alongside the letter she had written him. They were his only possessions. He felt for another letter, hidden in the stitching of his shirt, a letter that Johanna had once written him, telling him how much she loved him. He didn't need to see it to read it. He knew its contents by heart, and he recited them to himself as a sort of mantra. He could hear the voices. Johanna's voice. Once comforting. Now only a haunting memory. She was there somewhere in this world, if only he could find her.

There was a fire across the compound, and he shuffled closer, ignoring the smell of smoke and something else, something bitter he couldn't put his finger on. He was thankful for the warmth and for the first time in over a year he felt energy in his limbs. Even though the fire was dying down, it comforted him and reminded him of the fireplace at home. Oh, how he longed to be sitting in that room now, with the clock he had hated, wasting away the seconds as if they weren't precious.

There was a shape in the edge of the fire. He reached out thin, pale fingers for it, not caring that the heat burned his hands. They were weak and useless, covered in blisters and sores, so what difference would it make? The shape was wooden, carved from a larger piece but now charred and blackened around the edges. The density of the wood had kept its shape, but it had diminished in size as it had been forgotten. It was the shape of a horse, a wooden horse. The horse he had carved for Johanna on that Christmas so many years ago.

He dropped onto his knees next to the fire, crying out a curse. A pair of guards dragged him away as he was too weak to kick and scream. He never once let go of the horse, that last precious remnant of a life once lived.

The Island

December 1944

The SS *Vega* glided its way into the harbour in St Peter Port, its light grey hull reflecting the struggling winter sun. The giant red cross painted on its prow was a welcome sign to the Islanders who still struggled to live in Guernsey, but not so for the German soldiers who were still stationed there. Even after all this time they had not come to live together in harmony. Even though they were all cut off from the rest of the world by the war that had passed them by.

In a way Henrik was thankful for that. He and the other Wehrmacht soldiers who waited on the pier for the arrival of the Red Cross ship had been given what had initially been an ideal posting. Some had been angry at being kept from the glorious victory of the Reich, but he had understood from early on exactly what it meant; it had kept him from the fighting, and for the time being at least, it had kept him breathing. Call him a coward, he didn't care. Life was too short, and he had already seen too many friends die to care about anything like glory or honour. Those words were cheap in the face of mortality. He was just a man and like so many others he wanted to live.

As the *Vega* slid against the pier and the crew called down to the mooring points, he thought of what the ship contained and what it meant for them. Despite being an ideal posting, things had become increasingly difficult on the island and both his fellow Germans and the natives were on course for the worst winter yet. Rations had helped make what they had last longer, but it hadn't been enough. Both governments had resisted help while the war was going on, but the situation had grown perilous, the more isolated the islands had become. His uniform no longer fitted him and there was no thread with which to take it in. It hung loosely on his arms as he followed his compatriots to the *Vega*'s lowering gangway to help unload the ship.

When they had been given the order to unload the ship it had struck Henrik as cruel. And now, faced with the reality of the situation, it felt even worse. The supplies on the *Vega* were needed for the Islanders, but none of them would be given to the Germans. As his superiors had refused to surrender, the Red Cross had decided that they were still at war, and these supplies were only for the other Islanders. The soldiers would have to starve. He wasn't sure there was even any ersatz coffee left. They had almost given everything and for what? Hitler's ridiculous idea was in tatters and it wouldn't be long before the Allied forces came to the island to take them all.

*

Henrik had been coming to the church for a few years now, on and off when his duties would allow him to. He had never been particularly religious, especially after the efforts of the National Socialists had forced many religions underground and his parents had stopped talking about their beliefs, but coming here gave him some sense of comfort. Maybe it was the comfort of being close to people. Maybe because they were all equal here, all suffering together, closer than in the confines of their billets and homes. Many had come and gone in his time on the island, and his billet at the Collinette hotel now seemed more deserted than ever. He only saw the other Germans who lived there when they were on duty together, and they were sullen and quiet. Here in the church everything seemed different.

At the end of the service the locals gathered together at the front of the church and joined hands. Then they started singing. He recognised the words but didn't know their meaning. 'Should auld acquaintance be …' At first he was unsure, but the Islanders at the front of the church were holding their hands out for him and the others. His countrymen looked about awkwardly. But something made him jump up from the pew and step towards the singing group. In between words they smiled at him at beckoned him to them. His feet took him willingly, finally embracing the Islanders.

A tear threatened to fall onto his cheek, but he didn't care. They were all together in this, both German and Islander. The war had affected them all and through it they had found some common ground.

1945

Chapter 39

15 April 1945

He had lost track of how long he had been in the camp. The days merged into one seemingly endless world of torment. Even the nights brought no relief, only the cold realisation that they were doomed there, to die from starvation, forgotten like animals. At first the pain had grown, but it had reached its crescendo and there was nothing else left to feel, no more pain to add to that which he already felt. It brought about a sense of numbness, as if he were seeing the camp through external eyes. He no longer had a capacity to empathise with his fellow prisoners. When one shadow of a man fell in the dirt before him, the wheals visible through the scraps of curly hair that still clung to his scalp, Jack simply stared. The man he had been would have knelt in the dirt if only to provide comfort, but that man had gone.

He had thought that the island had been isolated, lost in the middle of the Channel. But this was something worse. The surrounding sea had given some sort of hope, hope that whatever happened there was a chance of escape. In the camp they were caged, like animals. There was no hope of escape. The only way Jack would ever get out of there was if the war ended and they decided that he was no longer a threat to them.

Without work to occupy his mind, Jack had fallen into a stupor. Days would go by without so much as movement, as he lay on a pallet and forced his mind to ignore the torment. If he had thought that the guards would drill them; he had been wrong. They no longer cared for the inmates, nor did it seem the prisoners cared for themselves. They had lost all hope.

Now even most of the German guards had gone. They had heard the sounds of fighting in the distance, the rumbling of war machines carried by the wind. Jack had thought it might have been his stomach protesting for food, but the sound had been enough to scare the Germans, or force them to join up with their compatriots. Only those who truly believed in their cause had stayed, the cruellest of their captors, with a crew of slave labourers who, like Jack and the others, had no choice but to stay.

With no one to feed them, they would surely perish. A part of Jack welcomed it, the end to his suffering. He longed for an end to the pain, so that maybe in the afterlife he might feel something again.

He sat as he always did, near one of the fences looking out at the line of trees.

The trees that surrounded the camp were crooked, turning away from the sun as if in disgrace, weak and fragile. The whole place felt like the island when the Germans had occupied it, the sense of oppression, a cloud hanging over everything even in the brightest sun, but much more pronounced. The war had broken everything, even here in northern Germany, almost at the heart of the beast. He wondered if he would ever get a chance to see Berlin, to see where all the evil had started, to maybe try to understand what had gone wrong. But he knew that would never happen. He was close to the end now. There was no turning back.

*

The gunfire was incessant, far from the controlled sound of the hunting rifles he had heard on Guernsey. It sounded angry, as if the very bullets themselves wanted to cause damage. An explosion boomed somewhere off to his right, the *whoomph* of a high explosive round from an artillery piece or tank. For a moment his hearing blared at him, a distortion that was every bit as painful as it was disorientating, then it came back to be filled once again with the chatter of machine guns and the occasional crack of a rifle.

It had taken all this time for the war to actually reach Jack. The area around the camp was usually so quiet, as if they were in another world, cut off from reality. The guards, those who were left, looked around themselves for some form of command or instruction. The camp inmates shuffled towards the gates. One of the guards shouted for them to get back but his shouts were drowned out by further sounds of gunfire. Then it fell silent. All Jack could hear was the hum of the assembled people, those who had once been men and women and now were reduced to nothingness.

Vehicles emerged from the tree line, their hulls blending into the green and brown landscape. They didn't rush towards the camp, even though Jack willed them to hurry. He was standing near the fence, but his body swayed, threatening to pull him down to earth again.

Shots rang out as the soldiers attacked those few defenders who were left. Then the rest of the guards dropped their weapons and raised their hands in the air, signalling that they were surrendering. Jack stumbled towards the nearest guard, noticing the tears in his eyes. With trembling fingers, Jack picked up the rifle. He didn't know what he was doing, but it felt good to find some control, to take charge again. The rifle was heavy in his hands, but as he racked the bolt back, he realised the cartridge was empty. The guard shrugged at him.

There were shouts as soldiers came nearer. It was the first time in a long time that Jack had heard a British accent, shouting orders, rather than the cries of desperate fear. It warmed his heart to know that his countrymen still had strength out there. He pushed himself towards them, willing his frail and beaten limbs to obey his commands. With stumbling steps he reached the fence, once a symbol of fear and now an object of hope.

Jack fell to his knees as he saw the khaki uniforms. It had been around five years since he had seen anything like it and he knew immediately what it meant. Tears fell down his cheeks as he looked on, unable to tear his eyes away from the soldiers in case when he looked back they had gone, a figment of his imagination. His knees hit the dirt, but he no longer felt pain as the ground came up to meet him. Somehow, far away from his home, he had finally found his freedom.

Chapter 40

His head stung with a pain he hadn't felt before. It was intense and cloying, making it difficult to think. Everything was a blur, like a dream, and he could never be entirely sure whether he was awake or asleep. The times when he thought he was awake were the worst; they were painful as his aching body protested. There were voices speaking to him. While they spoke English it wasn't with the accent he was familiar with – they were from somewhere else, or he was somewhere else. The room around him was awash with colour, bright like a migraine and just as painful. He couldn't lift his head in those waking moments, as if he no longer had a body, was just encased in some kaleidoscope of being. Thoughts came to him, but he didn't have the energy to pull on them, to help them manifest. Then he would sleep again, lost in the worlds of his dreams where, strangely, reality was more pleasant, and the pain was only a deep hollowness in his stomach.

Sometime later, he couldn't tell how long it had been, he came around and realised with clarity for the first time that he was in a small room lying on a bed. He was vaguely aware of the space he had been occupying for some time as if he had seen everything that had happened to him over to past few months as an outside observer. He tried to sit up, but couldn't. Jack sank back into the pillow.

After they had liberated the camps the soldiers had inspected the prisoners, trying to find out where they were from and calling in the doctors to see what illnesses they had. Jack had managed to avoid the worst of the dysentery and other debilitating illness. Others had not been so lucky. The man he had seen fall down had died on the very day the camp was liberated, a distinct lack of fortune that Jack had thought he himself had once had. After that the British prisoners had been separated out and taken up to Sweden. That time the trains had been much more comfortable, and they had been looked after with the care that only doctors could prescribe. Jack had had his trip through Europe after all, only he could barely remember it. He laughed bitterly to himself, which brought about a racking cough. Then he remembered where he was.

Somehow, either through his postcard or some other means, the authorities had managed to find his father's parents, his grandparents. They had cared for him these past few months, feeding him despite his protesting body. He coughed again at the memory of food.

A shape appeared in the doorway, lit white by the sunshine streaming in through the window. His eyes struggled to adjust as he saw an outline of curly red hair. The thought made him sob uncontrollably, thinking of Johanna. He had gone looking for her, but he had failed. She had died somewhere in a camp on her own, lost and desperate. He had failed her as he had failed so many others. For the first time in his life he closed his eyes and let the tears flow. He didn't care anymore; there was no reason to live, no reason to be ashamed. He let go until he felt a pressure on the bed next to him and he opened his eyes again. He was met with the fierce intelligence of brown eyes staring into his, and a hand on the back of his palm.

He would have recognised those eyes anywhere, but he couldn't believe it. He was hallucinating again, as he had done in the camp. His mind was broken and lost beyond reason, just like his mother's.

'Johanna?' he breathed.

'Yes,' she replied. 'I'm here, I'm not going anywhere. Never again.'

'How?' He didn't understand.

'You kept mentioning my name in your sleep.' Her voice was like salve on his wounded soul. She lay her hand on the back of his. 'You said Johanna, Johanna, over and over again. Your grandparents said it was the only thing that came out of your mouth through the long months of your recovery.'

'They found you?' His voice was a grating whisper. 'How?'

'Shhh,' she comforted him. She seemed frailer than he remembered, gaunt and malnourished like the people in the camp, but words could not convey how glad he was to see her. 'Your grandparents searched through the few belongings you had, and they found the list with my name on. Without it they would not have found me. They took a gamble and they managed to find me, through the war office. The camp they were holding me in was liberated before yours, and the English brought us here to recover. I'm here now, shhhh.'

She leant down closer and kissed him, pressing gently against his mouth. Her lips were warm on his and he closed his eyes, breathing her in, savouring the moment, the future he never dared hope would come.

Epilogue

After the War

The islands had been liberated after the rest of Europe, forgotten about and abandoned as they had been at the start of the war. The Islanders had suffered in that time, but they had come through.

Ghosts walked past as he walked down the High Street of St Peter Port and the memories flashed into his mind as he passed the buildings he was so familiar with. The shops and sights were almost as they had been before the war. The swastikas had gone from Woolworths and the Union flags were back on their poles, blowing gently in the cool autumnal breeze. He breathed in the salty sea air, not realising how much he had missed it. He had thought about never returning, but that seemed too much like admitting defeat.

The island had changed so much since he had first arrived as a child. Even though the Germans were now gone, the scars of their presence were still visible. There were still signs in German around the place, and the fortifications that they had added to the island were still there.

He thought of the number of people they'd lost over the years, the names running through his head. Too many. His grandparents, David, Henry, William, Frederic, Nicholas, Henrik … He didn't think he would ever see the German again. He would be a prisoner somewhere as Jack had once been. The rest were still on the island, but none of them would speak of what they had been through.

There was one person Jack had not thought of.

His mother.

He didn't blame her for what she had done. It had hurt at first, of course, but he couldn't think of it as the easy way out as so many others had done. What she did couldn't have been easy, and she was far from the only one on the island who had taken such measures. She couldn't take the darkness anymore, that much was clear, and he didn't blame her for that. If he blamed anyone, he blamed himself. He hadn't been there when she died, and he still wondered whether his mere presence could have done something to stop her. Johanna told him there was nothing he could do, that his mother's darkness was something that controlled her and wouldn't listen to reason, but a small part of him couldn't help but wonder. He would build a bigger memorial to her memory when he got the chance.

He took hold of Johanna's hand and led her across the street. Somehow, she had come back to him, and he would never let her go again. Neither of them had wanted to return to their old homes. They had come here to start a new life. It was a new world, still recovering, but full of hope. Their new house was in a part of the island where they had never really spent time together before. Here they would be allowed to rebuild their lives and maybe start some new ones.

They had been married in London now that the war was over, so that his grandparents could be involved. They had promised they would come and visit the island once he and Johanna had settled, and they were more than welcome.

The war was over, but it would be years, maybe even decades, before the recovery was complete. Some people would bear the scars for the rest of their lives. In a weird way it felt as if they had come full circle, but in reality many things had changed and would never be the same again. He had thought that he had lost everything, but there was still hope.

Would Europe ever be free from war? For Jack the scars of the war would always be there, but they would be able to start a new life together. A new start. Somewhere in this island there was a future for Jack and Johanna; they just had to find it.

*

9 May 1985

Alice Godwin walked into the church, nodding at the other parishioners as she went. The inside was cold and dark as churches always were, but she wasn't there for comfort. She was there because it was Liberation Day and she wanted to pay her respects to those who had suffered. Not just her parents, but her grandmother after whom she was named. She took up her usual space in the pews, in the middle, not too close to the front, but not at the back. One of the organisers had lit a number of candles that stood around the church, their flickering glow reminding Alice of the stories she had heard about the occupation as a child. Her father had been determined to talk about it as often as possible, determined that their pain would not be forgotten.

She looked around the church, noted the familiar faces and threw them a friendly smile. Her eyes fell on the back row. There was a man sitting there whom she didn't recognise. He must have been in his late sixties or early seventies. Old enough to have lived through the war. His tall frame was obvious as he sat down, once over six feet tall but now hunched and frail. Once-good looks still showed on his face, but time had given him many wrinkles. Piercing blue eyes shone under a heavy brow, showing intelligence and a wariness that spoke of the things that he had seen. He didn't smile when she looked at him, but merely nodded, a shallow movement that acknowledged her presence but didn't overstep familiarity.

Alice remembered the stories of the German soldiers during the occupation joining the congregations but sitting at the back to give the Islanders their space. The man reminded her so much of a German soldier her father had once shown her a picture of. German or not, she flashed him a smile as she had with the others and watched as his stony facade melted a little. There was a kindness there despite everything.

Turning back to the front she closed her eyes and thought through the words she had mentally prepared earlier that day. She wanted to thank all those who had helped her parents survive the war and remember all those who she knew had not made it, whether she knew their stories or not. She had just finished her whispered prayers when the service came to an end. Many others said their goodbyes and made their way from the church, but Alice stayed behind to light a candle for the grandmother she had never known. She watched from the corner of her eye as the old man did the same, closing his eyes and muttering something in German. Despite her best efforts her mother had never managed to get her to learn anything but the rudimentary elements of the language.

She smiled again as he opened his bright blue eyes and stared right at her. It was becoming a habit. For the first time since she had seen him, he smiled back, before placing a battered leather notebook next to the candle he had lit. With a heavy accent he uttered one sentence as he passed her, leaving the church.

'It was my liberation too …'

Historical Note

The thing that inspired this story was the photograph of a policeman in the uniform of a British bobby holding open the door of a car, clad in German identifiers, for a German officer. It begged the question: 'What must it have been like for the police in the Channel Islands to go from serving the British Crown to serving the Nazis?'

The story grew from that seed, bringing other aspects of the German occupation of the Channel Islands into it. I have gathered stories from across the islands, deciding to have them occur on Guernsey, rather than trying to stretch the story across multiple locations, which also provided that sense of being trapped on the island where all these horrible things were happening.

When I first pitched this story to my editor, we had no idea that I would end up writing it in the middle of a pandemic. Whether experiencing isolation, panic-buying, rationing, and overriding fear made the novel better or not, I will never know, but it certainly helped give me some perspective for the difficulties the people of the Channel Islands went through, on top of the sympathy I already felt for them during my research.

The story of the occupation of the Channel Islands provides something unique, that sense of a place that is very British being controlled by the Germans in a way that people on the 'mainland' never experienced. It helps us to see what life may have been like had the Third Reich made it as far as England, and it asks many questions that those living in Britain at the time asked.

The love between Jack and Johanna is central to the story, but there were so many other stories to be told, and many more that I didn't have space for. A number of the stories in the novel are adapted from real-life events. The German sergeant handing his pistol to a veteran of the First World War and ordering him to shoot did happen. (It's true what people say, sometimes the truth is stranger than fiction.)

Sadly, three Jewish women – Marianne Grunfeld, Auguste Spitz and Therese Steiner – were deported from Guernsey and lost their lives in Auschwitz, and they were not the only ones to lose their lives. The leader of the Frenchmen who landed on the beach singing the French National Anthem was indeed executed in Jersey for his role in the French Resistance.

Many Islanders were deported for various reasons, not just the policemen who were accused of stealing supplies from both the German and local stores, but also the English who were deported by order of Adolf Hitler himself as vengeance for the accidental shooting of a number of German POWs.

Towards the end of the war the Germans were abandoned on the island. Food became very scarce, more so than when they were making potato peel pies, and those in charge refused to surrender, instead ordering the soldiers to 'defend the island to the last'. As they were at war, the Germans were not allowed access to the Red Cross supplies brought to the islands by the SS *Vega*. The German forces did not surrender until after VE Day, on the 9th of May.

Other aspects of the story were simplified in order to help the narrative. I have kept the same kommandant throughout the story, while in fact there was more than one, and the trials of the policemen accused of stealing went on for a long time, being tried by both civil and military authorities.

It was important to show that not everyone in the German army was entirely unsympathetic to the Islanders, nor were they all card-carrying members of the Nazi Party.

As with all my stories I hope to show you, the reader, what happened to these people, but leave it up to you to question what was wrong or right. Things are never as simple as being a case of good versus evil, even if some are capable of great evil.

M J Hollows – July 2020

Acknowledgments

As the saying goes, it takes a village to write a novel. Thanks and love always goes to my parents, who have supported me at every turn. Without them, I would not have the opportunity to write this. I'm eternally grateful to Abi Fenton at HQ Digital/ HarperCollins for trusting me enough to commission this novel; Finn Cotton and Helena Newton whose insightful edits and suggestions helped to make *The German Nurse* the novel it is; and everyone else at the publisher. Thanks goes to my agent Robbie Guillory for his support and for being an excellent sounding board for my ideas and questions. Without the recommendations for reading materials of Judith Finnamore from the Priaulx Library in Guernsey I would not have been able to write this novel. So my sincerest thanks to her and all those that have taken their time to catalogue the occupation of the Channel Islands. As always, I thank James Friel and Jeff Young for their tuition on my MA in writing, for giving me the knowledge, the skills, and the confidence to write; my PhD supervisor Cathy Cole for her patience while I conduct extra-curricular writing and for reassuring me that I'm doing good work. Thanks to Cheryl Bellis for encouraging me to have a happy ending, for once. This is all your fault!

Final thanks go to the staff of Caffè Nero in Liverpool One for their bravery in opening up and going to work after the initial lockdown and providing me with enough coffee while I worked on the edits for this novel; and to anyone else I may have inadvertently forgotten. I'm grateful to all of you. But, most importantly, I thank you *the reader* for picking up this novel. Words cannot convey how much you reading this book means to me, and I sincerely hope you enjoyed it.

**If you loved *The German Nurse*,
try another heart-breaking WWII historical
novel from M. J. Hollows!**

**As Europe is on the brink of war, two brothers fight very
different battles, and both could lose everything ...**
While George has always been the brother to rush towards
the action, fast becoming a boy-soldier when war breaks out,
Joe thinks differently. Refusing to fight, Joe stays behind as a
conscientious objector battling against the propaganda.
On the Western front, George soon discovers that war is
not the great adventure he was led to believe. Surrounded
by mud, blood and horror his mindset begins to shift as
he questions everything he was once sure of.
At home in Liverpool, Joe has his own war to win. Judged
and imprisoned for his cowardice, he is determined to
stand by his convictions, no matter the cost.

Dear Reader,

We hope you enjoyed reading this book. If you did, we'd be so appreciative if you left a review. It really helps us and the author to bring more books like this to you.

Here at HQ Digital we are dedicated to publishing fiction that will keep you turning the pages into the early hours. Don't want to miss a thing? To find out more about our books, promotions, discover exclusive content and enter competitions you can keep in touch in the following ways:

JOIN OUR COMMUNITY:
Sign up to our new email newsletter: hyperurl.co/hqnewsletter
Read our new blog www.hqstories.co.uk
🐦 : https://twitter.com/HQDigitalUK
📘 : www.facebook.com/HQStories

BUDDING WRITER?
We're also looking for authors to join the HQ Digital family!
Find out more here:
https://www.hqstories.co.uk/want-to-write-for-us/
Thanks for reading, from the HQ Digital team

DIGITAL HQ

If you enjoyed *The German Nurse*,
then why not try another gripping
novel from HQ Digital?